STIRRING UP TROUBLE

Somewhere between the sexy curve of her mouth and the half dare coming out of it, Gavin flung his stalwart caution to the wind. He knew how to live life, dammit. Losing his mother with barely any warning had taught him just how quickly things could slip away.

This moment wasn't going to be one of them.

Gavin rounded the bistro table in a purposeful stride, stopping only when he was close enough to feel the rise of Sloane's chest over her sharp inhale of surprise. "I know how to have fun, and I don't have to run around in the rain to do it."

"You don't?" Sloane squeaked, but she didn't take a step back. Instead, she lifted her gaze to meet his head-on, and there was no mistaking the want in her eyes.

"I don't. Let's go."

Stirring Up
Trouble

KIMBERLY
KINCAID

ZEBRA BOOKS
KENSINGTON PUBLISHING CORP.
http://www.kensingtonbooks.com

ZEBRA BOOKS are published by

Kensington Publishing Corp.
119 West 40th Street
New York, NY 10018

All Kensington titles, imprints, and distributed lines are available at special quantity discounts for bulk purchases for sales promotion, premiums, fund-raising, educational, or institutional use.

Special book excerpts or customized printings can also be created to fit specific needs. For details, write or phone the office of the Kensington Special Sales Manager: Attn. Special Sales Department. Kensington Publishing Corp., 119 West 40th Street, New York, NY 10018. Phone: 1-800-221-2647.

Zebra and the Z logo Reg. U.S. Pat. & TM Off.

First Printing: October 2014
ISBN-13: 978-1-4201-3287-8
ISBN-10: 1-4201-3287-3

First Electronic Edition: October 2014
eISBN-13: 978-1-4201-3288-5
eISBN-10: 1-4201-3288-1

10 9 8 7 6 5 4 3 2 1

Printed in the United States of America

To A, J, and T.
Thanks for reminding me to put "be happy" first.

Acknowledgments

Writing is a delicious, crazy, wonderful adventure, and the writing of this book in particular was made so much richer by the following people:

Maureen Walters and Alicia Condon, who believed in both me and Pine Mountain from word one. Your support makes my enthusiasm possible. To Alyssa Alexander, Tracy Brogan, and Jenni McQuiston, who let me break both of my cardinal rules with this one and still read every word of every draft, I adore you. To Robin Covington and Avery Flynn, your conference calls and FMW themes get me through every day. Without you, I am lost!

To the Taste Testers for being the best street team a girl could ask for, and the BITE book club, who has cheered me on forever, you guys inspire me to be a better writer, and I'm grateful.

To my fantastic mother-in-law, Marie, for buying the purple boots that inspired the ones in this story, thank you for your keen fashion sense (and also, for your son, who is my real-life hero every day). To my mother, Marthe, who battled breast cancer like Gavin's mom in the book, and beat it like the warrior she is. I love you both.

To my three daughters, all of whom love to cook just like Bree, and my amazing husband, who lets them do just that while I write, you are my true north. Thank you for showing me that happily ever after does exist, and for living it with me every day.

Lastly, to my amazing readers. Without you, none of this happens. Thank you for your e-mails, your Facebook friendships, for loving Pine Mountain, and for letting me live my dreams. I cherish each and every one of you!

Chapter One

As far as Sloane Russo's family was concerned, if you were over eighteen, you were either happily married or dead, with no in-between. The distinct lack of a ring on her finger suggested she looked pretty damned fine, considering she'd been a corpse for nearly fourteen years. Not that it made a difference to her mother.

"Ma, do we need to have this discussion right now? I'm only in New York overnight, and I've got to get ready to meet with Belinda." Sloane riffled through the bright tangle of clothes in her suitcase, searching in vain for her black push-up bra. It was God's cruelest joke that she'd been gifted with the impossibly long legs of a runway model yet no bust to speak of, as if she was the living embodiment of *close, but no cigar*.

Wasn't that just the story of her life?

Her mother crossed her arms over her modest pink blouse as she scowled from the doorframe of Sloane's childhood bedroom. "I don't understand why you insist on meeting with that woman. You only have one night before you go back to Pine Mountain. What about going to a nice dinner with Joey Romano? He always asks after you."

Sloane swallowed a laugh. "You're talking about a guy who tried to get me to eat paste in the second grade."

"You and that crazy imagination." Her mother tsked, but no way was Sloane letting her creative streak take the blame for this one.

"I remember it like it was last week. He put it on a lunch tray and told me it was mashed potatoes. Said it would stick to my ribs." At least Sloane hadn't been thick enough to fall for it. Poor Frannie Bascom hadn't been so lucky, and the nickname Paste Face had stuck with her for years.

Her mother changed tactics. "That was decades ago! You can't at least call him to say hello?"

"It's probably not a good idea for me to date someone from Brooklyn." Sloane dodged the subject with well-practiced grace, although her mother put the screws to her on such a regular basis, there was no chance the topic was dead. She yanked her lingerie bag from the depths of her suitcase with a victorious flourish. Hello, instant cleavage.

"What's wrong with dating someone from the neighborhood?" Her mother's tone matched her expression in both intensity and temperature.

"Nothing, except I don't exactly live here right now."

Another sore subject, if her mother's frown was any indication. "Don't remind me. You're still back here enough to at least give it a try."

Sloane's hands flew over the sweaters and silk as she continued to rummage. "But that's only to visit. I just don't think it would work out."

As expected, her mother refused to be deterred. "Your father and I knew each other in grammar school. Even then, I realized he was something special."

"I know, Ma." Of course she did. The love-at-first-sight story was Russo family legend. But as sweet as it was, it certainly didn't translate to her marrying Joey Romano. After all, she hadn't been kidding about the paste.

"It's only dinner, Sloane Marie. And Joey is such a nice boy. Why do you have to be so difficult?"

Sloane's grip tightened over the lipstick-red sweater dress in her grasp. "I'm not being difficult. I've already got plans." Her hands kicked back into gear, just as fast and twice as purposeful. "To answer your earlier question, I'm meeting with Belinda because she's my editor. She wants to talk about the proposal for my next book. Once she gives me her feedback, I can start writing, which I'll probably do tonight. So I wouldn't be able to go out with Joey, even if he'd asked."

Sloane let the sentence hang, hammering home the unspoken *which he didn't*. Honestly, her mother's match-making was getting out of hand. So she'd rather see the world than settle down with a nice boy from the neigh-borhood like her sisters. In the grand scheme of things, there were worse things Sloane could be than capricious.

"Oh, no, you don't! You're not wasting a perfectly good chance to go out on a date. Who knows what the men are like all the way out in that tiny town you've landed in, or how long you'll even stay there? You move like the wind, never too long in one place. Pretty soon it's going to be too late for you to find a good Catholic boy." Her mother wagged a thin finger at her, but two could play at the stubborn game. Sloane put her hands on her nonexistent hips and forced a smile over her mouth.

"Living in different places makes me well-rounded, Ma. And Carly needed me in Pine Mountain. I'm happy staying there for now."

She didn't add that her mother was spot-on about the dating pool in the Blue Ridge. But Sloane had moved to the mountains to support her best friend through a horri-ble divorce and a career transformation. Lack of man candy aside, Sloane wasn't bending the truth when she said she enjoyed living there.

For the moment, at least.

"Five places in ten years isn't well-rounded, *bambolina*. You need to settle down."

"It's only been four places." Sloane pulled another dress from her timeworn and travel-battered suitcase, smoothing her fingers over the herringbone-print fabric in approval as she shook it out. "Europe doesn't count."

"You spent almost five months there," her mother argued, and Sloane had to bite her lip to keep from smiling in admission.

"What can I say? It's not every day you find room at hostels in Madrid, Venice, *and* Châteauroux. It made for a nice trip."

So nice, in fact, she'd written her first published book during those months. Being abroad had not only sparked her to study creative writing upon her return, but the research she'd done in the gorgeous locales had given her enough fodder to write two more bestsellers while she earned her master's degree. Not to mention springboarding her into the only career she'd ever had that didn't feel like a nine-to-five grind.

And Sloane had dabbled in more of those than she cared to count.

Using the details from whatever town she'd landed in as she toured Europe worked like a well-traveled charm, and had launched her quickly through the romance-writer ranks. She planned on changing things up for her latest series and writing about small-town heroes, although she'd fudged around with the exact details in her proposal. Still, once Belinda gave her the green light today, she'd be fine, and her muse would come out of hiding to get the ball rolling again. After all, Belinda had loved her European Bachelors series, and The Men of the Mountains books were going to be just as hot. As soon as she got started, anyway.

Her mother uttered an indelicate *hmph,* and she crossed the faded carpet to start folding Sloane's castoffs with military precision.

"What's so great about this Belinda, anyway? You can write anything you want. But you insist on *those* books." She paused, crossing herself and muttering a quick prayer in Italian. "You know what Mrs. Delvecchio calls them? *Bodice rippers.*"

Sloane bit back the rude noise welling up in her throat and unearthed a sweater from her suitcase with a snap sharp enough to test the delicate fabric. "Please. Tina Delvecchio used to swipe books from her mother's collection all the time. Mrs. D has no room to talk." Half the girls in Sloane's eighth-grade class had learned the logistics of French kissing from Mrs. Delvecchio's pilfered "bodice rippers."

"And you don't even use one of those . . . what are they called? Ah! Pen names! Anybody in the world could just get on the computer and see what you do. Don't you want to have a respectable job like your sisters?"

"They're both stay-at-home moms." Oh, hell. This conversation needed a handbasket, stat.

A look of triumph settled over her mother's stern features as she arranged the last of Sloane's garments into a ruler-straight row. "Exactly. You're nearly thirty-two. Your eggs might already be too dried up for making babies."

Sloane let out a belly laugh that burst through the tension brewing between her shoulders. "Guess it's a good thing I don't want any, then."

Try as she might, no way could she envision herself as the maternal type. Her one attempt at domesticity ended up with a cactus so dehydrated, it defied recognition. To fathom taking care of a kid was like asking her to sprout wings and fly.

Both were utterly crazy, and neither one was going to happen. Plus, why would she pin herself to one place when there was still so much of the world left to see? And more importantly, more books to write.

"Look, I appreciate your concern for my, um, eggs, but really . . . I'm not like Angela and Rosie." Sloane kept her smile, but crossed her arms over her non-chest so her mother would still know she meant business.

Again. Lord, this conversation was practically scripted, complete with Sloane's refusal to acquiesce and her mother's resulting chagrin.

Her mother paused, but her frown didn't lose any steam in the silence. "I only want you to be happy. You don't want to be single forever, do you?"

"Not necessarily." After all, you couldn't really do what she did for a living and not believe in some form of happily ever after. "But the right guy hasn't come along yet."

"Mr. Right could be just under your nose! You might find him, if only you'd stop moving long enough to take a look."

"Just because I do things differently than everybody else doesn't mean I want to end up alone. I write romance novels for a reason."

Of course Sloane believed in happily ever after. Hers just involved a beach in Cabo San Lucas instead of a white picket fence in the 'burbs, that's all. Until she got sick of the beach, anyway, and then she'd find it in another gorgeous locale.

Her mother crossed herself again, the fragility of her hand at odds with the strength and speed of the motion it performed. "Don't remind me. I should have known you'd give me fits over this. You don't do anything the regular way. You didn't even come into the world like most people."

A grin poked at the corners of Sloane's mouth at the reminder. "You're not really going to give me grief about how I was born again, are you?"

Ignoring the question, her mother barreled on. "Both of your sisters were born right on their due dates. Like clock-work."

"Mmm hmm. Just like the doctor said." Her smile picked up momentum as her mother continued, gesturing with her hands to emphasize the words.

"Looking back, you were never like them, not even in my belly. Your papa swore it was because you were a boy, the way you tumbled around. You were always kicking, always moving. So eager to get out and do your own thing." Her mother's expression flirted with a smile for an instant, before shifting into the knowing brow raise Sloane was so accustomed to. "But never in my wildest dreams did I think you'd be brash enough to be born in the back of a cab on Atlantic Avenue."

Ah, the pièce de résistance. Personally, it was Sloane's favorite part of the story. "See? The conventional route just isn't in my nature." She tossed a glance over her shoulder, calculating the trip to Manhattan with a grimace. "And as much as I'd love to rehash my offbeat childhood and have a discussion with you about the decrepit state of my eggs, I really do have a lunchtime meeting to get to. You might not like it, Ma, but Belinda's my editor. My job is important to me."

Her mother pursed her lips, her frown clearly suggest-ing the conversation wasn't a done deal. "Fine. At least promise you'll call Joey. A nice dinner out never hurt a girl. Not even one who marches to her own drummer."

She made a face, flipping a swath of too-long bangs out

of her eyes as she glossed over the request. "Gotta get ready, or I'm going to be late."

Sloane served her mother one last smile before nudging her out of the sun-filled bedroom and shutting the door. Flinging the contents of her suitcase around in earnest, she managed to get ready in record time. Fifteen minutes and two wardrobe changes later, Sloane smoothed her hands down her black and cream wrap dress, forgoing traditional pumps in favor of a pair of purple suede boots. At least her drummer had good fashion sense.

She hooked the clasps on her lucky fleur-de-lis earrings and breezed out the door, biting back a shudder at the frigid air sneaking past her coat to swirl under her dress. With her boots keeping steady time on the bleached gray pavement, her mother's words made a repeat performance in her brain.

You don't want to be single forever, do you?

She headed down the stairs toward the subway, the question tumbling to the tune of the staccato *clack clack clack* of the incoming train. Just because she wasn't conventional didn't mean she was dead inside—of course the idea of being a permanent party of one was unappealing. But equally unappealing was the thought of marrying a nice, steady man with a nice, steady income so they could raise a handful of nice, steady children. Not that there was anything wrong with settling down in a traditional sense, per se. Both of her sisters were thrilled to the teeth to live like that, and Sloane was thrilled for them.

But deep down, she knew that for her, settling down would be . . . well, settling for less.

A lump of dread roughly the size of a hippopotamus parked itself directly over Gavin Carmichael's sternum and refused to budge. He pressed the phone firmly to his ear, willing his composure to hold fast.

"I see. And how many times has my sister missed English class, exactly?" His dread morphed quickly into anger, but it didn't lose any intensity with the transformation. He took a deep breath, determined to bolster his resolve and deal with this calmly.

"Her attendance record says six," clipped the vice principal. "I assume she hasn't been ill, then."

"No." He raked a hand through his hair, counting to three before continuing so his irritation wouldn't show. "Thank you for being concerned enough to call. The absences are all unexcused, so please feel free to administer whatever punishment Bree has earned according to school policy. She'll also receive punishment here at home, of course."

Not that it would matter. Gavin could no more control Bree than he could coax table grapes into becoming Dom Pérignon. Christ, what a mess their tenuous relationship was turning out to be.

The vice principal cleared her throat. "Mr. Carmichael, I don't mean to pry, but . . . well, we have excellent counseling services here at Pine Mountain Middle School. Perhaps Bree might benefit from talking with one of our staff members." Her voice softened considerably. "Thirteen is a difficult age for all girls. To lose her mother and move to a small town on top of that is . . ."

"I'm grateful for your concern, Mrs. Wilkerson," Gavin interrupted, hoping he sounded like it. The woman probably meant well, but having a touchy-feely chat with a middle school vice principal he barely knew wasn't on his agenda. Talking with Bree herself was hard enough.

"I'll make sure she knows it's an option. In the meantime, can you let me know if she misses any more classes? I'll make sure she makes up all of her incomplete assignments."

He wasn't about to tell Mrs. Wilkerson how many times he'd asked Bree if she wanted to go to counseling in the last ten months. In hindsight, Gavin realized she automatically shot down anything he suggested, from where they lived to what they should eat for dinner. All this arguing couldn't possibly be what their mother had had in mind when she'd named him Bree's sole guardian.

Then again, she hadn't planned on breast cancer stealing her life at fifty-three and leaving both of her children orphans, either.

Gavin thanked Mrs. Wilkerson again and replaced the receiver with a deliberate *snick*. He was due at La Dolce Vita in less than an hour to get the waitstaff and the front of the house ready for tonight's dinner service, and prep for the upcoming weekend would entail all the usual insanity. Still, no matter how seriously he took his job, Bree took precedence over work. If he left now, he'd get to the school just in time to pick her up, saving her from the bus ride she always grumbled about.

Plus, even though he hated to admit it, if they were in the car together, she'd be a captive audience, and he wanted to deal with her latest defiance before Mrs. Teasdale arrived. While Gavin wasn't crazy about having the elderly sitter keep an eye on her while he worked, Bree's track record for troublemaking left him no choice. Plus, the babysitting service had yet to come up with a single decent candidate for a full-time nanny, and Mrs. Teasdale had agreed to stay until that happened. Even in sleepy Pine Mountain, he felt safer knowing not just that Bree was on the straight and narrow, but that she wasn't alone. Just in case she needed anything.

Not that she'd let on if she did. Why did she have to make it so hard just to *talk* to her?

The metallic scrape of a key in the lock cut his thoughts

in half, and the jolt back to reality mingled with his shock as Bree bumped the front door open with a jeans-clad hip.

"I was just coming to pick you up," Gavin said, voice flattening over the words before she could fully cross the threshold. The instant their eyes locked, her fluid movements screeched to a halt, and she reached up to pluck her earbuds from their twin perches beneath her honey brown hair.

"I was just coming to pick you up," he repeated over the tinny screech of music blasting through her now-loose earbuds. Bree made a face like she'd just gotten a whiff of something terribly rotten, but didn't move from the door-frame.

"You do realize that only the geeky kids get picked up by their parents. It's totally embarrassing." She squared her shoulders, defiant and too-thin, to fix him with a stare. God, when had she gotten so tall?

"I thought the bus was embarrassing," Gavin replied, a frown bracketing his mouth. "And anyway, I'm your brother, not your parent."

"*Half* brother," Bree corrected forcefully. "Who's supposed to be at work."

Gavin buckled down and blanked his expression. He should've known they were going to do this the hard way.

"And you're supposed to be in school. You don't get out until two-forty. It's barely ten after," he said.

Bree's arms shot around her rib cage, the knot of gangly limbs creasing the front of her army jacket as she held herself with snug resolve. "My last class is study hall. It's kind of optional, you know?"

Gavin's level voice met her hormone-fueled bravado head-on. "How about English class? Is that optional, too?"

Her chocolate brown eyes widened for an instant before she rolled them. "English is lame. The schools are so much better in Philadelphia. I don't see why we can't just go back."

Guess they were headed down memory lane.

Stellar.

"We can't go back because I have a stable job here that doesn't require me to travel." Had it really been only a year and a half ago that he'd gone from one glittering city to another, fixing up failing restaurants until their management staff could handle things on their own? San Francisco, Santa Fe, Chicago . . . the memories were already blurry around the edges, replaced by words like *stage 4, aggressive chemotherapy,* and *double mastectomy.* Gavin shoved them away.

"All my friends are in Philly," Bree said, unwrapping one arm to place a petulant hand on her hip.

He arched a brow, unable to help himself. "The same friends who tried to talk you into shoplifting?"

Bree's mouth settled into a hard scowl that contradicted the youthful prettiness of her face. "That was a misunderstanding. I didn't do anything wrong. The police even said so!"

As much as it irritated Gavin to get phone calls from the vice principal, it sure beat the day he got called to pick Bree up at the police station. "Still. Both of your so-called friends were happy to say you knew what they were up to when they stuck those CDs in your backpack." Thank God for the security tape, which clearly showed she'd been unaware of the other girls' actions.

"Like I said, it was a misunderstanding." She clapped her mouth shut, par for the course at this point in the discussion. Gavin had tried no less than a thousand times to get her to talk about it, but Bree never opened up. He'd spent weeks afterward alternating between being fearful for her future and highly pissed off at her lack of good judgment.

They'd ended up moving to more rural and definitely safer Pine Mountain less than a month after they walked out of the police station.

"I'm all ears if you want to clear the air." Gavin knew she'd probably shoot him down yet again, but still the offer came out anyway. Wearing her down wasn't exactly how he wanted to go, but at this point, he was nearly at the end of his rope. Bree gripped the sides of her jacket hard enough to blanch her knuckles, an odd, impossible-to-place expression flickering over her face.

"All the kids here think you're stupid if you don't ski."

"You want to learn how to ski?" What the hell? Thirteen-year-old girls should really come with a manual. "Is that what this is about?"

"No," she shot back, her rapid-fire blinking making it impossible for him to meet her eyes. The odd expression was gone from her face, painted over with an angry coat of frustration. "God, you just don't get it!"

He clung to his reserve like it was a life raft on raging seas. "You're not really helping me here, Bree. What does skiing have to do with you cutting English class?" Desperate, he sifted through a handful of possible parallels, each one more absurd than the last.

"Just forget it." She huffed out an exaggerated breath, angling her face away. Damn it, this was impossible. Maybe if he gentled his voice, they'd at least get somewhere.

"I can't forget it, Bree. You're cutting classes and failing English. If you need help, we can get you a tutor, but we're not going to fix this unless . . ."

"I don't need a tutor! And you can't fix this. Why can't you just leave me alone?"

The words flew out before he could stop them, low and quiet. "Because I promised Mom I'd take care of you, that's why."

Bree froze, midglower, her expression slamming shut. "I don't need anyone to take care of me. I hate this. I hate *you*."

Before Gavin could respond, Bree was gone, just a blur of olive drab and surly attitude whooshing down the narrow hallway toward her room. The tooth-rattling slam of her door a moment later punctuated the silence with a rude clap of wood on wood.

"Glad we had this little chat," Gavin muttered, pinching the bridge of his nose between his thumb and forefinger. Part of him wanted to go after Bree, to sit her down in a chair and wait out her anger with methodical precision so they could just deal with this and start moving on. But the more he tried, the tighter-lipped and more defiant she got. Even though she was no longer hanging out with a bad crowd, she was still toeing a dangerous line. If he couldn't figure out a way to get through to her, it was only going to get worse. He needed a way to reach out to her, some kind of bridge between them that they could both cross without stomping their feet.

Of course, the best shot he'd had at bridging the gap and having the family he'd always wanted had left him just shy of the altar.

"Knock, knock."

Gavin's head jerked around even though the voice coming from behind the storm door was gentle and familiar. "What? Oh . . . sorry, Mrs. Teasdale. Come on in." He waved the kind, elderly sitter past the storm door, dodging her crinkly-eyed look of concern with a stiff smile.

"I didn't mean to startle you, dear. You must've been off in your own little world. Is everything all right?"

The irony smacked against his ears, but he held his ground, determined not to let it get to him. "Absolutely. Bree is in her room. She's had a bit of a rough day."

Mrs. Teasdale bobbed her silver-gray head in a knowing

nod. "Well, don't you worry. I'll make a nice cup of hot cocoa and go check up on her. See if maybe she feels like talking this time."

Gavin exhaled a slow breath as he scooped up his keys and said good night to Mrs. Teasdale. As he drove toward the restaurant, he found himself praying harder than ever for that bridge.

If he didn't find a way to reach Bree soon, he was going to drown trying.

Chapter Two

"Hey! I was starting to think you'd forgotten me." Sloane softened the accusation with a playful smile as she rose from her plush seat in the reception area. Morton House Publishers didn't do anything halfway, and the gorgeously appointed offices served as case in point. Belinda flashed a smile as she took Sloane's hands and airily kissed both of her cheeks.

"You're a one of a kind, sweetheart. Nobody who meets you ever forgets it." She gestured to her office, already beginning to glide down the hall in a blur of ash blond and stylish navy blue. "Sorry I'm running behind. Things have been crazy, as usual. Here, let's make room for you." Belinda scooped up a foot-high pile of manuscripts from her client chair, and Sloane had to laugh.

"And I thought my work space was a mess." She dropped into the chair as Belinda moved yet another thick sheaf of paperwork from her own seat.

"Controlled chaos," Belinda said with a mischievous smile, although it didn't last. She tapped a folder on her desk with one perfectly manicured hand before sliding a handful of papers from beneath the cover. "Listen, sweetie. We need to talk about this proposal, and I'll tell you the truth. The news isn't good."

The back of Sloane's neck prickled as Belinda's words registered in her brain. "Okay." Come on. How bad could it be? She'd written three sexy bestsellers, for God's sake. They'd just walked past framed pictures of her book covers in the hallway.

"I hate to say it, but I just don't love the small-town vibe you want to go with. We've branded you as an author who writes about these exotic places and the exotic men that go with them. Your readers are expecting that, honey." She paused for another tap-tap on the proposal in front of her, this one accompanied by a frown. "They want hot Sven, the ski instructor from the Swiss Alps, not *Small Town, Big Love*. And I've got to say, I'm with them."

Sloane's gut bottomed out somewhere around her hemline. "I thought maybe a change of pace would keep readers from getting bored."

"The market is totally saturated with sleepy-town stories right now. And anyway, your readers are far from bored." Belinda shuffled through more papers on her desk, plucking a sheet from the pile and passing it to Sloane. "Just look at the latest reviews."

Her stomach did a twist and flip as she scanned the page. Phrases like *More of the same, Allejandro was smokin' hot!* and *Can the next hero be Greek? Please?!* leapt off the printout. "Okay, but when I was in Europe, I only went to France, Italy and Spain, and I used those in my first three books."

"But that's only three countries out of the entire continent. Think of this—we could even go with a world tour theme. The first three were so popular, the possibilities for continuing the series are really endless. Although, if you flip through all the reviews, Greece *is* the number one request for book four," Belinda said with a knowing smile.

Sloane's attempt at a swallow fell woefully short. "I've never been to Greece."

In order to really get a feel for something, she had to be immersed in it one hundred percent. Otherwise, no matter how well she researched the details, they came out flat, or worse, inaccurate. She'd never written anything set in a place she'd never been. It seemed impossible—how could she get it right without firsthand knowledge?

Belinda eyed her, a flicker of sympathy crossing her shrewd features before she pushed up her glasses and flipped back to business mode. "I know this is hard to hear, but it's better that we work through the strongest ideas now, at the proposal stage."

"I really thought *Small Town, Big Love* made the cozy setting feel exciting and fresh," Sloane said, working the last-ditch effort. Not that small towns really *were* exciting or fresh in reality. The most thrilling thing she'd experienced during her year in Pine Mountain was when the town approved turning the four-way stop at Main Street into an actual stoplight.

Damn it, Belinda was right.

"Being seduced in a gondola by a brooding yet brilliant Venetian painter is exciting and fresh. And it's what you're good at. It's what you do." Belinda paused, folding her hands over the proposal Sloane had sent her. "This just isn't good enough. I'm sorry."

Tears pricked at her eyes, but she blinked to keep them at bay. "So, what are you saying?" Oh, God. This couldn't be happening. It couldn't be . . .

Belinda's quiet tone did nothing to soften the blow of her words. "I need a solid draft of the Greece book within the next four months, five tops, otherwise we'll have to drop you."

All the breath left Sloane's lungs in a sharp whoosh.

"Five months?" She'd have to be in Greece no later than eight weeks from now, ten at the most, in order to make that fly.

"You can do this, Sloane. And if the Greece book passes muster like your other three, it could take your career to a whole new level." Belinda arched a flawlessly penciled brow at her. "I'm talking about the definite possibility of another multibook deal, and numbers big enough to add *New York Times bestseller* beneath your name. You could write your ticket, here. What do you think?"

Her gut jumped. It wasn't like Sloane was a stranger to living out of a suitcase, and she hadn't been to Europe in a while. She'd moved to Pine Mountain to support her best friend, but not only had Carly embarked on a hugely successful career, but she was getting married in less than two weeks, to boot. Just one thing stood between Sloane and a plane ticket out of Dodge, and it definitely wasn't small potatoes.

Her bank account had been running on fumes for the last few months, and she'd been counting on the advance for *Small Town, Big Love* in order to get by. If she couldn't even pay the rent in teeny-tiny Pine Mountain, how the hell was she going to haul her cookies to Greece to write a book?

Sloane swallowed past the tight knot of her throat. She should just open her mouth and tell Belinda that an extended trip to Europe wasn't financially feasible. After all, maybe Belinda would understand and they could work on some heavy edits to *Small Town, Big Love*.

Or maybe you'll lose the only career you ever truly loved because what you've got just isn't good enough.

"Sloane?" Belinda interrupted her rising internal panic with an expectant look, asking again, "What do you think?"

She pushed a too-big smile to her lips and brightly replied, "I think I'm headed to Greece."

The Great Hippopotamus of Dread was back, and Gavin's first reaction was that it had put on a few pounds since yesterday.

"I'm so sorry, Gavin. I know this leaves you in a bind, and I hate to think of Bree all by herself. Poor girl." Mrs. Teasdale worried her lip, tossing a glance over her shoulder at the car she'd left running in the driveway. "But there's nobody else to take care of my sister, and now that she's gone and broken her hip . . ."

"No, I completely understand. Family first, of course. And don't worry, I'll come up with something for Bree."

Exactly *what* he'd come up with was a bit of a freaking mystery, seeing as how he had to be at La Dolce Vita to supervise a liquor delivery in forty-five minutes. And of course it was Friday, their busiest dinner service of the week, so calling in sick—hell, even being late—wasn't an option.

"Bree keeps to herself, but she's a good girl. Oh, I wish I could be in two places at once. I just hate to worry about the two of you," Mrs. Teasdale apologized, already turning down the walkway in a rush. "I hope you find someone for her."

"I'll figure something out, don't worry. Drive safely." Gavin lifted his arm in a single wave, watching her car disappear down the road before exhaling a breath that resembled a steady leak.

Two hours. In two hours, Bree would get out of school, and he'd be damned if she'd cross the threshold into an empty house.

"Come on, Carmichael. Think."

Nope. Nada. The frustrated prompting only made his

brain go even more blank. Since they'd moved to Pine Mountain, Bree hadn't mentioned a single friend, and Gavin had been so busy at the restaurant, the only people he knew well and trusted were those he worked with. Without the babysitting service, he wouldn't even know Mrs. Teasdale.

Of course! The babysitting service. Surely, they could send him someone temporary. He scrolled through the caller ID until he found the number, nestled between La Dolce Vita and Pine Mountain Middle School. Highlighting it and punching *send,* he prided himself on his quick thinking. Parenting might not be instinctive just yet, but he was getting the hang of it. This was going to work out just fine. Crisis averted, no sweat.

Twenty minutes later, Murphy's Law had ganged up on him in an epic coup.

"You don't have anybody available at all? Not even temporarily?" Gavin raked a hand through his hair and slumped into a chair at the kitchen table.

"I'm sorry, Mr. Carmichael. The short notice makes it a bit of a challenge, and our sitters are in high demand as it is. At the very best, I'd say you're looking at a couple of weeks. I take it you want us to call if someone becomes available in the meantime?"

"Please." Gavin rattled off the number of the restaurant, a fresh wave of trepidation punching through his gut as he ended the call. He didn't even have hours, let alone weeks to wait for a sitter. He'd been so focused on finding someone for the day that he hadn't thought of the two fifteen-hour double shifts that followed. And that delivery truck was going to pass through the west gate at the resort in twenty minutes, which meant if he didn't leave now, he wouldn't make it.

If he couldn't find someone to come to Bree, she was going to have to come to him, like it or not. Flipping the phone over in his hand and scrolling back through the numbers until he found the one for the middle school, Gavin did the only thing he could think of.

"Mrs. Wilkerson? This is Gavin Carmichael, Bree Shelton's brother. I'm in a really big jam, and I was wondering if you could help me out."

Sloane stirred the steaming bowl of minestrone in front of her, propping one elbow over the table in La Dolce Vita's empty dining room as she watched the jewel-toned vegetables swirl through the broth like New Year's confetti in Times Square.

"Thanks for letting me come straight here. I don't think I could've handled going back to the bungalow just yet." She cast a look at her best friend, noting that Carly's chef's whites already bore dribbles of whatever she'd been working on in the kitchen even though the restaurant wouldn't open for another few hours.

"Like I'm going to turn you out. Plus, the dinner staff won't get here for another hour or so, and Adrian can handle getting the tasting menu started." Carly waved toward the propped-open doors leading to the kitchen, where the burly sous-chef in question was already creating both some incredible smells and a holy racket. Strains of Sinatra oldies filtered in around the metallic clatter of pots and pans, and although Sloane was tempted to smile, she just couldn't work it up.

"I hate to say it, but I was wondering when that wanderlust of yours was going to catch up with you. Greece, huh?" Carly cocked her head, sending her dark braid over one shoulder with a heavy swish.

The tinge of amusement sparkling in her friend's glance wasn't lost on Sloane, who wiggled her brows in a self-deprecating maneuver that was just as much knee-jerk reaction as it was defense mechanism.

"Yup. One more place to cross off my bucket list. As soon as I can figure out how to finance the trip, anyway." Each idea she'd come up with on the drive back to Pine Mountain had been worse than the last, to the point that despair threatened to seep past the bravado she normally wore like a fashionably perfect suit of armor.

"Your bucket list reads like a cross between a world-tour travel manual and a stunt double's daily agenda." Carly waved a breadstick with an accusatory flourish before taking a bite. She wasn't embellishing—Sloane had a bucket list as long as her leg, and at five-foot-ten, that was really saying something.

A tiny smile found Sloane's lips, and she let it stay for a brief moment. "Yeah, but you've gotta admit. I'm the only person you know who's hiked to the top of an active volcano *and* learned how to drive a motorcycle all in the same month."

Carly brushed the breadcrumbs from her fingers, casting Sloane a measured glance. "I know that when I moved in with Jackson, it left you without a roommate, and I wish I could help you with the money to make up for it. But even small, intimate weddings are bank-breakers these days." Her fingers moved absently to the engagement ring hanging on a gold chain around her neck, a definite safety precaution considering Carly's profession. Sloane's gut twanged at the remorse on her friend's face.

"Don't even think about apologizing for moving out of the bungalow! Plus, I'm not worried," Sloane said, feeling instantly guilty at the lie. But what kind of friend would she be if she burdened Carly with a sack full of issues a week before the woman's wedding? "Something will come up to get me on my way."

Carly set her jaw in thought. "Well, let's see. Maybe

you could teach another online class?" Her voice was hopeful, but Sloane cut her off with a decisive head shake.

"Nope. They take months to organize, and that's time I don't have." Sloane threaded her spoon around the bright pops of carrot and zucchini in her bowl without taking a bite. "Believe me, I've thought of everything."

"Everything?"

"Including trying to sell my eggs to a fertility clinic." Of course her mother had been right. The age cutoff for that was twenty-frickin'-seven. Her eggs really were too old for making babies.

Carly laughed. "I hate to see you leave. I knew you wouldn't stay forever—hell, I didn't think *I'd* be here this long." Carly's lips twisted into a wistful smile, reminding Sloane that the original plan had been to stay in Pine Mountain for a year, tops. Until Carly went and fell in love with a local contractor, her new job, *and* the tiny Blue Ridge town.

"Ah, true love," Sloane said without sarcasm. "Maybe I should write you into a short story. I could probably sell it in four seconds flat."

Carly's smile held the tiniest threat. "Don't even think about it. Anyway, are you sure about leaving? Maybe you could just write the book from here."

"Only if I want to kill my career in one swift move. Let's face it, I have to knock this book out of the park, and I haven't had a decent idea since I landed here. I don't just write on location, sweetie. I *live* on location, and it's time for me to be moving on. If I want to spark my creativity and write a bestseller, I'm going to have to pack my bags. It's the only way that works."

Her stomach began to ache, and she kept swirling her untasted soup. Forget Greece. If she couldn't come up with some money, and stat, she wasn't even going to be able to afford her current rent at the bungalow.

Which meant that her only available option would be to move home and try to write a career-saving book under her mother's disapproving nose. Talk about your hostile conditions.

"You know, selling a short story isn't such a bad idea. Maybe you could try that," Carly said.

"The whole problem is that small-town settings are off-limits, remember? And that's all I've got." As much as she hated to admit it, Sloane was utterly out of story ideas, other than the one Belinda had shot down. If she wanted exotic ideas, she needed the exotic locale to go with it.

Carly leaned forward, dropping her chin into her palms. "Maybe you just need a little inspiration." But the suggestion only prompted Sloane to bark out a sardonic laugh at the double entendre.

"Please. Do you have any idea how long it's been since I've had a little *inspiration?*" She hooked disdainful air quotes around the word, counting backward in her head to recheck her math.

Wait, was it January again? Already? Jeez, no wonder her muse was pissed.

"I'm sorry," Carly said. "Maybe that wasn't a good suggestion."

"Actually, it's a great suggestion." Sloane released her spoon with a plunk, and all the frustration swishing around in her chest burst forth in an emotional jailbreak. "Believe me, nothing would make me happier than to be earth-movingly *inspired* right now. As a matter of fact, considering the lack of inspiration going on in my life, I think I'm due for a downright out-of-body experience. Not that I've ever reached the summit of Mount O during the actual act. Nope, not me. If I'm gonna get there, I've gotta fly solo."

What a joke. She had to be the only romance writer on the planet who'd never achieved orgasm with someone else in the room. No wonder she had an epic-sized case of the writing blahs.

"Sweetie." Carly's eyes widened, coppery brown and full of astonishment. She reached a hand out, but Sloane had hit her limit. She lifted a hand right back, stopping her friend's motion cold.

"No, really. Karmically speaking, is it too much to ask for the powers-that-be to send some mind-blowing orgasms my way? I'm tired of doing all the work. Plus, it's all in the name of research. I mean, show a girl a little joy, for heaven's sake!" Sloane knew she was ranting, but blowing off the steam she'd slowly built up felt divine. "Just once, I'd like to give new meaning to the phrase *life imitates art*. After all the fumbling lovers I've put up with who couldn't find my hot spots with a map and compass, I deserve some really hot, toe-curling, religious-experience sex!"

"Um, Sloane?"

But the sinfully good release prompted her to continue without pause. "I mean it, *cucciola*. In spite of what I do for a living, I'm starting to think men who can dish up Richter scale orgasms are just a cruel myth."

Finally stopping for a breath, Sloane registered the odd look on Carly's face with apprehension. "What? Oh, God, don't tell me they really *are* a myth?"

The deep rumble of a throat being cleared cut Sloane's breath short in her lungs.

"Excuse me, chef. I don't mean to interrupt a . . . delicate conversation, but I've got an emergency I need to discuss with you."

The sound of the very smooth, very male voice over her shoulder froze Sloane into place and ignited every one of her nerve endings to a slow sizzle. Stunned, she whirled in her seat, only to find herself face-to-crotch with a pair of flawlessly tailored charcoal dress slacks. The wearer jerked backward, looking both startled and more than a little put out at her sudden movement.

Carly cleared her throat too late to hide the laugh beneath the gesture. "Sloane, you remember my restaurant manager, Gavin Carmichael, don't you?"

Knowing she should be utterly mortified and praying for a fault line in the earth to swallow her whole, Sloane threw on a cocky smile instead. Letting her gaze float slowly upward, she looked Gavin right in his stunning, melted-chocolate eyes and said the only thing she could think of.

"Nice pants."

Chapter Three

A thousand thoughts raced through Gavin's mind, not the least of which was a) he felt like someone had shoved a furnace under his skin and b) as pretty as she was, Sloane must be doing one hell of an indecent research project. He raked a gaze over the glossy black hair she'd tossed out of her eyes, feeling every inch of her water-color-blue stare as she returned the favor of an assessing up-and-down.

Damn, she really was pretty.

"It's nice to see you again." Oh, hell. If that stiff-as-a-board reply was the best he could do, he needed to get out more. After all, they'd met before, and he'd seen her a handful of times around the restaurant. Plus, this wasn't exactly his first rodeo. He could hold his own around beautiful women—hell, Caroline had been a former Miss Santa Barbara, with pretty to spare.

Right. Just look where that had gotten him.

Sloane slipped him a catlike smile, murmuring a breathy "likewise" in his direction before angling herself back toward the table, offering her long, cross-legged profile so as not to turn her back on him completely. She didn't look the least bit embarrassed that he'd overheard her highly personal discussion. It also didn't seem to fluster her that she'd swung her taller-than-average frame around so fast, he hadn't had time to calculate where her baby blues would land until it was too late to reposition himself.

Carly furrowed her brow. "Is there a problem with tonight's staff?"

"I'm sorry?" Despite his efforts, all Gavin could come up with was a pair of heart-shaped lips uttering the words *really hot, toe-curling, religious-experience sex*. The image conjured by Sloane's words and the fresh memory of her quick turnaround flashed seductively through his head, and the furnace under his skin cranked into over-drive.

"You mentioned an emergency," Carly reminded him. "Is everything okay?"

Reality yanked at Gavin with a vicious twist, and he jammed both hands in his pockets, moving his trousers from Sloane's natural line of vision even though she'd turned her attention back to her soup.

Was he out of his mind? How had he forgotten about Bree, even for a minute? His mother had trusted him to take care of her, and here he was, overcome with dirty thoughts for a woman with an even dirtier mouth.

Nice.

"Right. Actually, no it's not." Gavin paused, trying to think of how to explain things in as little detail as possi-ble. Mixing work with his personal life wasn't something he made a habit of, not that anything private ever ranked too high on his list of things to share. "My thirteen-year-old sister is on her way here from school. The person who usually looks after her had an emergency, and . . . well, do you know anyone who'd be willing to keep an eye on her for me, at least while I'm on shift tonight?"

Carly furrowed her brow while Sloane lifted her arms in a languid stretch. Gavin forced himself to ignore the briefly exposed sliver of skin between the hem of her long-sleeved T-shirt and the top of her jeans, focusing intently on the empty four-top just over Carly's shoulder.

"Just for tonight?" she asked, biting her lip in thought.

He shook his head. "I have a priority call in with the babysitting service, but there's a possibility they won't find anybody on short notice. I'll try to figure something out when I'm off on Monday, but I need somebody at least until then."

"Your mom's gone all weekend?"

Gavin met Carly's confused gaze and steeled himself. "I'm Bree's legal guardian."

"Oh! I'm sorry, I didn't know." She left the requisite pause for him to fill in the blanks, but he waited out the awkward silence until she continued. "Well, let's see. Jackson's cousins are all right about that age themselves, so they're out, and we only have eight days to go before the wedding, so his mom is up to her eyeballs in last-minute details . . ."

Despair crept up the back of Gavin's neck, booting the words right out of his mouth. "I'll pay really well. She just can't be alone all weekend."

"Mind if I ask why not?" Sloane unfolded her legs and turned to give him a quizzical look. "I mean, isn't thirteen old enough to stay home alone?"

Gavin stiffened. He had this argument all the time with Bree. He wasn't about to have it with some stranger, even if that stranger's liquid blue stare could ignite a kitchen fire faster than a faulty broiler. "Yes, technically it is, and yes, I actually do mind if you ask."

The words came out more clipped than he'd intended, and although Sloane's eyes flashed as she fastened them on him yet again, she merely lifted a thin shoulder and returned to her soup. "Okay, then. You're the boss."

Carly's glance flicked from Gavin down to her friend,

a slow smile breaking over her face. "Why don't you ask Sloane to watch your sister?"

"No!"

Gavin was about to apologize for letting the word rudely barge out, until he realized he wasn't the one who'd said it.

Sloane shook her head, adamant. "Look, I'm sorry you're in a bind, but I don't do kids. Plus, I have a ton of work to do. I don't have time to play Nanny McPhee." Her coal-colored bangs tumbled over one cheek in another firm head shake, and something in Gavin's chest leapt forward without his consent.

"That's just as well, because I didn't ask. Considering the conversation I just overheard, I don't think whatever you do for a living would make you a good fit anyway." Okay, so it was a bit chillier than was probably necessary, but still. Bree wasn't just some *kid*.

"Excuse me?" The ladder of Sloane's spine rose in an indignant line, and she leveled an icy stare at him.

"Okay, knock it off, both of you." Carly stood, knotting her arms over her chest in a way that said she meant business. "Gavin, Sloane writes romance novels. I can personally vouch for her character."

"And for the record, eavesdropping is rude," Sloane added on a grumble. "What'd you think I did for a living?"

Gavin's face went hot. "Well, it didn't sound too respectable. And I wouldn't have eavesdropped if you hadn't been so loud." Okay, so penning naughty books hadn't crossed his mind as a possibility, and it was a lot more reputable than what his imagination had cooked up, but still. A romance writer who seemed hell-bent on stirring up trouble wasn't exactly the kind of influence he wanted for his thirteen-year-old sister. He'd just bow out of this gracefully.

"No offense, but my sister's in kind of a rough place.

She's been struggling in school lately, and I'd prefer someone with more experience who can handle that kind of thing. She's got a lot of work to catch up on."

Sloane uttered an unladylike noise. "I can *handle that kind of thing* perfectly fine. I'd just prefer not to. Plus, like I said, I have a book to write." She pinched her thumb and forefinger together, motioning an imaginary pen across a page.

Oh, for the love of God. He'd been trying to be polite about it. Did she have to take it so personally?

"Look, I don't have time for this," he started, but Carly cut him off.

"No, you really don't. It's Friday, and as much as I'd love to tell you I can run the front of the house without you all weekend, the truth is that I can't. But I do think the solution is right under your nose." She tilted her head at her friend. "I meant it when I said Sloane's a good choice. You already know her, she's responsible, and she just happens to be looking for a little extra income." Carly shot her friend a look that dared her to argue.

Of course, Sloane's infuriatingly pink lips popped open in protest. "Well, yeah, but—"

"And Gavin," Carly interrupted with her best don't-fuck-with-me smile. "You said Bree needs help in school, right? What subject?"

"English, but—"

"Perfect," Carly continued smoothly, and he had no choice but to shut up. "Sloane's an excellent writer. Look, what doesn't make sense here? You need someone to look after your sister and tutor her in English. And you"—she pointed a warning finger at Sloane—"are a writer who has the time and could use the money. Hate to break it to you, but despite both of your misgivings, it seems you two need each other. Now if you'll excuse me, I've really got to help Adrian with the tasting menu." She narrowed a *help me out, here* glance at her friend, then lobbed a matching one in his direction before disappearing into the kitchen.

Gavin blew out a hard breath. The restaurant was no place for a moody preteen to spend thirty-five hours of her weekend, no matter how badly he wanted to keep an eye on her, but still. Miss I-Don't-Do-Kids couldn't possibly be his only hope.

"Just out of curiosity, what's the going rate for a babysitter these days? Not that I'm considering doing this," Sloane qualified with a lift of her hand. "Because it's a really bad idea."

"And why is that? You don't have a criminal record or anything, do you?" God, part of him wanted her to give up a reason that would make this conversation a done deal so he could come up with a decent fallback plan, one that didn't involve a candidate with a sassy mouth and bravado to spare.

Sloane shocked him with her quick burst of laughter. "Of course not. Carly wouldn't have recommended me if I was a degenerate, now would she?"

Okay, so she had him there. He wouldn't have asked Carly for help if he didn't trust her judgment. "Sorry. I guess you're right."

Sloane raised a shoulder toward the long, graceful line of her neck, releasing it noncommittally. "So you still haven't answered my question."

Gavin blinked, recalculating their conversation with a quick nod. "Oh, right." He told her Mrs. Teasdale's weekly rate, and her eyebrows shot skyward.

"And you just need somebody for the weekend?"

He hesitated. "Well, not really."

Her almond-shaped eyes crinkled with a look of confusion. "It's kind of a yes or no question."

Damn it, he was really out of options. "If it works out this weekend, I'd need somebody until the babysitting service can find a replacement. Probably for a couple of weeks."

Sloane's smile turned shrewd. "*If* I do this, I want time and a half." Her stare offered no quarter, but he met her head-on anyway. He wasn't *that* desperate.

"First of all, I still haven't asked. And secondly, what makes you think you're worth time and a half?" How much experience could she have if she didn't even like kids?

"Kid wranglers who double as English tutors don't come cheap, and this one in particular needs the cash. You said she has a lot to catch up on; plus, you need someone to babysit on top of it. You're getting two-for-one here. Take it or leave it."

He folded his arms over his chest, not quite convinced. "You're not going to teach her how to write trashy novels, are you?" Gavin asked, wary. Bree was only thirteen, for God's sake.

Sloane's pretty blue eyes shrank to slits. "The correct terminology for that perfectly legitimate subgenre is *erotica*. And of course I won't teach her how to write it—in addition to being inappropriate, it's not what you're asking for. If you'd ask about my background instead of just passing judgment, you'd find that I earned an MFA from NYU, and I've taught several creative writing courses for adults online. Like it or not, this *trashy* author is probably more qualified to tutor middle school English than anyone else in Pine Mountain."

He blinked. "You have a master's degree?"

She served up a smile more syrupy than dessert wine. "Summa cum laude, buddy."

Wonderful. All he wanted was to make sure Bree would learn Proust, not porn. So sue him for being a little protective and having his sister's best interests at heart.

The antique grandfather clock by the double-door entrance echoed three distinct chimes through the muted chaos of kitchen prep, a literal signal that Gavin was running out of time. "Okay, what do you say we start over, here? I didn't mean to offend you."

Sloane's saccharine smirk lost some of its caustic edge. "Well, you did a pretty good job of it."

A tiny quirk tickled the corners of his mouth, daring it to bloom into a full-blown smile. "Come on. It's a little tough to blame a guy for jumping to conclusions after overhearing all that talk about *orgasm* this and *toe-curling* that, don't you think?"

But rather than get defensive or try to change the subject, Sloane chuckled. "Okay, you might have a point. But just so you're aware, terms like *trashy* and *smut* are pretty derogatory. I take my job seriously, and I expect other people to do the same."

Jeez, he'd really put his foot in his mouth. "Understood. But for the record, I take my sister's welfare seriously, too. While I didn't mean to insult you, it's my responsibility to make sure Bree's sitters are good enough to take care of her."

Sloane's lips parted for a split second before she pressed them together and dropped her head into a tight nod. "I hope you find someone who fits the bill."

She shifted her body back toward the table and shouldered her bright red bag. As she stood and moved to scoop up her untouched bowl of soup, something high-pitched and fierce hollered at him to stop her. Risqué books aside, he really was out of options. Plus, despite Bree's complaint about not needing a tutor, letting her fail English wasn't an option.

"You fit the bill." The words flew out before Gavin could finesse them into an actual request, and he scrambled to try again. "I mean, ah, I'd really like it if you could help me out with my sister until the babysitting service can send someone to relieve you. Please."

Sloane looked at him with a shocked blink-and-start

combination, and her spoon plopped to the tablecloth with a velvety orange splash. "I don't know," she said, finally. "Like I said, I'm not really a kid person. To be honest, I might fit the bill less than you think."

"But you're responsible, right?" God, any second now, Bree was going to walk through the door with a truckload of attitude and a backpack full of English assignments. Sloane nodded. *Think . . . think!*

"If you need more money, I'll pay you double," he said, taking a step toward her.

Her mouth popped open, silent for only a second before she protested. "No, no, that's not what I meant. I'm not trying to bargain with you."

"But I'm trying to bargain with you." Gavin moved forward, taking steps until he was close enough to smell the spicy cinnamon notes of Sloane's skin. "Look, my sister might not be the easiest kid to deal with, but she took our mother's death hard. I just want someone to keep an eye on her so she doesn't have to be alone all weekend, and I don't want her to fail English. I'm worried about her."

It was more than he'd said about taking care of Bree since their mother had died, and as soon as he heard the words, he wished them back.

"Your mother passed away recently?" Sloane's long fingers migrated up her breast bone, splaying in a gentle arc as she pressed them over her chest, and the gesture caught Gavin's attention enough to fumble through an answer.

He nodded. "Ten months ago. She had cancer. But I'd appreciate it if—"

"I'll do it."

"You'll . . . what?"

Sloane's hand lowered in an abrupt drop, her hair framing her face in a shadowy fringe that rendered her eyes unreadable. "What can I say? You wore me down, and I really could use the cash."

A strange sensation Gavin couldn't quite pin with a name flooded his chest. "Thank you."

She laughed, tossing her bangs from her face to reveal an expression that was all business. "Don't thank me yet. I'll make sure she catches up with her schoolwork, but I'm holding you to that offer of paying double. And just so we're on the same page, despite the company I keep, I don't cook. Unless Bree has an unnatural fondness for PB and J, we'll be doing the takeout thing."

Gavin exhaled in relief. Finally, an easy fix. "Double the pay is fine; it's what I offered. And you don't have to worry about meals. We've got plenty at our place, and Bree is an excellent cook."

"You make your thirteen-year-old sister cook for you?" Sloane's eyes widened, the color of lush, ripe blueberries on a warm summer morning.

The corners of his own mouth twitched in response, surprising him with the repeat performance of a long-forgotten sensation. "Bree cooks with me, not for me." Well, she had before their mother died, anyway, but Gavin wasn't in the mood to split hairs. "I learned restaurant management in culinary school."

Okay, so the zinger felt better than it should. The look of pure shock on her face was priceless. "*You* went to culinary school?"

He nodded. "Three years. But I didn't graduate summa cum laude."

"Oh." She scuffed the carpet with the toe of one purple suede boot. "Sorry. I shouldn't have jumped to conclusions."

"I accept your apology." A quick glance at his watch reminded him that the newly delivered bar inventory wasn't going to tally itself, and he was behind as it was. "I'll be on shift tonight until about midnight, then back on tomorrow at nine. We have a guest bedroom, so you're welcome to stay if that's easier."

"No thanks, boss. I'm kind of particular about my space. Coming and going works just fine, but I can't make any promises about my mood in the mornings."

Great. Two moody females in the same house. What had he done? "Speaking of which, I should probably warn you. Bree's a little bit—"

Gavin's words were summarily cut off by a rush of winter wind, and the shrill voice that accompanied it from the heavy mahogany doorframe was no less bitter.

"Do you have any idea how embarrassing it is for the whole school to see you get a ride from the vice principal? *Do you?*"

He turned just in time to catch the flash of liquid hatred in his sister's eyes, and his gut churned like a stand mixer gone terribly wrong. "I was in a jam, Bree. I can't be in two places at once, and she offered to drop you off," he started, but her interruption was swift and merciless.

"How come you couldn't just send me home on the bus like normal? Anything would've been better than this!"

"I thought you hated the bus." He was dangerously close to losing his cool, so he scrambled to defuse the situation. Taking a breath, he calmed his voice, hoping she'd take the cue and at least listen to reason. "Mrs. Teasdale had an emergency, and I had to make other arrangements. If I'd sent you home on the bus, you'd have been alone."

"Like *that's* such a crime. Everybody thinks I'm a huge brown-noser now, thanks to you!" Bree jammed her hands over her hips, refusing to back down, but Gavin wasn't about to give in and make a scene, especially in front of someone he barely knew. He inhaled as deeply as possible and reached for his poise. Clearly, he needed enough for both of them.

"Don't be melodramatic, Bree. I'm sure it's not that bad."

But the voice that piped up didn't belong to his sister. "You sent her here with the vice principal?" Sloane cocked her shadowy head at him, her disbelief as plain as the afternoon sunlight pouring in through the windows.

"Yes. I didn't have a choice." Gavin crossed his arms in an unforgiving loop over the front of his dress shirt and stood firm. He didn't care how much he needed the temporary help. No way was he apologizing for the way he took care of Bree, not to Sloane or anyone else.

"Who are *you?*" The challenge in Bree's voice was punctuated by an obvious hint of curiosity, but she quickly canceled it out with a disdainful glance at Sloane's trendy clothes, right down to those crazy high-heeled boots.

"Bree, this is Sloane. She's going to look after you and help you catch up in English."

Bree's eyes glittered with anger. "Are you kidding me? You're making me work with a *tutor?* On the weekend? This is so unfair!"

Gavin winced. Okay, maybe he should've saved that part until she wasn't quite so worked up. "Not all weekend. Look, let's be reasonable about this. It's a great chance for you to improve your grade." Why did she have to be so difficult? He'd practically gift-wrapped a way for her *not* to fail English, only she was too damned stubborn to take it.

"Didn't you learn the last time that I don't need any help from your girlfriends? They don't stick around, anyway."

For just a breath, he was utterly paralyzed. The words were a dare, he knew, to admit things he'd tried to forget. But giving those things airtime now was pointless, and so was arguing with Bree.

As much as she hated it, he was all she had.

"That's enough," he said, putting enough frost on the words to catch her attention. "You can wait until tomorrow to start your classwork if you want, but Sloane's in charge while I'm here at work. Are we clear?"

Bree shrugged and mumbled a *whatever* under her breath, turning toward the front entrance. Gavin clenched his jaw hard enough that his muscles ticked, and he forced himself to meet Sloane's eyes.

"Sorry about that. Like I said, things have been rough." The last thing he wanted was to go into this now, with his nerves frayed and a late night ahead of him. He braced for a barrage of questions, but to his shock, only one came.

"You weren't kidding about that warning, were you?" Sloane pulled her bright red coat over her shoulders, flipping her keys into her palm with a jingle.

"No." This had disaster written all over it. She didn't have any experience with kids, and here he was, throwing her to a walking, talking pile of angry-girl hormones. He'd be shocked if Sloane didn't end their deal right on the spot.

But to his relief, she just smiled. "It's a good thing you hired me, boss. I love a challenge, and you need all the help you can get."

Chapter Four

It took less than five minutes of one-on-one for Sloane to realize she'd kicked a hornet's nest of epic proportions when she impulsively signed on for this job.

"Just so you know, I don't need a tutor in English, and I definitely don't need a babysitter." Bree slumped in the passenger seat of Sloane's Fiat, fiddling with the iPod in her lap.

"Good. That makes two of us." She eased the car onto the main road outside the grounds of the Pine Mountain Resort and tapped out an imaginary beat over the steering wheel with both index fingers. Maybe if she just played it cool, they'd get somewhere. After all, how hard could it be to have a casual conversation with this kid?

"Soooo, what've you got on there?" Sloane popped her chin toward the iPod, and Bree promptly lowered another three inches in her seat.

"Music."

"Anything I might like?"

"Probably not." Bree plugged her earbuds into place and looked out the window, flicking the round dial on the iPod to life with the pad of her thumb.

Right. So much for casual conversation. With the

exception of the GPS chirping out directions to the address Gavin had offered up just before they'd left, the rest of the ride passed in silence. Good thing Sloane didn't have to rely on her sulky passenger to get them there. Not that she could blame the kid for being a little bit hacked off about her day. Having to hitch a ride with a school official might've been the only way for Gavin to get her to the restaurant safely, but that didn't make it any less mortifying for Bree. Even Sloane, who didn't know squat about kids, could figure that one out.

On the flip side, Bree *had* lit into him pretty hard over it. Not that it had put a dent in his cool demeanor, but still. Sloane knew fighting words when she heard them. Her curiosity sparked to life as she tried to picture the ex-girlfriend-in-question. Pretty, no doubt. After all, what pretty girl wouldn't be a sucker for those melty brown eyes and classically handsome face?

Well, besides her, of course. Chiseled jaw line or not, the Ice King was so not her type.

"Anyway," she breathed, her cheeks flushing with too much warmth at the blast of heat cranking from the vent. She flipped it toward Bree in case she was cold, then pulled off of Rural Route Four to a winding residential road dotted with lakeside cottages, thinking all the way.

Although Sloane still wasn't quite sure what had possessed her to agree to it, she was about to spend the better part of two weeks with this kid. She needed a plan of attack, especially for the tutoring. She'd never worked with a preteen before, but she hadn't been bullshitting Gavin about those online creative writing classes she'd taught. In the grander scheme of things, this job couldn't be *that* different than teaching adults. If anything, the challenge might kick-start her creative juices. At the very least, this gig would pad her anemic bank account, which put her that much closer to packing her bags and saving her career.

If the kid would give her something more than the cold shoulder and a mountain of attitude.

"Well, here we are. Home sweet home." By the time Sloane had the Fiat in Park, both of Bree's black Converse All-Stars had hit the gravel drive in a blur of motion. She crunched her way to the single-story clapboard cottage, withdrawing a set of keys from the side pocket of her backpack without breaking stride. Only when she'd bumped the thick wooden door from its resting place in the frame did she turn back to look at Sloane.

"My home is in Philadelphia. This is just where I'm staying for now, because I don't have any choice. But I'm never going to call this place home." Her voice caught over the last word, making it softer than all the others.

Sloane's exhale puffed around her in a visible cloud, scattered by a sudden gust of wind. "Okay." She followed Bree's footsteps up the porch, stopping short of where the girl still stood in the doorframe. "You going in? It's pretty cold out here."

Bree eyed Sloane with obvious distrust. "That's it? You're not going to give me some line about how things will get better eventually? Before I know it, I'll love it here, and all that crap?" Bree's knuckles blanched over the matte brass doorknob, which she still grasped even though the door was already wide open.

"Nope."

Bree let go of the knob, but didn't commit to going all the way inside. She traced the outer edge of the lock with one short, electric blue fingernail. "How come? Everybody else does."

Sloane laughed, long and loud, making Bree jump. "Honey, we're about to spend the next couple of weeks together, so let's get something straight right now. If you're expecting me to be like everybody else, then you're gonna be sorely disappointed. And believe me when I tell you, you won't be the first."

For a fraction of a second, Bree's hot-cocoa eyes lit with the barest hint of a spark, but then she shrugged. Her enormous backpack listed awkwardly off one shoulder, and although it took effort, she hitched it back into place over her slight frame and walked inside the cottage. "Whatever. I'm going to my room."

"Okeydoke. Let me know if you need anything, I guess."

Sloane watched the girl retreat down the hall with a shrug. While it would be easier if they were civil to each other, especially for the tutoring part of things, she wasn't going to bend over backward to get the kid to open up if she didn't want to do it. All Sloane needed in order to get paid was to keep her out of trouble and get her up to speed in English. Being friends was optional.

Although how many friends could Bree have if she was hitching rides with the vice principal?

Sloane shook the chill from her favorite bright red pea coat and wandered into the cottage, pushing the front door snugly back into the frame behind her. The tastefully understated entryway split in two directions, the one in which Bree had fled and the other that led into a living room as understated as the entryway.

The only thing not painted stark white or lined in modern chrome were the hardwood planks beneath her feet, and although their black cherry color went beautifully with the décor, their warmth seemed at odds with the crisp, serious lines of everything above them. A series of black and white prints graced the walls, imposing oversized mats edged in elegant, glossy frames. They were all landscapes, and upon closer inspection, Sloane noted the curling, woody vines of different vineyards, some with rolling fields in the distance, others surrounded by groves of thin-leaved olive trees. A strange sensation worked its way up from the depths of her chest, unfurling like a favorite blanket on the first night of winter.

"Tuscany," she whispered, an involuntary smile forming on her lips as she examined each photograph in turn. Given his occupation, it made sense that Gavin had likely traveled to Europe, although she had to fess up to the fact that the culinary school thing had thrown her for a loop. Food was so evocative—hell, Sloane had seen Carly get so torqued up over plain old mushrooms that she'd cried in the middle of a farmer's market once. Gavin didn't really seem the type.

The adjacent kitchen showcased black granite countertops flowing seamlessly into stainless steel appliances, and Sloane meandered in with the rhythmic clack of boots on tile. Not a single dirty dish in the sink, no signs of a hastily eaten breakfast scattered across the table in the side nook. Even the matte silver trash can was devoid of fingerprints.

Okay, really? Did humans live here?

A quick inventory of the contents of the fridge told her Gavin hadn't been kidding when he'd said they were stocked, and she liberated a couple of grapes from a bowl on the top shelf. They burst on her tongue, their thin skin so taut, it crunched as she chewed. Three different kinds of mustard, assorted fruit, a half-wheel of Brie . . . okay, maybe culinary school wasn't that much of a stretch. She gave the pantry door a quick pull and promptly stopped short, blinking a few times to make sure her vision was working properly.

"Whoa." Sloane felt her eyes go wide, and she stepped back to take in the baffling visual inventory. The shelves had been removed from the bottom third of the widened pantry, replaced by a stainless steel and smoked glass

refrigerator that came up to her thigh. She folded her legs
beneath her in a quick kneel to get a better look, chewing
her lip as she thought.

"But why would you have two refrigerators?" Her
murmur caught on a surprised breath as she registered the
digital temperature readouts in the corner by the handle,
and she tugged the door open. The unit hummed its approval in a steady sigh, but it didn't take a genius to see
that this was far from an ordinary spare fridge.

Sturdy black shelves, set on tiny casters that allowed
them to roll out on a whisper, sat stacked one on top of the
other in neat rows. Rounded grooves marked the spaces in
every row like perfectly symmetrical waves, and Sloane
slid each shelf out for quick yet reverent appraisal. The
muted light from behind her spilled in to illuminate the
carefully reclined bottles, and she ran her fingers over
their slender necks gently, as if afraid to wake them.
Chardonnay, Riesling, Pinot Grigio . . . there had to be
nearly a hundred labels, all meticulously separated by type
and vintage.

Looked like the Ice King was passionate about something after all.

"I'm pretty sure he counts those, just in case you're getting any ideas."

Sloane jumped up so fast she nearly gave herself a head
rush, clapping a hand over her sternum as she released the
wine cellar door to whirl around. "Jesus, kid! You nearly
gave me a heart attack."

Undaunted, Bree glared at her from the doorway. "You
shouldn't snoop. It's rude."

"What are you, the pantry police?" Sloane volleyed,
dishing up a pinched face of her own. "And for the record,
sneaking up on people doesn't rank too high in the proper
etiquette department either."

"I came to get something to eat." Bree crossed the

kitchen, yanking the real refrigerator open with a huff. "I can't help it if I caught you poking around in my brother's stuff."

"Looking in the pantry isn't poking around. Riffling through someone's underwear drawer, now that's snooping." Maybe a little humor would loosen this kid up.

But Bree just rolled her eyes and reached into the deli drawer for a package of string cheese. "Save your energy. The only thing in there besides boxer shorts is a bunch of stupid pictures."

Sloane clamped down on her surprise, but only by a thread. "Like the ones on the walls out there?" She gestured to the living room. The vineyard shots seemed a lot more personal now that she'd gotten a glimpse of Gavin's extensive wine collection.

"Hardly." Bree buried her scoff in a bite of mozzarella, following up with a silence that gave Sloane no choice but to push or change the subject.

Oh, screw it. She was tired of beating around the bush with this kid. "Listen, it would probably make things easier on both of us if you dialed back on your attitude while you're stuck with me. Your brother is pretty adamant about you catching up in English class, and the faster we get you there, the faster I'll leave you alone."

"Right. Like you'd leave me alone."

"You're making it awfully tempting." The quip was out before Sloane could bite down on it.

Bree's eyes flashed. "If I let you tutor me and we get caught up with all my classwork tonight, would you really leave me alone after that?" Her disbelieving glance refused to waver.

Sloane hesitated. "You do know how much classwork we're talking about, right?"

Before they'd left La Dolce Vita, Gavin had mentioned at least four outstanding writing assignments, along with the required reading Bree needed to do in order to complete them. That alone would take hours, and Sloane suspected those four papers weren't everything on the to-do list of missed assignments.

Bree didn't flinch. "Yeah. Would you?"

She should've figured it would come down to bribery. "Well, your brother is paying me to keep an eye on you, so leaving you *alone*-alone is out of the question. However"— Sloane enunciated each syllable as if it were its own word, cutting Bree's pouty moue of protest off at the knees— "if you're willing to drop the 'tude and bust your buns to get that stack of work done satisfactorily, then sure thing, kid." She crossed her arms over her chest and looked Bree right in the eye. "Once we're square, you can stay in your room 'til school starts on Monday, and I won't knock unless the house is on fire. Fair?"

Without a word, Bree turned on her heel and walked out of the kitchen.

"Great." Sloane winced. If humor and bribery were out, she was going to have to resort to some pretty ugly tactics to get this job completed. Damn it, she should've known better than to think she could actually pull this off. But no, her stupid heart had to go and lurch like it had been cattle-prodded as soon as Gavin said their mom had died of cancer, just like her father. The next thing she knew, she'd impulsively agreed to do a job she knew nothing about.

Between her bank account and her heartstrings, Sloane had gone temporarily insane. Maybe she could call the babysitting service and explain things, see if they couldn't find someone, *anyone,* to come and relieve her. This had obviously been a mistake. Clearly, she wasn't—

"So can we get this over with?" Bree's voice startled Sloane as much as the request. She tried not to let it show as Bree swung her humongous backpack from her shoulder with a *whump*. Not wanting to waste the opportunity on a little thing like being shocked down to her toes, Sloane scrambled to answer in spite of her surprise.

"Um, sure. Will the breakfast bar work for you?"

"Whatever." Bree hefted the bag back up and headed to the nook, but Sloane stopped her cold, stepping in to place a hand on the girl's forearm.

"Uh-uh. Our terms were that you lose the attitude while we get the work done, kid. You don't have to shower me with platitudes, but that word's gotta go." She dropped her hand, but didn't step backward to let Bree pass.

She narrowed her eyes, her lashes drawing low in shadowy disdain. "That's censorship, you know."

"I prefer to think of it as a respect issue. No more *whatever,* otherwise the deal's off the table." Two could play at the not-budging game, and although Sloane really didn't want Bree to recant, she also wasn't going to let a thirteen-year-old push her around. No matter how much closer to greener pastures the money would get her.

"Then no more calling me *kid,* either. I'm not a baby." Bree's hands went to her hips in true I-mean-it fashion, and Sloane nodded. After all, she was right.

"Deal. But I don't do freebies. Slip up at your own risk." Despite trying to keep her poker face intact, Sloane couldn't help the satisfied smile tickling her lips. Maybe this wouldn't be so bad after all.

Bree measured her with a hard stare. "*Whatever* you say."

"I say let's get started." She paused just long enough to let Bree think she'd gotten away with one before amping her smile to grin status.

"You've got a lot of work to do, and I'm not *kid*ding."

At ten past midnight, Gavin gave in and admitted that the ache in his bones might be permanent. The fact that he'd been largely distracted by having sent his broody, moody sister home in the charge of a quick-witted child-phobe only added to his stress. He knew from his limited observations that Bree usually steered clear of Mrs. Teasdale, avoiding contact despite the sweet old woman's efforts to make Bree feel comfortable and cared for. Sloane was different, though—young and sharp and openly brazen. Clearly, Bree saw her as a repeat performance of Caroline, although Gavin had to laugh at the thought. If ever there was a polar opposite of his ex-fiancée, Sloane was it.

Besides the child-phobe thing, anyway.

Gavin pulled his Audi A6 into the gravel drive next to a sporty little silver Fiat and coughed out a laugh. Jeez, the damn thing was more clown car than real vehicle, with just a tiny bench behind the two front seats and a mere bubble of space parading as a trunk. With the assistance of the three-inch heels on her boots, Sloane had stood eye level with him at the restaurant, which was no small feat at six-foot-one. How on earth she managed to fold her long, lean frame into such a tiny car was mind-boggling. In fact, it had to be the last damned car on the planet he'd expect her to drive.

Then again, surprise might be par for the course where she was concerned. This was a woman who laughed when strangers overheard her talking about her most intimate secrets. Although they couldn't be that secret if she was willing to admit to them so freely. Take that orgasm thing, for example. Surely she'd been exaggerating. No way could she have meant *never* ever. She probably had her pick of men wanting to please her in bed.

Heat crept into a few long-forgotten places, lingering enticingly, and his eyes shuttered closed. The image of Sloane, with her sassy attitude and lips so full they were practically extravagant, hit him without remorse. The heat became a tingle, then a full-on tightening as he conjured

what he'd do if it were him in her bed, tangled in her
sheets.

That glimpse of exotically bronze Mediterranean skin
he'd caught earlier flashed like a wicked temptation in his
mind's eye, daring his imagination to touch her. He pictured trailing slow, languid kisses from that hot sliver of
her belly up to her high, firm breasts. He'd tease her
nipples in seductive, slow circles with his mouth, daring
her to dance on the edge of ecstasy before dropping past
the indentation of her navel to taste the scorching heat
of her—

"Jesus Christ." Gavin barked out a tight, involuntary
laugh. This exhaustion was seriously messing with him.
What Sloane did in bed was none of his business, specu-
lative or otherwise. Even though it was only temporary,
she was looking after his sister, which was only the cherry
on top of all the reasons it was a bad idea to entertain ex-
plicit thoughts about her.

Bracing himself against the dead-of-night January
chill, he made his way up the walk, forcing his inner
teenage horn dog to default to the reality of being an adult.
He was impressed to find the dead bolt tightly turned even
though Sloane was expecting him home, and he flipped
the key in the lock with a firm twist.

"Hey. I'm back." He stopped in the entryway to the
living room, purposely keeping his distance so his over-
active imagination wouldn't get any more crazy ideas.

Sloane blinked up from her cross-legged perch on the
couch, peering at him from beneath the brim of the same
kind of floppy sun hat his mother used to wear at the
beach.

"Oh, crap. Is it midnight already?" She slid the blue
and white striped hat from her head, and her tousled hair
looked worse for the wear, like she'd spent the evening
trying to tug it from its roots.

He nodded. "Quarter past." Curiosity gave decorum a nosy shove, and he gestured to the fabric in her lap. "Kind of cold for one of those, isn't it?"

She tucked her pencil behind one ear and frowned. "Writing ritual. Think of it like a lucky jersey. Only sometimes the luck is optional." Crumpled sheets of notebook paper circled her like a failed-attempt force field, and she dropped the legal pad she'd been cursing from her fingers to her lap.

Gavin shifted his weight from one loafer to the other. "I take it the tutoring didn't go so well." He gestured to the scattered yellow papers, most of which had been deposited at the foot of the couch, and tamped down the urge to pick them all up and head for the garbage can.

Sloane stretched, treating Gavin to the exact snippet of skin he'd just managed to block from his mind. "Oh, yeah, no. Actually . . ." She riffled around on the cushions, milling through several sloppy piles of paper before choosing a stack to hand over. "She did three out of her four missed assignments, and caught up on all of her reading, including this weekend's passages. She tried like hell to finish that fourth paper, but ended up falling asleep on the book so I cut her a break."

Hiding his shock was a complete impossibility. "Wait . . . I don't understand. Bree did *all* of her work? In one night?" In spite of Sloane's matter-of-fact nod, his brain refused to accept the possibility. He'd barely been able to get a list of assignments from Bree, much less get her to sit down and work on any of them. "How did you pull that off? It had to have taken all night."

"Almost five hours. And I've gotta tell you, the fact that she spoke to me as little as humanly possible didn't make it a walk in the park. But I think she's got the hang of it now. If what she did isn't up to snuff with her teacher, then the woman's crazy." Sloane scooped up the rest of the piles from the couch and stuffed them into her bag, tossing the legal pad on top of the melee.

A question poked at his conscience, getting increasingly louder until he finally gave it voice. "Look . . . don't take this the wrong way, but this is over three weeks' worth of work. I've got to ask, how much help did you give Bree, exactly?"

Sloane made a less-than-dainty sound and rolled her eyes. "I already passed eighth-grade English, and I'm not exactly eager to do any of the writing on my own again. Bree busted her butt, I assure you." She started to wad up the discarded pages at her feet, muttering a low oath as the ball got big enough to exceed her hand.

Okay, so that had come out more accusatory than he'd intended. He knelt to help her collect the crumpled pages. "Sorry. I didn't mean to imply that you did it for her."

"Sure you did. But like I said, you don't have to worry. I helped her, but only as much as she'd let me. Once we got started, she really did most of it without even talking to me."

Now there was something he could relate to. "Yeah, that sounds like her." The ache in his bones migrated to include everything beneath his sternum, and Gavin let out a tired exhale. He reached for the last scrap of paper at the exact moment Sloane did. Unable to change his course of movement without making contact, his fingertips brushed against the top of her hand as she closed a fist over the page, and the sheer heat of her skin under his hand registered in a jolt.

"Whoops, sorry." He withdrew his hand and looked up, only to discover his face about six inches from a pair of heart-shaped lips, parted in a look of surprise. "I didn't mean to . . ." A quick gesture to her hand completed the sentence. Her skin was so soft, like a stretch of perfectly golden caramel, warm and sweet and utterly decadent.

For a hot, impulsive moment, he wondered if she tasted the way she looked.

"No biggie," she murmured, not moving her eyes from his.

Up close in the soft lamp light, they looked even prettier, kind of a cross between a summer sky and gathering storm clouds, and the juxtaposition caught him square in the chest. His left knee pressed against her right thigh from when they'd both knelt down on the floor-boards, and even through the wool and denim, heat coursed from her body in waves.

He meant to lean back, to correct the mistake of acci-dentally invading her space and just let her go. Gavin commanded himself to move, say good night, and give her enough room to walk out the door.

But instead, he kissed her.

The warmth of Sloane's body was nothing compared to the rich heat of her mouth, and he fought back a groan as he brushed the surprise from her lips with his own. He traced the lush curve of her bottom lip with his tongue before drawing it in to savor it, and the softness hit him with a bolt of satisfaction.

His imagination had been spot-on. She tasted exquisite, and he didn't want to stop until he'd tried the rest of her.

As if she'd crawled into his head for a direct read on his thoughts, Sloane angled her body against his, cup-ping the back of his neck with deft fingers. Gavin's desire went from slow burn to liquid want as she parted her lips to deepen the kiss, searching his mouth with growing intensity.

He skimmed his teeth over her now-swollen bottom lip, and the hot sigh it called up from Sloane's chest made him want to do it until her soft breath tumbled into a scream. Slipping kisses across the perfect swoop of her jawline to taste the sweet divot behind her ear, he coasted lower to sample the honey-colored column of her neck, then the tight juncture where her collarbone met it.

Damn, this woman was a delicacy. Burning with uncut desire, he returned to her mouth, turning her sigh to a gasp.

"Oh. *Oh*." Sloane fisted his shirt hard enough to pull the fabric taut over his chest, and the click of a button hitting the hardwood registered in a vague corner of his mind. In one fluid move, her lap covered his, the heated seam of those infernally long legs notched over his aching erection in a way that left zero to the imagination.

"Gavin."

The way her voice shaped his name, with equal parts promise and raw desire, smashed into him like a sucker punch, and the undiluted shock of where they were and what they were doing—hell, what they *could've* been doing—made him skid to a stiff halt under her ministrations.

"Sloane . . . Sloane, we're in the living room." Was he out of his mind? How the hell had he let lust hijack his common sense so thoroughly?

"Okay." She lifted her head, fluttering her eyelids open as if she'd been knocked from a dream. Doing his best to ignore the sexy tumble of her hair and the throbbing protest in his pants, Gavin shifted her gently off of his lap.

"Wait, I didn't mean you should stop. I just . . ." Sloane's fingers flew to the bow of her lips, even more full from having been thoroughly kissed, and a flush crept over her high cheekbones. "Ah, I see. But you did."

Without pause, she stood and put on her coat in one fluid motion, heavy footsteps thumping over the floorboards in time with her brisk strides toward the door.

"Sloane, wait. I should apologize. It was . . ."

Amazing. Incredible. Hands down the hottest fucking

kiss I've ever had anyone lay on me in all my thirty-two years.

He shook his head. "It was impulsive. I was out of line, and I'm truly sorry."

She kept her back to him for just a breath before turning to look over one shoulder, throwing him a saucy smile that slapped the chagrin right out of him.

"A word to the wise, boss. If you've gotta apologize after you kiss a girl, you might want to rethink your strategy. See you tomorrow."

And then she was gone.

Chapter Five

After her alarm went off for the third time, Sloane ran out of swear words and had no choice but to haul herself out of bed. Chucking a handful of sleep-mussed hair from her eyes, she plodded to the coffeepot, pausing just long enough to hit the auto-brew button with the back of one hand. The memory of Gavin's scorching hot kiss slammed back into her conscious thoughts with all the grace of a stampeding bull, and she swiped a hand over her lips in an effort to get them to stop tingling.

Well, hell. It hadn't worked for the two hours she'd spent twisting around in her bed last night before finally dropping off to sleep at three A.M. What on earth made her think it was going to work now?

"Hrmmph." She directed the grunt at her cell phone, whose beep signaled an unread text message. Carly's number flashed across the top of the screen, and Sloane palmed her phone with a bleary grumble as she trudged to the bathroom. Time was of the essence, and while she drew the line at texting and driving, she could text and brush her teeth with the best of them.

How was babysitting? Money=good, yes? Gav is a
good guy. Trust me! PS, rehearsal Friday, 5 P.M. sharp!

She made a sour face around her mouthful of tooth-
paste, and not just at the prospect of attending her best
friend's wedding rehearsal, an event that would likely send
her mother into the stratosphere. If her sister Angela
wasn't ready to pop with baby number three any minute
now, Sloane's mother wouldn't hesitate to attend the wedding and make her life a living hell in person.

She made a mental note to send her sister Angela a
thank-you note and stuffed her mother's disapproval down,
knowing she'd have to cross the you-need-to-settle-down
bridge again soon enough. Dwelling on the inevitability
would only make it worse.

At any rate, Sloane thought as she rinsed her tooth-
brush, Carly was right. The money *was* good, and she
needed it desperately. She'd tried like hell last night to get
a workable idea on paper, or at least do a little legwork so
she could dive right in once she got to Greece, but her
muse had remained solidly unimpressed. So much for the
possibility of tutoring being the light for her creative fire.
Right about now, Sloane had all the spark of wet logs in
the wilderness.

Dry humping in the living room notwithstanding.

"Oh, forget the kiss, girl! And anyway, a deal's a deal."
Adding a temporary nanny gig to her résumé might not
have done much for her creativity, but at least the job got
her one step closer to packing her bags. Still, the rest of
the cash wasn't going to simply appear via Fairy God-
mother, and she was going to have to come up with one
hell of a fallback plan in order to get herself to book-
writing Nirvana.

Sloane made her way back to the kitchen, pouring a cup
of coffee with one hand while dialing her cell phone with

the other. Just because she'd dismissed her misgivings about playing Mary Poppins for a couple of weeks didn't mean she couldn't dish out a little well-placed attitude. After all, Carly had all but offered her up on a platter.

"If you're calling to give me a hard time, save your breath. You need the money, and I can't run a restaurant without a general manager." Her best friend's sleepy voice murmured over the line without the benefit of a hello, and Sloane bit back a laugh in response.

"Your preemptive strike will get you nowhere. I can't believe you threw me to the wolves."

"It was only one wolf, and besides, it's a perfectly workable solution." Leave it to Carly to be so matter-of-fact.

The dark, piercing gaze Gavin had sent right into her bones just before he'd kissed her last night shock waved through Sloane's memory, sending an electric hum through her blood like she'd been slapped upside the head with a tuning fork. "There is nothing workable about me and your GM. He's wound tighter than a Salvation Army drum, I swear to God."

She tucked the phone to her ear and flattened her palms over both forearms to give the goose bumps that had sprouted there a vigorous rub. After all, the kiss he'd planted on her had no sooner moved from oh-yes to oh-*hell*-yes when Gavin not only snapped out of it, but fell all over himself to make a formal apology. The whole thing had left Sloane in a moment of rare embarrassment, wondering if she'd conjured the sizzling passion out of thin air. Hell, she *had* been grasping for romantic ideas all night. She'd probably just been projecting on the nearest available male body.

Never mind that it had been the first male body to ever stir a potential orgasm between her thighs, and that she'd wanted him so badly, she'd climbed him like a tree.

At least her fight or flight instincts hadn't dallied in getting her out the door. Thank God some things still worked flawlessly.

Carly chuckled, yanking Sloane's sizzling thoughts back down to planet Earth. "Just because he takes his job seriously doesn't mean Gavin's a bad guy. Look at it this way, babysitting his sister is less painful than selling your eggs to a fertility clinic, right?"

"Marginally." Sloane headed down the hall to her bedroom with her cup in hand and the phone still tucked to her ear, shaking off the last of the weird ripple coursing through her. Arriving at her dresser, she set her hands to work in a flurry of motion, tugging a few things mercilessly from the drawers. "You know kids and I don't mix."

"It's only for two weeks. And besides, if anyone's tough enough to handle a thirteen-year-old, it's you."

Sloane made a disdainful noise and paused to slurp her coffee. "Please. The first and pretty much only thing the kid said to me was that she didn't need me." She hesitated before admitting, "And I have to be honest. She's basically right."

"I thought Gavin said she was having trouble in school," Carly said, sounding confused.

"Oh, she's failing. Or she was." Sloane sent another slosh of coffee down the hatch, cradling the mug in one hand while snapping up more clothing with the other. "But as soon as I started working with her, it became pretty clear she's no slouch in the smarts department. She had an F because she didn't do the assignments. Not because she couldn't."

The bewilderment in Carly's voice grew even thicker. "I don't get it. Why would she intentionally flunk a class if she knows it'll land her not just with a tutor, but in Gavin's poor graces too? It doesn't make any sense."

"It does if she's trying to work him down to his very last nerve. Now *that* is something this kid excels at." She threw back the last of her coffee and stuck the empty mug on her dresser next to two partially drained water bottles and a handful of Post-its bearing scribbled book notes. "Anyway, you're right. The gig isn't that bad. If I'm tough enough to stand up and give a toast at your wedding, then I am indeed tough enough to handle the next two weeks with a cranky eighth grader."

Carly's voice sparked with excitement. "Hey, speaking of which, did you pick a dress yet?"

Sloane shook her head even though Carly couldn't see it and padded into her closet for a pair of jeans. "I still can't believe you're not picking the bridesmaids' dresses yourself. Seriously, you're the most laid-back bride on the planet." At last count, Sloane had been in six weddings over the last ten years. She had the battle scars and the bad wardrobe to prove it.

"Are you kidding? We're lucky I picked a dress for me. No way am I picking yours too. Just wear black to go with the guys' suits, and you'll be fine."

Sloane turned, doing a ten-second run-through of the dresses in her closet that were fancy enough to pass muster. She stopped at a dark red garment bag, trying not to shudder as her fingers passed over the plastic. "Yeah, I'll probably just go with that satin A-line dress my sister Rosie had us wear at her wedding."

"You hate that dress."

Sloane bit her lip to keep from agreeing, heading down the hall to the bathroom. "It's not so bad."

A muffled snort filtered over the line. "You said it made all the bridesmaids look like statuary."

Sloane's laugh shot out in a quick burst before she

clamped her teeth over it. "I don't suppose you'll buy that I meant it as a compliment?"

"Ho-hum and fading into the background isn't a compliment," Carly accused, albeit jokingly. "If you wear that dress, you'll be miserable."

Sloane opened her mouth to argue, but she couldn't. The dress was so freaking boring, it didn't even put the *fun* in *functional*. But most of the gowns in her closet were total showstoppers. And while that was a perfect fit for her outgoing personality, her best friend's wedding was a different story. The only head-turning gown at this blessed event should be on the bride, period. For once, Sloane was determined to blend in to the wallpaper.

The leftover bridesmaid's dress from her sister's wedding should more than do the trick.

Carly interrupted her thoughts. "Why don't you wear that gorgeous dress you got in Madrid? It's black, and it looks so pretty on you."

Sloane snorted and cranked the shower up as hot as the dial would allow. "I can't wear my tango dress to your wedding."

"Why not? I love that dress." Carly let out a breathy sigh, but Sloane was unconvinced.

"I love it too, but come on. That dress is . . . well, it's . . ."

"It's perfect," Carly finished for her, her tone brooking zero argument.

Okay, fine. So the delicately beaded dress was a definite stunner, but it didn't earn any marks in the subtlety department. As a long, flowing column of ebony silk with a strategically placed slit up one side, it had come by its nickname honestly. Sloane had broken it in as she tangoed her way across Spain, gathering all the sexy fodder for her third book.

Maybe putting it on again was just the jump start she needed to begin getting words on the page.

"Come on, *cucciola*." Carly went in for the I'm-the-bride kill. "You have to wear it. It's so *you*, I can't imagine you standing next to me wearing anything else."

A smile tugged at the edges of Sloane's lips. The slinky, black sheath really was one of Sloane's favorite garments. If ever she'd felt comfortable in something, that dress was it.

"Fine. But I draw the line at walking down the aisle with a rose between my teeth."

"Deal. Now please get your ass to work. The last thing I need is for Gavin to be crabby because you were fashionably late."

"I'm always fashionably late," Sloane said, eyeing the clock. She hustled back into the bathroom, pulling her tattered New York Yankees sleep shirt over her head as she went.

"Not today, please. Now go." Carly's laugh echoed over the line for just a second before she ended the call, and within thirty seconds, the rest of Sloane's clothing had hit the floor in a jumbled heap. She closed her eyes, letting the near-scalding water roll over her shoulders.

Maybe today she could get something on the page. Just a sketch or a glimmer would be enough, an image of something that would spark the rest in her mind's eye. She shook her head, scattering a stream of warm water and scented suds down her back as she washed her hair and let her thoughts wander.

Sexy . . . sexy . . . she needed something sexy, but not obviously so, kind of like her dress. Sure, it was beautiful on the surface, but it was only when it was off the hanger and on her warm body that it felt truly sensual. Sloane needed a hint of something surprising in its seductiveness.

Something that heated and lingered all at the same time.

Water sluiced down her back, caressing the fold of her shoulder where it tucked into her neck and releasing all the tension knit tightly in her body. The image of lean, corded muscles, fitting perfectly beneath taut skin swirled in her brain, and she let the picture form more clearly. No extravagantly bulging muscles on this hero forming in her mind, uh-uh. His outline spoke of something efficient and direct, almost raw in how pared down it was.

Sloane's breath slid through her lungs more quickly as she pictured the guy against the backdrop of her closed eyelids. He was angular and silent and wicked in his intensity, the kind of man whose actions spoke volumes compared to his words. And those actions could make an absolute symphony of a woman's body.

"Yeah," she breathed, reaching a hand out toward the cool, slick tiles of the shower wall, steadying herself while fastening the passionate image securely into place. His hands would be the perfect combination of rough masculinity and agile grace, both strong and beautiful. He'd know just how to use them on a woman, coaxing her to perfection in deliberate strokes, like Michelangelo discovering the statue hidden inside a marble slab. And once he'd used those deft hands on every inch of her wanting skin, he'd start all over again.

With his mouth.

"Oh, God." The juncture between Sloane's thighs went tight and hot, spearing tendrils of want all the way up to her belly, and a keening sigh spilled from her lips. She needed to open her eyes and get this on the page, but the image was so lush and real, so goddamned *hot,* it was impossible to force her lids open.

Her brain gave another wanton shove, and suddenly, the man fit against her body, matching her warmth in all the right places. Sloane let her mind trail across the hard planes of his chest, pressed against her own with nothing but water and bad intentions between his slippery skin and hers.

His mouth was fast and unforgiving in her mind as he skimmed a hot line over her shoulder, setting the edge of his teeth to the slope of it with just enough pressure to balance the sensation with more excruciating heat. He lifted his eyes, locking them on hers, and for one suspended moment, Sloane lost herself in the depths of imaginary desire.

Until she connected the liquid brown gaze of her fantasy man with its real-world owner, and her breath slammed through her lungs in a hard gasp.

Chapter Six

Ten minutes after jerking the shower dial all the way into cold territory, Sloane was dry, dressed, and no less hot and bothered by the naughty images she'd conjured of the guy who was about to sign the only paycheck she'd seen in months.

Emphasis on *bothered*.

"Seriously . . . I'm losing my mind," she muttered into a travel mug the size of a fishbowl and elbowed her way out the door, only to be blasted in the face by sunlight so bright, it bordered on cruel.

"Gah!" Not even a full-bodied jerk-and-wince could save her completely, and Sloane had no choice but to shutter her eyes closed in an act of self-defense.

Gavin's smoldering glance popped back into her brain, as clear as a billboard on Broadway.

Sloane's lids flew back open to reveal the last remnants of a jewel-toned sunrise filtering through bare trees. Golden light played brightly on the frost-encrusted grass, sending sparkles bouncing in every direction like fresh-cut diamonds scattered on velvet. Surely, the view up here in God's country should be breathtaking enough to eradicate any other mental image, no matter how attractive.

Sloane settled her eyes closed once more, determined to replace passionate looks with pastoral landscapes.

Good *Lord,* the man's eyes were so sexy, it was just unfair!

"Okay, that's enough." Sloane huffed her way down the frozen concrete pavers leading to the driveway, sliding a pair of huge Tom Ford sunglasses up the bridge of her nose. The now-bearable sunlight folded around the trees that formed a perimeter around her rented bungalow, creating that pastoral scene in her head like an epic showing of *too little, too late.*

Oh, sure. The sun could do its best to turn her corneas to early morning toast, but ask it to do a little thing like help blot out a couple of ultrasexy images, and it just twinkled benevolently from behind a damned tree. Like racy thoughts of the person signing your paycheck were not only normal, but encouraged.

Sloane put the Fiat in Drive and commanded herself to get a grip. The last thing she needed was to blow the tiny shred of focus she'd managed to work up, thinking of a guy who wasn't even her type. The smoldering kiss he'd leveled at her last night—the one that was clearly wreaking havoc on her overeager neurons—had been a mistake, and she absolutely had to expunge it from her memory. Getting down to business was priority number one, and creating a paper hero who looked nothing like Gavin Carmichael topped that list.

She jammed her eyes shut so tightly they tingled, forcing away the image of those deep brown eyes, fringed with lashes as warm and decadent as a tray full of cinnamon rolls. Instead, she pictured Gavin scowling and holding a plaque that read YOUR NEW BOSS, AKA THE ICE KING beneath his handsomely chiseled jaw.

Well, *that* did the trick.

When she pulled into the familiar gravel driveway a

few minutes later, Sloane had adjusted her mental snapshot of Gavin to that of a regular guy with ordinary eyes and dime-a-dozen features. After all, she'd seen him a bunch of times at La Dolce Vita, and not one of those meetings had ever prompted illicit shower fantasies. She mounted the front porch steps with a decisive nod. Her imagination had just gotten the best of her, that's all. No harm, no foul.

"Good morning." Gavin stood in the open doorway, wearing a perfectly pressed blue dress shirt that emphasized his deep brown eyes like an unfair advantage, and Sloane nearly choked on her tongue.

"Bree's still sleeping, so I figured I'd catch you before you rang the bell." He held the door open, ushering her inside with a polite nod. Even though he looked like he'd sprouted from the pages of *GQ,* his tone was all business, and it gave Sloane's composure a kick-start in the right direction.

Okay, fine. So his eyes were definitely the color of satiny milk chocolate, shot through with just a hint of gold flecks around the edges. It didn't mean she was going to get all swoony over him. Her energy and imagination were strictly for book writing. And, hello. Boss, boss, boss!

"What kind of thirteen-year-old doesn't sleep like the dead?" She shook herself the rest of the way back to Earth as she hustled past him into the cottage, mentally adding one last *boss!* for good measure.

Gavin paused, shutting the door behind her and stepping into the entryway. The light, clean notes of his cologne filled her nose enough to entice but not overpower.

It was way too early for this.

"Sometimes she has trouble sleeping, plus she did all that work last night, so I thought I'd let her sleep in a little. Anyway, I put on a pot of coffee." He tipped his chin toward the kitchen, light brown hair glinting in the sunlight coming through the window. "Help yourself to a refill."

His crisp tone nudged the rational side of her brain, making it easier to shake her impure thoughts about his melty eyes. "Thanks." She toasted him with her travel mug, determined to duck past him without fanfare, but he stopped short, blocking her path.

"I . . . ah, I just want to make sure everything is okay." Gavin cleared his throat and examined his loafers, clearly uncomfortable as hell.

Well, that made two of them. Not that Sloane was about to show it. After all, a girl had her pride.

"Other than the fact that no human being should be up this early on a Saturday, life is grand." She flashed a bigger-than-necessary smile in his direction, but he didn't budge.

"I meant between us."

Sloane resisted the urge to look at the door. "We got a little carried away and kissed, Gavin," she said, forcing her voice to a breezy calm. "I can forget about it if you can."

He paused, and she sent up a fervent prayer.

Please don't dwell on it, because if we relive that kiss live in person, forgetting about it will be a complete and utter no-go.

"Okay," he said. Wait, was that relief or disappointment flooding through her veins? Clearly, she needed more coffee to keep her brain online.

"You said there's more coffee in the kitchen, right?" Sloane hauled in a deep breath, and was pleased to discover that it actually chilled her out a little.

"Coffee. Right. Yes." Gavin turned on his well-polished heel and moved through the entryway toward the living room. As she followed him farther into the cottage, the black and white prints on the living room wall snagged her attention again.

"These are pretty," she said, stopping to take a closer look. Gavin halted halfway across the living room floorboards, turning to lay eyes on her before sparing a glance at the photographs.

"Thank you."

"Did you take them?" Sloane edged close enough to the photos to run her fingertips along one polished black frame. A few years had passed since the trip abroad that had fueled her unbridled creativity. All the places where she'd written—tiny trattorias in Venice, grassy hillsides in Tuscany, and then later in cafés in Provence and Madrid— they all cascaded together now, a series of blurry fragments rather than the solid outlines and crisp details she used to know by heart.

She was losing her inspiration, bit by bit. And nothing short of being there was going to get it back.

"Yes."

"Florence?"

"Most of them." Gavin kept his gaze fixed on her, his expression as blank as if they were discussing the weather rather than one of the most beautiful places on the planet.

"Did you take them recently?" She was pushing, she knew. But as she stood there, grasping at the elusive memory of her own experience, Sloane suddenly ached so hard to unearth the spark again that she didn't care.

"Two years ago." Gavin's clipped answer was a clear indicator he'd rather not talk about it, but rather than clam up like anyone else would, Sloane closed her eyes and let her words flow.

"There are vineyards like this along the Via Francigena." Her mind's eye stuttered like an old movie projector, stirring up snapshotlike images of ancient stone-cobbled pathways and trees thick with the suggestion of summer turning into fall, but the pictures faded quickly, refusing to stay put.

"You traveled the Via Francigena?" Gavin's words were heavy with recognition and surprise.

She nodded, letting a smile touch her lips before opening her eyes. "Only from Tuscany to Rome. Do you know the route?"

"Of course. It's one of the most well-known medieval trade routes in history. I've just never met anyone who's traveled the actual path."

"It's time consuming, but worth every second."

His eyes turned wary. "Wait . . . you didn't *walk* it, did you?"

She barked out a quick laugh, watching Gavin's expression morph from doubt to outright shock. "The ancients walked the entire path from Canterbury as a pilgrimage," she said. "Getting from Florence to Rome on foot isn't as hard as it sounds. Really, it's just one step at a time. Plus, it's not like I did it in a day or anything. I was there for six weeks."

"Still, there's what? A hundred and fifty miles between Florence and Rome? And you just walked it?"

Jeez. You'd have thought she'd just told him she was a celestial being from the planet Insanity rather than copping to some extended sightseeing. Then again, it wasn't like she was unused to people thinking she was unorthodox. "Actually, I think it's closer to a hundred and seventy-five."

"You think?"

She shrugged. "I was a little distracted by the whole gorgeous landmark thing to count."

Okay, so walking the beautiful path of the Via Francigena might seem a little crazy in hindsight, but the sheer awe she'd felt following in the literal footsteps of so many people seeking enlightenment of their own had set her creativity on fire. She'd outlined and drafted her entire first book with her feet on that path. Crazy or not, there was simply no substitute.

"So you spent over a month of your life wandering the Italian countryside on foot, rather than hitting the major cities to vacation like pretty much everyone else?"

The fact that she'd surprised him felt oddly satisfying. "Oh, I spent time in Venice and Milan, too. But the whole point of the trip was to find inspiration. What better place to do that than a pilgrimage route, really? I mean, you thought it was beautiful enough to take these pictures, right?"

She paused, sweeping a gesture at the photographs lined up on the wall with all the austerity of the Queen's Guard. "All I really wanted to do was take things in, at my own pace, so I'd never forget it."

And yet, she had. Just like that.

God, this whole thing was stupid. All the tiny villages, every stone church and garden courtyard, all of it had been reduced to memories she could no longer bring forth with any sort of clarity. Gavin clearly didn't want to skip down memory lane, and anyway, all the reminiscing in the world wasn't going to bring her inspiration back. Sloane buttoned her lips, determined to drop it.

"There are a couple of incredible vineyards along the VF stops in Tuscany. I took these first two photographs in Barberino Val d'Elsa," Gavin said, so quietly she nearly missed it.

"What?" Surprise spurted in her chest.

"Barberino Val d'Elsa, just south of Florence." He pointed to the photographs closest to the entryway. "The chianti is unreal."

"Wait a second." Sloane leaned in so close that her breath fogged the glass, her pulse jackhammering through her veins. "I remember this village! There was a little hillside chapel, with a courtyard garden in the back, and a low wall, made up of these really old stacked stones I was sure would topple at the first sign of a stiff breeze."

Gavin nodded, his eyes going a shade warmer. "Definitely Val d'Elsa. That chapel is a couple hundred years old. Last I saw, the wall is still standing, but barely."

The memory of the courtyard, with its heavy slab benches and dark, flowering vines, flitted back to Sloane's mind like the soft cotton of a whisper, and she tackled it with glee. "God, how could I have not made the connection? It's just past this grove of trees, right here." She tapped the edge of the frame. "I must've outlined the first eight chapters of my debut novel sitting by that wall!"

Gavin cleared his throat in a masculine rumble. "So, ah, that's what you were doing last night? You know, with all the crumpled-up papers?" He indicated the floor with one hand, and the stark reminder of Sloane's failed attempts brought her squarely back to the present.

"Yeah. Obviously the process works better in some places than others."

"I'm sorry. I didn't mean to bring up a sore subject." He looked so truly remorseful that she had no choice but to smile. This pity-party crap was totally overrated, and anyway, she'd be back in Europe again, scribbling away before she knew it.

"No worries, boss. The next book always comes from somewhere."

Sloane's eyes dashed over the photograph one more time, where dappled sunlight filtered through the curling fingers of the grapevines and the weatherworn stakes securing them tightly into the ground.

She'd found inspiration plenty of times before. She'd find it again, no problem. Just as soon as she landed in Greece, she'd be as right as a cocktail on a Friday night.

Gavin scratched his head, and the slightly ruffled look

it left behind struck her as oddly endearing. "Well, it might not be ideal, but you're welcome to use the breakfast nook in the kitchen if you think it'll work better than the couch. The printer is right there in the kitchen, too. You could link your laptop to our wireless if you ever needed to use it. Then you'd at least have a little bit more workspace. Maybe it'll help."

She bit back a full-blown laugh so as not to wake Bree. The simplicity of the offer was ironic enough to overwhelm her, as if moving a few feet and having a little more room to stretch out would give her a whole new perspective. Hell, she'd moved her writing spot from one end of Pine Mountain to the other for a whole year, and it had given her nothing but stale ideas she couldn't use. Sloane opened her mouth to deliver a sarcastic response, something to the tune of if-only-it-were-so-easy, when the look on Gavin's face stopped her cold. His expression flickered with genuine niceness, not the cool indifference she'd seen for much of yesterday, and without thinking, she replied, "Thanks. I'll definitely give that a try."

There were a couple of tried and true places to catch a quick nap in between Saturday shifts at La Dolce Vita, provided you weren't claustrophobic or terribly picky. At his current level of sleep deprivation, Gavin was neither. Not only had he tossed and turned trying to burn the slideshow of Sloane's exotically golden skin and pouty lips from his short-term memory, but Bree had had a nightmare, her third one this week.

Hearing her cry from across the hall in the middle of the night was hard enough. Her refusal to talk about it, not even to let him comfort her, was nearly unbearable. But no matter how hard he tried, she uttered the same terse "I'm fine" before cranking her mouth shut and turning over in bed, and he had no choice but to give in to her silence and walk away. He'd given up even asking, simply padding across the floorboards to stand in her doorframe whenever he heard her sharp cries, waiting for her to acknowledge him and hoping her words would change.

They never did.

Gavin shook himself back to reality with a groggy blink. If he didn't get some sleep in the ninety-minute lull between his lunch and dinner responsibilities, he was going to end up making *Night of the Living Dead* look like a frigging beauty pageant. He maneuvered past the swinging doors at the pass, through the hushed quiet of the industrial kitchen and past the office where he heard the indistinct murmur of Carly's voice. With a silent prayer for solitude, Gavin made a beeline for the small but usually quiet staff lounge.

Mercifully, the lights were off, and he made his way into the lounge with an exhale of relief. Only fragments of muted daylight filtered past the blinds, and even those had turned a heavy gray with a cold front he'd heard some lunch-goers talking about. Not that the daylight mattered. He would probably fall asleep ten seconds after his head hit the throw pillow on the couch even if the sun itself showed up in the room for a song and dance.

Gavin bit back a groan as his frame sank to the cushions. His body was so overjoyed at no longer being vertical that he didn't realize he wasn't alone until the gruff sound of a throat being cleared interrupted his bliss.

"Oh, sorry." He levered himself up from his halfway reclined position on the couch, squinting at the well-muscled figure sitting in the far corner of the shadows.

The hulking outline could only belong to one person on La Dolce Vita's staff. Adrian Holt might wear chef's whites and whip up elegant meals with one tattooed arm tied behind his back, but the guy could easily pass for a pro wrestler turned lumberjack. Not the kind of person whose space you wanted to invade.

"It's cool. I was just trying to catch some quiet." Adrian's eyes flickered, barely visible in the low light of the lounge but for the stainless steel piercing marking his dark brow. "Chef's driving me nuts with down-to-the-wire wedding plans, so I came in here to escape. I'll be glad after next Saturday, when she's back to normal again."

"Yeah, a guy can only take so much discussion about bridesmaids' dresses and chocolate fountains before he's tempted to lose his mind," Gavin agreed.

"Planned a wedding recently, have you?" Adrian's response was laden with sarcasm, but it arrowed into Gavin's chest all the same. Damn it, he'd said too much. The thought of airing out those memories, even in a vague admission to a gruff coworker who probably wouldn't ask questions anyway, still made him uneasy.

"Just stuff I've overheard. Carly's wedding plans are kind of hard to miss." As tired as he was, Gavin pondered forgoing sleep in favor of a good, stiff drink. "Although I have to say, Chef seems pretty laid-back about it, as far as brides go."

Adrian nodded, a quick jerk of his platinum-dyed head. "Fair enough. She's too frickin' happy to go full-on Bridezilla, anyway." They sat in silence for a minute, and Gavin's lingering exhaustion left him unprepared for the shift in subject.

"Hey, she told me you hired Sloane to babysit your sister, huh? Interesting move."

His gut tightened, and he sat up straighter against the plush couch cushions. "Carly's the one who suggested it, and so far it's working out. I take it you know Sloane."

It made sense that he would, given that Adrian, Carly, and Sloane all had the same hard Brooklyn accent and that Adrian had been Carly's sous-chef for four years. But since Gavin made it a point not to share his own particulars, that usually meant not hearing anybody else's either.

Adrian's low chuckle was full of gravel. "She and Carly have been best friends since they were in kneesocks, man. It's kind of tough to know one without the other."

A picture of Sloane wearing kneesocks and one of those infuriatingly sexy short pleated skirts flashed through Gavin's mind with startling clarity, and he tamped it down with all his might.

"Oh, I, uh, guess so," he said, clearing his throat. Great. Sleep deprivation was making him insane.

Adrian rolled a thick shoulder, continuing, "I'm surprised she took the job, though. I thought she was writing the great American love story or something."

The image of the schoolgirl skirt was replaced by that of a floppy blue and white striped sun hat, and Gavin latched on to the quirky image to smooth out his demeanor. "She's only watching my sister temporarily. Our regular sitter had an emergency."

"Ah. Well, as off the wall as she seems, Sloane's all right." The words were as close to a ringing endorsement as Gavin had ever heard from Adrian, and they sparked his curiosity.

A beat of silence passed, then two before he had to ask, "She takes her career pretty seriously, huh?"

Adrian's laugh was like a growl without the anger. "Took her long enough to get there, so I guess so."

His inquiring mind did a slow burn, like embers just waiting for something to engulf in flames. "What'd she do before becoming a writer?"

"More like what didn't she do. In the time it took me and Carly to move up the ranks as chefs, Sloane's had some pretty unconventional jobs."

"More unconventional than writing romance novels?" It wasn't a dime-a-dozen kind of career, like being an accountant or a doctor or even a restaurant manager. She was definitely the only person he'd ever met to make a living writing steamy books.

"She taught ballroom dancing for a while. Oh, and then she was a hand model. You know, for jewelry circulars and catalogs and stuff?" Adrian's face split into a knowing grin.

The idea of Sloane teaching the waltz to some poor guy whose mother or wife insisted he take dancing lessons seemed kind of unfair. Hell, he wasn't half-bad in the dance department, and even he was tempted to trip over his imaginary friend at the sight of her.

Gavin cleared his throat. "That's not so bad," he said, although he couldn't deny that his curiosity was now at a full simmer. Adrian's lifted brows translated to a nonverbal *we're just getting started*.

"She also apprenticed in a glass blowing studio someplace in Arizona, ran deliveries for a bagel shop, and did a stint as a blackjack dealer in Atlantic City." He broke off with a shrug. "I could go on all day, and I'm probably forgetting half of it."

Gavin's curiosity skipped catching fire and went right for spontaneous combustion. "Are you serious?"

Adrian nodded. "As a heart attack, man. That woman is going places even in her sleep."

Unease nestled into the pit of Gavin's stomach in a series of sharp pokes. As flighty as she seemed, he hadn't thought Sloane irresponsible, otherwise he'd never have trusted her to look after Bree. Plus, her literary accomplishments were pretty impressive. Something wasn't adding up.

"So she's just writing to fill the time until the next thing comes along?"

"Nah." Adrian settled his kitchen-tested black clogs on the floor and stood to stretch. "She's been writing longer than she did all of the other stuff combined, so my guess is that it's going to stick. Still moves around like the freaking wind, though. It's not hard to lose count of all the places she's lived."

Sloane's story about traveling to Florence threaded through Gavin's mind, and realization dinged him hard. Of course she moved around a lot, single girl with no attachments. Why wouldn't she? Hell, his life had been the same way just a year and a half ago.

Watching his mother go through surgery and chemo had made it feel as if the intervening months had been ten times that long. Not that he would trade the chance to have spent those precious last days with her, or the opportunity to be with Bree, no matter what it had cost him. In truth, he'd missed them both every time he got on a plane to start up a new restaurant, and as much as Gavin loved his job, the traveling part always took a toll on him. His mom and Bree were the only family he had ever known, and he'd have gladly lost everything, including the shirt off his back, before he'd give up caring for them when it really mattered.

Adrian cracked a grin, examining him so closely that he was tempted to flinch. "Don't worry about Sloane. Like I said, she's all right. Worth having on your side. For as long as she's around, anyway."

Gavin nodded, swallowing thickly but cementing his standard cool facial expression into place. The last thing he wanted was to let the weird feeling swirling in his gut show on his face. Why should he care about Sloane's whereabouts? Where she went and how long she stayed— or didn't stay—was none of his business. "I'll keep it in mind. Thanks."

"No problem. Get some shut-eye. Tonight's gonna be a killer."

Adrian pulled the door shut with a tight click, and

Gavin sank back into the couch, releasing a slow breath. He'd come in here to find a few minutes of respite to get his head back on straight, but between his restless mind and his churning gut, the chances of it actually happening looked pretty bleak. Cold rain trickled down the window across from the couch, and a stark memory tugged at the corners of his mind, demanding the forefront.

When Bree had angrily compared Sloane to his ex-fiancée, his first response had been to laugh. On the surface, the two women were nothing alike. Yes, they were both pretty, career-driven women—Caroline had taken her job as an interior designer for the Gourmet Network's makeover show, *Five Star Restaurant,* very seriously—but their personalities seemed like a light, crisp Riesling compared to a full-bodied Merlot. Sure, they were both great wines, but hell if you could find any other similarities.

Gavin closed his eyes, letting the image of Caroline's blond hair, brown eyes, and petite frame solidify and flood back into his mind's eye. It had been cold and rainy that night in Philadelphia, when he told Caroline he wanted to put off leaving his family. Not just until his mother recovered from her mastectomy, not only to see her through the last-chance round of debilitating chemo, or to hold her fragile yet steadfast hand when her oncologist gravely told her it had failed. No, he told her. He was done traveling from city to city. He wanted to stay indefinitely.

He wanted to take care of Bree, not just because his mother had begged him to make sure she'd be okay, but because he loved them both, and caring for her felt right. Hell, if he'd been around more often instead of jet-setting all over the planet with his high-profile job, maybe his mother wouldn't have been too busy to schedule her regular mammogram in the first place. He knew then that he belonged with Bree, as her family, and he wanted Caroline to be part of that. To marry him like they'd planned so they could have a family together.

As soon as the words had come from his mouth, he'd known she wouldn't stay. Of course, she supported him as he grieved for his mother, and promised to do whatever he needed to help care for Bree. Gavin never doubted that Caroline loved him and that her promise was well-intentioned, but he'd seen the tiny flicker of shadows that had darted through her eyes like a quick jolt of panic, and in hindsight, he knew.

Of course, Bree hadn't made it easy, fighting Caroline to the teeth at every turn. Add the pressure of Gavin not being able to find a job in the saturated Philadelphia restaurant market, and the inconsistency of Caroline's breakneck travel schedule for her own job, and it was a recipe for disaster. Things with Bree became increasingly strained, and the nicer Caroline tried to be, the harder Bree fought her kindness. After three months of trying to make things work, Caroline finally admitted that maybe taking care of a child with such an emotional background wasn't in her future, and he'd had no choice but to watch her go.

An angry gust of wind scattered hard raindrops against the glass, bringing Gavin back to the staff lounge with a start, and he bulldozed the memory into the back of his brain.

Dwelling on Caroline and all the what-ifs was pointless now. What he needed more than anything else was to figure out a way to connect with Bree, to help her past the grief that was clearly still bogging her down. If a woman came along who had the sticking power to help him with that, then great. But no way was he going to roll the dice on anyone who wouldn't be around for the long haul, especially when that long haul involved the ups and downs of an emotional preteen. So maybe Sloane had more in common with Caroline than he'd thought.

Which was all the more reason he needed to stay the hell away from her.

Chapter Seven

By the time Bree emerged, bleary-eyed and still yawning, from her bedroom at ten forty-five, Sloane had amassed a brand-new pile of failed attempts at a paper hero—or a paper *anything*—by her feet.

"Oh, hey." She scratched out the latest horrible idea with a sigh and poked the brim of her hat from her eyes before looking up. "You're awake."

Bree rubbed her sleep-swollen eyes with one hand. "How come you didn't wake me up?"

"Um, I didn't know I was supposed to." Damn it, Gavin had never said anything about waking her up eventually. How was she supposed to know she had to wake the kid up at a certain time? It seemed kind of mean, considering it was Saturday, but then again, what did she know about this kind of thing?

"Mrs. Teasdale usually wakes me by nine. She says it's good for me to have a regular sleep schedule."

Sloane took off her hat and pushed her pencil behind her ear, looking at Bree with interest. "Who's Mrs. Teasdale?"

"The lady who normally babysits me." Bree's face bent into a disdainful frown.

Ah, the regular sitter. Of course that lady probably knew how to take care of kids in her sleep. "You don't like her?"

"She's okay, I guess. She says getting up at the same time every morning makes for a happy, healthy day."

Sloane barely bit back the rude noise bubbling in her throat. What a load of happy, healthy crap. Then again, she was probably a teensy bit biased, being that she was as far from a morning person as a girl could get. "And what do you think?"

Bree's eyes widened. "What do you mean?"

"I mean what I said. It's your schedule, right? Do you think waking up at nine is a good idea?"

While Sloane could admit she didn't have a clue how much sleep a thirteen-year-old was supposed to get and that her own sleep schedule had all the twists and turns of an ancient treasure map, not asking Bree what she thought about her own sleep habits seemed kind of stupid. If the kid was tired on a Saturday, who was Sloane to wake her up?

"I'm usually up anyway." Bree pulled at the hem of her pajama top. "Plus, it makes it kind of hard to get up for school and stuff if my sleep schedule on the weekend is all messed up."

Huh. Okay, so that made sense. Still . . . "But that doesn't answer the question. Do you like getting up early on the weekend?"

Bree measured Sloane with a wary glance, yanking the hem of her top even harder to twist it around her thumb. "Well, it's hard to get up sometimes. Especially if . . ." She jerked her words to a halt, letting her shirt fall loosely from her fingers. "No. I guess I don't like it."

Sloane nodded, looking down at her legal pad. The scratched-out words sent weariness into her bones, and she cast it aside in favor of a good stretch. "I can relate.

Lucky for you, you've got the whole day to go back to bed if you feel like it. After that last assignment gets done, anyway."

"Are you seriously going to let me do whatever I want if I finish that paper?" Bree's skepticism was evident in both her tone and her expression, but Sloane wasn't about to renege on their deal. How much trouble could one kid stir up at home, anyway?

"As long as it's not illegal or dangerous, sure." She shrugged.

"Turn my stereo up as loud as it'll go?"

"Something tells me if you blow out your speakers, your brother won't buy you new ones. But if you've got the cash to spare, knock yourself out." Maybe a little loud music would nudge her creative juices into flow-mode. That could be a good idea for both of them.

"Okay, what about letting me wear black eyeliner, red lipstick, and a miniskirt that comes up to *here*." Bree indicated the top of her thigh in a dramatic sweeping gesture.

Sloane laughed, trying to picture such a brash look on the fresh-faced, sullen preteen. "If you want to Goth up in the privacy of your own home, go for it," she said. What could it hurt to let the kid parade around the living room dressed like Lady Gaga? It wasn't like they were going to go anywhere with her looking like that. All in all, a little Gaga never hurt a girl.

Bree's eyes glinted. "Okay. What if I want to drink a whole pot of coffee?"

"Get me some while you're up."

"Go all weekend without taking a shower or brushing my teeth?"

"Um, eww. That's up to you, but don't be mad when I nickname you Stinky Sue."

"Say the f-word ten times in a row at the top of my lungs?"

"Freedom of speech, sweetheart. And I've heard it once or twice before." As a matter of fact, Sloane had hurled the f-bomb at her alarm clock in three different languages before getting out of bed mere hours ago. "Anything else you want to do today?"

Bree's face flushed, her eyes darkening with emotion as she delivered her next words. "What if I smash the two-hundred-dollar bottle of Merlot sitting in the wine cellar? Then what?"

Whoa! Sloane jerked her spine to ramrod status, a bolt of fear traveling through each bone before dispersing outward with a hard tingle, like a heat signature. "Why would you do that?"

Bree blanked her expression, taking a step backward toward the kitchen as she averted her eyes. "I . . . I was just kidding. You know, trying to come up with something crazy. Forget it."

But Sloane couldn't. "Bree . . ." Thoughts clogged her brain, but none of them made sense. Everything else had been fun and games, silly stuff that any budding teenager might want to try. But not this. This was hurtful, designed to push someone away in anger. And from what little Sloane knew of Gavin, it would more than do the trick.

Why did she want to piss him off so badly?

"I'm going to go finish my paper." For just a breath, Bree didn't move, almost as if she was daring Sloane to try to stop her. Sloane opened her mouth to do just that, when a thought clattered unavoidably into her brain.

Sloane's maternal instincts couldn't even fill a thimble. What the hell would she say if Bree actually stopped to listen? Clearly, the kid knew she'd crossed the line, and she couldn't even go down the hall to pee without Sloane knowing her whereabouts, anyway. That made actual bottle-smashing seem highly unlikely. What was more, Sloane honestly didn't believe she'd follow through on her destructive suggestion even if she did have the chance.

Damn it, this was exactly why she steered clear of kids. How was she supposed to handle this? An argument with a thirteen-year-old wasn't really on her wish list, and somehow she didn't think Bree was in the mood for a lecture, either.

Finally, she just went with, "Okay. Do you want any help?"

Bree's gaze winged upward, as if commanded by the surprise evident on her face. Her eyes betrayed a hint of soft, childlike vulnerability, and in that instant, Sloane actually thought the kid would say yes.

But then she turned back toward her bedroom, not even bothering to slow her steps as she answered, "No. I'm fine all by myself."

Gavin trudged up the porch stairs on Sunday night with the firm knowledge that the ache he'd felt a few days ago had merely been child's play. At least Sunday's dinner service was abbreviated by an hour, and he'd managed to finish tallying receipts at eleven rather than the usual midnight. For all its tedium, though, his number crunching paid off in efficiency. They could run inventory just as easy as breathing at La Dolce Vita now that he'd implemented a system that worked. Gavin had no worries that his assistant manager would keep things running smoothly tomorrow on his much-needed day off.

He flipped the dead bolt, and just like the last two nights when he'd dragged himself home, the living room was the only illuminated space in the tiny cottage.

Similarly, a freshly minted host of crumpled papers lay scattered by the arm of the couch.

The piece of furniture itself, however, was decidedly vacant.

"Sloane?" A beat of silence passed, then two, without even a hint of movement in the rest of the house, and Gavin's breath quickened in his lungs. He took three strides to double back to the foyer and headed down the darkened hallway, his pulse popping with every step. Bree's bedroom door was shut tight, but he nudged it open for a quick check anyway.

Relief flowed through his veins as he caught sight of her curled soundly in bed, and he whispered the door shut so as not to wake her. A quick perusal revealed that Sloane hadn't opted for a snooze in the guest bedroom, and as usual, his bedroom door was firmly closed. Repeating his steps back to the entryway, Gavin's mounting worry edged out his irritation by only a hair.

Where the hell was she?

"Hello? Sloane?" There were only so many places to hide in the cottage, and unless she was sitting in the dark kitchen all by her lonesome, he'd exhausted the short list of choices. Gavin's frustration quickly surrendered to cold, hard panic, however, as he finally rounded the empty couch.

Sloane was lying on the floor in front of the coffee table, eyes closed and completely unmoving.

"Sloane!" His heart slammed in an honest effort to shoot free of his rib cage, and he dropped to the hardwood with an unforgiving *thunk*. Dread clutched at him with clammy fingers, and he grabbed her shoulders in a rough hold, lowering his head to instinctively listen for a breath.

Oh, fuck, please let her open her eyes, or take a breath, or something. Please let her . . .

A bolt of white-hot pain cracked from his nose all the way to the back of his skull.

Somewhere in the distance, he heard a familiar, feminine voice gasping his name, but he was too fascinated by the pretty, winking lights in his vision to try to figure it out.

Sparkly.

"Gavin! Oh God. Oh God oh God oh God. I'm so sorry." A flurry of movement rushed past his ears, and somewhere amid the crushing pain reverberating between his temples, he felt himself being eased backward onto a soft surface and covered with a warm, wonderful blanket.

Wait a second . . . the blanket had breasts. Nice ones.

Make that *really* wonderful.

"Gavin? Can you hear me?" The woman's voice rose and fell over inflections he vaguely recognized, and understanding snapped back at him like a rubber band on raw skin.

Clearly, Sloane was just fine, because she was practically straddling his chest.

"Yeah, of course I can hear you. You're right in my— *ow!*" Okay, so sitting up was a bad plan. He eased ungracefully back to the floor, highly aware of the heat of Sloane's body notched against his.

"Okay, shh. Just relax for a second." Her fingers coursed gently over the back of his neck, and he caught a nose full of the spicy, seductive scent of her skin.

Huh. Relaxing somehow got a little easier.

"What were . . . what were you doing on the floor?" His fragmented thoughts began spooling back together, and finally, blessedly, the marching band in his cranium started to tone things down.

Sloane's body tensed, a slight shift in the body weight still perched over him the only sign of her hesitance. "Um, meditating."

He cracked one eye open to catch her gesturing to a

bright yellow yoga mat beneath the tangle of their bodies. "Meditating?"

"Yeah. I thought it might give me some good ideas for my book, mental clarity, all that rot. I had my earphones in and didn't hear you come home. And then, well, you scared me half to death, and I guess I . . . I must've head-butted you." She bit her lip in apology, but then her attention seemed to snag on an unspoken thought. "Wait, what'd you think I was doing?"

Well, that explained the raging face pain. How had he not noticed the damned yoga mat? "I . . . well, never mind."

Of course, she didn't relent. "Seriously, why else would I crash on your floor?"

"Please," he said, letting his exasperation lead the way. "You're hardly predictable, Sloane."

She tensed, her muscles coiling tight against his body, and he instantly wished for the words back. Yes, he was irritated with her for scaring the shit out of him like that, but it was no excuse for taking a verbal jab at her.

"I'm sorry. It's just dangerous for you not to hear things like that. What if I'd been an intruder?" A bit of a lame recovery, but all told, not completely unfounded. What if something happened to her and Bree when they were alone at night?

"Then I'd have cold-cocked you just the same, making the cops' job easy?" Sloane released the words on a shrug, without the tiniest hint of remorse or worry that he could've been some thug with nasty intentions. Her face settled into a rare frown. "You don't have to worry about a repeat performance, anyway. It's not like it worked."

A pang shot through Gavin's gut. Maybe he *was* being a little tough on her. After all, he had slipped into the house pretty quietly. "I really am sorry," he mumbled, wincing at the residual twinge in his upper lip.

"No, you're right. I should be more careful. Are you sure you're okay?"

The streak of vulnerability on her face caught him so much by surprise that he spoke without thinking. "Sloane, you're sitting in my lap. Honestly, I've forgotten about my face."

"Oh!" The start-and-wiggle combination caused by her realization that she was indeed suggestively pressed against him destroyed any remaining irritation that she'd scared him. In fact, watching her flail to her bottom on the floorboards would've probably been downright amusing if he wasn't so busy mourning the loss of her body covering his.

Gavin levered himself to a sitting position, face hot with guilt. He hadn't meant to embarrass her, but surely he must have. He opened his mouth to say something reassuring, but she cut him off at the pass with a burst of throaty laughter.

"Sorry! I'm sorry, it's not funny." Sloane giggled even harder. "I didn't . . . mean to . . . you know, sit on you, but . . . God, I'm an idiot. I'll just go. Really . . . I can . . ."

The rest of her sentence was cut off by her unmitigated laughter, a sound so musical and full of unexpected happiness that Gavin had no choice but to start laughing with her.

"You're not an idiot. And for the record, I'm the one who acted like a jerk. Call it even?"

She nodded, and their laughter twined together for a full minute before subsiding. "So you're really okay?" she asked again. She reached up to brush her fingers over his cheekbone in a gentle sweep, and even though the touch was benign, he felt it in the darkest places of his body.

God, he wanted to kiss her again; only, this time, he wouldn't be an idiot and stop. She tilted her face toward his in the smallest gesture, her teeth pressing against her bottom lip to interrupt the lush shape of her mouth. The soft pads of her fingers coasted to a stop over his temple, lingering as her eyes met his.

Gavin shifted his weight with the intention of touching her back, of pulling her in and not letting go. But just as he moved, Sloane dropped both her hand and her chin, slipping away from him as if she'd realized the mistake of her proximity and meant to make good on her promise to leave. Already in motion, he had no choice but to do *something*, so he skimmed a clumsy palm over his own face in the wake of her now-absent hand.

"Yeah. You've got a pretty hard head, though." Everything seemed to be back in working order, except for maybe the rational section of his brain, and he nodded slowly as he let go of the desire brewing in his gut.

Sloane snorted, but the gesture sounded way more endearing than rude. "Gee, I've never heard that before." She popped to her feet in a shockingly fluid move, offering him a hand. Getting vertical was decidedly less graceful on his part, but he managed well enough.

"Thanks." Gavin watched her roll up the yoga mat, and the silence between them stretched out like a napping cat. "So how did things go today? Okay?" he asked, in a lame attempt to fill it.

"If by 'okay' you mean, 'Bree ignored me while I came up with a bunch of epic-fail ideas for a book', then yes. We were very okay, all day long." Sloane's easygoing tone erased any heat that her words might've carried, as if it were simply her way of saying *sure, we had a great day.*

Gavin nodded. He hadn't figured Bree would be an open book with her, but at least the weekend hadn't been a disaster. And the tutoring part had gone better than he'd expected, which was an added bonus. At least her grades were safe, for now. Maybe he was getting the hang of taking care of Bree, bit by bit.

"I really appreciate your help, especially with the tutoring," he said. "But I'm sorry about the book ideas thing."

Sloane bent to gather the scattered lumps of paper by the arm of the couch. "No problem. Like I said, Bree did most of it herself. I just refereed, really."

"Well, I'm glad she didn't give you any trouble. She can be, ah, difficult sometimes."

"She was okay. Actually, she spent most of today in her room, watching movies as far as I could tell. Oh, that and she tried on a bunch of red lipstick and black eyeliner." A sly half grin crossed Sloane's lips, as if wearing a ton of makeup was perfectly normal behavior for a middle schooler.

Panic uncurled in Gavin's chest. "Are you serious?"

Weren't girls supposed to be older than Bree before they wore makeup? Like, thirty, maybe? Why would Sloane let her do something like that? Christ, he was ill-prepared for this.

Sloane's grin faltered before fading completely. "Sorry. I didn't know you'd feel that strongly about it. We stayed here all day, so it didn't seem like a big deal. And honestly, the only reason I even saw it was because she came out to grab some water with it on."

"Bree knows I'd never let her do that," he muttered. Why did she have to be so defiant all the time? It was like she was trying to make him angry on purpose. Only that was ridiculous.

"Well, that explains her motivation. She had to know I'd tell you," Sloane said with a nonchalant shrug, as if the explanation made all the sense in the world.

Would he ever understand anyone with an XX chromosome?

"Why on earth would she do something she knows I'll get angry over, and then go out of her way to get caught?"

The logic made no sense at all. How come Sloane seemed to understand it so perfectly?

"She's just pushing your buttons to see how far she can go."

Gavin had a bad feeling he was gaping, but that didn't stop him from asking, "Did she tell you that?"

Sloane's good-natured belly laugh plucked its way through him with enticing warmth. "Of course not. But I was a teenage girl once, too, you know. When I was fourteen, my mother flat-out insisted I wear these annoying pants underneath the skirt of my school uniform."

Great. He was never going to get rid of the image of her in those damned kneesocks. Gavin cleared his throat. "That seems a little extreme for a fourteen-year-old."

She popped a shadowy brow, sliding a hand over one denim-encased hip. "Not once she heard from Joey Romano's mother that the boys had taken to going under the bleachers to look up the girls' skirts."

The image in his head caught fire and exploded. "You wanted the boys to look up your skirt?"

Sloane meted out an insouciant smile. "Please. I kept my legs crossed like everyone else once we figured it out. And anyway, you're missing the point. It was totally embarrassing to wear pants under my skirt like a little kid, and I wanted my mother to know I could take care of myself."

"You were fourteen." He looked at her dubiously.

She pointed to herself with both index fingers, grinning. "Hello, figured it out, remember?"

Gavin's curiosity got the best of him and he gave in. "Okay, so how'd your mother find out you didn't listen to her if all this went down at school?"

"Because rather than leaving home with the pants on and just taking them off once I got there, I left them folded up, right on top of my bed every morning. It was standard teenage boundary testing, and I bet it's exactly what Bree's doing. She just wants to prove she's growing up."

His gut gave a hard yank at the thought. She didn't have to grow up *that* fast. "Well, it wasn't a good idea to let her put on all that makeup. You should've said something to her."

Sloane's laid-back expression shorted out like a faulty fuse, and she set her jaw in a firm line. "We stayed here all day, so nobody saw her except me. It just didn't seem like such a big deal."

"Well . . ." Okay, so she had a point. Still, the idea of makeup on his little sister's face, especially red lipstick with all its grown-up connotations, made him more than vaguely nauseous. He couldn't let it happen again.

"We'll just have to agree to disagree, I guess. But thanks for letting me know."

Sloane's smile returned, albeit at half the wattage of before. "I don't think you have anything to worry about. After the novelty wore off, she muttered something about looking like a clown and then she wiped it off."

"Oh. Good, then." His words were like overstarched shirts, stiff to the point of breaking.

God, when had he gotten so old?

The urge to talk about it, to air his frustrations with someone who might get it—hell, someone who'd just listen—pushed its way to the surface.

"Sloane?"

She froze, one arm encased in the red wool of her pea coat, the other one halfway in the sleeve. "Yes?"

For a split second, he wanted her to stay. She seemed to have some insight on Bree, and the simple snippets of conversation they'd shared both yesterday morning and again tonight had strummed up a long-forgotten feeling of ease in his chest. Gavin opened his mouth to ask her if she wanted to stay, maybe have a glass of wine, when his conversation with Adrian punched through his memory with startling clarity.

That woman is going places even in her sleep.

Who was he kidding? She wasn't going to stick around, and after Mrs. Teasdale returned, he wasn't going to see Sloane again. There wouldn't be any more conversations, and anyway, airing out his personal life would only stir up trouble. He'd have to figure this out on his own.

Gavin served up a cool, professional smile, one that he knew from experience didn't reach his eyes. Walking her to the door, he said, "See you on Tuesday. Have a good night."

Chapter Eight

Gavin spared a glance at the clock, as if the numbers would change simply because he'd willed them backward.

Nope. Six A.M. pretty much sucked no matter how you sliced it. And when it followed a restless night's sleep spent trying to get rid of a gut full of unease, getting out of bed on his day off was just that much tougher.

He padded across the cold floorboards to place a hand on Bree's door, only to find it open and her room vacant. A faint glow edged out from the bathroom doorframe, and the steady hum of running water confirmed the fact that Bree was already up and getting ready on her own. Damn, he simultaneously loved and felt sick at how well she could take care of herself, like it had snuck up on him and transformed her from a kid in a car seat to a capable preteen overnight.

Then again, considering some of the choices she'd made in Philadelphia, plus failing English here in Pine Mountain, *capable* was a bit relative. The whole makeup escapade with Sloane yesterday was really just the cream in the cannoli, hammering home the fact that he couldn't leave her alone. No matter how much she hated him for it.

Gavin swept a hand over his sleep-mussed hair and

headed for the kitchen, putting just enough water on to boil before beelining for the bag of coffee beans behind the sleek, white cabinet doors. The stainless steel coffee grinder released a chorus of soft clicks as he poured the beans into its belly, and the familiar, calming sound polished the rough edges off his nerves.

The rhythm of being in the kitchen, of filling the French press with precise tablespoons of fresh grounds, the earthy, complex aroma of the hot water meeting the coarse coffee grounds as he poured it into the pot—all of it unfolded over fresh calm. By the time Bree trundled into the kitchen wearing a pair of faded jeans and a scowl that looked more sleepy than surly, Gavin had assembled half a dozen ingredients on the rolling butcher block island. The comfort of feeling the food beneath his hands fled at the sight of Bree's frown.

"You don't have to get up early just to make sure I get on the bus, you know." The intensity of her expression slipped a notch as her eyes rested on the carton of eggs lying open on the smooth wooden square of the butcher block, but she didn't move from the doorframe.

Ah, right. Their favorite morning argument. Only today, something told him not to bite. "I'm making omelets. You want one?"

"No." The word crossed Bree's lips at the same moment her stomach growled, and she surrendered a heavy sigh. "Okay, maybe."

Gavin bit back his urge to smile in case she caught it and decided to flee after all. "French okay with you?" He slipped a knife, thin and gleaming, from a slot in the side of the island, and the smell of fresh-chopped parsley met him like an old friend at the door.

"Whatev—I guess." Bree corrected herself with a shrug, and although the noticeable hitch made his curiosity uncoil, Gavin didn't pursue it.

"Anyway, I don't get up early just to make sure you get on the bus." He meant the words as a peace offering, but her disdainful eye roll negated his good intentions.

"I'm not going to do anything stupid with you right down the hall. Plus, you'd wake up if I did." Bree kept her focus firmly on the butcher block, her frown locked into place.

Gavin's irritation spurted. "I said that's not why I get up early." He looked down, only to see that his hands had stopped moving and his knuckles were as blanched as raw almonds. Shit. This was so not the early morning chat he'd envisioned. Time for a redirect.

"Anyway. How was your weekend with Sloane?" he asked, pulling the thin leaves from a sprig of tarragon a lot more smoothly than he'd changed the subject.

"Fine, I guess. She's kind of weird."

The sound of Sloane's quirky, full-bodied laugh ribboned through his memory, and the potshot it took at his gut made him glad he'd put the knife down. Talk about ruining a guy's concentration.

"Weird how?" Gavin knocked two eggs together in his palm, splitting them into a shallow dish one right after the other before repeating the process with the four remaining eggs.

Bree lifted one shoulder in a birdlike flutter. "She likes Shakespeare."

"She's a writer, Bree. All in all, that's not too shocking."

"She went on for like ten whole minutes about how *Romeo and Juliet* was the quintessential love story with tragic elements. And she cited direct quotes. In a British accent."

Gavin choked out a laugh. "Really?"

"It's not as much fun as it sounds," Bree said, although a smile twitched over her lips. "And anyway, only geeks know that much about Shakespeare."

Huh. She kind of had a point. Sloane struck him more like the naughty limerick type. The fact that she seemed to house a vast knowledge of Shakespearean plays was as much a surprise to him as it was to Bree.

"That knowledge helped you get all your work done," he offered, starting to whisk the eggs. "So it can't be that bad."

Another shrug. "Yeah."

They lapsed into silence while Gavin finished prepping the omelet mixture, then melted a pat of butter into a rich, golden river across the bottom of his skillet before starting to cook. The conversation, while neither deep nor terribly meaningful, had been one of the longest they'd had since their mom died that didn't encompass an argument. Bree had once been the kind of kid who would burst into laughter just as soon as look at you. When had it become so difficult for them to just talk?

"So, ah, you want to flip these when they're ready?" Gavin dipped his chin at the stove, giving the batter in the skillet an expert tilt. Omelets were finicky as hell, and if you didn't keep a careful eye on them, they went right from hot breakfast to hot mess.

Bree crinkled her nose. "I don't think so."

He knew he should let it slide, but something about the small success of their earlier conversation made Gavin push instead. "Come on. You always ended up with the most perfectly folded eggs when we'd make these at home. You're a natural."

"Uh-uh." Bree's protest chilled by a few degrees, but she didn't shut down or walk away. Maybe teasing her a little would bring her out of her shell, and he could unearth one of those fantastic smiles he knew she was capable of.

"Don't be so modest, kiddo." He tossed in some ham and Gruyère, giving the pan another slanted shake as he pulled it off the burner with a flourish and a smile. "Here, it's already starting to slide. C'mon! Go for it."

"I said *no!*"

The shrill burst of the word hit him with all the force of an actual blow, and for a minute, neither of them spoke. Not knowing what else to do, Gavin flipped the omelet gracelessly and deposited it onto a plate.

"Sorry," he finally managed, and the brief ease he'd felt just moments before went completely numb. God *damn* it, he was in so far over his head. He didn't even know how to communicate with his own sister.

"I don't . . . I just don't want to cook, that's all." Bree's voice cracked over the words, as broken as the eggshells on the butcher block between them. "Okay?"

Gavin started to say no, it was definitely *not* okay for them to keep going like this, fighting each other at every freaking turn, when her expression knocked the breath from his lungs.

Rather than wearing her customary scowl, Bree looked at him with genuine pleading. Tears tracked down both sides of her face, so silently that if he hadn't looked with care, he'd have missed them altogether.

"Okay. Just let me know if you change your mind."

Sloane peered down at her cell phone and willed herself not to throw up. What had she been thinking when she'd signed up to get those stupid reminders about her bills being due?

"Are you okay?" Carly's voice startled Sloane from her reverie of debt, whirling her back to one of the most posh suites Pine Mountain Resort had to offer. Sloane straightened from her perch in a tastefully fancy silk and damask chair, stuffing her phone into her tiny purse.

"Yeah, of course." While she didn't make it a habit to

lie, she was pretty sure there was a special circle in hell for people who bogged their best friends down with personal issues on their wedding day. Although if Sloane got kicked out of the bungalow for not paying her rent, moving back in with her mother would make that circle of hell look like a carnival ride at Coney Island.

Shit.

"Are you sure? You look like you just saw a ghost."

Sloane pasted on a smile and shoved her purse out of sight behind a lamp on the side table. "Nope! I'm totally fine."

Okay, so she wasn't *fine*-fine, but she wasn't exactly screwed, either. As of this morning, she had a whole week's worth of babysitting under her belt, and Gavin had written her a check for it that would help cover the bungalow for this month, at least. But paying rent would drain her account, tossing her back to square one on her ticket out of Dodge, and with the rest of her bills, next month's rent was iffy at best.

She had to be on a plane by then.

"Anyway," Sloane continued, mashing down her dread, "the last thing you should be worried about is me. You're getting married in a few hours."

Her next smile came a lot more easily, and she let it take over. The absolute glow suffusing her best friend's face canceled out any remaining unease churning in Sloane's gut, and she exhaled over the temporary reprieve. She was about to take part in a gorgeous wedding and spend the entire night in one of the luxuriously appointed hotel rooms the resort executives had blocked off for their star chef's special guests. Just for tonight, Sloane was going to send her troubles packing. No worries, no stress, and no distractions, period.

Including her brooding, sexy, calm-cool-and-collected boss, and the fact that she could *still* feel the kiss he'd laid on her nearly a week ago, even though they'd been all business, all week long.

Carly popped up from her chair and smoothed a hand over her jeans. "Wow, is it already that late? I know we're done with the hair and makeup thing, but I should get dressed." She headed for the white garment bag perched on a stand over by the full-length mirror in the suite's dressing room, but Sloane stopped her in her tracks.

"You have to wait for your mother," she protested. She might not ever be destined for the altar herself, but Sloane sure as hell knew the rules of the game. Unless you had a death wish, inciting the wrath of an Italian mother on her only daughter's wedding day was just plain stupid.

Carly laughed. "Since when are you so sentimental?"

"It's self-preservation, not sentiment. Your mother will kill us both if you get into that dress and she's not here. Plus, it won't be long. She and Bellamy should both be here any second." Bellamy Blake was the only other female chef on Carly's staff, and Sloane's compatriot in bridesmaid duties.

"You're probably right. I guess we can wait another minute or two." Carly shrugged. "I have to be honest, it's kind of nice not to have such a big production. The first time through was a lot different."

Sloane couldn't help it. She scoffed. "The first time through, you married an asshat."

Carly's laughter echoed through the luxurious suite, bouncing off the peach-colored walls to land happily back around their ears. "Yeah, but I found my swan, so it all turned out fine in the end."

She should've known sharing that metaphor would come back to bite her. Swans mated for life, so calling the happily-ever-after guy a swan had made sense to Sloane. Of course, she usually reserved it for her books, since real-life swans seemed more legend than likelihood. But as hard as it was to imagine Carly's six-foot-four fiancé as an elegant white bird, there was no doubt in anyone's mind Jackson was her swan.

"Did someone slip you a happy pill? You are way too laid-back for someone about to get hitched." Sloane's nerves did a jump-and-jangle in her belly, as if to make up for Carly's nonchalance. While the week she'd spent tutoring and looking after Bree had been uneventful, Sloane's unease at not being able to write a single useable word had gone from niggling worry to flat-out dread.

Nope! No worries tonight, remember? La la la la! Sloane metaphorically plugged her ears and drowned her worry in a deep, calming breath.

"There's no point in being nervous." Carly's grin took over, recapturing Sloane's attention as her best friend kept on. "Marrying Jackson is the easiest thing I'll ever do."

Sloane lifted a brow. "Now who's sentimental?"

"Give me a break. I'm getting married."

As if on cue, Bellamy poked her head past the dressing room entryway. "Hey, sorry I'm late. I just wanted to make sure the catering guys had everything under control in the restaurant for the reception."

Bellamy's at-ease smile was an unspoken testament to the fact that everything downstairs was running smoothly. Otherwise, knowing her, she'd probably have thrown some chef's whites over her bridesmaid's dress and started whipping up the perfect cocktail sauce with one hand while rolling crisp-tender asparagus spears in prosciutto with the other.

"They're being careful in my kitchen, right?" While Carly's smile remained in place, her words came out on a serrated edge, making Sloane laugh.

"So much for laid-back," she said.

Bellamy leapt into chef mode, reassuring Carly with a detailed account of the food prep. With most of La Dolce Vita's staff attending the wedding, it had only made sense to have the reception in the restaurant itself. Getting management to agree to the deal would've been tough for anybody other than their star chef, but the stack of rave reviews that kept rolling in for La Dolce Vita along with a reservation log that was booked a solid month in advance sealed the deal. If Carly had asked for the moon on a plate, the resort execs would've been on the next rocket out of town.

Sloane watched Carly's face melt back into relaxed bliss as Bellamy described the food, right down to the little sprigs of dill on the cucumber-salmon canapés. Carly's usual no-nonsense expression softened with pure happiness, but rather than giving Sloane the warm fuzzies, the sentiment panged through her as if it was covered in barbed wire.

What the hell? Her hand flew to her breastbone, as if she could extinguish the strange sensation with a simple cover-up. Sure, Sloane put stock in happily ever after, but it wasn't like her to get all gooey at a simple wedding. Plus, seeing Carly get the fairy tale ending she so deserved was a good thing—no, make that a *great* thing. She and Jackson were perfect for each other, and Sloane hadn't been kidding when she'd said their story was bestseller material. It was the very stuff romance novels were made of, for God's sake, and it couldn't have happened to two people more deserving of real-deal, forever-and-ever love.

So what was with her rib cage trying to impersonate a corkscrew at her best friend's joy?

"Ah! Here's the bride. Let me look at you, eh?" Carly's mother, Francesca di Matisse, bustled into the dressing room, and the warmth on her face was unmistakable. Her thick Italian accent, laced with a nonsubtle Brooklyn cadence, was all-too-familiar, and it sent Sloane's unease into rapid descent.

Their home-turf neighborhood had a grapevine as thick as one of the fifty-year-old oaks shadowing Sloane's current residence at the bungalow. Even though her own mother was in New York, squawking over a hugely pregnant Angela, she'd surely hear every last detail of Carly's wedding before the week was out. Which was certain to kick off the latest round of Sloane's least favorite game: Why Aren't *You* Getting Married?

Okay. So maybe that explained the corkscrew.

Carly leaned in, letting her mother fold her into a quick embrace. "Hi, Ma. Is the minister all set downstairs?"

"Of course. Although when he walked in, I had to assure him it was the same room we were in for last night's rehearsal. It's so beautiful, the way it's all set up for the ceremony. But not more beautiful than you." Francesca kissed both of Carly's cheeks before pulling back to level Sloane and Bellamy with a proud smile. "You see this glow on her face? This glow comes from only one thing." Francesca hooked a knowing finger at her daughter and smiled.

"*Mama!* Jeez. I haven't even seen Jackson today!" Even though Carly could boss around a team of muscle-bound, tattooed chefs twice her size, her mother's good-natured teasing stained her cheeks bright red. Bellamy clamped her teeth down on her bottom lip, surely in an effort to maintain decorum, but Sloane wasn't so lucky. Eh, she'd never been big on etiquette, anyway.

"Wow, Mrs. D," she murmured, the weird unease in her chest having been momentarily kicked to the curb by a fit of laughter. "That's, uh, awesome."

"Get your mind out of the gutter, Sloane Marie. You've been writing too many naughty books. I'm talking about love. It's as plain as the nose on my face." The shine in Francesca's eyes was unmistakable as she looked at her daughter, and the obvious maternal pride boomeranged hotly through Sloane's gut.

"Oh, right. That's exactly what I thought you meant." She put on a cheeky grin, but Carly's mother didn't buy it for a second.

"Save your smart answers, *cucciola*. You'll find out one of these days, and all the sass in the world won't save you from looking the same way."

Sloane swallowed a sardonic laugh. "Did my mother put you up to this?" Lord, she couldn't even get a reprieve when her mother was a whole state away.

"Come on, Ma. Let's leave Sloane be, huh?" Carly put a hand on her mother's arm, casting an apologetic glance in Sloane's direction, but Francesca arched an unwavering brow.

"I know what I know. You might move around like a little hummingbird, but you have a good heart. You'll find a man worth staying still for. Your mama can rest easy."

Right. And then they could all ice skate in Satan's backyard. Sloane's mama didn't even rest easy on Sundays. Plus, why would Sloane stay in one place when she could see the world?

"Tell you what, Mrs. D. When I find him, you'll get the very first wedding invite. Promise." Sloane crossed her heart, her fingernail gently clicking over the delicate beads of her dress, and helped Bellamy lift Carly's gown from the garment bag.

Any focus on Sloane's love life—or lack thereof—was summarily snuffed out by the sight of the simple, elegant confection of ivory silk. Sloane's heart lifted right along with the layers of delicate fabric and intricate, subtly placed lace, and she breathed a sigh of relief. Finally, she could ditch the weird feelings and get on with what was important.

Which turned out to be no less than four billion pictures,

the lighting of twice as many candles in the room where the ceremony was being held, and a host of other small chores that added up to three hours' worth of big exhaustion.

"You sure you don't want to skip this and go to Vegas?" Sloane asked from the side of her mouth as the wedding planner finally guided them all into a line outside the double doors leading into the ceremony room.

Carly's chuckle came from behind her, soft but definite. "Let's save that for your wedding, what do you say?"

"I say it's a good thing I already knocked Vegas off my bucket list. If we're waiting for my name on the Elvis Chapel o' Love, it's gonna be a while."

"What's the matter, Russo? Afraid of the altar?" Adrian's gravelly voice teased her from where he stood next to Carly, and Sloane turned to look at him. Adrian's giant frame was imposing on a good day, and even in his suit, he looked menacing as hell. But rather than shrink, Sloane simply snorted and curled her fingers to mimic a telephone.

"Hello? Pot, this is the kettle calling. You're looking a little dark over there."

The wedding planner interrupted Sloane and Carly's hushed laughter, as well as a few choice swear words from Adrian, with her cue for Carly to step back so they could open the doors.

"Last chance," Sloane whispered, turning to look at her friend.

God, she was radiant, and the corkscrew hit Sloane again, full force.

Carly grinned. "I'm all set. Believe me."

The room was truly breathtaking, with the fifty or so guests' chairs swathed in rich ivory fabric, and the lights overhead softening the pale yellow walls down to a deep glow. Creamy white flowers and fresh pine greenery were interspersed around a wide, understated archway at the end of the aisle, and Sloane focused on a thick bough as she put one foot in front of the other. Low light spilled from crystal-encrusted chandeliers, offering enough illumination to see clearly, yet just the right amount of ambiance to make everything seem lit from within.

Oh, yeah. Ditching her issues for one night was going to be a piece of wedding cake, because everything about this felt perfect. By the time Sloane got to the end of the runner to fix Jackson with an exaggerated wink, she was full to the brim with happy excitement. She settled into place on the other side of the minister, and the dulcet cello music that had accompanied her down the aisle drifted to a graceful stop.

Everyone in the tightly knit crowd stood expectantly, turning their faces toward the back of the room, and the electric anticipation sent a prickle over Sloane's nearly bare shoulders. The music started again, signaling the bride's imminent walk down the aisle, and undiluted goodness splashed through her chest. She was sweeping her gaze over the small sea of profiles, all eyes on the now-open double doors at the back of the room, when her vision caught on the only face not turned to take in the bride floating down the aisle.

Gavin stood in the middle of the third aisle on the bride's side, parked between Carly's aunt Daniela and Bree. She knew she should be amused that crazy Aunt Daniela was wearing a god-awful hat festooned with black feathers, or that she should take in all the nuances of how shockingly pretty Bree looked without her trademark scowl.

But the beautiful, sinuous notes of the cello faded as if they'd been suddenly plunged under water, and the faces around her shrank and receded before turning into nothing more than indiscriminate blurs. Only one thing snapped into sharp relief, and it hit her with such intensity that all the air left her on one razor-sharp breath.

Gavin's liquid brown stare was locked on her as if she was the only person in the room.

Chapter Nine

Even though they hadn't been in a church, Gavin was fairly certain he'd go to hell for the hard-on he'd sported the minute Sloane stepped past those double doors to move down the aisle.

Thank God he hadn't taken off his suit jacket before the ceremony. Not that the image of her had grown any less intense in the three hours that had passed since the minister had said, "You may now kiss the bride."

Come on, Gavin thought as he stood in one of the shallow alcoves dotting the perimeter of La Dolce Vita's bar area. There was no chance he could fight that kind of reaction when her dress was sex with a designer label. Go the extra step of putting it on Sloane's lean silhouette instead of a padded hanger, and of course he was going to take notice.

Often.

Gavin's gaze drifted across the restaurant's warm green and terra cotta dining room, landing on the lady in question for the hundredth time tonight. His breath went haywire in his lungs just as it had the other ninety-nine times he'd clapped eyes on her, but he was well past trying to do anything about it.

The slip of black fabric molded to Sloane's body, its skinny little straps and the long stretch of silk hugging her lithe angles as though she'd been poured into it inch by inch. It shimmered when she moved, not in a flashy way, but with the suggestion that there was something warm and decadent built into the fabric. The plunging neckline and side slit revealed just enough to drive a guy crazy wondering what she had on—or more to the point, didn't have on—underneath it.

Sloane's intoxicating laugh, both musical and robust, filtered across the candlelit dining room. As hot as the dress looked, it was nothing compared to the lit-up purity of her smile, like she'd simply bucked biology and decided to exhale happiness instead of carbon dioxide. Any guy with a pulse would be helpless to do anything but stare at her.

But then, she hadn't caught just any man with a pulse shamelessly staring at her as the ceremony began. She'd caught him, and *red-handed* didn't even begin to cover it. No wonder she'd only given him and Bree a drive-by hello as she mingled with the crowd during the reception.

Gavin grabbed a glass of sparkling water from a passing server and filed the thought under *forget about it* in his brain. Whether or not Sloane caught him staring, it didn't matter in the long run. Yes, she looked unbelievable in her dress, but it wasn't as if he was going to do anything about it.

No matter how badly he wanted to.

"Can we go home yet? They already cut the cake." Bree's grumble interrupted his heated thoughts, and for once, he was grateful for the churlish distraction.

"Glad to see you made it back from the bathroom with your good mood intact." His attempt at humor fell prey to her frosty stare, leaving him to silently lean a forearm against one of the bistro-style tables in their nook by the bar.

"It's hard to be in a good mood when you're the only kid hanging out with a bunch of old people. I totally stick out."

"You did just fine talking with Bellamy and her fiancé, Shane, during dinner," Gavin said, purposely ignoring her jab. He had strategically chosen to sit with members of La Dolce Vita's staff in order to increase the chances that they'd stick to polite, work-related conversation. That way, there would be less of a chance that someone would ask questions about their mom that might make Bree uncomfortable. For the most part, it had worked like a charm.

She sighed, a long, drawn-out sound he'd been hearing a lot of lately. "No, *you* did just fine talking to them. I don't have anything to say about food, or cooking."

Bree crossed her arms in a petulant knot and leaned forward on her bar stool, dropping her elbows to the table. Things had gone back to normal since their kitchen incident five days ago, with her offering the usual litany of complaints and him doing his best to counter them with patience he had to summon from somewhere around his toes.

Gavin's smile tightened a notch, but he refused to let it fade. "Still, I work with a lot of nice people. You should give them a shot."

Her frown was ever persistent. "None of them even know me. I don't see why I couldn't have just stayed at home."

"Because I needed a date, remember?" Damn, his supply of calm was running low. Where was the happily social kid he used to call his sister?

She resorted to one of her dramatic eye rolls, but Gavin refused to let it bother him. "Come on, Bree. I know it's not ideal, but could we at least try to enjoy the party, a little bit? We don't have to stay much longer."

An oddly familiar, cinnamon-spicy scent preceded an even more familiar feminine voice by less than a second.

"But where's the fun in that?"

Sloane's words hit him with a jolt, and he made an abrupt half turn toward her, only to find himself inches from her sparkling blue eyes.

"Hi, Sloane. You look nice." His inner voice let out a serious snort at the understatement, but he smothered it with what he prayed was a casual smile.

"Thanks, boss. You look . . . like you always do. Fantastic suit, serious face."

His smile broke into genuine territory. "Thank you, I think."

"You're very welcome." She turned her attention to Bree, and Gavin noticed with surprise that his sister's sour face had softened a notch. "Don't tell me you two are ditching out on Pine Mountain's event of the year before it really gets started," Sloane teased. "Now that I've finally gotten all the requisite socializing out of the way, we can kick things up a bit. Come on, Bree. I won't even ask you to write an essay about it. Cross my heart."

She leaned in farther, and oh hell, her dress was even sexier up close, with a scattering of glossy beads emphasizing the deep V of the neckline. And did she have to smell so good, all dark and sweet like a decadent crème brûlée?

Gavin cleared his throat and double-checked to make sure his jacket was buttoned. "Bree's a little concerned because she doesn't know anybody, that's all."

Bree's cheeks turned pink, her flush paving the way for a brand-new scowl. "And Gavin's a little concerned because he doesn't have a real date," she flipped back with an overly angelic smile.

Damn it, why did she always think he was picking on her? He scrambled for something to smooth over Bree's attitude, but Sloane just laughed that infernally hypnotic laugh that told him getting her out of his head was a complete impossibility.

"Lucky for you, I can help on both counts. Come on." She jutted a slender arm, elbow first, in Bree's direction.

Bree's frown was heavy with suspicion. "Where are we going?"

"Jackson's cousin has twin daughters about your age. They're right over there, by the entryway to the main lodge. If you want, I can introduce you."

Bree snuck a glance past the stacked stone fireplaces and cozy seating arrangements in La Dolce Vita's front room, unable to hide the interest lighting her eyes. "Anything's better than hanging out with a bunch of geriatrics. Okay, I guess."

Across the room, the two blond girls giggled together in typical preteen fashion. Maybe if Bree finally made a friend or two in Pine Mountain, she'd hate it here less. Still, Gavin felt a little burble of worry.

"Don't go too far, okay?"

"I can't believe you don't trust me to walk across the restaurant without getting into trouble." Her whisper came out more like a hiss, and she whipped her arms back over the front of her sweater. "I'm thirteen, not three!"

Oh, for the love of God, couldn't they go one day without having a blowout? Why did she have to turn his concern into the Spanish freaking Inquisition?

Gavin lowered his voice, willing false calm over every word. "I trust you. I just want to make sure you'll be okay, that's all."

Bree looked poised for a fight, her lightly freckled brow furrowed in determination, but before she could open her mouth, Sloane took Bree's hand and folded it into the crook of her arm.

"Oh, Sadie and Caitlin will take good care of her. Plus, Bree's a smart cookie. She won't do anything she's not supposed to. Right?"

The move seemed to shock the argument right from Bree's lips, and after a pause she said, "Right."

Sloane shifted her focus back to him, brows raised. "Okay?"

She made it sound so easy, so no-big-deal, that he softened. He hadn't meant to overreact, and after all, Bree was right. She wasn't a little kid anymore. Gavin worked up an apologetic look for Bree, startled to see the same sentiment sweeping over her face, too.

"Sure. Go have fun. Just come find me if you need anything," he said.

With the scowl wiped from her face, Bree agreed with a nod. The resolution prompted one corner of Sloane's mouth to kick up into a victorious smile.

"Okay, then. I'll be right back for you."

"For me?" Gavin blinked.

Her smile curled into a smirk, sparking a gleam in her crushed-velvet eyes that shot right through his body.

"I promised to help both of you, didn't I? As soon as Bree here is comfy with her new friends, you've got yourself a real date."

Gavin didn't know whether to be taken aback or turned on, but as he watched Sloane's hips swivel in the same flawless, drop-dead sexy rhythm that had been driving him mad all week long, he had the feeling he was in for a long night. While he'd managed to tamp down the memory of their heated kiss enough to avoid a repeat performance, something about Sloane's pouty, pink mouth and the unadulterated laugh that spilled from it without warning made him want to chuck the rules. In another life, that might've been okay, but now? There was more to think about than simply what he wanted.

Even when what he wanted was packaged in a dress that could cause nations to crumble.

From his vantage point by the bar, Gavin surreptitiously watched Sloane lead Bree past groups of people knotted in conversation to arrive at their destination by the door. After just a couple of animated gestures and a deep peal of laughter that shot through him from halfway across the room, Sloane had managed to single-handedly integrate his standoffish sister into the small group of girls standing by the entryway.

For someone claiming to be the antinanny, Sloane was one hell of a quick study.

He was about to turn his attention elsewhere and give Bree a bit of privacy when she leaned her head in to listen to something one of the blond girls said. Her lips tipped upward, breaking into a sweet, unabashed smile. The sight of Bree's face, lit with something other than anger or sullen nonchalance, detonated in Gavin's gut like a firecracker with a too-short fuse.

He couldn't remember the last time he'd seen that smile.

"Occasionally, I have a good idea, don't you think?" Sloane reappeared at his side, nodding over her shoulder at the girls, who clustered together like brightly colored grapes on a summer vine.

How bad for him could Sloane really be if she was willing to do something like that for his surly sister?

"Or do you not think it was a good idea? I mean, they're right over there, and I just thought . . . well . . ."

Gavin had been so distracted by his thought that he'd almost failed to notice the strange expression trickling over Sloane's face, as if all her seductive certainty had been carried away by a stiff breeze. For a breath, she seemed unvarnished, like a completely pure version of the brazen woman he knew, and his pulse log-jammed in his veins.

With that vulnerable look casting shadows over her face in the low light by the bar, he wanted her now more than ever.

"Oh, uh, no. Not at all," he said. Okay, no matter how attractive that glimpse of her had been, stammering wasn't going to earn him any points in the suave category. "I should thank you, actually. If I'd encouraged her to go over there and make friends, she'd probably have told me it was an epically stupid idea."

"Ouch. That's a pretty steep price to pay for putting her on the spot," Sloane observed, slipping her graceful frame into one of the two tall chairs in the cozy nook.

Gavin drew back in surprise. "I put *her* on the spot? She's the one who gave me a hard time."

Sloane leaned in, splitting the distance between their bodies by half. "I'm going to let you in on a little secret. Pointing out a lady's unease in public tends to make her feel self-conscious. Especially if the lady in question is full to brimming with preteen hormones."

It took Gavin a few seconds to attach the label *lady* to his kid sister, and then a full minute to link the ideas together in a way that made sense. "So, wait. All that attitude was because I said she was uncomfortable?"

Sloane sighed like he was a lost cause. "You said she was uncomfortable because she didn't know anybody. As far as she's concerned, you might as well have told the whole room she has no friends."

"But I didn't say that." And damn it, as much as he hated it, Bree *didn't* have any friends. Not that he'd have ever said so, because he wished like hell it wasn't true.

Sloane's words seeped past his automatic defenses and he paused as they soaked in. Wait a second . . . had he inadvertently said so?

Seriously, there had to be a secret decoder ring for this stuff.

"Of course you didn't." Sloane lifted her shoulders as if all of this hormone-fueled cloak-and-dagger business made perfect sense.

"That's a hell of a logic leap for someone who claims to have no experience with kids," he said, realizing only after the words were out that they might offend her. Wonderful. At this rate he was going to piss off the entire room, one woman at a time.

But Sloane just laughed. "Oh, my knowledge about kids is nil. All my experience in this matter comes from the belligerent-daughter department."

"You?" he asked, certain she was pushing the boundaries of the truth. "Come on. You're an independent woman with a successful career. That hardly qualifies as belligerent."

Like any red-blooded guy hiring a romance novelist to watch his sister, Gavin had Googled Sloane the first day she'd spent at the cottage. Her writing credentials were as impressive as she'd claimed; in fact, she'd left out the little tidbit about her last book hitting the *USA Today* bestseller list. How could her parents not be proud of that?

"Yeah, my mother missed the news flash on that one. According to her, my business cards should read *Sloane Russo, black sheep of the family*." Sloane's smile stayed firmly attached to her face, but her jaw ticked ever so slightly, betraying the effort she was making.

"Because you're a writer?" Something about it just didn't compute. "What does your father think?"

The hitch in Sloane's movement was noticeable, but

she answered softly, "I don't know. He died of colon cancer when I was nineteen."

The words punched him right in the gut. "I'm sorry." Somehow, the default answer didn't feel like it was enough. Especially now that he knew first-hand how hollow it could be.

"Thanks." She measured out a tiny smile. "Anyway, embarrassment notwithstanding, Bree's still a little hard on you, huh?"

The observation prompted a sharp tug from deep in his belly that hollered at him not to share. "I'm getting used to it."

Desperate to shift the focus of the conversation, Gavin plucked a glass of champagne from the tray of a passing server and pressed the flute into her hand. "Sorry, I'm not really doing a good job here. I'm supposed to be your date, right?"

"Now *you're* being hard on you, too. And for the record, I'm supposed to be yours." Sloane grinned, taking a healthy sip from her glass. Her dark brows popped in surprise. "Wow, I was too nervous when I made my toast to actually taste this. It's really good."

His lips tingled with the urge to break into a satisfied smile at her approval. "I know. I chose it."

"You took it off the tray, Gavin. Let's not get crazy." Sloane's laughter folded around him like sun-bleached laundry, fresh from the line, and for the first time, he didn't fight the streak of goodness it left in its wake.

"No, I really chose it. As in, Carly asked my advice on the best champagne to serve, and this is what I picked."

"Huh. Guess she hired you for more than just your chiseled jawline."

Gavin cocked his head, a little bit surprised and a whole lot intrigued. "My what?"

Sloane clamped down on her bottom lip in a move he

swore would undo him, but before he could prompt a more detailed answer, an unfamiliar voice uttering Sloane's name snagged his attention.

"Sorry to interrupt your conversation," the woman said, smiling pointedly at both of them. "But I thought I should come over and say hi."

"Hey, Jeannie! You're not interrupting at all," Sloane chirped, a little too eagerly. "Actually, I guess I should've introduced you two before."

Remorse flickered over Sloane's face while Gavin was certain that confusion covered his. The petite blonde snuffed out both with her all-American smile.

"Oh, honey, please. You've been a little busy tonight, don't you think? Plus, it's my job to annoy the girls and go around introducing myself to their friends' parents." She swung her attention to Gavin and extended a slender hand. "Jeannie Carter. I'm Sadie and Caitlin's mom."

Realization trickled in as he followed her gaze to the spot where Bree stood with the two blond girls, along with a grateful rush. At least he wasn't the only person who wondered about other kids' parents. "Gavin Carmichael."

"Nice to meet you, Gavin." Jeannie flashed her pearly whites again, making her look more like a former cheerleader than the mother of two preteen daughters. "Though I hate to admit, I'm not without ulterior motive."

"That sounds kind of ominous," Sloane said, lifting a glossy brow.

The back of Gavin's neck prickled. "Is everything okay?" He turned to scan the restaurant again for Bree, but Jeannie shook her head, her sleek ponytail swaying emphatically.

"Oh, nothing's wrong. I just promised Sadie and Caitlin that I'd take them to the Main Street diner tonight. Apparently, it's *the* place for middle schoolers to hang out.

Now that dessert is over, they're raring to go. We thought we'd ask Bree to come along."

Well. It looked like he and Bree were even in the putting-each-other-on-the-spot department.

"I'd hate to put you out," he said, in an effort to ease into a polite decline. After all, letting Bree roam Main Street on a Saturday night wasn't high up on the list of things he felt comfortable with. Even if Main Street was less than six blocks long.

"Are you kidding? There's plenty of room in our car. And, as stodgy as I am, I only let them stay an hour or so. One milkshake and a handful of songs on the jukebox are about all this lady can handle anymore," Jeannie said with a genuine laugh. "I can even drop her back home when we're done, if that's easier for you."

Gavin shot a quick glance across the dining room, zeroing in on the spot where he'd last seen Bree. She hadn't budged, and neither had her smile. She wiggled her fingers at one of Jeannie's daughters, taking one of the earbuds attached to the girl's iPod and popping it into place on her own ear. They leaned in, joining their heads together at the free ear, and started bobbing in perfect unison.

Something Gavin had no name for turned over in his chest.

"Why don't you have her give me a call when you're ready to leave? I'll swing by the diner and pick her up on my way home."

They spent a few minutes exchanging cell phone numbers, and although Bree's cheeks flushed a shade when he gave her some money and reminded her to call him for a ride home, the frown that had etched her face all evening didn't make a single appearance as they parted ways.

"So it looks like you've got some time to kill," Sloane ventured as soon as they were alone at the table.

"Guess it's a good thing I have a date." He tipped his glass of water at her in a grateful gesture, and she tilted her flute toward him in return.

The fluid lilt of her wrist made the bubbles dance like lazy sparks against the crystal. "So the wine thing, I take it that's more pleasure than business."

A safe topic if ever there was one. He could talk wine all day without getting bored, and it would keep his emotional family life firmly in the shadows.

Gavin nodded. "Mostly, although I've created the wine lists for almost every restaurant I've managed."

"I bet the chefs love that." Sarcasm rang clearly through Sloane's reply, reminding him that while she wasn't immersed in the restaurant world firsthand, she knew a thing or two about how it worked. Most head chefs had egos the size of ocean liners, and he'd tangled with more than a few at the idea of taking their restaurants' wine lists into his hands.

"Some are more receptive than others. But pairing the right wine with a dish can take the whole experience from good to great. And in the end, they all want to be great." He broke off with a shrug. "We usually start on the same page, or at least in the same ballpark. It doesn't take much convincing once I put everything together, since good chefs have excellent palates and can taste all the nuances the wine adds."

"Yeah, Carly can wax poetic about the 'toothsome complexity' of plain old apple pie." She cradled her champagne flute between her pinky and ring finger to crook air quotes around the phrase. "All the fancy terminology is enough to blow a civilian's mind. I mean, it's *pie,* for God's sake."

Sloane crinkled her nose, although not with disdain, and Gavin's sudden good mood prompted him to take the thread and pull.

He faked a serious expression. "Actually, you might be on to something there with deconstructing one of America's most revered desserts. Apple pie is full of different flavor profiles, not to mention the varying textures in the crust versus the filling. If you consider the—"

"Oh my God, you're worse than a chef! I love dessert as much as the next girl, but come on. You don't deconstruct pie, you eat it!" she cried, swatting at him with her free hand. The contact of her fingers, even over the wool of his suit jacket, sent a snap of heat up his arm, leaving a definite trail of want behind it. It made his next words taste even more delicious as he cracked a smile, lifted his brows and said, "Sloane, I'm kidding."

Her eyes, nearly navy blue in the ambient light of La Dolce Vita's dining room, went wide. "Wait . . . what?"

The look on her face, so caught up in confusion, was priceless, and he started to laugh. "I'm kidding. You know, giving you a hard time?"

Whatever impulse had dared him to turn the tables and tease her for a change had been right on the money. With her Cupid's bow mouth parted in surprise, she was damn near irresistible, and the sheer pleasure of catching her off guard drew out his well-meaning chuckle.

"You're kidding. As in, making light of things, ha-ha, very funny, kidding?" Sloane looped her arms over the daring neckline of her dress, but there was no hiding the smile brewing on her lips like rich, warm French roast.

"Yeah. How'd I do?" he asked, although her cat-in-cream smile was all the answer he needed.

"Not bad, although I'm compelled to ask if you're feeling okay." She leaned her glass of champagne against her lips, but didn't take her eyes from his as she sipped. "I mean, that whole lighthearted laughter thing didn't hurt, did it? You didn't strain anything? Because I could see if there's a doctor in the house."

Oh, come on. He wasn't that serious.

Was he?

"Just because I don't go stirring up trouble all the time doesn't mean I'm incapable of having fun," he said, but the words were so measured with caution that they snagged in his ears. Okay, so he'd never been a social spotlight kind of guy, but he knew how to have a good time.

"Really? When was the last time you stayed in your pajamas and watched movies all day?"

He wrinkled his brow in confusion. "What?"

"You heard me. When?" The cluster of tiny candles on the table between them cast a shimmery glow on Sloane's face, emphasizing her mischievous smile.

He hesitated, but after a minute he was forced to admit the truth. "I don't know."

"Mmm hmm. And when was the last time you ate breakfast for dinner?"

Gavin laughed, releasing some of his pent-up tension. "Okay, now you're getting weird."

"I'm not getting weird. I'd be willing to bet next week's paycheck you can't remember the last time you laughed so hard you could barely breathe. Or that you've never taken a trip without planning it in advance, or run out into the middle of a rainstorm instead of running away from it."

His gut plucked with unease, but he swallowed hard to cover it. "How is getting purposely drenched fun?"

Sloane raised an inky brow. "If you tried it, you'd know."

Somewhere between the sexy curve of her mouth and the half dare coming out of it, Gavin flung his stalwart caution to the wind. He knew how to live life, dammit. Losing his mother with barely any warning had taught him just how quickly things could slip away.

This moment wasn't going to be one of them.

Gavin rounded the bistro table in a purposeful stride, stopping only when he was close enough to feel the rise of Sloane's chest over her sharp inhale of surprise. "I know how to have fun, and I don't have to run around in the rain to do it."

"You don't?" Sloane squeaked, but she didn't take a step back. Instead, she lifted her gaze to meet his head-on, and there was no mistaking the want in her eyes.

"I don't. Let's go."

Chapter Ten

"This is your idea of stirring up trouble?" Sloane asked, certain she was missing a crucial piece to the cool yet sexy-as-hell puzzle that was Gavin Carmichael.

"Yes. Now watch and learn."

Gavin rolled up his sleeves with precise, even turns, either unaware or uncaring that she was watching him. The corded muscles of his forearms stood out in lean relief under the light spilling down from the cozy half kitchen in her hotel suite. He shot her a quick glance before starting to rummage through one of the well-stocked drawers.

She chewed her bottom lip, torn between guilt and rampant curiosity. She'd been kidding when she'd given him a hard time about being so serious, and anyway, he'd been the one to start teasing her first. No way had she thought he'd actually *do* anything about it. Even though grabbing two glasses and a dusty old bottle of wine from La Dolce Vita's wine cellar and finding a quiet place to indulge didn't exactly qualify as wild and crazy.

"Technically, Bordeaux is supposed to breathe for a while before you drink it, but this one is old enough that we'll be fine with a shorter breathing time." Gavin stopped to examine the bottle, then the glasses, with careful precision. The reverent attention to detail in his liquid brown stare made her wonder what it would feel like to be the crystal in his hands.

Sloane cleared her throat and eyed the plain-Jane bottle. "How old is it, exactly?"

"1999."

She should've known that Mr. Calm, Cool, and Collected wouldn't get squirrely enough to pop open a vintage that was too old.

"So, how come you took glasses from downstairs? Aren't they all the same?" Sloane gestured to the narrow shelf above the sink that housed assorted glassware.

"Not even close. We use these downstairs when customers buy a bottle of nicer red." He unearthed a no-frills manual corkscrew from a drawer with a wry smile. "Guess we're going old school here, though. Good. I'm not really a fan of those fancy wine keys for something like this."

"Does it really matter how you get the cork out?" Sloane watched him uncork the wine, unable to ignore the flutter in her belly at the way he held the bottle so gently, yet maneuvered the corkscrew with such efficient, purposeful strokes.

She squirmed, trying with all her might to disperse the heat in her body to someplace other than between her legs. The cork slid from the slender neck of the bottle with a soft murmur, and Gavin paused for just a fraction of a second before starting to pour.

"No. But I'm a traditional kind of guy."

"Shocking, that," Sloane said with lighthearted sarcasm. It was already hard enough to keep her mind from flashing back to the dark, openly seductive look he'd laid on her when they'd left the restaurant. If she didn't keep it light, the suggestive twinge working through her was going to rip loose and have its way with him.

"I hate to break it to you, but you're no stranger to tradition yourself." Gavin set the bottle carefully on the counter and cast a glance at the clock on the microwave. "Five minutes should be good, and then we can drink."

She laughed, and it scattered the odd tension building under her skin. "Oh, goodie. That's plenty of time for me to tell you you're nuts."

Sloane had been called a lot of things in her thirty-one years. This was definitely the maiden voyage for the word *traditional*.

"Why am I nuts?"

Her laugh came out with a heavy edge of disbelief. "Gavin, I change my mind like most people change their pants. As quaint as traditions are, they're so not my speed."

He crossed his arms, a note of satisfaction creeping over his face. "What about your writing hat?"

Sloane froze. "What about it?"

"You wear it every time you write, don't you?"

The satisfied smile kicking up at the corners of Gavin's mouth did nothing to cool the unmitigated want swishing around in her nether region. She hauled in a breath both to relax and argue with him at the same time.

"Technically, yes. But that doesn't make it a tradition." Sloane traced an imaginary circle on the countertop, picking at the flecks in the swirled granite.

"Really? I thought a tradition was something a person did without fail, time after time." He picked up his wineglass by the stem, and although his eyes focused on the deep, plum-colored liquid in front of him, she got the distinct feeling that the grin on his face was solely at her expense.

No way. No *way* was she going to let him use her hat against her.

She narrowed her eyes and scraped the toe of her shoe over the marble tile beneath it. "I wear my hat every time I write because I like it. It feels like me. Real traditions seem more . . . I don't know, constricting. Like eating the same sweet potato casserole on Thanksgiving year after year. How boring is that? I just don't want to be stuck with the same old stuff and no chance of trying something new, that's all."

Gavin leaned silently against the counter for a minute. "So have you always had the same writer's hat? Or do you swap it out whenever you feel like it?"

Her laughter popped out in a burst. "I've written all my books with that thing firmly on my noodle. No way am I swapping it out for a new model."

"Same thing, time after time. Sounds like a tradition to me." He shrugged, but his nonchalance only kicked Sloane into high gear.

"That's different. My hat is more like a superstition. I wear it because it brings me good luck. I could still change it at any time and that would be okay."

"And yet you don't. Hmm." His chuckle teased her ears, and Sloane's skin prickled involuntarily. Damn, and she'd thought the I-told-you-so *smile* was bad! This rumbly laugh was going to send her over the edge.

"Can we drink now?" Sloane did her best not to scowl as she snatched up her glass and raised it to her lips.

"Wait!" Gavin's hand was on hers in a flash, staying her from tipping the glass toward her mouth. "If you want to really savor it, you have to do it right." His voice turned to gravel, but was far from harsh.

"O-okay." Suddenly, she realized how close his effort to stop her from taking that sip had brought their bodies.

Only a sliver of space separated them, but he didn't take a step as he lifted his glass next to hers.

"If you give it a gentle swirl, you can see the depth of the color. It's opaque, but not too thick. And see how it clings to the glass? It's a good sign for this vintage."

Sloane blinked, examining her glass. "Oh, yeah! That's pretty cool. Do all wines make those streaky marks like that?" She peered at the thin layer of amethyst liquid sliding down the interior slope and back toward the center of the rounded goblet.

Gavin nodded. "Those are the legs. All wines leave them to some degree or another. But with a lot of reds, like this Bordeaux, they're really noticeable." He lifted his glass, but not to his lips. "Now we breathe it in, to check the aroma."

"For . . . what?" She had a sneaking suspicion it was a far cry from sniffing the milk in her fridge to make sure it wasn't spoiled, but hell if she could think of any other reason to smell something you were going to drink.

Gavin answered her patiently. "Your nose and your palate work together. Breathing in the bouquet primes your taste buds, which heightens the flavors once you start to drink. It's why your mouth waters when you smell good food."

"Huh! And here I thought breathing in wine was just a snobby maneuver designed to draw out the inevitable." She lifted her glass and mirrored Gavin's serious expression as she gave it another look.

He cracked a wry smile. "You can't just throw this stuff back like Jell-O shots."

"You've done Jell-O shots?" She lifted a doubtful brow, totally unable to picture it.

"I went to U Penn before culinary school, Sloane. I've done a lot worse than Jell-O shots." His smile darkened with suggestion, and her pulse did a perfect imitation of a hummingbird stuck in a small space.

Gavin continued. "The idea is to draw out the experience to enhance the enjoyment, not get it over with before you know what hit you."

"For you, maybe. But I don't have a clue what the bouquet is, or what it's supposed to smell like," she said with a laugh. "Most of the wine I drink comes packaged in a box, you know."

His shudder was probably visible from the moon. "I'm going to pretend you didn't say that."

"Whatever helps you sleep at night, boss."

"Anyway." He drew the word out, his voice teasing each syllable. "You don't have to know what a bouquet is in order to enjoy it. Proper wine tasting is an evocative experience, completely unique to each person. You might not recognize the bouquet for what it is when you experience it, but it will affect you just the same."

Sloane bit her lip, searching her mind for a parallel. "How can something affect me if I don't even know what it is?"

"You're a romance writer. Think of it in terms of sex."

A nervous bubble of laughter rose from her chest. "Excuse me?"

"The journey is the pleasurable part. Not the destination." Gavin pinned her with one of his seductively serious looks, leaving her to wonder who had hijacked her knees.

"Oh." The word escaped her on a breathy sigh, and she cleared her throat in an effort to cover it. "Well, I don't know. Isn't the whole point to get to the destination?"

"Let's find out." He motioned toward her glass, gaze unwavering. "Now breathe."

Sloane's inhale got partway in at best.

"Yeah. Perfect," he murmured, his eyes lowered over

the glass so his spice-colored lashes left just a hint of sexy shadow over his face.

Her exhale fared poorly too.

"So now do we drink?" It took Sloane a minute to comprehend that the trembly voice asking the question belonged to her, and she forced herself to even out her nerves. After all, it was a measly bottle of wine, plus, they were adults. She could do this, no big deal.

"Now we toast," Gavin corrected, but then fell silent.

After a silence that lasted just a breath too long, Sloane understood that he was waiting for her to say something.

"Oh! I've already made one of those tonight, and anyway, this is your moment, isn't it? You go ahead," she said.

"Okay. To traditions." He guided his glass to hers, the flawless ring of crystal tickling the silence.

"Touché," Sloane said, unable to reel in her smile. She pressed her glass to her lips.

"Salut," he answered, his glass unable to hide either the perfectly cultured accent of his French or the mischievous smirk on his face.

It was the last thing she saw before every one of her taste buds wept with joy.

A rich, seductive taste filled not just her mouth, but all her senses with a rush of something so intense, she was tempted to moan. Far from syrupy, the wine was smooth velvet. She tilted the rim to her mouth again, and although the flavors sliding over her tongue were familiar, they scattered through her brain like a deck of cards spilled on the floor, just out of reach. They lingered even after she swallowed, as if to give her another chance to figure them out, but she couldn't.

"Oh my God." Fine, so any hope she might've had for eloquence had gone out the window as soon as the glass had left her lips. But please. This wine was making a flavor playground out of taste buds she never knew existed. Even if she didn't have a clue what she was tasting.

"You like it?"

Although she didn't remember closing them, her eyes fluttered open to reveal a picture as seductive as the wine in her glass. Gavin stared at her, wearing a smile of dark satisfaction that said he was just beginning.

Stick with the wine, stick with the wine.

"It's incredible," she admitted, pressing her lips together so as not to let the last of the taste escape before taking another sip.

"What do you taste?" he asked, nodding down at the glass in his hand.

"I have no idea." Sloane didn't waste her energy blushing at the admission. She'd never claimed to know anything about wine, and she didn't need a bunch of fancy terms to say what she liked. "I mean, there are all these different flavors, and they're all amazing. But I don't have a clue what they are. I just know they're good."

Gavin chuckled. "Let's give this a try, then. Take another sip."

She did, and damn if it wasn't just as good as the first.

"Now close your eyes and picture the flavors."

Sloane couldn't help it. She started to giggle. "*Picture the flavors?*" She cracked one eye open, just in time to catch the hint of warmth in his gaze as he took a taste from his own glass.

"Just tell me what you see when you think of the way the wine tastes," he said, and the sexy smile playing on his lips made her close her eyes.

"Okay. I see . . . summertime." She sipped her wine and pressed her tongue to the roof of her mouth, making a slow circle to capture the flavors before swallowing them down. "Plums in August. The jam Carly used to get at Greenmarket in the city."

"Anything else?"

Pictures swirled over her mind's eye, taking shape with bright colors. An image flickered in the deep recesses of her brain, barely a faded scrap of thought, but she didn't let it go. She swallowed again, catching a hint of something smoky and sweet and so familiar . . .

"Oh! Licorice!" Her eyes flew open, heart hammering with pure excitement. "When I was a kid, there was a candy shop by our house in Brooklyn. It was one of those old-fashioned places that made everything from scratch; right there in the front where you could watch. My father used to buy licorice and sneak it to me before dinner when my mom wasn't looking. But then she always caught us, because it turned our teeth blue."

She raised her fingers to her mouth as if it could keep the sudden memory locked in place forever. "Nobody else in our family could ever stand the stuff, but he and I always loved it."

"This vintage is known for definite notes of licorice, although the dark fruit flavors you caught on to first are easier to identify. You must have a really discerning palate to go with your good memories."

Sloane shook her head, and the emotional punch of the memory folded back into her mind. "You're probably giving me way too much credit. I'm sure I just got lucky."

Gavin leaned one hip against the gleaming countertop as he searched her with another heated gaze. "I doubt it. Taste is very emotional, and sometimes it triggers memories. That's why I asked you to picture the flavors. They tend to go hand in hand with specific experiences, and picturing them can heighten the tasting experience."

Not even the lovely flavors still dancing around in her mouth could mask the lump in Sloane's throat. "I never thought about it like that."

He examined his glass with a smile before taking a

healthy sip. "It's also a two-hundred-and-fifty-dollar bottle of wine, so that helps."

"Oh my God, Gavin!" Sloane's first instinct was to let go of her goblet, but the mistake had dollar signs written all over it. "Are you out of your mind?"

"Nope. I'm having fun, remember? And call me crazy, but I much prefer a really nice bottle of wine and the company of a pretty woman to running around in crappy weather."

Oh, hell. Of course she'd goaded him into this. Gavin was the least likely candidate for stepping outside the box, and what had she done? Dared him right over the line.

"I didn't mean for you to take it like this. We can't—"

He stepped in, cupping his free hand firmly over the shaking fingers that still held her glass. "We can, and we are. The bottle's already open, Sloane, and life's too short for cheap wine. All that's left to do is live a little and enjoy it."

"Enjoy it?" She cast a doubtful glance at the bottle sitting benignly on the counter, and the promise she'd made earlier in the evening echoed front and center through her brain.

No troubles, no worries. Just for tonight.

Gavin lowered their entwined fingers, releasing her glass to the counter but not letting go of her hand. "Look, it might not be the wild and crazy thing that you had in mind, but this is my version of running around in the rain. So, yeah. We're going to enjoy it."

His seductive expression kicked up a notch, and in that moment, Sloane knew two things. The look on his face had nothing to do with the bottle of wine, and if she raised her eyes to fully meet his, she was going to take forgetting her troubles for just one night to a whole new level.

She didn't think twice.

Chapter Eleven

Gavin's mouth tasted smooth and rich as Sloane pressed her lips against his in a heated rush. Impulse mixed with her sheer desire for more, and she boldly skipped tender pleasantries in order to get it. Gavin obliged, deepening the kiss to run his teeth over her lower lip with just enough pressure to make her gasp.

"You've been killing me all night in this dress." He sent the words, along with an appreciative exhale, into the ultrasensitive skin of her neck, and the suggestive glide of his tongue derailed any last shred of rational thought from her brain.

"This dress?" she asked, hooking her thumbs beneath the thin shoulder ribbons to slide them from her body.

Gavin's rich brown eyes darkened to near-black, but he replaced her hands with his own, stilling her. "This dress is so hot, it's a fire hazard."

Slipping the straps to just barely expose the naked expanse of her shoulders, he lowered his head to follow the path forged by his hands. Sloane's nerve endings sparked and sizzled, igniting sensations not just where he touched her on the surface, but deep within her, like a glimmer of electricity suddenly bursting into a dangerous, white-hot flame.

She wanted more.

"You're right. It's a complete menace," she said, her voice betraying her shocking level of arousal. Her nipples beaded into tight points as Gavin trailed kisses over the top curve of her breasts, and she arched into his touch to give him unfettered access.

"A societal threat," he agreed, answering her intensity by wrapping one arm around her back to hold her fast beneath his eager mouth. Though it was soft, the waterfall of silk on her skin heightened the friction from his hands, and when he skimmed a palm over the small weight of her breasts, an unbearable, urgent ache flared to life between her legs.

Oh, God, he couldn't possibly . . . there was no way he could make her—

He slid his hand deep inside her neckline, and every one of Sloane's thoughts completely shorted out from wanting him.

Gavin moved the strap of her dress just far enough to expose one needy breast, still cradled in black silk. The arm around her back tightened, and he angled his body against hers while he cupped her bare skin. The ache in her core became a hot throb as he dipped his mouth lower, trailing over the fluttering expanse of her chest to encircle her nipple. The heat of Gavin's mouth alternated with the cool strength of his fingers, and both worked her with flawless strokes. His gentle touch gave way to the merciless ministrations of his tongue, and holding back became as impossible as moving the moon.

Sloane didn't care how much he loved her dress. She wanted more of him *right now*.

"Oh, God, take it off." She fumbled for the zipper, briefly considered just tearing the damned thing to have more of him on her, but he captured both of her wrists so quickly, she jerked to a stop.

"No."

Shock trickled like ice water down her spine. "What?"

Gavin cast a head-to-toe look at her as palpable as any touch. "Your body in that dress is like the Bordeaux. It's perfect, and I want to savor the hell out of it. Just not in this tiny kitchen."

Before Sloane could even moan outright, they'd covered the space between the suite's kitchen and the bedroom, maneuvering various articles of clothing and kissing as they went. She worked quick fingers over his shirttails, freeing them from his pants in one deft move before liberating the buttons and lifting the T-shirt beneath. Gavin's chest was a perfect match for the hard, lean muscles of his forearms, and Sloane's attempt to bite back a second moan as he eased her to the bed failed miserably. He trailed one hand up her bare leg, following the side slit of her dress, but his movement screeched to a halt as his palm curled over her hip beneath the silk.

"Jesus. You're not wearing anything under here."

"Under this dress? Are you kidding?" The tango dress left nothing to the imagination, including panty lines.

His breath rasped by her ear. "And I thought you were killing me before."

Gavin nudged the edges of the fabric apart, tracing the natural curve of her hip before inching over her belly, and Sloane canted the cradle of her hips toward his touch. She reached out impatiently to snag the button on his pants, but he drew back.

"You said something last week that made me curious." He brushed his fingers over the seam where her inner thigh met her core, frustratingly close and yet miles away from the ache building within her. She made another bid to free him from his only article of clothing, but he dodged her again.

"It's kind of an odd time for a trip down memory lane, isn't it?" Heat lay banked beneath her skin, desperate to be kindled, but Gavin didn't relent.

He moved to put them face-to-face, dropping a slow touch from his lips to hers. "You said you've given yourself every orgasm you've ever had, and I want to change that."

Sloane's eyes flew open, her surprise complete. Her partners in the past hadn't been *completely* lacking, and sex was enjoyable enough. But by the time she got really warmed up, well . . . the game was usually over. She'd long ago chalked it up to just another version of *close, but not good enough.*

She couldn't come up lacking. Not again.

"Gavin, really, what we're doing now is fine. I don't even think—"

He cut her words off with another soft kiss. "This is about really living, right?" His fingers dallied in that excruciating spot on her inner thigh, and the suggestive touch sent a merciless throb right into her center.

Yes, yes, yes.

Gavin slipped his hand right over the apex where her legs came together, and his seductive smile in the light from the hallway was Sloane's only clue that she'd murmured the word out loud.

"Then let me do it right. Let me give you the moment."

His fingers found the heat of her sex at the same time he claimed her mouth in a punishing kiss, and she nearly flew off the bed at the intimacy of both touches together.

"Oh." The word hummed out of her, daring her forward, and she followed without thought. Gavin teased her with languid sweeps of his tongue, and she bowed up to meet him, experiencing the kiss in every part of her body

just like she'd tasted the wine right down to her toes. Each movement, each breath that moved seamlessly from his body to hers, pulsed through her, hot and deliberate.

He paired tender kisses above with firm, purposeful touches below, then traded off with harder kisses to her mouth and lighter strokes on her body to create beautiful, unbearable tension. Oh, God, the way he touched her, with a flawless combination of soft strokes and deep hunger, set Sloane on fire in ways she'd only written about. His eager fingers seemed to memorize her on the spot, paying such sweet attention to nuances that she herself hadn't even known existed, as if they were both unraveling them together. Sensations rushed to the surface, propelled by the deepest parts of her, and Gavin quickened his pace in response to her pleasured gasps for more.

"Gavin . . . if you don't stop . . ."

The realization that she was truly on the razor's edge of an orgasm hit Sloane like rising from the bottom of the ocean, with the shimmering surface tantalizingly close. His lips parted over her skin, spilling a smile over her neck with a wicked breath.

"I'm not stopping."

Just like that, the beautiful, unbearable tension coiling through Sloane came wildly undone. Sensation, dark and rich and forbidden, came at her from every direction, and she gasped for air as if her lungs were brand-new. For a moment, she felt wrapped tightly in nothing and everything all at the same time.

Sweet God in heaven, if *this* was what she'd been missing out on, she had some serious catching up to do. Like right now.

"Please let me touch you," she gasped when she could speak again. Want began rebuilding under Sloane's skin, just as relentless as it had been the first time, and she slid her hands down the lean expanse of his chest.

"You don't have to." Gavin's voice was gravel over satin, prickling all the way down her neck as he kissed her. "It's fine if we don't—"

"But I want to," Sloane said, pushing her fingers against his lips. "I want *you*."

Arching up, she pushed her way to sitting. With a quick reach and twist, the zipper of her dress hit the small of her back and the silk fell away from her body in an inky pool. She slipped it the rest of the way off in one fluid pull.

"You're a goddamn banquet. Do you know that?" He reached out, skimming her waist with patient fingers, and the deliberate touch made her shiver.

It's the journey, not the destination.

But Sloane wanted the destination so badly, she could taste it.

She dodged him gracefully before coming back around to push him to his back against the bed. "Flattery will get you everywhere."

She undid his pants, removing them with a few well-placed tugs, and swung her body over his to straddle his lap. Only the thin cotton of his boxers stood between them, and he thrust his erection against the cradle of her hips in an agonizing promise. Another thrust, and a heady sigh spilled from Sloane's lips, unbidden. She pushed back, enhancing the glorious friction.

Gavin tightened his hands over her hips, guiding her into a perfect rhythm, and her sigh became a moan. She leaned over him, placing her palms on his shoulders and covering his bare chest with her own, not stopping the movement between them. The slide of his fabric-clad arousal, so hard against her aching center, sent her breath tripping through her lungs.

"Ohhhhh, Gavin, I don't want to wait. I want to—"

The unmistakable chime of a cell phone interrupted her without ceremony.

For a split second, time froze, and Sloane floated, suspended in the hazy passion of the moment. Then reality careened into her senses, pasting the rest of her words to her throat.

"Sloane, I'm so sorry. It might be Bree. I have to get this." In one economical move, Gavin lifted her gently from his lap and unearthed his cell phone from his discarded pants. He spoke in hushed tones, and although she tried not to eavesdrop, it was damn near impossible since he was sitting right next to her.

"Okay, that's fine. Make sure Jeannie waits with you until I get there, okay?" He paused. "I know you'll be fine, Bree. I'll be there shortly."

Sloane's face heated with stark realization. Of course. It had been easily an hour, maybe even an hour and a half since Bree had left with Jeannie and the girls. How could she have possibly lost track of that?

Forgetting her troubles was one thing. Going so far over the line that reality was a distant memory was quite another.

There wasn't enough damage control in the world to kill this much awkward. She needed to get out of there, and fast. Sloane reached for her dress, shaking it from its puddle of silk on the floor.

"Hey." Gavin's quiet sincerity froze her movements against her will. God dammit, sitting here, naked and vulnerable as hell, was so not on her agenda.

Why couldn't she make herself *move?*

"That was Bree." He sounded truly torn, but it did nothing to ease the weird feelings swirling about in Sloane's chest.

"Right, of course. You should get going." Finally, blessedly, her limbs got the move-it memo, and she stepped into her dress. Bree was absolutely Gavin's number one priority, as she should be. No way was Sloane going to pretend otherwise.

"I'm sorry, Sloane," he said, and the apology only hammered her resolve into place. She tried on a shaky smile.

"No. I should be the one apologizing. You know me, totally flighty. It wasn't fair to goad you into something so impulsive." She smoothed her palms over the thin straps of her dress twice, even though they were perfectly in place. Now where the hell was her purse?

Gavin jerked to a stop, his arms halfway through his crumpled T-shirt. "Is that what you think? That you goaded me into this?" He stared at her in the barely there light filtering in from the kitchen, clearly waiting for an answer.

For a ridiculous split second, Sloane wanted nothing more than to tell him no. Her devil-may-care attitude and the crazy vow she'd made to forget her troubles tonight had nothing to do with how much she wanted him.

But saying yes would get him out the door, and really, hadn't she already screwed up his normally calm life enough tonight?

"Really, Gavin, it's fine. I just got caught up in the moment, that's all. No harm done." Sloane smoothed a hand over her hair in an effort to hide her wince. The words tasted like a two-day hangover, but it was too late to take them back now. As much as she hated it, sticking to her retreat was best for both of them.

"I see," he said, pulling his T-shirt all the way on with a solid yank. "Well, glad I could help you out with that."

Ouch. Okay, so she might've earned that one. "I didn't mean it like that. I just—"

"No, you're right." Gavin had his shirt buttoned and tucked in so fast, Sloane barely had time to blink. His tone harbored no heat; in fact, it didn't harbor . . . well, anything.

Just like the rest of him.

"I should've kept my cool, and I didn't. It was my mistake. Like you said, no harm, right?"

She nodded, her next word merely a whisper. "Sure."

"Okay. See you Monday, then."

Chapter Twelve

Gavin drifted slowly, vague snapshots of black silk and reckless, wanton curves flickering through his memory in individual frames. Velvet laughter unspooled in his ear, and he reached out, wanting to kiss the lush, pink lips responsible for the sound and ravage them until they parted in a perfect *O* of needful surprise.

But then his hands landed on empty space and thoroughly rumpled covers. The sunlight stabbing past the blinds in his bedroom sent a rude good-morning jolt, an all-too-stark reminder that he'd spent the night alone.

"Shit." Gavin jammed his eyes shut in self-defense, and the image in his mind's eye scattered. For a moment, he wished hotly for it back, but then everything surrounding last night's events tripped into place in a series of resounding thuds. The sheer, open joy on Sloane's face as the wine delivered an obviously cherished memory from her palate to her brain . . . the feel of her skin, softer and more electric than the dress that covered it . . . wanting to please her, not for the primal satisfaction of it, but because he craved the sound of *her* satisfaction even more than his own . . .

And the harsh realization that everything that had happened between them was just her latest impulsive experiment. Come on, had he really fallen for that orgasm thing? It had probably just been the bow on top of the sure-why-not package, a bending of the truth that meant nothing more to her than a night of sinfully good rolling around.

"Doesn't matter." Gavin's grumble fell flat against his pillow. The truth was, Sloane had no obligation to him other than to temporarily take care of Bree, and he'd hadn't exactly discouraged the I-know-how-to-have-fun banter when he'd grabbed that bottle of Château Belle-vue Mondotte from La Dolce Vita's wine cellar. They were probably equal in the blame department. He really should just chalk it up to no harm, no foul.

Except that he couldn't get her out of his head for all the grapes in Tuscany.

A quick glance at the clock told him he'd lingered in bed a lot longer than usual, and he threw back the covers with a start. He hadn't slept past ten since before his mother had gotten sick, and the fact that he'd let himself do it today sat like a brick of unease in his gut. Going through the familiar motions soothed his nerves, and by the time he made it down the hall in search of coffee, he'd relegated the memory of that sexy black dress—and the woman who wore it—to the back of his mind.

His routine hit the skids as soon as he reached the kitchen.

"Whoa." Gavin blinked, uncertain he was in the right house. A stainless steel skillet cooled over a dormant burner on the stove, empty save for some dregs of bacon grease streaking the bottom. Shells from a couple of eggs lay, cracked and discarded, on the butcher block, and a carton of orange juice stood crookedly next to them like a sentry gone askew. Bree sat, perched in one of the tall chairs at the counter of the breakfast nook, a single earbud tucked beneath her sloppy ponytail and a piece of bacon halfway to her mouth.

"Did you . . . make breakfast?" His words were hushed by complete surprise, but she jumped anyway.

"Oh!" Bree silenced her iPod with an abrupt flick and dropped the bacon back to her plate. "Um, yeah. I was hungry, and you were asleep. Sorry about the mess."

Gavin shook his head, still trying to process it. "How long have you been up?"

"I don't know. Not that long," she said, shrugging a shoulder from beneath the ocean of her hooded sweatshirt.

"You're dressed," he pointed out, remorse seeping past his foggy shock. He should've set his alarm.

Another shrug, this one less pronounced. "So are you."

He opened his mouth to counter that he was *always* dressed in the morning, when something on the counter in front of her yanked at his attention. "Are you reading the paper?"

Bree straightened as if she'd been caught doing something wrong. Finally, she said, "Yeah," but didn't elaborate.

His curiosity spurted, and although he didn't want to push her so hard she clammed up, he couldn't let it go. "That's new," he said, keeping his voice purposely casual. Maybe if they had a no-big-deal conversation, she'd open up a little.

Much to his surprise, the impromptu tactic actually worked.

"Yeah, well, it's important to be informed. I don't want to be an idiot." She shrugged, but rather than aiming herself toward the door, she resumed eating her breakfast.

Gavin bent his emerging laughter into a wry smile, not wanting to scare her away by seeming too eager. "I guess not. I've got to give you some credit, though. Reading the paper is a smart way to go." He crossed the kitchen to dig for the coffee beans and the grinder.

"It was Sloane's idea. She said it's a good way to practice interpretive reading. You know, telling the difference between opinion and facts?"

Surprise streaked through him, but he buried it in the cabinet under his hands. "That's why she's the tutor." The bag of coffee beans hit the countertop with a plunk, but he forced his hands to steadiness. He was an adult. Of course he could handle this accordingly.

"Oh, yeah, speaking of people who take care of me, Mrs. Teasdale called while you were sleeping." Bree took a bite of bacon while his stomach plummeted to the vicinity of his kneecaps. How had he missed the phone ringing?

"She did?" Gavin's stomach kept descending. Something told him it hadn't been a social call. "Did she leave a number?"

Bree nodded, a wisp of hair falling over her eyes. "Yeah, but she told me everything you need to know."

"What?"

"I'm a teenager. We're really good at talking on the phone," she said with a matter-of-fact eye roll. "She said that her sister's insurance wouldn't cover a full-time caregiver, so she won't be back for another six weeks."

"Six?" He fumbled the lid to the bean grinder, and it clattered to the floor with a noisy rattle. "Are you serious?"

"Yup. She was really apologetic and stuff. I had to tell her three times I'd be okay. She said she'd try you back later to talk to you herself."

Gavin blew out an extended exhale, sorting through the options. "Well, I guess I can put in a call to the babysitting service and tell them I still need someone temporary." It had been over a week since that first call. They had to have a line on someone he could use by now.

Bree busied herself by folding the paper into a crisp rectangle. "Or we could just keep Sloane."

Gavin's muscles pulled tight over his bones in a totally involuntary response. "I'm not sure that's such a good idea."

"Why not? I mean, she's already taking care of me, right?"

Suddenly, he had the urge to put something stronger than coffee in the French press. "It's not necessarily that easy. She's not a full-time sitter. And anyway, it's just six weeks. I'm sure the agency can send us a great temporary sitter."

"If it's *just* six weeks, then why can't you *just* ask Sloane?" she asked, her frown deepening. In spite of the sassy delivery, the question made sense, and Gavin knew it deserved a legitimate answer. After all, she was old enough to have at least a little bit of say in the matter.

He was just fairly certain that *because she makes me want to flush caution down the toilet* was outside the realm of an appropriate response.

"She's writing a book, Bree. She might not even be able to do it." Gavin paused. "I thought you said she was weird, anyway."

Bree dropped the last bite of bacon to her plate and shoved it away. "She is." Her chin and her voice both dropped a notch, and she refused to meet his eyes. "But she's nice, too. And, you know . . . I just thought since I'm getting good grades now, and since it's not permanent anyway, that it wouldn't be such a big deal."

Several emotions flooded through him all at once, and each one took a whack at his composure. Bree wasn't wrong about her grade in English. Her teacher had sent him a glowing e-mail detailing Bree's progress in class. Hell, she was even reading the Sunday paper of her own accord. While Sloane might consider herself the antinanny, Gavin had to admit that she wasn't the bad influence he'd feared in the beginning. But more importantly, in the ten months since their mom's death, Bree hadn't asked him for a single thing.

And she was asking now.

"Bree, I—"

"You know what, forget it." She jumped down from her chair in a rush of gangly limbs. "It was a stupid idea. It doesn't really matter who my babysitter is. I don't need one, anyway."

"I'll ask her first thing tomorrow morning."

Bree stopped halfway across the kitchen floor, a look of true shock painted on her girlish features. "You will?"

Gavin released the breath he hadn't realized he'd been holding. "You're right. You've done great work with Sloane, and the two of you already know each other. It makes sense to ask her first." He took the plate from Bree's hand, meeting her eyes before turning to walk it to the sink.

In a move that shocked him to stillness, she fell into rhythm next to him, popping the carton of orange juice closed and returning it to the fridge. After a minute, she said, "Then why don't you want her to do it? Don't you like her?"

Damn. Gavin didn't know which was worse—having her moody and monosyllabic, or having to answer the really hard questions. He raked a hand through his hair, trying to decide how to proceed.

"I just know she's pretty busy with her book. I don't want you to get your hopes up, in case she has to say no." Okay, so it wasn't the entire answer, but more than a kernel of truth lay at the heart of his words. While he'd do his best to put his impulsive foray with Sloane firmly in the rearview mirror, asking her to stay on might not be enough. He'd found out the hard way how fickle she was, and there were no guarantees that she'd agree to six more weeks of babysitting when she'd made it clear it wasn't her forte.

She wasn't exactly the kind of girl who stuck around.

Bree curled her arms over her chest, and for the first time, Gavin noticed not just that she was vulnerable, but how badly she wanted to hide it.

"Oh. Well . . . do you think she will? Say no, I mean?"

The look on her face sliced through him without warning, and in that moment Gavin knew he'd do anything to erase the painful lines etched around her eyes.

Including whatever it took to get Sloane to say yes.

"I don't know. But I'll do my best to work it out."

Monday morning hit Gavin with more than its usual vengeance, and he threw an extra scoop of grounds into the French press even though he'd already had three cups and it was going on eleven o'clock in the morning.

Yesterday's conversation with Bree seemed to have exhausted their monthly allotment, and she'd lapsed back into paltry one- or two-word answers to his questions before her mad scramble for the bus a few hours ago. Still, something about her had softened just slightly around the edges, and her scowl wasn't quite as caustic, even though she'd still aimed it at him a few times for good measure during breakfast.

Okay. So maybe breaking into a celebratory mood over a little less attitude from his sister was a bit much. But for now, he'd take it.

The sound of a car door slamming in the driveway drew his attention, and he headed toward the front of the house, pausing only briefly to give his tie a quick tug in the living room mirror before opening the door.

"Good morning." Gavin leaned into the brilliantly chilly

late morning to usher Sloane inside the house, and she breezed past him with a wide smile.

"Good morning, yourself. I got your message to come a little early. Does Bree have a half day at school or something?" She peeked out at him over the edges of the fluffy white scarf that swallowed her up to her chin, and Gavin found himself wondering how on earth anyone's eyes could be so blue.

"Oh, ah, no. Bree will be home later." Unrelenting heat stirred to life at the sight of her, and when she unwound the scarf to reveal the sleek, bare column of her neck and the snug sweater beneath her coat, he nearly forgot the intended topic of conversation.

Knock it off. This isn't about you, he hissed at himself, but apparently his dick had been absent on the day they taught obedience.

"Okay, then I have to admit that you've got me confused. Is Bree okay?" Sloane's shadowy lashes swept upward, marking her surprise as she hung her coat in the foyer and followed him toward the back of the cottage.

Gavin took a steadying breath. "She's fine, but I wanted to talk to you when she wasn't here."

The dainty riot of Sloane's bright red heels came to an abrupt halt against the hardwood. "If this is about the other night, I—"

"Actually, it's not." His gut tightened. Okay, so cutting her off bordered on rude, but there was no need to waste time and risk an awkward conversation over something she meant to sweep under the rug, anyway. They'd agreed to move on, so that's exactly what he'd do.

"It's about Mrs. Teasdale," he said, turning to meet Sloane's eyes.

They rounded, right along with her mouth. "Your regular babysitter?"

"It looks like her family emergency is going to keep her

out of town for another six weeks. The circumstances are pretty unexpected. She just let me know."

Gavin had finally spoken to Mrs. Teasdale yesterday afternoon, and the poor woman had sounded genuinely upset that she wouldn't be able to return as promised. It was easy to see why Bree had jumped to reassure her, and in the end, he'd done the same. After all, taking care of her family should be her number one priority.

"Oh," Sloane said, her eyes crinkling around the edges. "That sounds bad. Is she okay?"

He nodded his head to reassure her. "She's fine. But it leaves me in a bit of a jam with Bree." He paused. "One I was hoping you might be able to help out with."

A look of realization crossed Sloane's face as she finally connected the dots. "You want me to stay? For six more weeks?"

"I understand that you've got other obligations to consider. But yes. I was hoping maybe we could work something out."

Her expression rippled with a hint of something odd that he couldn't quite pin down, and it looked out of place on her pretty face. "Like what, exactly?"

Gavin aimed for nonchalance. "Well, since everything went so smoothly last week, it would essentially just be an extension of our arrangement."

Sloane's brow kicked up. Now *that* was an expression he was familiar with.

She said, "What about the babysitting service? I'm sure they could come up with someone a lot more qualified to look after Bree for six weeks."

"Last week went well, plus Bree has made some pretty impressive strides in her schoolwork since she started working with you. I'd say that makes you pretty qualified." Damn it, he should've known Sloane would balk at sticking around. She probably had some impulsive to-do list she was raring to get back to or something.

Nope. No way. He'd sworn to do his best to convince her, and this passive complimentary stuff wasn't going to cut it. He took a step toward her out of instinct.

"Look, I know you've got a book to write and a life to live. Kids aren't your thing, I get it. But Bree asked for you. She wants you. So I'd be really grateful if you'd consider it, because Bree's well-being is *my* thing, and I promised her I'd do what I could to make it work."

Sloane's lips parted, and shock commandeered her features. "But that's . . . that's crazy. She's barely said ten words to me that I haven't had to coax out of her with a bribe. Why would she want me?"

Gavin took another step, stopping right in front of her in the sun-filled kitchen. "The why of it doesn't matter. Whatever you've been doing, it's good enough for her."

"What?"

Oh, hell. He must've said something terribly wrong, otherwise why would she be looking at him like he'd just kicked her puppy? He cleared his throat. "I'm sorry. I don't want to strong-arm you. I know you've got a book to write, and—"

"I do. I have a book to write." She blinked, and the words seemed to kick-start her into gear. She looked at him, her face suddenly shrewd. "You're sure it would only be for six weeks?"

"Yes." Mrs. Teasdale had been pretty adamant, plus he didn't want to scare Sloane off. If worse came to worst, he'd figure something out. "I'm sure."

She nodded, and when she met his gaze with her crystal blue stare, he felt it deep in his gut.

"Okay. I'm in."

Chapter Thirteen

"Hey. It sounded important, so I came bearing food."

"I don't know about *important*," Sloane said, taking the white paper bag from Carly as her friend hustled into the bungalow they used to share. "Can't a girl kill a couple of hours before work with her best friend?"

"Yes. But it usually encompasses gossip." Carly cocked her head expectantly, tossing her coat over the back of the couch in the cozy living room.

"How's Jackson? Are you guys making do with postponing your honeymoon until spring, when ski season is over?" Sloane took the bag into the kitchen and started flipping through the cabinets in quick movements, her skin prickling from Carly's eagle eyes on her every step of the way. She should've known Carly would read too much into the whole let's-have-coffee routine.

"He's fine. How are you?"

Sloane placed two dishes on the counter and popped the paper bag open, taking a big inhale that made her mouth water. "I'm fine. Mmmm, cinnamon raisin muffins. You know these are my favorite. They're the best."

Carly frowned, placing a firm hand on each hip. "Are you trying to distract me with flattery and niceties?"

"Distract you from what? Coffee should be done in a minute," Sloane said, jutting her chin at the burbling pot.

"You forget how long we've known each other, *cucciola*. Something's going on with you. I know a cry for help when I hear it."

"More like a cry for sanity." Sloane's mutter got lost in the depths of the incredible aroma drifting up from the paper bag. "Good God, these really do smell amazing."

Carly's attention wavered to the food, tempting Sloane into a sigh of relief. "They're better warmed up. They only need a couple of minutes." Carly motioned for the bag, and Sloane dutifully passed it over so Carly could put the muffins into the oven.

"So do you want to tell me what's going on?" Carly threw a glance over her shoulder as she moved through the kitchen and suddenly, Sloane felt like one of those butterflies pinned down to a board, waiting to be labeled.

"Nothing's going on. Don't tell me you're so mired in marital bliss already that just hanging out with your best friend on your day off is out." Sloane laughed in an effort to cancel out any heat the words might carry.

Carly snapped a dish towel at her menacingly. "Don't hate on married people. You never know if you'll end up as one someday." She let Sloane's laughter run its course before continuing. "Of course I don't mind spending part of my day off with you, but we haven't had breakfast together in a while. Seriously, is everything okay?"

"Technically, I think this is lunch. And yes, everything is fine. Really fine, actually. I solved the rest of my cash flow problem."

Carly stopped with her hand halfway to the coffeepot and stared. "You did? How?"

Sloane paused. She sucked at beating around the bush, and with Carly, there was no point, anyway. Plus, this wasn't that big of a deal. She said, "I'm going to keep the nanny gig for another six weeks so I can pay my way to Greece."

Much to Sloane's surprise, Carly's expression was way more satisfied grin than horrified shock. "I thought kids weren't your thing."

Sloane snorted, unable to help it. "I'm not going to *have* any. I'm just going to keep track of one for a little while. And like I said, it's only temporary. Bree's regular babysitter had a bigger emergency than she expected, and I really need the money, so I said I'd stick around and help out. It'll make things tight for the book, but I should be able to get on a plane with just enough time to make it work."

"You *are* quite the literary Fembot. I bet the minute you get there, the ideas will flow like the Aegean. You'll crank that book out in no time."

A rich, comforting aroma wafted across the breakfast bar as Carly poured twin mugs of coffee, but it did little to cancel out the feeling of unease brewing in Sloane's belly at the mention of the b-word. God, getting down ideas for this book had been like trying to suck peanut butter through a cocktail straw. Finally having a solid plan to get to Greece and let the words loose on the page should be sending her into a joyful frenzy. And yet something she couldn't identify still had her breath hopscotching through her lungs instead.

The longer she stayed in Pine Mountain, the worse it was getting.

"Well, I don't have anything solid yet, but I've spent a lot of time thinking about it. And now that everything's falling into place, the words should follow suit," Sloane agreed, punctuating her words with a reinforcing nod.

After all, this was how it always was. Her books started out as tiny glimmers in her head, growing and percolating and swirling around until the next thing she knew, she immersed herself in a locale and inspiration slammed into her like a literary hurricane. If Sloane showed up in Greece and soaked in her exotic surroundings, the words would spill across her screen, just like they always did when she arrived on location. She was sure of it.

The timing, the circumstances, the possibility for success—all of it was perfect, really. Except . . .

"So Gavin only needs you for six weeks, huh? Or did you tell him you're on a deadline?"

Sloane took a gulp of too-hot coffee, choking it down with a sputter. "No, I, uh . . . I didn't mention my trip to Greece."

Carly's brows winged upward. "Any particular reason?"

Sloane hesitated. "I . . . I was afraid that if I told Gavin I was leaving, he'd just rely on the babysitting service and get someone with more experience," she said, rushing to add, "I mean, don't get me wrong. I intend to take care of Bree for the whole six weeks like I said I would. But it doesn't make me look very dependable if I have an expiration date stamped on my forehead, you know? I don't want to push it and lose my chance."

"True." Carly canted her head in thought. "But it's not like traveling isn't a regular part of your lifestyle. You think he'd care that much?"

Sloane's breath thickened in her throat. "Aside from winning the lottery, I don't have any other way of getting to Greece unless I do this, and I can't risk finding out the hard way. Plus, Gavin already has reason to think I'm a little . . . impulsive. I don't want to make it worse."

She booted herself with a mental kick for the hundredth time today. Sure, she'd just *had* to blame their heat-of-the-moment rendezvous on her capricious nature. Since when had marching to your own drummer become such a liability?

"Reaaaaaally? And what would make Gavin think you're so *impulsive?*" Carly's eyes sparkled over the word as if it rated a perfect ten on the naughty scale, and Sloane realized her gaffe too late.

"Well, it's possible that he . . . has some firsthand knowledge in that department." Her cheeks heated, no doubt highlighting her guilt with a blush of admission.

"Sloane," Carly intoned playfully. "Is there something you want to tell me?"

"No?" It came out like a question, and Carly's jaw popped so wide, her molars flashed.

"You're a terrible liar!" She broke into a grin that would make the Cheshire cat slink away in defeat. "You besmirched my restaurant manager, didn't you?"

"No!" The laughter welling up in Sloane's chest rode a tide of nervous energy, but she knew when she'd been beat. She admitted, "We may have, ah, kissed, but technically, there was no besmirching."

Carly shook her head with a laugh of her own and bent to slide the warm muffins from the oven. "To be honest, I can't say I'm all that surprised."

Sloane made a rude noise and turned to stare at her friend. "Excuse me? Unless I'm mistaken, I don't have a habit of . . . besmirching the people you work with." She might be a touch impetuous, but come on! It wasn't synonymous with *easy,* for Chrissake!

"Oh, don't get your panties in a tangle. I didn't mean it like that. It's just that with all the sparks flying between the two of you at La Dolce Vita last week, I figured you'd either end up killing each other, or in bed together. That's all."

"Sorry to disappoint you, but it's going to be none of the above." While Sloane didn't have too many personal limits as a rule, she knew better than to mix business with pleasure. "The last thing I need before getting out of Dodge is to be distracted."

"Distracted, huh? Sounds like a hell of a kiss," Carly

said, and although Sloane recognized the subtle bid for information, her resolve didn't budge.

"Even good distractions are still distractions. Now fork over that muffin, would you? I'm starving."

Sloane dug into the crumbly cinnamon perfection with a less-than-dainty grunt, losing herself in thought as the jamlike sweetness of the warm raisins and the rich, dark cinnamon melted in her mouth. Okay, so she'd left out a teensy part of the equation, and it rattled around in her brain like a marble in a glass box.

Gavin thought she was good enough to look after the one person in life who meant more to him than anything else. He'd even said so, and the words had nearly derailed her to the point of saying no. But then he'd mentioned her book, and everything had whipped into startling focus.

Trying to write a book in Pine Mountain had been an exercise in futility. If she wanted to save her career, she had to go to Greece. And that meant she *had* to say yes. So not only would she stay, but for the next six weeks, she'd be the best damned babysitter to ever set foot in the Blue Ridge.

Sloane couldn't let Gavin see how wrong he'd been about her being good enough. Her livelihood depended on it.

Sloane crunched her eyebrows over the scribbled notes on her legal pad, rereading each of the six pages she'd written with growing confusion. The words made sense— in fact, they made *wonderful* sense, evoking an excitement from deep in her belly that she hadn't felt in far too long.

But she had no idea where they'd come from, and the word *Greece* didn't appear on the pages. Not even once.

"Great. Now what am I supposed to do with it?"

Her semisarcastic mumble was punctuated by the sound

of a key in the lock, and Sloane tossed her legal pad to the couch just in time to catch the blur of haphazard ponytail and threadbare jacket that signaled the arrival of her charge.

"Hey, you. How was school?" She pulled her writing hat to her lap, twisting the thick cotton edges absently between her fingers.

"It was school." Bree shrugged, slinging her backpack from her waiflike shoulder with a heavy thud. She made her way to the kitchen, and Sloane followed suit.

"At least it's Friday," Sloane volunteered with enough shiny enthusiasm to make herself slightly nauseous. All week, she'd been pouring effort into making sure Bree was one hundred percent well-cared for, stopping just short of tucking the kid in at night. And all week, Bree had given absolutely zero indication that she cared one way or the other, let alone liked Sloane enough to specifically request her for a babysitter.

Who knew kids were so damned infuriating?

"I guess." Bree lifted an arm to slide a glass from the cupboard, revealing a quarter-sized hole in the underarm of her shirt.

"Whoa, your shirt needs a little surgery there." Sloane gestured to the split in the fabric, and Bree jerked her head toward it for a churlish inspection.

"Again?" She mashed her arm flat against her side as if to smother the hole into submission, shifting her weight to accommodate her new stance.

Even though she knew she risked Bree's ire by doing it, Sloane gave the girl a long, up-and-down appraisal, and her heart panged with realization. It took a close inspection to realize it, but the sleeves on Bree's shirt revealed just enough of her wrist to be too short, and the fabric sat a touch too snugly over her arms. If she lifted a hand just right, she'd pop that underarm seam like a grape.

How long had it been since Bree had gone shopping for new clothes?

Sloane opened her mouth to put words to the question in her mind, but Bree's pink cheeks and reinforced scowl made her stop midbreath. It wasn't exactly a secret that Bree embarrassed easily, and putting her under a microscope, even with good intentions, certainly wouldn't get Sloane in her good graces. Maybe she should just let it go.

Bree stooped down to pull a soda from the fridge, and the gap between her shirt and jeans revealed the bunchy, shapeless waistband of her underwear. Lord, they must be clinging to life by a literal thread. No way could Sloane turn the other cheek. But how could she possibly make headway with this kid without getting shot down, just like she had all week?

Unless . . .

"Hey, did I ever tell you that when I was thirteen, I grew so fast that my father tried putting *The Complete Works of William Shakespeare* on my head to get me to stop?" Sloane cocked her hip and leaned against the countertop, trying to look as bored as possible.

Bree's eyes flashed, chocolate brown and wary, but she didn't say anything. Sloane's gut gave a twinge of defeat, but she stuffed it down.

"He was kidding, of course. But man, I think I grew four inches that summer alone. I was the tallest kid in the eighth grade."

"Even taller than the boys?" Bree's voice sifted past the hum of the fridge, barely audible.

"Oh, yeah," Sloane said, meeting the question with an easy laugh. "They totally made fun of me."

Bree's brow folded over a look of disbelief. "Of *you?*"

She nodded, putting up her hand as if taking a solemn oath. "Yup. Too-Tall Sloaney Baloney, at your service."

A burst of genuine laughter spilled from Bree's lips to

fill the kitchen, and Sloane felt a bolt of shock at how girlish it made her look.

"So what did you do? To get them to stop, I mean," Bree said.

"There wasn't much I could do, really. My older sisters told me the boys were just embarrassed that they hadn't grown so tall yet, and that made sense, but it didn't help much. Once we got to high school a year later, lots of the boys were as tall as me, even taller by the time I graduated. And everyone kind of forgot about it."

"Does anyone still call you Sloaney Baloney?"

Sloane cracked a self-deprecating grin. "Not if they want to live to tell the tale." She paused, dipping her chin to meet Bree's eyes across the counter space.

It was now or never.

"You're growing too fast to keep up with your clothes, aren't you?"

Bree wound her arms around herself in a flash of long limbs. "Nobody's calling me names over it, if that's what you're asking. It's not that big a deal."

"Well, I'm glad no one's calling you names. But I respectfully disagree about it being a big deal. Can I ask why you're hiding it from Gavin?"

"Who says I'm hiding it from him?" She angled her body away from Sloane on the other side of the breakfast bar, but didn't flee, so Sloane proceeded with gentle caution.

"Because if he saw that shirt, he'd take you shopping in about ten seconds flat." Sloane had no doubt Gavin did his best to take care of Bree. But if she'd been hiding her ill-fitting clothes from him, he wouldn't have the chance. Plus, noticing the length of her shirtsleeves was probably the last thing on his mind, considering everything they'd been through.

Bree huffed softly. "Would you ask your older brother

to take you shopping for clothes? For . . ." She lowered her voice to a thready whisper. "For *underwear?*"

Eh. The kid had a point. Sloane sighed. "I hear what you're saying, Bree, but maybe you should give him a little credit. It might not be as bad as you think. And pretty soon, you're going to run out of shirts. You need clothes that fit."

"I can fix this." Bree lifted her arm again, twisting to get a closer look at the tear. Something utterly strange ripped free in Sloane's chest, and before she could even process the sensation, she was moving with swift intention. She pushed away from the counter and took a step around the breakfast bar, then another and another until they were close enough for her to see the shock in Bree's eyes.

"I know you can, but you don't have to. Now go get your coat."

"What? Why?"

Sloane marched over to the kitchen cabinet where Gavin kept the coffee and propped it open with a decisive tug.

"Because your brother has a hundred dollars in here in case of an emergency, and today's emergency is a trip to the mall."

Chapter Fourteen

Gavin raked a hand through his hair as he made the turn onto Rural Route Four, finally succumbing to the delicious exhaustion that signaled yet another successful Friday night shift. He'd never been a nine-to-five kind of guy, and while the weariness wasn't exactly relaxing, it was the sign of a job well done. At some point, he'd probably pay for it, but come on. He was only thirty-two. There was plenty of time before he had to worry about his body yielding to the long hours and brutally hectic nature of his job. Of course, he'd thought there would be plenty of time for other things too. Things that could vanish in the blink of an eye, without warning.

Things that mattered a lot more than a couple of aches and pains from a double shift or two.

"Great attitude there, Carmichael," he grunted, guiding the Audi up the shadowy driveway toward the cottage. While things with Bree weren't all hearts and flowers, there had been some hopeful glimmers lately, and in truth, those tiny moments had saved him. She wasn't the fun-loving little girl he'd left behind with their mom in Philly, although the three years he'd spent traveling for work had gone by so fast, they'd been reduced to a smudgy blur of cities with restaurants desperate for rescue attached. The bakery bistro in San Francisco—his first big break into management—had been a grueling series of trial and error for eight months. But after going to culinary school and doing his time to move up the ranks in Philadelphia's bustling restaurant scene, he was hungry for the back-breaking work of managing his own place. When that job opened up in San Francisco, he'd pounced on the chance to go.

Gavin put the car in Park, and rather than fighting his thoughts like usual, he let them spin backward, into his past. The success he'd felt at righting the bistro, at going in to fix what needed fixing in order to make the place flourish, had been addicting, so much so that he'd wanted to do it again. San Francisco became Santa Fe, which then morphed into Chicago, and before Gavin could turn around, over three years and just as many restaurants had passed, not to mention half a summer's worth of European wine tours in between.

In spite of the fact that he'd made it home to Philly for a grand total of seventy-two hours over the course of those years, his mother still encouraged him. He'd cultivated a passion for something he truly loved, and he felt right at the helm of a restaurant, restoring it to former glory.

Yes, he missed his family, and was in awe even then of how fast Bree seemed to slingshot from a gap-toothed little girl to the cusp of adolescence. But his own father had left when Gavin was five, and Bree's father died when she was a toddler. Gavin could barely remember a time when it wasn't just the three of them, and he owed it to his mother and sister to make a good living, to support them the best he could, even if it had to be from afar. He wasn't crazy about being absent for such long stretches, but there would be plenty of time to make up for that later. Doing whatever he could to bolster his mother's single-parent salary while gaining the experience to write his own ticket had seemed like a win-win of the first order.

Until his mother got sick, and he realized he'd failed both her and Bree miserably by not being there until it was too late.

Gavin shook off the wad of guilt building in his gut and got out of the Audi, welcoming the snap of cold night air around him as he stalked up the porch steps. No matter how badly he wanted to, he couldn't change the past. The most important thing now was to take care of Bree, and while their talk earlier in the week seemed like small potatoes on the surface, the relief he felt at finally making progress tasted more like a four-course banquet. He might not be perfect parent material, but he was getting the hang of things, slowly but surely.

The sound of voices floating into the foyer from the living room hit him like a thick web of confusion, and concern immediately pinpricked his senses. Frozen to the threshold between the porch and the cottage, he tried to place the voices. Bree's light timbre mixed in with Sloane's deeper cadence, and the concern upgraded a level. He hadn't told Sloane about Bree's nightmares, but what if she'd had one? It was after midnight, and a nightmare might explain why she was up. A curl of laughter shot from the kitchen right into Gavin's chest.

If Bree had woken from a nightmare, no way would they be laughing over it. So what the hell was going on?

Stuck to his spot between outside and in, he listened. The actual words were unintelligible, but the way Bree's girlish voice layered over Sloane's throaty laughter took a potshot at his gut. The sounds held strains of something he hadn't heard in far too long.

They sounded so happy.

Realizing that he was standing in an open doorway with a subarctic chill at his back, Gavin stepped all the way into the cottage with a quick head shake. He pulled the front door shut behind him, and the resulting noise reduced both voices in the kitchen to hushed whispers.

"Hey!" Sloane poked her head in from the doorframe, eyeing him mischievously. "You're home."

"Is Bree okay? She's not normally up this late." He nodded toward the back of the cottage. Although his fear had downgraded after hearing the sounds of happiness coming from the kitchen, it wouldn't hurt to be one hundred percent sure everything was fine. And to find out why on earth Bree was awake if nothing was really wrong.

Sloane's eyes widened, fringed by her sooty lashes. "Oh! I know it's late, but . . . well, it's Friday night. And Bree wanted to stay up until you got home."

Gavin's pulse stuttered with shock. "She . . . what? Are you sure everything's okay?"

Sloane released an overdrawn sigh, clucking her tongue. "You are such a pessimist. Of course everything is okay. She just has a surprise for you."

"What is it?" He swallowed tightly, tamping his feelings into a smooth veneer.

"Please. Didn't anyone ever tell you how a surprise works? You have to close your eyes."

The worry he'd felt when he'd walked through the door gave way to a startled laugh. "You're serious."

"No, *you're* serious. But I'll try not to hold it against you." She walked into the living room, and the sway of her hips beneath her dark, low-slung jeans made Gavin's libido yawn and stretch like a bear coming out of hibernation.

"Gee, thanks." Damn, Sloane looked pretty with her face all lit up in excitement. And clearly, the surprise was something good. How bad could it be to just play along?

Sloane sidled up to him, wearing that infuriatingly sexy grin he simultaneously loved and wished she'd keep to herself, and said, "Come on, close 'em. I promise I won't lead you astray."

Every single one of the just-business defenses he'd built over the course of the week disintegrated into dust. He jammed his eyes shut, more of an act of self-preservation than obedience. "Okay. They're closed."

Sloane's obvious buzz of happiness was catching, and despite the reluctance he'd felt just minutes ago, Gavin found himself giving in to the bolt of eager curiosity running through his veins. If the conversation he and Bree had shared earlier in the week was a glimmer of hope, her staying up late to surprise him with something was an out-and-out bonfire of possibility.

"Okay, Bree. Are you ready?" Sloane's voice lilted past his ear, and his anticipation amped even higher when Bree chimed in.

"I guess. Okay, yeah." Traces of something soft folded over Bree's voice, and Gavin scrambled through his mental Rolodex to try to place it.

But before he could put a finger on the hushed emotion cradled in her words, Sloane said, "Okay. Open your eyes."

Gavin raised his lids, but the image in front of him made no sense. Blinking didn't offer any help in the clarity department, and finally, after ten seconds of full-on staring, recognition flattened him like a steamroller moving downhill.

No way.

"Bree?" The word thudded past his lips, laden with shock.

"Ta-da." She gave an awkward twirl, not meeting his eyes when she returned to stillness. The Bree standing in the doorframe was an altered version of a beloved familiar image, and he went back to blinking in an attempt to reconcile the two in his brain. But the more he did it, the less it worked.

He barely recognized her.

"What did you do to your hair?" Gone was the light brown ponytail he'd watched her pull into place just this morning, replaced by a sleek new haircut that barely grazed her shoulders. And wait, how did it look so much lighter than it had just hours ago? She looked just like the older girls she'd been hanging out with in Philadelphia, and the realization made his unease return with a nasty vengeance.

Bree's cheeks flushed. "I . . . I got it cut."

"It's a different *color*." Anger welled up, demanding release, but it was circumvented by a fresh wave of shock as Gavin registered the trendy new jeans and V-neck sweater she was wearing. And was that lipstick shaping her mouth into a sheer pink frown? "How did you do all of this?"

Bree's eyes darted over his shoulder, her frown flattening into a thin line. "We just went to the mall."

His anger ratcheted higher, and he swung around to face Sloane. "You did this?" God *damn* it, Sloane being impulsive with herself was one thing—she was an adult, even if she didn't always act like one. But letting Bree go from zero to grown-up in an afternoon was totally over the line.

Sloane took a step back, eyes as wide as dinner plates. "She needed a couple of new outfits for school, so we went to the outlet mall in Riverside."

"Funny, last time I checked, hair color wasn't on the school supply list." His tone could've inspired an ice age, but he was well past giving a shit.

"There's a training school for stylists around the corner from the mall. The highlights are only temporary—they wash out in a couple of shampoos, and they offered to do them free with her haircut. They're not that much different from her natural color, so I didn't think it was such a big deal. In fact, I thought you'd be happy."

"Happy?" The word reeked of sarcasm, but Gavin made no effort to rein it in. "You thought I'd be happy about the fact that she looks like she's eighteen? You've got to be joking!" Temporary or not, thirteen was way too young for hair color. Those shampoos needed to start happening, pronto.

Before he could draw enough breath to tell her to get scrubbing, Bree threw her hands up with a shout, startling the hell out of him.

"Are you ever going to stop treating me like a baby? It's my head, and I'm standing right *here!*"

He slashed a hand through his hair in frustration, but refused to budge on the argument. "I know you're not a baby, Bree, but you're not an adult, either. You can't just run around getting makeovers like you're grown up."

A niggling thought trickled into his consciousness, and the entirety of what Sloane had said hit Gavin like a delayed reaction.

He turned to narrow his eyes at her. "Wait. You said the highlights were free. Where exactly did you get the money for the rest of this little excursion?"

Sloane's wince was so slight, he would've missed it if he hadn't been staring her down. "From the cabinet in the kitchen."

"The money I left for emergencies?" It was all he could do to drag in a deep breath and let her answer.

"Yes."

He turned toward Bree, reaching for as much calm as he could muster under the circumstances. "Go to bed. I need a word with Sloane in private."

"But—"

"I'm not arguing with you about this." His tone sounded as frostbitten as he felt, but his cool was bound to be short-lived if he kept looking at this transformed version of her. "We'll discuss it in the morning."

"What's the point?" Her knuckles flashed in a thin string of bright white as she tightened her fists at her sides, and every ounce of progress they'd made over the course of the week evaporated into thin air.

"You never let me do anything, anyway! Don't even bother grounding me. I'm not coming out of my room *ever!*"

Before Gavin could tell her to stop overreacting, she ran down the hall toward her room, punctuating her departure with a bone-jarring slam of her door.

Which left him alone in the living room with Sloane.

"Gavin, I'm sorry. I just thought—"

He stopped her apology midbreath, unable to hold back. "You didn't *think* at all! Hair color? Makeup? There's nothing about this that's okay."

Sloane bit her lower lip hard enough to leave two crescent-shaped indentations in the curve of pink skin. "It's only a little lip gloss and temporary hair color. They're both easily undone."

"But your bad judgment isn't," he pressed, taking an angry step closer. "You're supposed to be taking care of her, not stirring up trouble. Just because you go through life like there aren't any freaking rules doesn't mean it's how her life should be."

"I said I was sorry." Although Sloane's words were nothing more than a whisper, they assaulted his senses as if she'd bellowed them like a drill sergeant.

He snapped, "Sorry isn't good enough!"

Sloane flinched visibly, and the rest of his anger jammed to a halt in his throat. But rather than apologize again or back down, she met his gaze head-on.

"Maybe you're right. Maybe the way I do things makes me a crappy candidate for a babysitter, and maybe I did use poor judgment when I took Bree to the mall without asking you first. But that kid opened herself up to you tonight. I might not know squat about how to raise a thirteen-year-old, but let me tell you what I *do* know. If you push her away for the sake of what you think she *should* be doing, she's going to shut you out completely."

Gavin stood, stunned into silence by Sloane's words as she picked up her things in a swift grab and walked toward the door.

"And you can trust me one hundred percent on that."

Gavin knew he should make his feet move, that in spite of how much she probably hated him right now, he should go check on Bree, or do *something*. But he couldn't remove himself from his spot in the living room.

No way had he pushed Bree away. If anything, it had been the other way around. And anyway, it was his job as her guardian to consider her well-being. She couldn't just throw on makeup and get her hair colored on a whim, no matter how subtle and natural-looking the result might be. She was thirteen, for Chrissake!

She's going to shut you out completely.

Despair welled up inside him like a cut in need of attention, stinging mercilessly as it rushed to the surface. With the singular exception of asking Sloane to continue as her sitter, every time he tried to do his best for Bree, they ended up further and further apart. No, she didn't make things particularly easy all the time, but she wasn't a bad kid, either. Was he honestly that terrible a parent, just because he worried about what would happen if she grew up too fast?

Was he keeping her from growing up at all?

"Okay, Mom, help me out here." Gavin's whisper rasped through the postmidnight silence in the cottage, tugging its way from his lungs. "I want to do what's right for Bree, but I don't know what that is."

God, this was crazy. After a few minutes of forcing his breath to shift from shaky to smooth, he scrubbed a hand over his face and ushered his thoughts into rational order. The odd recollection of old memories that he'd shuffled through in the driveway, the bittersweet pang of coming home to happy, feminine voices—he cataloged each of these things in his brain, turning them over and over like waves on a shoreline.

The note in Bree's voice just before he'd opened his eyes flickered back to his memory, winding through the corners of his brain until the emotion behind her familiar cadence plowed the breath from his chest.

Hope. Oh, God, Sloane was right. It had been hope, and even though he'd never hurt Bree on purpose, he'd pulled that hope out from under her all the same.

Gavin's purposeful stride had him halfway down the hall before his brain registered the movement, but it didn't matter. All the forethought in the world wasn't going to make what he had to say any easier, and even the most eloquent speech could be shot down by a righteously indignant thirteen-year-old.

He really was a terrible parent. How could he have missed this?

"Bree?" He knocked in an awkward thump. "Hey, are you awake? It's important."

After an excruciating minute that felt ten times as long, she mumbled, "It's open, but I'm not coming out."

Undaunted, Gavin turned the knob. Bree had scrubbed her face and put on her pajamas, and she kept the book on her propped-up knees open, as if to highlight the idea that she felt intruded upon. The sparse light cast down from the bedside lamp kept her expression in the shadows, and he noticed with a sharp pang that Bree had tried to pull her hair back into a ponytail, only now it was too short to cooperate. Tawny wisps framed the angles of her cheekbones, and she swiped at them in vain.

"Hey. I was hoping maybe we could, um, talk a little." He shuddered inwardly. Eloquent he was not.

"You're mad, I'm grounded. What is there to talk about?"

"You're not grounded. And while I'm not thrilled, I might've . . . jumped the gun on the mad thing."

Bree's head snapped up, and another chunk of hair feathered from her sad excuse for a ponytail. "What?"

"Got your attention with that one, huh?" He shoved his hands in his pockets. Damn, he hadn't felt this inundated with guilt since he'd missed her solo in the fourth grade choral concert because he'd had to cover a busy holiday shift at the last minute.

"No." She turned toward him, so slightly that it was barely perceptible. "Okay, maybe."

It was as much of an invitation to start talking as Gavin was going to get, so he took it. "Look, before I say anything else, you need to know that first and foremost it's my job to make sure you're taken care of. Sometimes that means I need to make decisions that aren't popular with you. I'm not going to apologize for wanting to make sure you're safe and okay."

Bree grimaced and wrapped her arms around herself, but he held up a hand. "But I am going to apologize for yelling at you. I shouldn't have done it, and I'm sorry."

She examined him with a wary flick of her eyes. "It's no big deal."

"It *is* a big deal," Gavin argued, earning a startled glance that held his rather than dropping like the first. "Yes, I was mad, but yelling at each other doesn't solve anything. And even though I didn't intend to, I hurt your feelings, which isn't okay. It's just . . ." His throat tightened, but he forced his words to persevere. "There's kind of a steep learning curve to this parenting thing, and I'm not always very good at it."

After an interminable silence that scraped at his ears, she said, "You're okay."

He fought off the urge to heave an obvious sigh of relief. "So do you think maybe the next time you need something, you could try asking your *okay* brother? If I'd known you needed school clothes, I'd have taken you to get them. It's part of taking care of you, Bree."

"Yeah, but some stuff is embarrassing. Like . . ." She dropped her eyes and mumbled something that sounded suspiciously like *buying bras,* and his knees became momentarily undependable.

"Um, well, yeah." Christ, he was wholly unequipped for this. But it was more headway than he'd made in the ten months since their mom had died, and he refused to abandon the conversation, even in the face of unmentionables on his sister. "Maybe we can let the saleslady at the store help you with that. But at least I could take you to the mall. And take care of the other things."

"You never would've let me get my hair cut off." Bree made a face, and her arms migrated from around her rib cage to cradle her hips as she shifted against her pillows to look at him fully. A quick slice of worry cut through him at the streak of pain on her freshly scrubbed features, but then it was gone.

"I wouldn't have let you get it colored, no. But we could've talked about the haircut." A wave of fresh guilt splashed through him, prompting him to boldly sit next to her on the edge of her bed. "I was a little busy being thickheaded before, so I didn't say this, but you really do look pretty."

Bree's face flushed all the way to her ears, but the smile tugging at her mouth gave her away. "You're such a dork."

"Thank you. But I'm being serious." He gestured to the back of her desk chair, where the sweater she'd been wearing earlier was neatly draped. Although he hated to admit it, there was nothing provocative about the stylish garment, and the deep blue color had looked becoming on her.

The image of her wearing it, looking like the grown-up version of herself, flashed through his mind with a tug to his gut. "That sweater looks nice on you."

"Oh. Well, Sloane picked it out. I liked a different one, but she said this was more appropriate preteen couture, whatever that means."

Dread descended, low and horrible in Gavin's belly.

What it meant was that he wasn't done on the apology front just yet.

Okay, so Sloane should've come to him rather than taking Bree on an impulsive trip to the mall, but still. Bree clearly felt a connection with Sloane, and while he wasn't sure how he felt about that, it didn't change the fact that Sloane didn't blow off his sister. She'd taken care of Bree in her own, well-intentioned way. And wasn't that all he'd been trying to do himself?

Shit. Why did all of this parenting stuff only make sense after the fact?

Gavin cleared his throat. "Well, it's nice. You probably need more than one of them, though. Maybe next week I can take you back on my afternoon off. You know . . . if you feel like it."

"Maybe." But her word held no indecision, and her smile, albeit slight, stayed in place. But then she coasted a hand over her stomach, and the pained expression from a few minutes ago returned and lingered.

"Are you okay? When was the last time you ate?"

"We had Pad Thai for dinner at that place in the mall," Bree said. "Probably not the best idea."

It was Gavin's turn to grimace, and he held nothing back. "Ugh. No wonder you've got an upset stomach. You want a cup of chamomile? I can go put some water on real quick."

"Yeah, okay." She swung her feet over the edge of her bed and followed him toward the door, but after a few steps, she stopped short. Her face bent into another painful frown, followed quickly by a look of shock so disconcerting that his pulse clattered through his veins.

"What's the matter?" he asked, cursing the very nature of fast-food Pad Thai. "Do you feel sick?"

"No." But then her eyes widened with something he couldn't place. Without elaborating, she turned and darted across the hall, slamming the bathroom door behind her.

"Bree! Open the door. If you're sick, I can help you." Oh, God. If something was really wrong with her, he'd never forgive himself for all the stupid head-butting they'd been doing lately. "Bree, I mean it!"

"It's not the Thai food," came the muffled cry from behind the door. "I'm not sick, but you can't help with this. Just . . . I'm sorry. Could you please go away?"

If he lived to be a hundred and fifty, he would *never* make sense of these ridiculous hormones. Hadn't they just made a truce?

Gavin tried as hard as he could not to just whip the door open anyway, digging his fingers into his palms instead. "Remember what I just said about taking care of you? I really can't go away until I know you're all right."

"I'm fine," Bree choked on a sob, making his heart twist with both fear and the desire to protect her from whatever was making her voice sound so shattered.

He put a hand over the door, pressing against the cool

wood as if it could give him oaklike strength. "All I want to do is help you, Bree. Please just tell me what's wrong."

Bree's words were barely audible through the door, but they punched all the way through Gavin anyway.

"I don't think you can help with this. I . . . I think I got my period."

Chapter Fifteen

After twenty minutes of rabid tossing and turning, Sloane gave up and got out of bed. She wasn't exactly a stranger to one o'clock in the morning, and anyway, there had to be some bad-karma rule against going to bed this full of piss and vinegar. She padded down the hall toward the hush of the kitchen, grabbing a water bottle and the growing stack of mail she'd been ignoring for the better part of two weeks.

"Electric bill . . . credit card bill . . . oh, look, I may have won a cruise. Details inside." She tossed the sheaf of junk mail and bills back to the counter with a disgusted plop.

While Gavin hadn't come right out and fired her, it had to be just a technicality at this point. Good money said Sloane had doomed her fallback plan for getting to Greece the minute she'd popped off at the mouth and left him standing speechless in the middle of his living room floor. While it was unlikely he'd find a replacement babysitter overnight, there was sure to be one on the near horizon, which meant her chances of getting on that plane were slim and none.

And slim was looking pretty anorexic.

But come on! She'd apologized not once but twice, only to have her decision to take Bree for a simple trip to the mall tossed back in her face like dirty laundry. It wasn't as if she'd dragged her bar-hopping or anything. Taking Bree shopping got her what she needed while still keeping her pride intact, and the last thing Sloane had wanted to do was out the poor kid. Plus, deep down she knew that if she put a spotlight on how Bree had hidden her old, threadbare clothes from Gavin, he'd feel horrible that he hadn't noticed, and as sappy as it was, Sloane had wanted to spare his feelings. All things considered, she'd just tried to make the best possible decision for the circumstances.

Of course she'd never admit that to the Ice King, and not just because it would betray Bree's confidence. They might not be buddy-buddy soul mates or anything, but Sloane had been around Gavin Carmichael long enough to know what he thought of her ability to think rationally. Anything she had to say—no matter how reasonable or grounded in good intentions—would probably just make him madder. The thickheaded, chiseled-jawed, hot-melty-eyed jackass!

Although . . .

Okay, so maybe it was possible she'd gone a teensy bit over the line with the hair color. Temporary highlights definitely fell under the category of No Big Deal for a thirty-one-year-old, but Sloane hadn't really thought of it that way in the fun of the moment. In hindsight, she should've known Gavin would go ballistic over it. Heck, he'd freaked out last week at the notion of Bree wearing a face full of makeup in the privacy of her own home.

Why hadn't she remembered that until *now*?

The blinking red light on Sloane's answering machine snagged her attention, and relief cascaded through her at the distraction. She took a hearty swig from her water bottle and hit the button, determined to come away with at least a shred of something good from the last couple of hours.

"Sloane, it's your *mama*. The one you never call."

She let out a groan and slumped over the counter, dropping her forehead to the cool granite while she winced and listened. Would this day ever end?

"Carly's mother came by to show me some pictures Dominic took at the wedding. You couldn't wear a shawl over that dress? A person could see what you had for breakfast if you so much as leaned over!"

Truly, Sloane didn't know whether to laugh or cry.

"Anyhow, I thought you should know that Angela's doctor finally decided to induce labor in the morning, so she's going to the hospital at ten. I'll call you as soon as the baby comes. Maybe you'll come to Brooklyn for more than a day when there's a new baby, eh? Until then, I hope you're behaving yourself. And keep your body covered!"

A wicked image of Gavin's hands delving beneath black silk lashed across her memory without warning, and she yelped as she slapped the machine into silence. Okay, tossing and turning aside, she absolutely needed to go to bed, if for no other reason than to put this freaking day out of its misery. She capped her water bottle, replacing it in the fridge before turning to plug her cell phone into the charger and trudge back to her rumpled bed.

It rang in her hand, scaring the crap out of her.

"Jesus!" Sloane splayed a hand over her chest, and she sent a string of colorful invectives at her merrily chiming iPhone. "Whoever this is had better be really drunk."

The name on the caller ID sent a streak of confusion through her, followed quickly by a bolt of pure shock.

No way. Gavin was going to fire her now? In the middle of the night?

Over the *phone*?

Oh, hell, no. She wasn't going down like this. He'd said he trusted her, for God's sake. And like it or not, she'd made her choice with Bree's best interests at heart!

She whipped the phone to her ear in a huff. "Look, I get that you're mad, okay, and that I might've screwed up, but if you'd just *listen*—"

"Sloane—"

"Don't interrupt! You're so jacked up over what you think is right that you don't—"

"Sloane—" Gavin tried again. God, he was so infuriating!

"No, let me get this out. You don't stop to think that there might be more at play than what you think or feel. That there were *reasons* for what I did. You just—"

"Sloane!"

The dire urgency in his voice jerked her words to a graceless halt. Whoa. Had he sounded this bad the first two times he'd tried to interrupt her?

The absence of anger, of any variety of heat as he spoke her name, made the hair on the back of Sloane's neck stand at eerie attention. "What?"

"I, um . . . I know it's late, but I need you to come back. Tonight. Please."

The words were simple enough to compute, but they deflected off of every part of her brain that might process them rationally, leaving her to stammer, "You . . . you what?"

"I need help with Bree."

"From me? I mean, I think we've established I'm not the best person for that," Sloane said without any trace of sarcasm.

"You're better equipped to handle this than I am, trust me," he said.

Wait . . . he sounded *serious*.

Sloane pressed the phone against her ear even tighter,

certain she'd misunderstood. "Gavin, none of this is making sense. I know you're mad, but—"

"Bree got her period."

Oh, *hell*. Sloane brushed her free hand over her rumpled sleep shirt to rest over the ache suddenly spreading out from her sternum. "Has she ever had it before?"

Gavin let out a quick, cheerless laugh. "I don't think so. I mean, I've never gotten her, you know, stuff to take care of it or anything. So no. Right?"

"Right." Keeping some well-worn clothing from him was one thing, but there was no way Bree could hide needing feminine supplies from her brother, no matter how mortifying she'd find asking. This had to be the first time. "Where is she right now?"

Gavin paused, and even though he cleared his throat, his words still came out hoarse and strained. "She's locked in the bathroom, crying her eyes out. I wouldn't bother you, but she won't let me help her, and I don't know what else to do."

Sloane was halfway down the hall before her reply was all the way out of her mouth.

"Tell her to hang tight. I'll be right there."

Sixteen minutes and a backpack full of supplies later, Sloane climbed the steps to the porch to find Gavin waiting with the door open.

"She's still in the bathroom. I told her you were coming, but she didn't answer me."

Oh, Lord. Sloane had to admit it. He looked as defeated and stressed-out as he'd sounded on the phone.

"Okay. I can't make any promises, but I'll give it a shot." She tipped the bag from her shoulder to take off her coat. In her haste to leave the bungalow, she'd slapped a pair of flannel lounge pants beneath her Yankees sleep shirt and called herself dressed, but if Gavin noticed her lack of proper attire, he gave no indication.

"Okay, yeah."

Sloane flipped the backpack open, rummaging with determined fingers until she found what she was looking for. "First things first. This will help."

Gavin passed a confused stare from the item in her hand up to her face. "Bree's thirteen," he reminded her with a look that suggested she'd lost her faculties. She kept the bottle of Jim Beam extended anyway, lifting a sardonic brow.

"It's not for her, boss. Go grab a glass. You look like you could use a stiff drink."

The weariness etched on his face slipped, but only by a tiny degree. "Oh. Right."

Sloane propped the backpack all the way over her shoulder again. "Trust me, you got the most fun thing in the bag." She turned toward the hallway, but Gavin stopped her with a gravelly whisper.

"She's going to be okay, right? I mean, dealing with this with just me around."

Sloane's heart smacked against her rib cage, but she forced her voice into her standard glib demeanor. "She's going to be fine." She let a smile ghost over her lips in an effort to reassure him, hoping it would do enough to calm them both, and gave his arm a quick squeeze. "Whether or not *you* make it, well, that's a different story."

By the time she got to the end of the hallway, however, Sloane's signature bravado had pulled a disappearing act. Pure impulse had sent her out the door of her bungalow twenty minutes ago, and it had autopiloted her back here before she could register the gravity of the task at hand. But now that she stood in Gavin's hallway, wearing her pajamas and armed with nothing more than her waning moxie and a jumbo box of maxi pads, the idea of having The Talk with Bree was pretty freaking daunting.

Maybe she should try to coach Gavin through it instead. After all, he was Bree's guardian, her *brother,* who had known her for all of her life. While Sloane might be better versed on the firsthand particulars, having a welcome-to-womanhood talk with a sullen, scared preteen she'd known for two weeks was way beyond her comfort zone.

A sheen of nervous perspiration formed on her temples. She really was the last person on the planet who should be offering advice, and anyway, Gavin was only relying on her because he had no one else to ask. She could talk him through the basics well enough. Honestly, setting her loose on Bree without the big-brother filter might do more harm than good.

A loud sniffle sounded from the other side of the door, and every trace of Sloane's hesitance bit the dust.

"Bree? It's me. Um, Sloane." She scooped in a steadying breath that did nothing to calm her. "I brought you a couple of things. Do you want to let me in so I can give them to you?"

"O-okay." Muffled movement sounded from behind the door, followed closely by a hard click. "It's open."

Sloane nudged her way past the door, whispering it closed right behind her. Bree sat on the bath mat with her back pressed against the tub and her knees under her chin, and Sloane's heart double-knotted in her chest.

"Hey." She placed the backpack on the floor and gestured to the unoccupied half of the navy blue bath mat. "Mind if I sit?"

Bree shrugged, but scooted over to make room. Sloane wedged herself against the bathtub, the coolness of the porcelain seeping through her thin shirt to ground her. She could do this.

She had to. Even if she had no idea *how* to.

"Listen, I'm not quite sure of the best way to have this conversation, but I'm certain you have questions that you think are embarrassing."

Bree gave a slight nod, and it bolstered Sloane's confidence that they were at least heading in the right direction, so she continued. "But I promise it's all really normal, even if it's kind of scary. Getting your period is actually your body's way of agreeing with you when you say you're not a kid anymore."

Bree lifted her head. "It doesn't feel normal."

"It takes a little getting used to," Sloane agreed.

"But it . . . kind of hurts. And it's gross."

Sloane clamped down on the urge to smack her own forehead. Of course the poor kid was probably uncomfortable. "I guess we should get you, um, situated first, and then we can talk about it. Okay?"

Sloane explained the basics of feminine hygiene and gave Bree some supplies and privacy to adjust. A few minutes later, Sloane ushered her from the hallway to her room, where two mugs of tea sat cooling on the nightstand.

"Oh, perfect," she murmured, pulling back the covers so Bree could crawl gingerly back beneath them. An odd sensation rippled through her like a whisper, but Sloane shook it off in favor of getting Bree settled. She handed over one of the mugs and sat on the edge of the bed.

"You'll probably feel pretty crummy for a day or so while your body gets used to things," Sloane said, taking a sip of honeyed chamomile.

"Like right here?" Bree laid a palm below her belly button and grimaced, but Sloane simply nodded.

"Yup. Totally normal. It might move around to your back, too. Sometimes a hot bath helps."

"I can still do that? I mean, like . . . this?" Her gaze flicked to her abdomen with disdain.

Sloane pressed a smile between her lips. "Sure. It won't hurt you." She unearthed a bottle of pain reliever from the depths of the backpack and put it in Bree's free hand. "This and the tea will make you feel a little better tonight."

Bree squinted at it with a look of confusion. "Isn't this stuff for headaches?"

"It works on cramps too. Think of it as a multitasker."

"Oh." Bree paused, fiddling with the lid. "Sorry. You probably think I'm pretty dumb for not knowing that."

"I don't think you're dumb at all." A thought careened into Sloane, slicing through her in a wide path of panic, and she looked at Bree carefully. "So, um, I guess I should ask how much you already know about . . . why women's bodies change . . ."

Bree flushed. "We did Life Studies back in Philadelphia. I know all about where babies come from and stuff."

Sloane exhaled, her relief audible. "Okay. That's good."

"They just . . ." Bree broke off, scrunching down against her headboard. "They told us what would happen, but no one ever said what it would be *like*."

Sloane paused. She'd had two older sisters to pave the way with information, plus Carly and a handful of other neighborhood girlfriends who all went through puberty right alongside her. Although they butted heads on a regular basis now, Sloane could even remember her own mother drawing hot baths for her when her body adjusted to those first scary cycles.

All the women in her life had been a given. The only female Bree had, right in this moment, was Sloane.

She swallowed hard, but her voice was unwavering. "I can help you with that."

Thirty minutes, both mugs of tea and countless questions later, Bree's eyelids drooped so heavily that Sloane had no choice but to pull the quilt up around the girl's shoulders and turn off the light. She hooked her index finger through the ceramic loops of both empty mugs, nearly dropping both as she stepped into the darkened hallway to meet the unyielding wall of Gavin's chest.

"Oh!" Sloane clapped her empty palm over her mouth at the same time Gavin's hands flew to her shoulders to steady her.

"Sorry." He dropped his voice to a whisper, and his palms felt hot on her arms even through her cotton sleeves. "I didn't hear you coming."

Her brain spun, quickly putting everything together. She whispered, "How long have you been standing here?"

Even in the dark of the hallway, the guilt that flashed over his features was obvious. He dropped her shoulders to pull Bree's door quietly shut before answering. "A couple of minutes. I wanted to make sure she was okay, but then I heard you talking and didn't want to interrupt."

Sloane tilted her head. "So you were eavesdropping?"

"A little. Yeah."

The admission startled her, and she couldn't rein in the empathetic smile it brought to her lips. "So you know she's okay, then?"

He shifted his weight, and in that moment Sloane realized that they were standing inches away from each other in a darkened hallway in the middle of the night.

"Thanks to you, she is."

His whisper caught her with the force of a yell, and she clutched the mugs so tightly that they clanked together. "I don't know about all that. I mean, I kind of fumbled my way through most of it."

Gavin refused to relent, cupping his hand beneath hers to take both mugs from her fingers. "No, you didn't. And I owe you a pretty big apology on top of my thanks."

"You . . . what?" Despite her effort to control it,

Sloane's pulse jackhammered through her veins as his words sank in.

"After what happened earlier, most people might've been tempted to tell me to go to hell, but you came back out here anyway."

"Well, yeah, but you said Bree wouldn't talk to you, and you didn't have anybody else to call. I couldn't just leave you guys hanging out to dry."

"Yes, you could've. But you didn't." Gavin's eyes glittered over hers in the barely there light filtering in from the living room, and his expression rendered her knees completely useless. "While I'm still not crazy about the hair thing, I shouldn't have accused you of stirring up trouble. I overreacted when I yelled at you, and I'm sorry."

"Oh." Her response came out as little more than a sigh, and she cleared her throat in an effort to get her neurons to do something of value. "Well, all things considered, I screwed up too. I should've asked you first. In hindsight, I overstepped my bounds."

"What do you say we call it a draw, then? Fresh start in the morning?"

Sloane blinked. With everything that had filled the last hour, she'd completely blanked on the notion of Gavin firing her. "Oh. Um, sure. I guess I'll see you tomorrow, then."

"Sloane, tomorrow is only a handful of hours from now, and you've got to be as exhausted as I am. I don't suppose you'd humor me and just stay in the guest bedroom." He took a step toward her and gestured to an adjacent doorframe farther down the hallway. Her muscles tightened at the unexpected closeness, sending warmth like a slingshot right between her hips.

Whoa.

"How would that be humoring you, exactly?" Okay, so she'd been unable to keep the hitch out of her voice on that one, but Lord almighty, had he really just asked her to *stay?*

Gavin stood so close she could practically feel the dark smile break over his face as he answered, and it did absolutely zip to help her gain her composure.

"We traditional guys tend to feel pretty uneasy at the idea of sleep-deprived ladies driving home at two-thirty in the morning."

A wisp of hushed laughter escaped from her lips without her permission. "It's ten minutes up the road. I think I can handle it."

"That's where the humor me part comes in. Look, there's no way Bree is going to wake up before I leave for work. If you stick around, you'll be able to sleep late rather than having to get up and drive right back out here in a few hours." Gavin capped his words off with a nonchalant shrug, but Sloane didn't buy it for a second. She crossed her arms and gave him a hard stare through the dusky light.

"Low blow, using my predilection for uninterrupted slumber against me like that."

"Guess it'd really be below the belt if I offered to throw in breakfast too, then."

Her stomach rumbled with awareness. "Doughnuts. Double glazed," she challenged, her resolve weakening by the second.

He scoffed. "Please. I make an omelet that'll make you forget baked goods even exist."

Under normal circumstances, she would be flat-out irritated at being manipulated this way. But as it stood, she was too busy being turned on like Christmas lights to notice. "I bet you're going to tell me it's nice and cozy in there, too, huh? The guest bedroom gets the nice linens, and all that jazz?"

A tiny voice warbled at the back of her mind, screeching at her to march herself down the hall and get the heck out of there. The offer was well-intentioned, sure, but in ten minutes, she could be back at home, in her own bed. Where she belonged.

Gavin grinned. "Ever pick up fifteen hundred thread count sheets when you were in Italy?"

Sloane fought back the moan growing in her throat at the mere inkling, and it shut her inner flight risk right up. Damn it, why did her limbs feel so heavy all of a sudden?

She swallowed hard and wavered. "No."

"Pity. I highly recommend them. But if you insist on heading back out into the cold . . ."

"Oh, come on. You had me at breakfast." Sloane made a show of releasing an exaggerated sigh as she padded toward the guest bedroom, but her smile canceled it out. After all, how many chances was she going to get to sleep on sheets that probably cost more than she spent on an entire month's worth of groceries? In the grander scheme of things, staying in the guest bedroom for just one night wasn't that big a deal.

"Hey, Sloane?"

The sound of Gavin's husky whisper trailing over her name as he turned toward his own door halted her feet on the floorboards.

"Yeah?"

"Sleep tight."

As he pulled his bedroom door shut behind him, Sloane knew it didn't matter if the sheets were spun from pure gold.

Exhausted or not, she wasn't going to sleep a wink.

Chapter Sixteen

Sloane climbed between the sheets in the darkened guest bedroom, but the sigh on her lips had nothing to do with the thread count enveloping her body. Even though the sheets did feel like butter.

She twisted beneath the covers, trying to drift off to sleep to no avail. The room was perfectly quiet, with no sounds from within the cottage or the boundaries beyond to distract her efforts. Likewise, the bed was comfortable to the point of decadence, a factor which normally would've had her inner sleep goddess preening with sleepy-time bliss. Hell, even the room temperature was wonderfully climate controlled, splitting the difference between not-too-cold and just-warm-enough with flawless precision.

Too bad Sloane was so hot and bothered, she didn't notice.

Wanting Gavin this much was a bad idea. Okay, yes, he was good-looking, and double yes, he could turn her insides to tapioca with just one of those dark, seductive smiles, but come on. She was watching his sister, which might not be so bad in itself, but she was doing it to finance a trip abroad in an attempt to resuscitate her dying career. And as of this moment, that trip had no return date *or* return destination, which was just how she wanted it. Getting tangled up in anything right now would just be epically stupid.

And epically hot.

Sloane kicked off her pajama bottoms and rucked her night shirt up around her rib cage in a last-ditch effort to let the sheets cool her overheated body, and to her surprise, it actually worked. The fabric was downright luxurious, cradling her legs and gliding over her belly as if its sole purpose for existing was to indulge her skin. She snuggled lower to enhance the contact, unable to keep the deep tingle of pure, sensual goodness from radiating down between her thighs. The heater kicked on in the cottage, providing a rhythmic rush of hushed sound that tickled her ears. *Tap tap tap tap . . .*

Someone was at her door.

She opened her eyes, certain she was just hearing things, but then it came again, followed by the click of the knob and the sigh of the hinges. The door opened to reveal Gavin's shadowy outline, barely visible in the muted moonlight spilling past the curtains, convincing Sloane that now she was seeing things, to boot.

"Hey." His voice was more innuendo than whisper, but it was a very real, no-you're-not-imagining-this sound. She blinked, feebly trying to keep her pulse from working overtime.

"Hey." Her whisper emerged like a question, and Gavin shifted his weight just slightly before answering.

"I was just lying in my bed, staring at the ceiling when it occurred to me that no one's ever slept in here before. So it only seemed right to make absolutely sure the sheets are okay."

"You came to check my sheets?"

He nodded, a bare rustle of movement. "You can't be too thorough about these things."

"I see." Her mouth curved into a completely involuntary ear-to-ear smile, and she propped herself up on one elbow to fully face him. "You're quite the gracious host."

Gavin laughed, just a soft chuckle, but she felt the sound in her bones. "That's me. Mr. Hospitality."

Sloane tightened with realization. If agreeing to stay had been a bad plan, then being half-naked and chock-full of lust for the guy while he flirted with her in the dark was a recipe for utter ruin. Especially when they'd both run the emotional gamut tonight as it was. The urge to hightail it back to the meager percale sheets on her bed at the bungalow made a repeat performance in her mind.

Oh, who was she kidding? Her girly bits were too busy doing backflips of joy at the sight of him, and he hadn't come across the hall in an act of goodwill. It might be impulsive as hell, but she was done fighting the attraction between them.

"Well, the best way to test for quality assurance is to find out firsthand," Sloane said on a whisper, pulling the comforter back in a clear invitation.

Gavin's seductive smile was nearly palpable through the dark. "Outstanding point."

He was next to her in less than a breath, his fingers in her hair and his mouth finding hers in the shadows. He cupped the back of her neck to bring her closer, and their kiss took on a life of its own as he drew her from the covers to his lap, seating her there tightly as he leaned back against the headboard.

"Sloane." Gavin parted from her mouth to trail hot kisses down the column of her neck, slipping his palms to her hips to anchor his hard angles to her swelling curves. "Damn, you taste incredible."

She splayed her fingers over his back to hold him close,

and he slid his tongue along the taut line of her collarbone, edging toward her breasts. Her nipples strained beneath the loose neck of her nightshirt, rasping against the fabric. Wanting nothing between her body and Gavin's glorious mouth, she crossed her arms between them and peeled the garment off in one swift motion.

"You *feel* incredible. Don't stop doing that."

His eyes flashed up at her, dark and glittering, and the naughty grin she felt on her skin sent a shot of uncut want through her.

"Hold that thought for two seconds." He maneuvered her from his lap to the sheets, crossing the room to lock the door with a decisive click.

"You didn't lock it on your way in?" Sloane asked, her body already mourning the loss of his intoxicating heat.

"I didn't want to be presumptuous." He traced back over the space between the door and where she lay in three strides, and she nearly groaned with pleasure when he eased her against the lush pillows, returning his attention to her aching body as if he'd never left.

"Presume, presume! Oh, God, that's good." The pure luxury of the sheets had nothing on Gavin's mouth, and Sloane arched from one to the other with hot abandon. He braced himself over her, dropping his head down the midline of her chest to divide his attention between her breasts. Each swirl of his tongue over her nipples dared her closer, coaxing her soft skin into hard peaks so quickly, she couldn't hold back.

"Please tell me you're at least presumptuous enough to have condoms." Sloane reached down and curled her hands into fists over the hem of Gavin's T-shirt, desperate to feel his body on hers without hindrance. She sent up a fervent prayer that he wasn't *that* much of a gentleman, and was rewarded with a gravelly chuckle that had her nearly crying with relief.

"There's a difference between being presumptuous and being stupid." He hovered over her body, close enough for her to feel the heat coming off him in waves. "But you're getting ahead of yourself, don't you think?"

"No." Sloane pushed her hips up in a maddening thrust, a wicked smile of satisfaction on her lips at the groan it produced from Gavin's chest. "I'm done waiting. I want you right now." She slipped one hand between his hips and her own to wrap her fingers firmly around his fabric-clad erection, and his groan grew deeper in her ear.

"We don't . . . have to go so fast." He arced into her hand, belying his words, and she reached her free arm around the other side of his body for leverage. "Christ, that's hot."

She released a satisfied sigh without stopping her movements, stroking his cock with rhythmic care. Need swirled, deep and low in her belly, and she guided him right over the spot at the apex of her thighs that begged for attention, every inch of her body sparking from the heat of contact. His fingers joined hers in the sliver of space between them, sliding beneath her panties to find the tight bundle of nerves at her core.

Oh, God, she was either going to shatter or scream.

"Gavin, please. I want you inside me. Don't make me wait."

Their remaining clothes became a blurry tangle, and in a handful of seconds Gavin retrieved the condom he'd put in his pocket. Sloane's body hummed in greedy anticipation as he settled back over her, slanting his mouth over hers. Urgent need flared under her skin, pushing her recklessly, and she listed her knees open as if to punctuate her desire.

"Now, Gavin. *Please.*"

He filled her in one swift thrust, so shocking in its intensity that for a second, Sloane couldn't breathe. But then a moan issued from her throat, both husky and delicate, and she widened her knees even farther, rising up to meet him like the sun slipping over a gorgeous horizon. Every last inch of her reveled in the feel of him inside her body, in the primal, pared down electricity of it. Gavin angled himself against the cradle of her hips, pushing into her over and over again, and Sloane answered every move without thinking.

She arched tightly off the sheets, and his hand flew beneath the sinewy curve of the small of her back as he breathed out her name, holding her so close that no space existed between them. Pure pleasure wrapped around every inflection, and she sank her palms around him to lock him into place, lifting the insistent threshold of her body with thrusts so exquisite, she had to bite back the gasps in her throat for fear of screaming out loud.

Her senses reached their limit, not gradually, but with a shock of undiluted awareness, and her eyes flew open just in time to watch Gavin's shadowed expression go hooded with pleasure. His ministrations became faster, more focused, and they pushed her over the edge, into an unexpected free fall of release.

"Sloane." Her name was both ragged and reverent as he placed it in her ear, breathing it into the heated fold where her shoulder met her neck. Gavin gripped her hips and tightened above her with a shudder, and her body went taut in acknowledgment, still singing with the awe of her own residual bliss.

They lay together, tangled in the skein of bedsheets, while their breathing slowed and time dropped off the clock. A thousand thoughts spun through Sloane's head, but none of them formed words that made any sense, so she said nothing. What had started out as impetuous want was now something entirely different, and it slipped beneath the circle of Gavin's arms, whispering right into her brain.

Even as he held her in a beautiful knot of arms and legs and quiet, she felt the urge to run.

Gavin hummed under his breath, chopping fresh herbs in time to the wordless rhythm. He cracked a couple of eggs, then a couple more with a swift tap and release. The familiarity of the motions, of the seamless string of tasks one after the other, piggybacked with scents he knew by heart, and he grinned into the egg mixture as he started to whisk.

Spending the night in bed with a beautiful woman will do that to a guy.

His head popped up like he'd been caught doing something forbidden, and his grin became a quiet laugh that fell over the empty room. While he hadn't exactly planned the bold move that brought him across the hall to Sloane's room, he sure as hell wasn't sorry for it after the fact. The look on her face in the half-darkened hallway, so uncharacteristically vulnerable and yet still edged with her trademark strength, had made him want to unravel her, bit by bit. Before he'd even realized it, he'd been in the shadows of her room with every intention of doing just that.

Ironic, then, that he'd completely abandoned the notion of that slow discovery the minute she put her hands on him.

Gavin shook his head and gripped the stainless steel whisk handle tighter, meting out a rhythmic *tat-tat-tat-tat* against the glass bowl. Yes, Sloane was a beautiful woman, and the chemistry between them was obvious. But ditching caution in all its forms wasn't something he could do, no matter how much he liked her. He had more than just himself to think about now, and anyway, he'd gone the serious relationship route once before with disastrous results.

Good thing the only thing serious about Sloane was that she was *seriously* sexy. Plus, it was plain that Bree felt comfortable with her, and having someone in his corner there would definitely help. While he wasn't about to spill all his feelings à la Dr. Phil, having someone to talk to about the everyday stuff wouldn't be a bad thing.

And there was no way around the fact that she'd well and truly blown his mind in bed last night. Denying his attraction to her would be like trying to convince a magnet to stick to plastic. It was pointless, so he might as well enjoy what they had and see how things panned out.

Maybe next time they'd pan out slower. Or twice.

By the time Bree made her bleary way into the kitchen, Gavin's goofy grin had returned in full force. For once, he didn't care about wearing a little emotion on his sleeve. Or in this case, on his slightly stubbled face.

"Breakfast?" he asked, transferring the egg mixture to the omelet pan with a flourish. "I don't have to leave for the restaurant for another hour."

Bree eyed him with equal parts curiosity and disdain, tucking a lock of hair behind her ear. "Why?"

Nope. Not gonna let it bug me. He gave the handle a solid shimmy, swirling the egg mixture around the pan in an even layer. "Because I closed last night, so I get to go in a little later. I don't have to be there until lunch shift starts at eleven."

"No, I meant breakfast. Are you cooking because Sloane stayed?"

Gavin dropped the pan to the burner with an unceremonious clank. "What?"

"I heard you guys talking a little in the hallway before I fell asleep. You told her you'd make breakfast, right?"

Bree asked, her matter-of-fact expression the polar opposite of the panic brewing in Gavin's chest.

Well, *shit*.

He'd been able to listen in on the tail end of Bree's conversation with Sloane last night easily enough. How the hell had he not put two and two together to realize that thin walls worked both ways? The spare bedroom was at the end of the hall, with the bathroom between its walls and those of Bree's room.

What else had she heard?

Gavin tested the waters with extreme care. "If I'd known you were awake last night, I'd have come in to say good night to you."

Bree let out a professional-grade sigh, but she backed it up with a look of slight chagrin. "Okay, I get it. I shouldn't eavesdrop. But you guys were right outside my door. And anyway, I fell asleep like ten seconds later, so I didn't think it was such a big deal. Sorry."

Gavin finally allowed himself to exhale. "It's okay." He paused before going for the redirect. "So you didn't answer the question. You hungry?"

She nodded, taking three plates from the cabinet over the sink and putting them on the counter next to the stove-top. "You didn't answer the question, either. How come you're making omelets?"

"Oh." So much for changing the subject. He pondered the question and grabbed a spatula to have at the ready. "Well, I did promise. Plus, I always make omelets."

In fact, he made them so often they'd been a staple item on the family menu before he left Philadelphia. He continued, his words coming out softer now. "You used to help me cook all the time, remember?"

"I remember." She crossed her arms over the front of her pajamas, not elaborating, but not turning away, either.

"Do you want to help now?" he asked, holding out the spatula with more hope than he should.

Bree's eyes widened. "No." A beat passed, then another before she said, "I'll get the juice."

It wasn't a moment of total defeat, so Gavin latched on to it. "If you're not up for omelets, maybe next time we could change it up." As much as it sent an ache through his chest to let go of something they'd always done together, clearly there was something about it that she wanted to avoid.

She lifted her head, and her brows followed suit. "You mean make something different?"

"Sure." The mixture in the pan bubbled merrily, and Gavin gave it a purposeful flip.

Bree frowned, but it looked more like deep thought than a mark of irritation. "Like what?"

"How about doughnuts? Double glazed."

Okay, so maybe he had Sloane on the brain a little more than he should. But then Bree's eyes sparkled with interest, and he found himself not caring how they got that way.

"Doughnuts might be okay." She poured three glasses of orange juice with a shrug, but the spark in her eyes stuck around.

Gavin put her omelet on a plate and passed it over, trying—and probably failing—to keep his idiot smile in check. "Okay. We could even shoot for Monday, since you have the semester break from school and I'm off work."

She took a sip of juice, but was just a beat too slow to hide her smile with the glass. "Sure."

"Great. I'll grab the ingredients from Joe's Grocery tomorrow, and we'll be all set."

They ate their omelets in quick and relative silence, and even though part of him wanted nothing more than to wake Sloane just to catch her sleepy-eyed and thoroughly mussed, Gavin made the executive decision to let her sleep. After all, he *had* promised her some undisturbed slumber, and although he'd promised her breakfast too, he had the feeling she'd appreciate the sleep more.

He covered her omelet in plastic wrap while Bree rinsed the dishes in the sink, and the harmony of the simple movements surrounded him with easy calm. His mood, which had been good to start with, skyrocketed into the realm of sheer excellence, and as he left for La Dolce Vita an hour later, Gavin felt a sense of relief that had been too long in coming.

Finally. Finally, Mom, I'm starting to get it right.

Chapter Seventeen

Sloane scanned the sixteen pages of hand-scribbled notes, spreading them out over the normally pristine kitchen table like a sunshine yellow quilt of words. She gathered all the Post-it notes she'd rapidly accumulated over the course of the evening and stuck them with meticulous care around the pages, rearranging them as if they were all pieces in an intricate puzzle.

The refrigerator hummed its nighttime symphony as Sloane's pencil flew over the unfurled pages, marking more notes in fluid shorthand and peppering in enough Post-its to ring the entire perimeter of the table. Finally, with one last brightly burning detail deposited from her brain to the page, she stepped back to take the whole thing in.

Apparently, her muse had one hell of a soft spot for Gavin Carmichael's brand of inspiration. Which would've been great on several levels, except the outline spread in front of her was the polar opposite of what Belinda had asked her to write.

Sloane had discarded the ideas from the surprised handful of notes she'd written yesterday afternoon about as quickly as she'd churned them out. Yes, they'd been the only worthwhile pages she'd managed since Halloween, but still. Nothing she'd jotted down had anything to do with dashing, adventurous heroes or exotic, whirl-wind escapades. She needed to gear up for the Greece book, and she couldn't afford even a couple pages' worth of distraction, even if they were good pages. So she'd done what any writer in her position would do. She shoved the notes in her bag and mentally filed them under *maybe someday*.

But as soon as she'd woken up this morning, sur-rounded by the memory of what had happened just hours before, the ideas on those pages burst right back into her brain, mashing down last night's desire to leave and ren-dering it useless. The thoughts on those pages called to her in barely audible whispers as she wandered down the hall to discover a surprisingly good-natured Bree sitting in the breakfast nook, reading the newspaper.

Those loose threads she'd scratched out tiptoed through her brain, weaving themselves together while she ate the omelet Gavin had left for her in the fridge. By the time she and Bree field-tripped back to the bungalow so Sloane could shower and change, then took a quick trip to the drugstore to cap off their afternoon, those vague ideas had become loud snatches of insistent suggestion she could no longer ignore.

What had started out as a glimmer became a thousand-watt light show in a matter of hours, and the six pages had nearly tripled before Sloane knew what hit her. The more she tried to purge the ideas for the sake of clearing cere-bral real estate for her Greece book, the sharper and more wonderful the new outline became on the page.

It was the most finely crafted outline she'd ever come up with, bar none.

Sloane snapped a bunch of close-ups of her handiwork

with her iPhone, then flipped her laptop open over the counter in the breakfast nook. Images vaulted from brain to fingers to screen, all without so much as a mental tug to move them along, and despite her misgivings on the subject matter, she didn't fight them. After months of having to drag the words out of her brain kicking and screaming, watching them spill over the page without effort was a huge relief. Even if the whole shebang was set in none other than a cozy mountain resort town, with not an ancient ruin or breathtaking exotic view in sight.

She'd just have to deal with the fact that they were the *wrong* words later.

"Wow. It looks like you got over that writer's block pretty fast."

The sound of Gavin's voice filtering in from the entry-way to the kitchen yanked Sloane on a one-way trip back to reality, and she pulled the canvas hat from her head with a series of blinks.

"Oh, sorry! I didn't hear you come in." Whoa, when had nine-thirty turned into midnight? And when had she passed the heading for Chapter Two?

And more importantly, how did Gavin manage to look so freaking sexy, all buttoned up in that serious navy blue suit? He gave a mischievous smile that ratcheted his sexy factor even higher, and Sloane's muse giggled like a schoolgirl.

The rest of her tightened with awkward indecision, and she dropped her eyes to the floorboards, gripping her hat with a little too much enthusiasm. She'd always been ter-rible at the whole morning-after thing, to the point that she avoided it whenever she could. But steering around this was impossible, and the heat in her veins suggested that part of her didn't even want to avoid it.

Of course, that was the part that got her into this in the first place.

Gavin's easy smile stayed constant, though, and it chipped away at her unease. "At least you didn't head-butt me this time," he said. "Looks like we're both making progress."

Progress. Right. She closed her laptop with a snap and a soft laugh. "More like running in circles, I'm afraid. At least as far as this is concerned."

He gestured to the literary cyclone covering the kitchen table with a shake of his head. "It doesn't look like running in circles to me. But between the paper and the Post-its, you might want to buy stock in 3M."

Sloane unwound herself from her cross-legged position at the breakfast bar, eager to head off the invasion of awkward that was sure to drop back in any second now. Though she had zero regrets about spending the night being righteously inspired by Gavin, things would probably just be easiest if they skipped a repeat performance.

Probably.

She started talking, the words tumbling out just a touch too fast. "Yeah, sorry about the mess. I just need to number these pages really quick and then I'll be out of your hair."

"You don't have to rush." Gavin's eyes locked on hers. "You could take your time. Or stick around for a while, if you want."

Ohhhhhh, Lordy, did she ever want. "Oh. Well, I wouldn't want to keep you up or anything." Her cheeks flamed at the insinuation, while her inner voice went right into *liar, liar, pants on fire* mode. "I mean, you know. If you're tired. From work."

Dammit, she knew all that awkward was going to sneak up and bite her. Sloane clamped down on her lust-addled tongue and leaned over the table to mark each page in sequence for quick removal.

"I'm not." Gavin paused, clearly catching the look of disbelief that had emerged on her face without her consent. "Well, I *am,* but . . ." He turned his attention toward the splayed-out sheets, clearing his throat and changing the subject without fanfare. "So, this is how you write a book, huh?"

She took the change of topic and ran like a third grader at recess. "It's kind of sloppy in the beginning, but yeah. More or less."

"It looks like a hell of a process." His eyes lit with interest, and he edged closer to the table. "How does it work?"

Sloane's heartbeat stuttered. "What?"

"Sorry, is that taboo or something? To ask a writer about a book she hasn't written yet?" He averted his eyes, as if the toes of his loafers had suddenly become fascinating.

An unexpected laugh welled up at his genuine concern. "They're not top secret FBI documents or anything. You don't have to worry." She paused, trying to dislodge the curve ball from her chest. Aside from a smattering of writers in her online courses, nobody had ever expressed that much interest in the particulars of what she did. And why would they? Half the people in her family were expecting her to change careers any minute now, and the other half were just hoping.

"Oh. So how come you use five different colors of Post-it notes?" Gavin loosened his tie and moved to stand next to her, as if it were the most normal thing in the world for her to tell him about her job.

As if her answer truly mattered.

"Well, obviously I have a heroine and a hero." Sloane lifted the pink and blue squares of paper accordingly, moving a few of them from the outer rim of the table to the pages of legal paper as she continued. "And then there are internal conflicts, which are the issues they each bring to the story." She motioned to the scattering of green notes in front of them.

"You mean like emotional baggage?" He leaned in closer, so their shoulders touched.

She smiled at both the contact and the question. "Exactly. But if you've got internal conflict then that also means . . ."

"External conflicts," he finished, and Sloane gave the pages of legal paper beneath her hands an affirming tap.

"External conflicts. Otherwise known as all the things that happen to keep the hero and heroine apart." She tossed the remainder of a half-used stack of yellow Post-it notes to Gavin, which he caught with a confused frown.

"But it's a love story, right? Why are the guy and the girl apart?"

A fair question, to be sure. "Because people who fall in love too easily make for really boring romance novels."

"So much for happily ever after," Gavin said, arching a caramel-colored brow.

"Funny you should mention that." Sloane ran her thumb over the edge of purple Post-its, fanning herself in an exaggerated sweep. "Purple is for the steps they take to get to the resolution. See?" She pointed to the last four sheets of legal paper, all flanked by notes on purple squares. "Happily ever after."

"I had no idea it was so involved." He skated a glance over the whole thing again. "So how does it get from this to an actual book?"

"I start out with the handwritten pages, just to gather my thoughts in one place, but then as the idea grows, I add finer details with the Post-it notes. That way I can shuffle them around if I want, or remove them easily if I decide they won't work. Then, once it all starts to gel, I have to get on the laptop in order to keep up with myself. But it's nice to have the written notes to go back and cross-reference as I draft."

His soft whistle emphasized his surprise. "It sounds pretty fast-paced."

"Sometimes. This is nothing compared to being on deadline, though." Sloane winced at the realization that she might have seen the last of her deadline days, but she shoved the awful sensation aside. Five weeks from now, she'd be the living embodiment of getting things done, and the book in front of her would be long gone from her system.

Losing her job because her creativity went off on a lust-induced tangent just wasn't an option. No matter how strong the outline was.

Or how delicious the lust.

"Whoa. From the look on your face, I'd guess meeting deadlines isn't the most fun part of your job," Gavin said, and Sloane pasted a smile onto her face.

"Actually, it is." She hauled in a breath, forcing herself to relax. "But you're right. Sometimes it's just kind of fast-paced."

"You really love it, don't you?"

The question startled her right down to her socks, but she answered it without hesitation. "Yeah. It just . . . fits me."

He lifted a hand, barely skimming it over her cheek-bone. "It's written all over your face."

"That is a terrible metaphor," she said with a soft laugh. But she curved into his palm anyway. Oh, God, she felt exquisite with his hands on her, even in the most benign of touches.

"Sorry." His look said he wasn't, but who was she to argue? "It's true, though."

Sloane stared at him through the late-night quiet of the kitchen and said the only thing she could think of.

"Thank you."

Gavin kissed her with none of last night's urgency, but every ounce of the intensity. He brushed her lips with light touches, exploring her with patience that sent a hot tug right between her hips.

"You're welcome." He kissed her again, and the tingle of want became a strenuous demand. She wrapped her hand around his loosened tie to pull him closer, opening herself up to the sheer goodness of his mouth, so hot on her own.

"Do you always go so fast?" His murmur fell into the stretch of skin behind her ear, and she arched up to greet it.

"Yes. That feels incredible."

He pulled back, and Sloane had to either swallow hard or whimper out loud.

"I'm glad. But in order to make you feel *really* incredible, I want to take my time. And I can't exactly do that here in the kitchen with my sister down the hall." Gavin paused. "Bree heard us talking last night."

Every last inch of her froze. "Talking?"

"In the hallway. She didn't hear anything else."

Sloane sagged with relief. "Good."

His smile went dark with suggestion. "But it *is* something we need to keep in mind for the next time you stay."

Yes, yes, yes. She shoved her muse aside. "Next time?"

"Yeah. Next time." Gavin shifted his weight, putting them eye to eye.

Something strange filtered through Sloane's chest, and it mingled with the pure goodness there like oil and water. Being impulsive was a far cry from being crazy. In five weeks, she'd be not just out the door, but out of the country, with no solid plans to return.

So why couldn't she just say so?

Gavin brushed a thumb over her bottom lip, bringing that feeling of goodness back to the forefront. "Look, I'm not going to lie. Bree likes you, but she's not the only one. And rather than keep trying to swim upstream to fight it, we might both save a little energy if we just admit it."

She blinked, a smile twitching at the corners of her lips. "That's awfully laid-back for someone so serious."

"What can I say?" He leaned in, and the heat from his body so close to her own sent everything rational in Sloane's brain completely offline. "You're rubbing off on me."

She groaned, only half in jest. "You wish."

He captured her mouth, parting her lips with a single stroke and kissing her until she felt too breathless to move. Finally, with one last slide of his tongue, he pulled back to pin her with a sexy look that brimmed with promise.

"You have no idea. Now go home and get some sleep. I'll see you tomorrow."

Chapter Eighteen

Gavin took the porch steps two at a time, juggling a couple brimming bags' worth of groceries on one hip while unlocking the front door.

"What are you doing here?" Sloane poked her head out from the entryway to the kitchen, decked out in that ridiculously endearing sun hat and a look of pure surprise.

"Great to see you, too," he teased, moving past her to offload the bags to the counter. Damn, she made even a simple hoodie and jeans look hotter than naughty lingerie.

Although knowing her, he wouldn't be entirely shocked to discover she was wearing some racy scraps of lace beneath all that cotton and denim. She was a walking contradiction, a complete puzzle.

And he wanted to undo her one piece at a time.

"You know what I mean." A flush crept up her cheeks, topping off the hot-look thing with subtle perfection. "It's only three-thirty. You're not off work for another eight hours."

Gavin unpacked a bag of flour with a grin. "We have a lull between lunch and dinner shifts, and I promised Bree we could make breakfast together tomorrow. I just ran to the grocery store to grab a few things."

"I bet she'll be excited to see this stuff when she gets back." Sloane eyed the box of powdered sugar in his hand, but he stopped short of the pantry where it belonged.

"Bree's not here?"

She shook her head, starting to unpack the second bag. "Nope. Still at the movies with Caitlin and Sadie. Jeannie's bringing her home any minute now. Actually, I thought you were her when I heard the key in the lock."

"Oh, right." When Bree had texted him to make sure the trip out was okay, it had been such a no-brainer that he'd forgotten all about it. "So we're alone?"

"For the next five minutes, anyway. Where do you want—"

Gavin's hands were on her in an instant, stilling both her words and her swift movements. "The groceries can wait five minutes." He snaked an arm around her from behind, uncaring that the move was bolder than their usual repertoire. Her breath coasted into a sigh, and he dropped his mouth to taste the skin on the back of her neck to see if it would make her cross the threshold into a moan.

Bingo.

Sloane gripped the counter in front of her with both hands. "Five minutes, huh? I bet that's just a blip in your slow and steady world."

He wanted to spend an hour just testing the nuances of the fold between her neck and her shoulder, to run his tongue over the sharp angles and soft curves until she screamed.

He slanted his mouth just above the rim of her ear. "Barely milliseconds. Which is a damned shame."

She turned the tables on him before he could even breathe back in.

"Sure you don't want to come on over to where it's fast and furious?" Sloane tipped her head to give him better access to her neck, surrounding him full force with the spicy cinnamon scent of her skin. "We could make those five minutes really count."

Jesus. He'd give his left arm for the ability to stop time right now. Gavin's usually stalwart resolve wavered like tissue paper in a stiff breeze. "We could?"

She nodded, canting her hips back into his and turning him rock hard in an instant. "Mmm hmm. From where I sit, five minutes is an eternity."

Five minutes sounded like paradise coming from those heart-shaped lips, and the promise of it dared him right over the line. "Turn around and prove it."

Her throaty response vibrated against his mouth as he trailed kisses from her neck to the velvety landscape of her shoulder, and she arced back into his arousal in another wanton slide. "How about I stay right here and prove it backward?"

Fuck it. Slow was overrated, anyway.

"Sloane," he said, the word going to gravel in his throat. "If you don't—"

The front door banged open, and they catapulted apart like dry leaves in a wind storm.

"Hey, I'm back!" Bree's voice floated in from the foyer, and Gavin cursed the hardwiring that had let a part of his anatomy other than his brain temporarily make his decisions. Although he doubted either one of them would've ended up really giving in under the circumstances, he still should've kept a more level head. Getting that lost in the moment when he knew full well that Bree was on her way home was just a bad idea, no matter how enticing the flirtation leading up to it.

And god*damn,* had it been enticing.

"Hey! How was the movie?" Sloane's voice was just a shade too bright, but Bree didn't seem to notice as she cruised into the kitchen and headed toward the fridge. Gavin busied himself with sorting the rest of the groceries, hoping that the task—along with the sudden presence of his sister—would be enough to loosen the image of what he'd been doing a few minutes ago from the impulsive clutches of his brain.

"It was good." Her eyes glimmered with surprise as she caught sight of him at the counter, and she stopped short on the floorboards. "Hey, what are you doing here?"

Sloane did a poor job of stifling a laugh, lifting her hands palm-up as if to say, *See?*

"Last I checked, I live here," Gavin said, rebounding with a chuckle. "How come everybody keeps asking me that?"

"Um, because it's a good question?" Bree crinkled her nose in true smart-ass fashion, and he snapped a dish towel at her, prompting a dodge-and-giggle maneuver that made his heart consider exploding.

"Told you." Sloane winked at Bree in like-minded approval, scooping up the twin containers of vegetable oil and heading for the pantry.

"Since you so eloquently asked, I made that run to Joe's Grocery to grab the ingredients for breakfast tomorrow. All I have to do now is dig up the fryer and mix the dough in the morning, and we'll be all set." The idea of spending time with Bree, doing something he'd once taken for granted but now missed like crazy, sparked something pure and good in his chest.

It flickered hard as soon as he caught her expression.

"Oh, doughnuts." Bree shifted her weight from one boot to the other, and Gavin paused.

"You still want to make breakfast, right?" Disappointment knocked his gut down a peg, but he refused to let it show. Considering how touchy Bree had been about cooking with him in the first place, he'd tried to prepare himself for the possibility that she might recant. He was learning the hard way that thirteen-year-old logic could change with the wind.

Bree dropped her eyes, but nodded. "I do, but, um . . ."

"Maybe you'd feel more comfortable if we invited Sloane."

Okay, so he'd blurted the suggestion without consulting the reasonable part of his brain, but he only wanted to make things easier for Bree. Maybe all she needed to feel untroubled about letting him back in was a buffer.

Asking Sloane just made sense. It felt . . . right.

"I don't want to intrude on a family thing," Sloane started, her blue eyes as wide as the ocean, but Bree shook her head, emphatic.

"No, you wouldn't. I mean, it's not that." She wrapped her arms around herself and scuffed a boot against the floorboards. "It's just that Caitlin and Sadie invited me to go skiing with them tomorrow, and I kind of wanted to, you know. Go."

Gavin frowned. "But you don't ski."

"I know, but they do, and they're both really good. And they promised to lend me their extra gear and help me on the easy trails until I get the hang of it. There's even a beginner's class for people who have never skied, so I won't look totally stupid." Her words rushed out, but as hard as he tried, Gavin couldn't quite latch on to any of them with a whole lot of clarity.

"Okay, but the resort is a big place, Bree. There are twenty-three trails. You can't just expect me to drop you off at the gate with your friends and say, 'See you later.'" The more the idea made it past his what-the-hell filter, the less he liked the thought of it. No less than a billion things could happen to her out on those trails, way more of them bad than not.

Bree flattened her mouth into a thin line, but her voice stayed calm. "I knew you'd say that, so Mrs. Carter promised she'd stay at the resort. And that we'd have to check in with her during the day. In person, not by cell phone."

Score one for Jeannie. He'd have insisted on the same thing. Still, something about the plan didn't quite add up. "How long are we talking about this trip lasting, exactly?"

She mumbled something, and Gavin's jaw popped.

"Sorry, did you say overnight?" The whole notion of what-the-hell went into overtime.

"It's just easier if I sleep over there. Then we can get up and head out early tomorrow morning before the crowd gets too bad. They're even making fresh snow tonight."

"Sounds like you have it all figured out." The words came out less noncommittal than they'd sounded in his mind, but come on. She'd practically blindsided him, for Chrissake! What was he supposed to do?

Bree let out an exasperated breath. "Only because I knew you'd want all the details. You would've said no right away if it wasn't planned out!"

"I might say no anyway, Bree. To be honest, I'm not really crazy about the way you're springing this on me, and I have to be back at work in less than an hour. I don't have time to talk to Mrs. Carter about this, or take you over there, or anything."

"Sloane could take me, and find out everything you want to know." Bree turned toward the pantry, and damned if Gavin hadn't forgotten Sloane had even been standing there. "Couldn't you? Please?"

Time hiccuped for the briefest second, but before he could get the protest brewing in his brain all the way out of his mouth, Sloane shocked the hell out of him by going totally Switzerland. She said, "That's not really my call to make."

Bree swung back to Gavin, exasperation hardening her girlish features. "But it's totally unfair. They didn't invite me until today, otherwise I would have asked before now!

You're going to say no without even talking to Mrs. Carter, and all my friends are going to know it's because you think I'm a total baby." She stomped a booted foot on the floorboards, throwing her hands into the air. "Just because I got all excited and forgot about the doughnuts!"

Gavin's head snapped up. "It doesn't have anything to do with that." His composure simmered, threatening to boil over from the heat of aggravation flowing freely through his veins. The last thing he wanted was to have yet another argument with her, especially in front of Sloane. He had to tie this up, pronto, so he made his voice as calm as possible. "Look, I'm not going to apologize for wanting to make sure nothing bad happens to you. It's the same thing Mom would do."

Bree's eyes flashed for just an instant, brimming with unshed tears, before she struck, angry and swift.

"You're nothing like Mom! At least with her, I got a say in things. But with you, it doesn't matter whether I'm good or bad. You never *hear* me. I don't even know why you bothered to take me if I don't make a difference to you!"

Thick silence soaked through the air while Gavin tried desperately to rebound from the serrated slice of her words, but all he could do was grasp for steady breath. Tears tracked down Bree's cheeks, and any peace of mind he'd had about finally getting it right disappeared like a cheap parlor trick.

He didn't know shit about taking care of her.

"Bree." The voice that cut across the kitchen was soft, but meant business.

And it wasn't his.

"Bree, look at me." Sloane moved soundlessly, but stationed herself so close that Bree had no choice but to do what she'd said. "Do you trust me to tell you the truth?"

The question made Gavin's thoughts feel like molasses

stuck in the back of the cupboard for too long. Turning them into words was going to take nothing short of a miracle, and he had no choice but to listen by shocked default.

Bree's eyes went wide, her lashes stuck together. "Yes."

Sloane's hesitation was barely perceptible, as if she hadn't quite been expecting that answer, but she didn't falter. "Good. Then let me tell you this. Your brother loves you."

"But—"

"No." Sloane put a hand on Bree's arm, barely making contact. "No buts. He does. You can be mad all you want, but you can't doubt that."

Gavin watched, completely poleaxed, as Bree's lips softened from a scowl to a tremble. "I don't. It's just . . ."

She hesitated, and in that moment, Sloane slid back out of the way so Bree could look at him, unimpeded. Fresh tears coursed down her face, and even through all the emotion running rampant in his head, he had the urge to cut the conversation off in order to protect her.

But instead, he listened.

"It makes me mad. I keep telling you I'm not a baby anymore, but you treat me like one anyway." Her breath sobbed out of her, but she continued in a torrent as if she'd been suddenly uncorked and spilled hard. "I hate being the new kid, the different kid. The kid . . . with no mom. I just want to be normal, like everybody else. But I can't. I can't change any of that stuff, and I don't . . . I don't . . ."

She choked out another sob, and Gavin's feet moved before his brain commanded them to. He covered the steps between them without breathing, only exhaling after Bree let him pull her close.

"I don't know how to be normal anymore," she cried into his shirt. "Everything's so backward and weird, and nothing feels right without Mom. All this stuff keeps happening without her, like you making omelets and me getting my stupid period, but it's all so different without her here. I hate it. I *hate* it. I don't want to change! I want her back." She shook in the cradle of his arms, and as much as her weeping ripped at him, he refused to let go.

At the very least, he could protect her in this.

"Okay." Gavin repeated the word until he lost count of how many times he'd spoken it, his earlier anger completely obliterated by the need to erase the hurt sawing out from Bree's lungs in cries so deep, they belied her size. God, how had he missed the level of her grief? How could he have not seen all this hurt that was so clearly in front of his face?

She'd been right here in front of him the whole time. He should've known.

"Bree, listen," he said, pulling back to look at her only after her sobs had subsided into intermittent hitches of breath. "I'm so sorry. I didn't realize you felt this way. Well, not like this, anyway." Christ, even now he was botching this. "Why didn't you tell me?"

Bree shook her head and wiped her face with the back of one hand. "I was mad at you. We were a family, but then you left, and you didn't come back until Mom got sick. I didn't want to tell you anything private because I thought you'd just leave again anyway. I thought she'd get . . . better . . . and you'd go back to Chicago . . ."

She paused for a shaky breath. "But then she didn't. And then after she died, you were busy with the grown-up stuff, like bills and work, and I thought you'd think I was weird because I was still sad."

"You think I'm not still sad about Mom?" Gavin stared at her, unable to say anything else.

Bree hesitated, then eked out a tiny nod. "You just seemed so normal, so calm. And then you were at work a lot, like nothing had ever happened. So I felt weird that I still missed her so much."

"I think about Mom every day," he insisted. "No matter what it looks like." God, all those hours he'd spent researching his mother's treatment plans before she died, the mind-numbing details he'd had to sort through to plan her funeral—not to mention all the times he'd walked out the door to go to work just to get away from his grief for a couple of hours—Bree had been stuffing her own grief down the whole time.

It had been well over a year since he'd come back from Chicago. Over a *year* of her thinking he didn't care.

And he hadn't realized how deep her distress was.

Brand-new tears tracked over the light smattering of freckles on her cheeks. "I didn't know how to tell you the part about, you know. Wanting to be like everybody else. It's embarrassing, and I feel stupid. It's hard to be normal without a mom."

"None of that is stupid. I wish you'd told me." Gavin brushed a hand over her face and forced strength into his voice. "I know it's not ideal. I know I'm not . . . Mom." He swallowed hard over the understatement. "But you're right. If I'd listened better, I might have been able to help you with some of this."

Bree sniffled. "I shouldn't have said what I did about you taking me in." She dropped her head, her words threaded through with emotion. "I know you love me."

"I do love you, Bree. But it's *because* I love you that I do what I do." He worked up a small, self-deprecating smile. "I know it doesn't always feel like it, but I really do have your best interests at heart. It's my job to take care of you. And that includes keeping you safe and making decisions that you're not ready to make yet, even if you don't like what I decide."

Bree furrowed her brow. "Like whether or not I need a babysitter?"

Every cell in Gavin's body froze, and he whipped his head toward the spot where Sloane had stood—God, had that only been twenty minutes ago?

But it was empty.

He blinked back at Bree, who was clearly waiting for an answer. Discovering Sloane's whereabouts would have to wait.

"That's one thing, yes. It's not that I think you can't take care of yourself. It's just that a lot could happen while you're here alone, including you just being lonely. And I don't want that."

Her lips parted. "I thought you didn't trust me."

"You've got to admit, kiddo, some of the things you did before we left the city didn't argue well for you in the trust department."

"Oh." Bree dropped her chin to her chest, but the gesture became a nod. "I know the whole mess with those older girls was stupid, but I really didn't steal those CDs. I wouldn't have done that."

"I know," Gavin said, and meant it. "But I still have to do what I think is right to make sure you're cared for. And for now, that means having someone stay with you when I'm not here."

"I guess having a babysitter isn't a horrible idea." She slipped a glance around the kitchen. "And spending time with Sloane is okay. She doesn't make me feel like a kid, even though she still has rules." Bree's gaze flicked to the spot where Sloane had stood. "And she's pretty smart. I like her."

His gut clenched. "I like her, too." The truth was, they wouldn't even be standing here having this conversation if it weren't for Sloane's intervention. It hadn't taken much, but she'd somehow known exactly what to say to get them to talk to each other rather than yell.

So where on earth was she?

Bree tried on a tiny smile. "So it's okay if she comes over for breakfast tomorrow? That kind of sounded like fun."

Just an hour ago, nothing would have made Gavin happier than spending the morning in the kitchen with Bree, getting back to something that had once been so easy-going and right.

But now, the right thing was to back up his words with his actions.

"How about this? Why don't I call Mrs. Carter on my way back to work and talk to her about the ski trip. If you promise to be careful and check in when you're supposed to, I can ask Sloane to drop you off tonight and then I'll pick you up from the resort tomorrow when you're done. Then we can have breakfast together next week. Sound okay?"

Bree blinked. "Y-yeah. Are you sure?"

His heart lurched against his ribs with an ungainly thud, but he nodded. "You and I still have a lot of talking to do, and that will come in time. But you're right. You're old enough to do things like this. If Mrs. Carter is going to be there, I don't see a problem with you going skiing with your friends."

She threw her arms around him, and both the force of the movement and the emotion behind it knocked into him like a battering ram. "Oh my God! Thank you thank you thank you. I promise you won't be sorry! Can I go call Caitlin and Sadie and tell them? Please?"

Her burst of happiness was infectious, and Gavin chuckled by default. "Go. I've got to get back to the restaurant, but I'll work out the particulars with Mrs. Carter and call you in a little while."

"Okay." Bree rushed to the entryway, excitement visible on every one of her features, but she paused when she got to the door. "Thank you. I really mean it."

"You're welcome. And hey"—Gavin paused for a second, the words sticking to his throat with emotion—"no matter what happens from here on in, just promise you'll talk to me."

She nodded. "Okay. I promise."

Gavin stood in the middle of the kitchen for a moment after she was gone, simply inhaling the quiet. So many thoughts flung themselves at his brain, and even more at the spaces in his chest and his gut, that trying to process them would take hours he didn't have.

Getting this parenting thing down was going to take his entire life. Even then, the odds were good that he wouldn't get it completely right.

Then again, did anybody?

"You did a really great thing, you know."

Sloane's voice startled him halfway to the ceiling, and he whipped back to reality with a graceless jerk.

"Sorry," she said, not moving from the kitchen doorframe. "I was in the living room. I know I should've given you complete privacy, but . . . I wanted to make sure you two were okay. So I overheard a little of what you said."

Even if she hadn't copped to being within earshot, her red-rimmed eyes and quiet tone would've been a dead giveaway. He nodded, but it did nothing to bring order to his thoughts.

"Oh. Yeah, we're, ah . . . okay." The word didn't touch the tip of the iceberg of what he felt, but he was too overwhelmed to go into further detail. Hell, he was too overwhelmed to spell his own name right now. Despite the fact that he and Bree had made more progress today than they had since their mom got sick, he still had no clue how to parent her. After all, Sloane had done more in five minutes than he'd managed to do in the last year, and she had no experience with kids whatsoever.

Words snapped around in his brain, trying so hard to form phrases, thoughts, *something* to let her know how he felt, but it was all so overpowering that he couldn't get out from beneath the guilt of not having seen it all sooner.

So he covered it up instead.

Gavin blanked his expression, save for a small, perfunctory smile that was as forced as it was uncomfortable. "If you could drop Bree off at Jeannie's in a little bit, I'd be really grateful. Then we'll just see you on Tuesday morning, I guess."

"Gavin, wait." Sloane looked right through him with those beautiful summer-sky eyes, under his skin, past the wall he'd desperately thrown up, and God damn it, she saw everything.

"You're not really okay, are you?"

Something larger than his desire to cover up all of his emotion pushed words to the forefront, and he took a step toward her to say *no* and bury himself in her arms, knowing he'd feel right there. But his cell phone rang, jolting him from his reverie.

And his feelings went right back where they belonged.

"I appreciate all your help today, Sloane. I've got to get back to the restaurant. Just give me a call if you need anything, okay?"

And then he was gone.

Chapter Nineteen

Sloane flipped the collar of her cherry-red pea coat over her ears to ward off the biting wind and hit *send* before she lost either her nerve or the feeling in her toes.

Gavin picked up on the third ring. "Hello?"

"Hi!" she chirruped, perky enough to make herself cringe. She bit her tongue into submission and clutched her fuzzy merino scarf tighter around her neck to trap her dwindling body heat before it made a jailbreak. Next time she chose a place to live, it was going to have an average temperature in the mid-eighties, minimum.

"Sloane? Is everything okay?"

God, his seriousness knew no bounds. She pulled in a breath, but cut it short when it froze to her throat and refused to migrate down to her lungs. "Sure. Why do you ask?"

"Um, because it's ten-thirty on a Sunday night and you sound like you're in a tin can. What's going on?"

Well, crap. Best to just come out with it then. Otherwise she was going to end up with a serious case of frostbite to go along with her idiotic impulses.

"Well, you said I should call you if I needed anything, and as it turns out, I need something." She swallowed a mouthful of subarctic air, wondering how on earth her palms could still sweat in weather like this.

Gavin stammered. "You . . . what? What do you need?"

No going back now. Sloane straightened in her spot on the weatherworn porch boards.

"I need you to open your front door."

After a telltale click, the door swung open, bringing them face-to-face. "What are you doing here?" he murmured with a look of pure surprise. A flicker of something she couldn't identify glinted in his melted-chocolate eyes, and suddenly, the cold felt like it was on some faraway planet rather than invading her personal space right down to her bones.

"I thought you might be hungry, so I brought you something to eat." She lifted two thick paper bags bearing La Dolce Vita's name and logo, and his cinnamon-colored brows moved in the direction of his hairline.

"We don't do takeout at the restaurant."

"Yeah, well, I have friends in high places," she said, allowing a saucy grin to emerge on her lips. "And they told me you haven't eaten anything since lunch. But unless you want piccata Popsicles, I'd invite me in."

"Oh! Sorry. You must be freezing. Come in." Gavin took both bags from her frozen fingers and ushered her into the cottage. "These friends of yours didn't happen to mention that chicken piccata is one of my favorite dishes, did they?"

She followed him into the kitchen, rubbing her hands together in an act of utter futility as he lifted the bags to the counter. She slanted him a look and debated her answer.

Screw it. Subtlety had never been one of her strong suits.

"No, but they did mention that you left early, and after

what happened before, I was a little, um . . . worried about you."

Gavin's hands stopped with a Styrofoam container halfway out of the bag, but it was a momentary glitch. He popped the lid off the container to check the contents. "I appreciate it. But I'm fine."

Sloane's bullshit meter erupted like Vesuvius on a bad day, but instinct told her not to push him. Not yet, anyway. "So what kind of wine goes best with chicken piccata?" she asked, moving toward the cupboard to take out a couple of plates.

It got a grin out of him, albeit a small one. "French Chablis. You want some?"

"Well, that depends. Is it two hundred dollars a bottle?" No way was she getting suckered into that again. At least, not without knowing it up front.

"No." Gavin passed her a container full of salad greens and the bowl he'd just pulled from the counter, and his grin kicked up a notch. "Not even close, although it's still good."

"Whew. Drinking wine that expensive makes me sweat."

"Wine is supposed to lower your stress levels, not jack them higher."

She snickered and gave the emerald green leaves a toss as she put them in the bowl. "Only if you drink enough of it to forget your problems."

"I wouldn't waste good wine just to get drunk. That's what liquor is for." He crossed the kitchen and popped the pantry door open, barely looking at the bottles before sliding one from a rack in the wine cellar.

"Come on, you're the quintessential wine guy. Surely you've overindulged on occasion."

He shook his head. "Nope. Not on wine."

Sloane laughed for just a beat before she realized he wasn't kidding. "Oh, no way. You're serious." She deposited the salad on the pristine white tablecloth with a residual smile.

"So you keep reminding me." Gavin brought the bottle of wine to the breakfast bar and placed it on top of the counter. "I'm not saying I've never been drunk. That's asinine. But drinking wine just to *get* drunk seems wasteful to me. It blurs everything good about it."

He cast a glance at her and continued. "And anyway, is being serious really that bad?"

"On you, it's perfect. On me, not so much. Then again, I've never really been a go-with-the-crowd kind of girl."

Gavin chuckled as he moved through the kitchen for a corkscrew and a pair of delicate pear-shaped glasses without stems. "Yeah, you do have a penchant for stirring up trouble. But it suits you, and plus, you seem happy just like you are."

"I am." The words sounded strange without the usual defensive coating she had to slather onto them, and she busied herself by leaning against the opposite side of the counter and watching while he uncorked the bottle with seamless movements. "So I'm not quite sure I buy into the theory that wine is good for you."

"What makes you doubt it?" Rather than coming off as a challenge, his question was edged with genuine curiosity, and he eased the cork from the bottle with a muted pop.

"It just sounds hokey. I mean, isn't the whole drinking-is-healthy thing just an excuse to go to happy hour instead of the gym?"

He laughed, and the pure richness of it stoked a fire under her skin. "Not entirely. The theory is based on the idea that there are some health benefits to drinking wine in moderation. Some kinds of wine contain antioxidants that can help knock down cholesterol levels. Other kinds work to lower your blood pressure, making you feel less stressed."

"Ah. And what does this kind of wine do?" she asked, pointing to the glasses of golden liquid Gavin held in either hand.

"This particular label tastes good and promotes relaxing conversation. It's your turn to toast." He placed the glass in her hand, and although their fingers didn't touch as he pulled away, the heat of him was suggestive enough that Sloane felt it regardless.

And she wanted it. Badly.

"Oh," she murmured, wishing it had been something more eloquent. She flushed. "Don't we have to let this breathe or something?"

He shook his head, leaning across the breakfast bar so she had no choice but to look right into his liquid-brown eyes. "That's usually with reds and drier wines. This Chablis is more full-bodied and crisp, so its flavor profile won't benefit from breathing."

"Translation, please?" Sloane wouldn't know a flavor profile if it socked her in the mouth.

"It's going to taste the same in an hour as it does right now."

She lifted her glass, noting the pretty shimmer of the wine inside it as it met more light from overhead. "In that case, here's to testing theories."

"To testing theories." Gavin raised his glass and inhaled once, chasing his breath with a sip of the wine. Sloane followed suit, and the sweet scent of the wine mixed perfectly with the crisp flavors in her mouth, one turning over the other only to layer back again, until they melded together into a wonderfully mellow glide down her throat.

"Oh, wow. It tastes like . . . summer." Sloane slipped

her eyes closed, where inviting images of warm sunshine and dipping her toes into the cool, dark green water of Big Gap Lake rose to meet her. She took another slow sip, and suddenly she was in the lake up to her knees.

Gavin countered quietly. "This vintage gets a lot of its sweetness from the notes of apple and pear. That fruitiness is what makes it so crisp."

Her eyes popped open in a rush of recognition, and she slapped the counter in front of her with glee. "Yes! The apple flavor makes it kind of spicy, too."

"Now you're catching on," he said, a smile evening out over his face. "What does it make you think of?"

"Sticking my feet in Big Gap Lake." She grinned. "How about you?"

He tipped his glass, taking a long sip before asking, "Me?"

But letting him off the hook was the last thing on her mind. "Yes, you. I'm not the only one who's supposed to be relaxing here, remember? Come on, tell me what you see."

"Okay, okay." Gavin closed his eyes, and his eyelashes cast slight shadows over his cheeks. For a heartbeat, Sloane wondered if this was how he looked when he slept.

And then her heartbeats grew decidedly faster.

"I see an apple grove." He drew in a breath and nodded. "Yeah. There's this apple orchard, way out past the suburbs in Philly. Trees as far as you can see, full to bursting with Jonagolds, Braeburns, you name it. The air smells brand-new, like no one's even breathed it before, and you can taste the sun on the apples when you bite into them."

Sloane's senses prickled with awareness as Gavin opened his eyes and continued. "One time, when Bree was eight, she begged for the apples from the top of the tree. She swore they must taste better, and we couldn't convince her that all the apples were the same. So I climbed fifteen feet up to the top of this apple tree, and the whole time I remember thinking I must be crazy for risking my neck over a handful of apples."

"Was she right?" Sloane breathed, unable to tear her gaze from him.

Gavin's expression softened around his upturned mouth, becoming a warm chuckle. "Hell if she wasn't. They were the best damned apples I've ever had."

"She's lucky to have you."

Her words stopped the laughter brewing in his throat, prompting a tight shrug. "Sometimes I'm not so sure."

"Are you kidding?" She pulled back with surprise and stared. "I mean, I know it's not all rainbows and unicorns and stuff, but anyone can see how much you care about her."

He released a slow breath. "I do care about her."

Silence unspooled between them as Gavin looked away, raising his glass with a faster-than-necessary jerk, and even though she didn't want to, Sloane took the hint.

"I guess we should warm the food up before we eat, huh?" She put her glass on the counter and made her way back to the heart of the kitchen, reaching for the plates she'd taken out of the cupboard.

Gavin turned to fall into place next to her. "Sure. How about you plate, and I'll man the microwave?"

"Look at you, breaking out the fancy techniques. You're a culinary tour de force over there." She handed him a plate loaded with chicken, capers, and artichokes, and even lukewarm from the restaurant, it smelled divine.

He took the plate, stepping close enough to fill her senses with the masculine scent of his skin and the dark, seductive smile that was like her own personal brand of Kryptonite. "I'm trying to impress you. Is it working?"

"Not even a little bit, Microwave Man. I'm not that easy." But the traitorous tingle of heat percolating at the seam of her jeans negated every last syllable.

Well. Didn't that just add a whole new dimension to the *pants on fire* part of things?

"Guess I'll just have to try harder," he said, bringing the microwave to life with a handful of touches. Oh, God, if she didn't come up with a distraction, stat, he was going to find out exactly how easy she was, right here in the kitchen.

Cut it out! She'd come over here in an honest-to-God act of concern, not to get laid. So she blurted out the first thing she could think of that didn't make her want to whip off her shirt just to feel him on her skin.

"So, um, how'd you get to be such a wine expert, anyway?"

His shoulders eased up by a fraction and he took the second plate from her. "Not the flashiest answer going, but it started in culinary school."

A tiny smile poked at the corners of her lips, and she enjoyed another sip of Chablis before answering. "Come on. Of all the things you could've become an expert on, you chose wine?"

"Hey, don't knock it," he said, handing her the first plate with a wry smile. "Why, what would you pick?"

"Something different every day. And I'm not knocking it. I just meant there are a bazillion things you could've chosen. Why wine?"

"Oh. Well, I think it kind of picked me, to be honest. We studied a lot of different regional cuisines, and I always came back to the ones that centered around wine pairings—mostly Italian and French, but of course there are others. I was fascinated by how the wine enhanced the meal and made it an experience. It didn't take long for me to discover that wine could actually *be* the experience."

"I never really thought of wine as its own complex thing," Sloane admitted, turning the idea over in her mind as she walked the steaming plate to the table.

"Most people don't. We're conditioned to do things as quickly as possible, eating and drinking included. It's just a means to an end. But wine is one of those things you've got to take your time with, otherwise you miss the point. It's the journey, remember?"

Her face flushed at the reminder of his words from the night of Carly's wedding, but looking away from Gavin's piercing stare right now wasn't even on her menu of options. "I remember."

"Isn't writing the same way? I mean, you don't race through it just to get to the end, do you? You must enjoy the process part a little bit, too. Look at how hard you work on putting it together." He pulled his plate from the microwave, crossing the kitchen to place it on the table across from hers, and Sloane's gut twanged at the reminder of the book she shouldn't be writing.

She was tempted to button her lip and brush the whole thing off. After all, the wine was flowing, and they were supposed to be relaxing. Talking about the fact that her writing process vaguely resembled a fricking corkscrew right now was only going to jack her stress-o-meter sky-high. She'd tried all afternoon to start an outline for her Greece book, just as she had for the last couple of weeks. For four hours straight, she'd trolled travel Web sites in the hopes that one of the images would serve as the spark she'd so desperately been searching for. Her pencil was sharp, her Post-its were at the ready, just begging to be scribbled upon.

But the only thing Sloane could think about was the outline for the other story, and before she could even blink twice, she'd cranked out another chapter and a half.

"I do enjoy the process," she started slowly, liberating her wineglass and moving to sit across the table from Gavin's inquisitive stare. "But it's not always that easy. Book ideas move fast, and they don't always obey the laws of logic or reason. Sometimes, the end result arrives first, and it's right there in my brain. If I don't rush for it, it might disappear, or change, or *something,* and then I'll miss it entirely."

"So you just keep your eye on the prize and never stop moving." He cut his chicken with surgical precision, each stroke swift and efficient, and Sloane wondered how something so mundane could be so unexpectedly sexy.

"I can't stop moving," she said, emphasizing her point with a shake of her head. "There's too much to soak in. If I go slow, I'm bound to miss something important."

Gavin took a few bites, his brow pulled low in thought before he said, "Did you ever stop to think that if you go too fast, you might miss what's right in front of you?"

Sloane took a bite of her own, and not even the rich, earthy flavors of the food could distract her from the irony of it all. "If that's the case, then I can't win either way."

"Not necessarily." He settled his gaze on her, and her muscles gave an involuntary tug around her bones as his words darkened with suggestion. "It's possible that you could have the best of both worlds."

"How's that?" Sloane managed, but her heartbeat had already kicked into full hammer mode. A small part of her warned that she still didn't need the distraction of getting involved with someone, even casually, right now.

But the part of her that wanted him to kiss her until she could no longer stand canceled that other part right out.

"You just have to strike a really good balance." Gavin pushed back from his spot across the table from her, and there was no mistaking his destination. She stood so fast that she forgot to put down her fork, and he took it from her fingers with a lazy smile.

"If you slow down just enough, I bet you'll find what you're looking for."

Reason flooded her senses now, reminding her that she

could blame sleeping with him once on a flight of fancy, a mutual heat-of-the-moment thing. But sleeping with him twice—hell, *feeling* the way she felt right now—well, that bypassed impulsive and went right for the heart of stupid. Five weeks from now, she'd be living out of a suitcase, writing an exotic novel and saving her hard-earned career.

But right in this moment, she wanted his hands on her.

Sloane arched toward him in one swift motion, searching and finding all at the same time. Gavin's breath left him on a heated exhale while he slanted his mouth over hers, diving in for just a brief taste before cupping her face.

"We need to work on your idea of balance," he murmured, smiling against her lips. She fought back the whimper being generated by her chest—and a couple of parts due south.

"But I don't want to miss what's right in front of me." She angled her body closer, dying to drink in the electric feel of his touch, but he drew back just before she made contact.

"Then slow down and find it."

Gavin tilted her face so their lips met again in a gentle rush of skin and heat. But rather than coaxing her mouth open to delve farther, he kissed her with soft intention, letting the place where their mouths came together rise to a slow simmer. When she parted her lips in encouragement, he didn't give in. Instead, he slipped a palm around her neck, stroking her sensitive skin with just enough pressure to make her bite back a groan.

He swept his tongue over her bottom lip, drawing it gently between his teeth before letting go to start over again, and holding back went from unlikely to impossible. Urgency flared, deep in Sloane's belly, and it guided her arms around the leanly muscled landscape of Gavin's shoulders. His body tensed under her hands, but he refused to be swayed. Instead, he kissed her with just enough sweet persuasion to move the breath from his body to hers, teasing her lips and tongue with a dark suggestion that made every cell in her body spark to life.

Sloane arched up even higher, tightening her hands into fists over his navy blue T-shirt. Gavin pulled back just enough to look at her, gifting her with a mischievous smile.

"If you keep that up, going slow isn't going to be much of an option," he said, not advancing, but not pulling back either. Oh, God, the hard plane of his chest was as close to her body as it could be without touching, and the innuendo of that delicious contact forced her to close the space.

"You say that like it's a bad thing." Her murmur fell into the spot where his collar met his neck, and she turned to trail eager kisses along his angular jaw. She skimmed her lips back toward his, searching for more, and the friction of his freshly emerging stubble beneath her hypersensitive mouth tightened her nipples to hard points.

"It's not a bad thing." He caught her face between his palms, his eyes glittering a dark, sensual brown. "But I don't want to rush. Not this time. Not tonight."

Gavin placed the barest hint of a kiss on her mouth like a promise. "I want to show you what's right in front of you, Sloane. But you're going to have to let me. What do you say?"

Chapter Twenty

"Yes. God, yes."

Sloane whispered the affirmation against Gavin's mouth, and even though he hadn't thought it possible to want her more than when she'd shown up unexpectedly on his porch, flushed with cold and yet so blazingly hot at the same time, his body proved him wrong. The idea of finally being able to have her slowly, to learn and relearn what she sounded like when he touched the gentle hollow above her collarbone, skimmed his fingers around the divot of her navel, grazed his teeth over the perfect slope of her breasts—all of it made him hard without so much as a touch from her. The look on Sloane's face as she'd talked about plowing through life at warp speed had only made him want to slow her down all the more.

Starting right here in the kitchen.

With his chest still molded to hers, Gavin swung her around. He guided her backward through the kitchen until they reached the first available flat surface, which turned out to be the refrigerator. *Good enough,* he thought, angling Sloane against the smooth expanse of stainless steel, gently trapping her body there with his own.

"Oh!" Her Cupid's-bow mouth parted over a shocked

gasp as he pressed her more tightly to the cool surface, and he dropped his lips to hover right over her ear.

"Don't worry. I'll keep you warm." He couldn't resist tracing the outline of her bare earlobe with his tongue, sampling the way she tasted there, and she moaned over his shoulder.

"It's not that it's cold," she said, turning her head so their gazes were level. Her eyes went dark with desire, the color of cut sapphires, and she dropped her hand to the tight fragment of space between their bodies to cup his erection with nimble fingers. "It's humming."

His eagerness to take his time and pleasure her superseded the screaming want surging through him, and he reached down to capture her wrist. With a careful yet firm gesture, he crossed it over her other one and pinned them over her head with a wicked grin.

"Let's see if we can make you hum, too."

With slow ministrations, he worked the buttons on her plain white shirt, popping them open one-handed while letting his mouth follow their path. He dipped past the indentation at the base of her throat, committing her throaty sighs to memory as he brushed his tongue over the delicate vein in her neck where her pulse fluttered like a live wire.

The small swell of her breasts, honey-colored and perfect, found the curve of his mouth as Sloane pressed against him with a groan that came from deep in her chest. Gavin nearly matched it when he freed enough buttons to expose her bright red lace and satin bra. He should've known he'd find something completely unexpected beneath that demure top, but the sexy shock of discovery filled him anyway.

"God, you're beautiful." He kissed the top curve of one breast, just enough to tease himself with the spicy taste of her skin, and she bowed against him in a wordless reply.

With the last of the buttons on her shirt liberated, Gavin was able to focus his free hand on the space between her breasts, where they rounded together like soft summer peaches.

There wasn't enough time in the world for this.

"You're driving me crazy," she breathed on a ragged voice. "I mean it. I'm going to lose my mind like this. Please let me touch you."

He paused, trailing a fingertip along the low-cut crimson lace that barely covered the modest rise of her cleavage, and grinned into her hot skin. "Nope. You'd better get used to it, because I'm going to do this to you in every room in the house before the night is over."

Sloane arced up into him at the same moment he closed his lips over one taut nipple, swirling the fabric out of the way with his tongue, and she cried out at the intimate contact. Fueled by nothing more than the desire to taste her indefinitely, Gavin dropped her wrists, sliding his palms behind her shoulder blades to undo the closure on her bra.

Her nipples were tight peaks, exquisite beneath his hands and mouth as he alternated between them, learning every subtlety with care. He touched and nibbled and stroked, ghosting over the outer rim of her areola with the pad of one thumb, tightening with need of his own when she shuddered at the barely there touch. But it wasn't until he cupped her with both hands and slid his tongue to the fragile, dewy skin in the tight space between her breasts that he almost lost his composure entirely.

Because Sloane was losing hers. Oh, fuck. She was going to kill him like this.

So he did it again. And again.

"Oh my God. You're . . . you can't . . . oh *God*." Her jumbled words spilled over the top of his head, and she reached between them, not to touch him this time, but to touch herself. She cradled her breasts in her palms, angling up to encourage unfettered access to her body, and with one final pass of his tongue over her gloriously hard nipple, she came undone on a keening sigh.

Gavin lightened his touch by lazy degrees, bearing the weight of Sloane's body as she went from arched tightly against him to languidly wrapping her arms around his shoulders. Without thinking twice, he hooked one arm under her shoulders and used the other behind her knees to lever her off her feet.

"What are you doing?" The combination of velvety satisfaction in her voice and the way her sinuous hip slid against his aching cock nearly made him veer off course, but he managed to make it through the living room and toward the darkened hallway that led to his room.

"Relocating. I want to watch you come like that until the sun rises." His purposeful stride hitched as Sloane tensed beneath his hands, and he slowed to a stop in the shadowed archway of the foyer. "What's the matter?"

"Nothing." She buried her face in his neck on the pretense of kissing him there, but her muscles were too stiff, making the movement almost wooden.

Dread pinched at him, and he settled her on her feet. As badly as he wanted her, he couldn't live with himself if Sloane regretted any of this tomorrow. "If you don't want to do this, it's okay. We don't—"

"No! It's not that at all." She hugged her arms around her body, crisscrossing her open shirttails over her chest to cover up. "I just, um. I'm fairly certain that was . . . it for me. Not that we can't still . . ." She trailed off, squeezing her eyes shut on an exhale. "I just don't want to disappoint you."

Snippets of past revelations slowly filtered through Gavin's brain, falling into place one by one until the whole picture hit him like a sucker punch.

She really *hadn't* ever had an orgasm with anyone else

before. And if she'd never had one, she sure as hell must think that having *more* than one was nothing other than pure fiction.

He was going to change that if it was the last thing he ever did.

"Sloane, listen to me." Gavin touched the side of her face as though he could soak up her vulnerability through his skin. "You are a lot of things, but believe me when I tell you, disappointing isn't one of them."

"But I—"

"You're beautiful." He stepped in to kiss the space behind her ear. "You have this great laugh." Another kiss, this one on the soft line where her neck met her shoulder. Christ, he'd never wanted to make love to anyone so much in his life. He twined his fingers around hers and lifted both to his chest. "It gets me right here. And you never, ever do what I think you're going to." He cupped her face between his hands, kissing her gently so the words became reverent, but she pulled back anyway.

"I'm sorry."

Gavin laughed, just a soft expression to mark the irony of it all. "How can you apologize for the best thing about you?" He kissed her again, this time with the firm intention of punctuating his words. "It's not your fault nobody ever took the time to really find you in there. That nobody showed you what a goddamn treasure you are." The words tumbled out, intense and fierce, but he meant them. And what was more, Sloane had clearly never heard them.

She was a canvas, covered with all these bold strokes and brilliant colors, and she had no fucking clue how stunning she was.

Their kiss became as pure as his words, and once again, Gavin found himself completely caught up in her. The lush bow of her mouth, the way her tall, lean frame fit against his like two pieces of a puzzle, the vibration of her sigh when he finally gave in and kissed her hard. He'd known he wanted her the minute he heard her voice on the phone tonight, like a beacon of goodness in the middle of his still-roiling emotions.

He just hadn't known he wanted her to stay.

Sloane kissed him then with so much tenderness wrapped in her trademark heat that he couldn't wait any longer. He guided her down the hall and through his bedroom door, not stopping until they'd reached his bed. He undressed her slowly, reveling in the way that she had a different response for every touch, every taste. And each one of her answers made him desperate to pleasure her, not just for the satisfaction of it, but to show her firsthand what he saw when he looked at her.

Gavin moved over her with excruciating care, laving attention on every inch of her body, listening to each nuance with his hands and mouth. Only when he was certain he would lose it if he didn't feel the silky heat between her thighs did he let his hands travel the length of her legs, parting them gently to test her depths.

"Don't *stop*," Sloane cried, her hips canting off the bed to surround him with that gorgeous tightness. It took every ounce of control he could muster to do as she asked, sliding his thumb to the top of her core in search of the spot he knew would take her home.

"You are incredible like this. I'm not stopping." Another swirl of his thumb, and she wrapped her fingers around the biceps of his free arm, digging her nails in with a bite that made him so hard, he groaned right along with her. Her body was strung with so much tension that Gavin could feel it both on her skin and inside her body, and when he lowered his mouth to hers, the tautness shattered in waves. The look of vulnerability, washed over with the pure bliss of discovery, made him realize how badly he wanted to watch her do it again and again. Not just tonight, but unceasingly.

For now, though, he'd start with tonight.

Gavin let his fingers slip from her body, giving her time to come down even though his cock begged to be inside her. Sloane's eyes fluttered open as if she were waking from a long sleep and didn't quite know where she was. She stared at him, her crystal blue eyes flashing in the moonlight overflowing past the blinds.

"I want you. I want you right now."

Her words were a soft proclamation, more of a pared down admission than a sexy demand. She pushed herself up to sitting, gently lifting the hem of his T-shirt over his head with quiet fingers.

"I want to make you feel like that. I want to make you feel . . . perfect." Sloane's hands moved over him like smoldering coals, just yearning for something to touch to make them burst into flame, and when she stroked his cock over his jeans, he let out an involuntary shudder. "Please, Gavin. Let me have you."

He couldn't say no even if he wanted to. And the only thing he wanted was Sloane.

Between the two of them, the rest of his clothes never had a chance. Gavin paused only long enough to take a condom from the drawer on his bedside table, kissing her just briefly before settling against the delicious cradle of her hips. She angled her body to his in a seamless fit, and they came together in a rush of heat that made his bones consider turning to dust. Sloane answered every one of his movements with a dare to go further, to let go and have her completely, and he complied without thinking.

The more she cried out, the sweeter it became, until he swore he would drown in the thrill of making love to her. He rode the razor's edge of his orgasm for a long, delectable second before it took him over, guiding him to stillness inside her body as the intensity of it stripped him bare and filled him up all at once.

Sloane reached up, threading her arms around his sweat-slicked shoulders, and pulled him down so his forehead rested on hers, kissing him with soft flutters of her lips.

"Thank you." She sealed the whisper with another bare touch of her mouth to his, and he settled onto his side to look at her, surprised.

"What?"

She kissed the shock from his face. "For finding me."

In thirty-two years, Gavin had never felt anything that even touched this, in bed or out. And even though it scared the shit out of him, as they lay together, still kissing quietly on the bedsheets, he knew he wouldn't stop wanting it anytime soon.

Chapter Twenty-One

Gavin had been a man of his word when he'd said he was going to make love to her in every room of the house, a fact that Sloane didn't find herself bemoaning in the least. After all, honest men weren't exactly a dime a dozen.

And neither were men who made her feel that good, that many times. As a matter of fact, Gavin bypassed being a rarity in that department and went straight for being the one and only. He was as incredible out of bed as he'd been in it, as if he could bypass the layers of her tough exterior and see right through to who she really was. Not only had he unearthed her, but he'd polished what he found to a flawless shine.

Sloane knew she should run, but it felt too damned good not to.

"I'm pretty sure these are yours." Gavin arched a brow at her from the side of the couch, where he lay breathlessly sprawled, holding her red satin panties in his hand. Late-morning sunlight streamed in through the foyer windows, illuminating the living room with a soft glow that made what they'd just done on the couch all the more naughty.

"Mmm. I'm starting to think there's not much point in

putting them back on," she speculated on a blissfully sated sigh. Gavin had been all too happy to prove over and again that he was a quick study when it came to learning every curve of her by heart, and she'd never felt so brand-new in her life.

He placed a soft kiss on her mouth, holding the garment in question just out of reach. "Are you sure? Because I was kind of looking for an excuse to remove them with my teeth later. But if you want to go without . . ."

"Fork 'em over." Sloane popped up from the cushions, her movements suddenly quick and agile. Proper motivation was *everything*.

Gavin chuckled, and the sound beat a nonstop path to her chest. "I thought you said you weren't easy."

"I'm also not stupid." She slid into her unmentionables while he pulled a pair of sweatpants over his boxers. He looked just as comfortable and composed after a night full of passionate sex as he did walking out the door to go to work, but it only ratcheted her desire to ruffle him even higher.

"You want some coffee?" He inclined his head toward the kitchen, and she jumped on the chance for both the pick-me-up and the distraction.

"Oh, God, yes." Sloane let a good-natured laugh fall from her lips as she buttoned her shirt, letting it fall over the tops of her bare legs as she padded behind him to the kitchen. She watched carefully as Gavin put some water on to boil. God, it was so like him to be meticulous about something as simple as morning caffeination.

She grinned, gesturing to the French press on the counter. "So what's with the fancy coffee thing? You can't brew java like the rest of us?"

"It tastes better this way," he said. Even though he measured the coffee beans by sight as he poured them into the grinder in front of him, Sloane was willing to bet there was a very precise method going on in his head. She waited out the metallic buzz of the bean grinder before answering.

"I'm all for a great cup of coffee, but this is pretty time-consuming. You really think it's worth it?" she asked, propping her elbows over the cold, sleek granite of the breakfast bar.

A lopsided smile tugged at the corners of his mouth. "And here I thought I might've changed your mind a little on the whole slowing down thing."

Her cheeks heated, along with a few of her other, more delicate parts. "Sorry." She shifted her weight against the stool and willed her bits into submission. At least he wasn't wrong about the quality of the coffee. She'd noticed the difference between the ho-hum, standard brew she brought with her in the mornings and the rich, lovely blend of flavors he coaxed into perfection every time she refilled her travel mug with the coffee he made each morning.

"I guess you're right about the coffee tasting better," Sloane conceded, although giving in entirely wasn't on her agenda. "But don't you ever get impatient with the process? I mean, it's not always bad to go the instant gratification route."

"Maybe not for some people. But I'm a think-it-through kind of guy. I like to take my time."

Did he ever. Good Lord, the man's restraint bordered on legendary. Sloane cleared her throat. "So you don't ever just do something without thinking?"

"No." He filled the French press with coffee grounds and jiggled the handle on the saucepan, moving through the kitchen like water.

"Never?" The concept was totally foreign to her, and the idea of being so calculated piqued the hell out of her curiosity. "Like never ever, in the history of ever?"

"Still no." His laughter filtered softly between them, and he poured the perfect amount of steaming water over the grounds without measuring.

Sloane's curiosity amped even higher. There had to be *some*thing that would set him off. She frowned and hooked her toes over the bottom rung on the bar stool where she sat. "So if I said I'd take you to Fiji, all-expenses-paid, but we had to leave right this second, you wouldn't go?"

"Sloane, I'm not even wearing real pants right now. Come on."

"Are you kidding? I'm not wearing *any* pants and I'd go," she said, only half-jokingly. After all, she'd never been to Fiji, and swimming naked in the South Pacific was number sixteen on her bucket list.

"You would seriously walk out of this cottage right now, without clothes on, just to go to Fiji on a whim?" The sinewy muscles in Gavin's forearms flexed slightly as he manipulated the French press to create a pot of perfectly brewed coffee, and the aroma steeped through Sloane's senses with a relaxing, earthy scent.

"Sure. Why not?"

"Uh, because it's crazy?"

She bit her lip, thinking. "Okay, so you might have a point about the no-pants part. It is kind of winter here, and let's face it. I'd need pants eventually. But otherwise, who knows when—or if—I'd get another chance to go to Fiji?"

"You sure do go against the grain, don't you?" He turned to grab a pair of plain white coffee cups from the cupboard, and Sloane laughed.

"Yeah, that's me. Irresponsible and loving it."

But rather than agree just like everyone else on the planet, Gavin thunked the mugs to the counter, pinning her with a look that was impossible to decipher. "You're not irresponsible."

His quiet tone threw her off-kilter in the face of all the

joking they'd just been doing, and she blinked for a second, mired in shock. "Oh, it's okay. I mean, I'm used to it."

"Let me ask you something. Do you think I'm stupid?"

The question was so unexpected that she coughed out an involuntary laugh, even though his face suggested he was as serious as a heart attack. Not that *that* was anything new.

"Of course not," she said, eyeing him carefully. "Why would I think that?"

"Because only an idiot would hire an irresponsible babysitter." He poured two cups of coffee with efficient movements, sliding one in her direction as if they were discussing something as irrefutable as the color of the sky.

But Sloane shrugged. It wasn't like this was shocking territory, after all. "It's not exactly a secret that I'm pretty flighty. I'm just used to being labeled the black sheep, I guess."

"That's different than being irresponsible." Gavin paused before turning to cull a couple of spoons from the drawer in front of him. "Just because you don't do things like everyone else doesn't mean there's anything wrong with you."

"Remind me never to take you to a Russo family reunion," she said, leaning forward to reach for the sugar. "That's not exactly popular opinion among my family."

"So you've mentioned. Care to elaborate? I'm not sure I quite understand the Russo logic here."

Something about the easy way Gavin moved around the kitchen, sauntering to the refrigerator for the milk and treating the topic like it was no great shakes, put her at ease rather than on guard. The answer tumbled from her lips.

"From the time I was little, I always did everything a little off-center. Not like anybody else. Which might've been okay if I didn't have a mother, two sisters, and a family tree loaded with cousins who all did things the 'normal' way." She paused just long enough to hook air quotes around the word. "So marching to your own drummer isn't exactly an endearing trait where I come from. At least, not to anyone but my father."

"You two were close, then?" The steady calm in Gavin's words was catching, and it loosened more thoughts like a torrent.

"Yes. I mean, don't get me wrong, I love my *mama* and my sisters." Sloane's face flamed with guilt, just like it always did at the implication that she and her father were closer than the rest of her family. "But my *papa* was different. He didn't push me to do things like anyone else unless I wanted to. Even when it turned out that I never wanted to."

"I don't have trouble seeing that," Gavin said over a wry smile. "But isn't it just a question of individuality?"

"Not when you buck tradition as hard and as often as I do." A nagging voice deep in the folds of her brain whispered at her to shut up, that if she pinpointed all the ways she was different from everybody else, it would hammer home the fact that he should find someone better to take care of Bree. Not to mention someone better to spend the morning making love with.

But all it took was one look into those melty brown eyes, and Sloane's resolve was toast.

"It's not just the little stuff. My career, my lifestyle, my personality, all of it is wildly different from everyone else's in my family. It's not that I don't want to be like my sisters. They're both smart and successful and happy. But what everyone in my family sees as the natural order of things, the way things *should* be, just feels stifling to me."

"You're smart and successful and happy too. I still don't see how you're so different. Not in that regard, anyway." Gavin palmed his coffee cup to take a sip, the action so normal and soothing that she didn't think twice about spilling her innermost vulnerabilities like water all over the floor.

"It took me ages to choose a career, and believe me when I tell you, I tried some doozies while I was figuring it out. The fact that I settled on something my mother finds socially unacceptable doesn't exactly add to my blend-in factor. Never mind that it's the only thing that I've ever really had a passion for." Well, until lately, anyway. The idea of leaving for Greece twanged a path of unease up her spine, but she thrust it aside. She'd figure out a way to deal with the book she couldn't write later.

Right now she had bigger fish to fry. Namely airing her emotional laundry in front of a man who had already coaxed something physically astounding out of her and discovering it felt better than it should.

It felt safe.

Gavin reached out to touch the hand she'd wrapped around her otherwise untouched coffee mug, skimming her knuckles with his thumb. "Your mother doesn't approve of you being a writer?"

She lifted an eyebrow. "Neither did you when I first told you, remember?"

His hand froze on hers. "I was wrong."

God, he was too good to be real. Sloane gave a sardonic smile. "Don't be sorry for your gut reaction. Reality is, some people don't take what I do seriously."

"They've never seen your Post-it collection. You work really hard, Sloane. You deserve credit for that."

An ache migrated up from deep in her belly, lodging itself beneath her sternum. "Thanks. But the truth is, I could probably be president of the United States and my *mama* would still think it's a phase. She's insistent that all I need is to get married and raise a handful of babies in the suburbs like my sisters, and that'll cure me of my crazy lifestyle like it's a disease. Marrying my father is what made her happiest in life. From the day I turned eighteen, the pressure's been on for me to follow in the family footsteps."

A look of shock splashed over Gavin's face. "That's kind of young, huh?"

Sloane shrugged. She was so used to the Russo legacy of getting married and having scads of babies that she was no longer fazed at how antiquated the notion was. "My oldest sister Rosie got married on her twenty-third birthday, and my other sister Angela wasn't that far behind. It's not like they had to or anything. But they both knew, beyond a doubt, that it was right for them, just like it had been for my parents. It only made me all the stranger for not doing the same."

"The black sheep of the family," Gavin murmured.

"Exactly. And no matter what I say, my mother doesn't get that it's not ever going to happen her way."

"So you don't *ever* want to get married and have kids?" The tiny crease that emerged between Gavin's eyes belied his calm tone, and Sloane had no choice but to lay out the rest of the truth.

"How could I ever have kids? I'm not even good daughter material, Gavin. Chances are pretty slim that I'd make anything other than a disastrous parent." Sadness welled up from the dark folds of her chest, filling the fresh space her words had just carved on their melancholy exit path, and she put her hand over her breastbone as if it could cover the surprise.

It wasn't that she didn't want a family. But she was a complete disappointment as a daughter, and she couldn't even hold on to her beloved career with both hands.

Holding on to a husband and kids would be impossible.

"None of this makes you a bad daughter. Or a potentially disastrous parent," Gavin said, and his eyes flashed as if he was poised to argue.

But there was no point in arguing something she knew down to her marrow. "It doesn't matter. I'm not cut out for that anyway. Like you said, I'm happy the way I am, even if I have to take flak for it."

"It *does* matter," he challenged. He pushed back from the counter so fast that she didn't have time to react until he was right next to her on the other side of the breakfast bar, but by then it was too late for shock. "You've spent all this time believing something that's just not true, and someone's got to set you straight. You're not unworthy just because you do things your own way. In fact, it's the most beautiful thing about you. I just wish you knew it."

In that moment, Sloane wanted nothing more than to deny his words with the fierce vehemence they deserved.

The only problem was, when he said she was worthy and beautiful, she believed him.

"I've felt like a failure as a daughter for so long, I don't know anything else," Sloane whispered, startled by the clarity of the confession. "No matter how hard I try or what I throw at it, I'm not going to be good enough."

Her throat knotted, threatening to close over an unexpected sob, and she swallowed hard in a last-ditch act of defiance. But then Gavin gathered her into his arms, and all her sadness and vulnerability poured out. It emerged from her throat on jagged edges, making her shake against the solid plane of his body, and with each cry, he only held her tighter.

"You're good enough, just as you are, Sloane," he whispered into her hair, and she shook her head against the tearstained cotton of his T-shirt.

"I'm not. I'm—"

"Stop." Without letting go of her, Gavin slipped the soft pad of one finger to her lips. "I don't care what you've been told or what you've got planted in your head. You're good enough. Christ, you're beyond good enough."

The words cradled her, deep and warm, as though they were made to fit against her skin. Habit, ingrained and merciless, reminded her he couldn't be right. As pure and good as the words felt when he said them, Gavin simply didn't know the whole story. Except she'd just told him, and he was holding her reverently anyway.

And with his arms wrapped around her as he held her tight and told her she was deserving in her own right, for the first time in her life, Sloane let go and believed it.

Chapter Twenty-Two

"I am the world's biggest idiot." Sloane threw herself against the pillowy couch cushions in her bungalow. As hard as she tried, she was unable to bite back the smile that poked the corners of her mouth upward. God, even her idiocy was tinged with bliss.

Spending the last two weeks having fantastic sex and better-than-fantastic conversations with Gavin had put a huge damper on her ability to be cynical about anything. How could the world be anything less than stellar when she felt so warm and happy and downright good?

Ugh, now she was a sap *and* an idiot. Fabulous.

"If having mutually exclusive sex with someone who actually happens to like you for who you are makes you an idiot, I don't even want to *know* what that makes me," Carly said with a laugh. She placed a huge bowl of popcorn on the coffee table, but not even the delectable smell of double-butter and sea salt could keep Sloane's reply from barging out.

"I haven't told him about Greece."

Carly froze with her hand halfway over the bowl. "Are you still going?"

"Yes. No. I don't know." *Way to be decisive there,*

sweetheart. She raked a hand through her tangled hair. "I mean, Gavin only needs me to watch Bree for a couple more weeks, so no matter what's going on between us, I'm still out of a job. I've tried countless times to write this book here, only the exact opposite of what my editor wants keeps popping out. If I stay in Pine Mountain, I'm afraid it'll only get worse, and I wrote my other three books on location. So nothing has really changed. If I want to save my career, I have to go. I've tried everything else."

Carly hesitated. "What about the book that keeps popping out?"

"What about it?" Sloane buried her fingers in the bowl of papery kernels even though her appetite was nonexistent. Despite her efforts to focus on mapping out a usable outline for the Greece book, the other story kept muscling its way into her brain, demanding airtime until she had no choice but to surrender in the hopes that it would clear out space for other ideas.

The space-clearing exercise had turned into a mind-blowing eleven chapters in just two weeks. Not even on her best days in Europe had she ever produced so much.

"Has Belinda read any of it? I mean, you said it's good, right? Maybe she'll like it even better than the Greece book." Carly's expression was loaded with optimism, but Sloane's frown watered it down a few degrees.

"She asked for something very specific, and she's been in the business for freaking ever. If there's anything I trust her on, it's what sells. And if she says Greece sells, I can't very well give her anything else, *especially* something she's already rejected. No matter how good it is, I'd be committing literary hara-kiri."

Carly slanted a glance at Sloane as if weighing her words, then broke into a shrug and eye roll combination that signaled her decision to ditch caution altogether.

"Okay, but you said yourself that it's better than anything you've ever come up with. Don't you think that makes it worth taking the chance? What's the worst-case scenario if you just run it by her?"

Sloane's thoughts hitched, causing her to open her mouth even though nothing came out. She'd toyed with the idea no less than a million times over the past week. She was becoming utterly captivated by the unexpected book spilling out of her, and she knew in her heart that even though it was different from anything she'd ever written, it was also better. Something about the words on the page simply spoke to her in quiet voices, weaving together in ways that felt effortless and right. The more she explored those words and ideas, the more layered they became, and with every chapter she clacked out, the book just became richer, more vibrant. As if it was growing from the inside out.

"I don't know," Sloane finally admitted. "It's one thing for me to think this other book is good, but let's face it. I wrote it. I'm not exactly unbiased here. It's a huge risk, and I'd have to really, really trust myself before I did something as dicey as give Belinda something so far from what we discussed." Although technically, they *had* discussed it back in New York. And Belinda had given Sloane a resounding *no*. God, this was a recipe for disaster.

But every time she went to put the kibosh on the new book completely, she heard Gavin's voice, sure and strong in her head.

You're good enough. Just as you are.

And with that, she surpassed sapdom and dove head-first into total lunacy.

Carly bit her lip over a sigh, knocking Sloane's thoughts back down to Earth. "Either way, maybe you should at least tell Gavin what's going on."

And to think, Sloane had been certain she couldn't fit

any more unease into her chest. "Nothing's going on. Plus, I can't really tell him what I don't even know," she hedged, and the dark seed of doubt looming in her mind squashed the purity of Gavin's words right out of her memory.

She couldn't take the risk, only to find out he was wrong.

"I guess," Carly said, although the look on her face outlined her doubt. "But if you guys are serious, then—"

"I'm not cut out for serious, *cucciola*." Sloane's words felt like rocks as they thudded past her lips. "And Gavin's not cut out for anything else. Especially since he has Bree to think about. So as much fun as I'm having with him in the here-and-now, blowing it up into something it's not will only confuse things."

"And you don't think keeping the truth from him will confuse things more?" Carly's question came out without a hint of accusation, but it stung nonetheless. Sloane rubbed a palm absently over her breastbone, but sat up tall as she sealed a lid on the topic.

"I'm not keeping anything from anybody. It's just the way things are. In a couple of weeks, Gavin won't need a babysitter anymore, and I'll need to leave to write a book. It's not like my personality or my profession is a huge secret. In truth, I don't know that he'll be all that shocked."

"Sloane." Carly's voice was one notch above whisper territory. "Is it possible that maybe Gavin is your swan?"

"No!" The word made Sloane flinch in both its intensity and its volume, even though she'd been the one to deliver it. No *way* was Gavin her happily ever after. As good as he made her feel in the moment, they wanted completely different things in the long run.

And what he wanted, she couldn't deliver.

Sloane cleared her throat. "No. He can't be. I mean, he's not. He's got his life here, and I've got to go my own way. It's just temporary."

Carly tipped her head, and years of best friendship told Sloane that she was about to push the issue in her typical, no-nonsense way. But then Carly shocked the hell out of her by giving in. "If you say so."

Sloane blinked, but stood firm. "I do."

"So do you want to watch some TV? I don't know about you, but this girl could use an hour of quality vegetation. As a special treat, I won't even make you watch The Food Network."

As Sloane slapped on a smile and watched Carly dig for the remote, the sensation running through her was way more impending dread than relief at being let off the hook. Everything Sloane had said was true, and yet the words had left her mouth with the hollow feeling of a lie. She wasn't afraid Gavin would be mad at her for not divulging her plans sooner, although he likely wouldn't be thrilled. No, it was the alternative that had Sloane's motto switched firmly into *don't ask, don't tell* mode.

If she told Gavin everything, there was a chance he'd try to convince her that the unexpected book—the one pouring from her heart—was worth the risk. That she should trust herself because she was good enough. And there was part of her that wanted so badly to believe him, the way she had when he'd held her in the kitchen. But if it turned out he was wrong, she wouldn't just lose her job.

She'd lose everything.

Gavin shot a gaze of total disdain at the coffee table before darkening his expression and lifting it toward Sloane.

"I think I deserve handicap points. Playing Scrabble with a writer is unfair." He gestured to the board, but his stalwart frown was slipping by the second. "I mean, *zealot?* Really? You're killing me, here."

Her deep, from-the-toes laugh made it impossible to keep the feigned irritation on his face. She folded her long legs as she knelt, her voice as sweet and simple as maple syrup over pancakes as she said, "Triple letter score on the *Z*, just so you know."

He tossed his pencil down with an exaggerated groan. He might not give a shit about Scrabble, but a guy had to defend his pride. "You're awfully pretty for a cheater."

"And you're awfully cute for a sore loser." Sloane placed her palms on either side of the board and leaned over to plant a quick kiss on his lips. On second thought, this might not be so bad.

His frown returned when she pulled back. "Hey, where are you going? I was just about to use my charms to try and earn bonus points."

"Please. You're too honest for bribery." She flicked a glance down at the board. "And good as you are, all the charming on the planet won't save you. Admit it, Wine Boy. I totally stomped you."

Gavin opened his mouth to protest, but one look at the score sheet told him he needed another angle. He rounded the coffee table from his seat on the couch in a matter of seconds, looping an arm around her to hold her close. Damn, her body felt good on his. "You totally stomped me. I don't know how I'll survive."

Sloane's pulse fluttered beneath his mouth as he kissed the delicate slope beneath her jaw. "I'm sure you'll think of . . . oh, God, that feels good."

Oh, yeah. This tactic was *much* better. "If you like that, then you should see—"

The squeal of the storm door riding its rusty hinges sent them in opposite directions in about two seconds flat. The familiar creak-and-bang combination coming from the foyer told Gavin that either a tornado had touched down at the front of the house or Bree was home from school. How a kid of her size and stature could make so much noise was beyond him, but hell if he wasn't grateful for it right now.

"Hey, you guys." Bree made her way into the living room, the sight of her flushed pink face and longer-by-the-day form catching him with a bittersweet pang. Damn, she was going from gangly to graceful in what felt like seconds.

He grinned from his regained position on the couch. "Hey. How was school?"

"Riveting." She made a face that suggested otherwise, swinging her backpack to the floor with an ungainly thud. Her eyes lit a path over the coffee table and she let out a small laugh. "Oh, she whipped you at Scrabble, too? Nice."

Gavin arched a brow at Sloane, who blinked sweetly, the picture of innocence. Oh, how he could call her bluff ten ways to Sunday. If only Bree wasn't standing right there to wonder how exactly he'd gathered that kind of intel.

"I thought you said you didn't play that often," he said instead.

"I don't. It's not my fault I'm good without practice." She lifted one shoulder in a demishrug and started to clear the board, glossy wooden tiles clicking in her hand. But the wink she snuck in Bree's direction didn't escape his notice.

Gavin knew his frown didn't stand a chance, so he didn't even bother. He tipped his chin at Bree, switching gears. "I was thinking of heading into Riverside this afternoon to do some shopping since I'm off work. You interested?"

Bree's toffee-colored eyes sparked, despite what looked

like her best effort to appear bored. "You throwing in dinner?"

Gavin helped Sloane clear the remaining tiles, pretending to think about it. "Possibly. What do you say?"

"Okay, but can we take your car? I mean, the Fiat's cooler, but the backseat is nonexistent."

Sloane's head snapped up in perfect unison with his, and Bree split her look of confusion between the two of them. "You *are* coming too, right?" she asked Sloane, who was suddenly very absorbed in tidying up.

"Oh, um. Well, I wouldn't want to intrude on you guys spending time together or anything."

Man, she had a hell of a game face. If he hadn't spent just about every waking, nonworking hour with her over the course of the last week, he'd probably miss her just-too-tight smile or the fact that her hands were moving a hair faster than usual.

"But you're always here anyway," Bree said, both hopeful and matter-of-fact. "And if you come, it won't be intruding. It'll be fun." She stopped, looking at Gavin for either confirmation or assistance. "Right?"

He didn't hesitate. "You do kind of have the market cornered on fun, Sloane. What do you say? You want to blow your evening off with us?"

A slow smile, this one genuine, spread across Sloane's pretty face, and whoa, did he feel it right in his gut.

"What can I say? You twisted my arm." She nudged him ever so slightly with one curvy hip as she moved past him toward the hall closet for her coat, and he couldn't help but send a grin in her wake. He was turning to get his keys when Bree leveled him with a question from square out in left field.

"So when are you guys going to tell me what's going on between you?"

Her words hit Gavin with all the subtlety of a sledge-hammer, and he nearly tripped on his way across the living room floor.

"Uh, what?" He winced at the ineloquence of his answer, but under the circumstances, he was damned lucky to have been able to manage even that. He'd struggled all week with what to say to Bree about him and Sloane, but in the end, he'd had to settle for staying mum.

After all, he was pretty sure *I tend to ruin personal relationships when things get emotional, but I'm crazy about your babysitter* was going to sound ridiculous. Even though it hit the nail on the head.

Bree bit her lip, but her expression betrayed her rampant curiosity. "Sorry. But you guys are kind of obvious."

Gavin clutched. "Obvious?" he finally croaked, and yeah, he was stalling, but it couldn't be helped. Christ, what had she overheard this time? And more importantly, how on earth was he going to explain his way out of it?

"Well, yeah," Bree said on a shrug. "You look at each other all weird and stuff."

"Are you okay with that?" Sloane's voice, so simple and matter-of-fact, snagged him out of his stupor long enough for him to be grateful she'd intervened.

Bree shot a startled look at Sloane. "What do you mean?"

"I mean what I said. Are you okay with us looking at each other like that?"

Bree's honey brown brows knit together in confusion. "But what I think doesn't matter."

Gavin dug deep and found his voice. "Sure it does." He took a step forward at the same moment Sloane moved back, and he found himself caught between gratitude and wonder that she'd been able to peg just the right thing to say to ease him into the conversation.

He took a deep breath. "Look, I'm not saying you get

the only vote here, but Sloane's right. What you think does matter."

"Oh." Bree shifted her weight from one scuffed boot to the other, transferring her gaze from his to Sloane's. "So you guys like each other, right? I mean, *like* like?" She twirled a finger, encompassing him and Sloane in an imaginary circle.

He gave a careful nod. "You could call it that. Yeah." Until now, whatever was going on between him and Sloane had felt too good to pin down with words and labels, but Bree's thirteen-year-old interpretation seemed about as good as any. As afraid as he was that he'd screw things up by getting involved with Sloane, Gavin couldn't deny the truth.

He wanted her. Even enough to risk his emotions.

Sloane's nod reinforced his words, digging him in deeper. She said, "I think that's a fair assessment."

Bree heaved a sigh, but her lips twitched upward, betraying her efforts. "Okay. But could you guys try not to do anything gross, like kiss in front of me and stuff? The faces are bad enough."

Gavin's gut tightened as he anticipated the awkward admission that yes, he and Sloane would be kissing, and *hell* yes, they'd do their best to keep it under wraps, but Sloane's rich laughter canceled out his unease.

"I'm sure we can manage that. For the sake of not embarrassing you, and all." Sloane lifted her eyes to meet his, all blue and sparkling and so damned beautiful. "Don't you think?" she asked, a smile as delicate and boldly sweet as spun sugar on her mouth.

In that brief slice of time, Gavin felt like someone had snuck into his chest to steal every last ounce of breath from his lungs. Yes, the room existed around him, with its familiar photos of Europe lining the walls and the relentless afternoon sunshine streaming in through the front windows. He knew that Bree was standing mere feet away, just as she had been seconds before. But this moment felt different despite its simplicity, as though all the moments that would fall off the clock after it would surely become a lot more complicated.

Because when he nodded in agreement and Sloane's smile twisted all the way through him with its perfect mixture of sensuality and vulnerability, he knew he was falling in love with her.

Chapter Twenty-Three

Gavin gripped the Audi's steering wheel with a dipping sense of unease. He'd been chock-full of emotions lately with Bree, and while he managed them just fine, they definitely weren't his thing. Surely all those residual feelings were rattling his brain. Otherwise he'd never have jumped to that crazy falling-in-love conclusion about Sloane in the living room.

She turned in the passenger seat next to him, delivering the warm, sexy smell of cinnamon spice right to his nose, and he couldn't decide whether to laugh or just plain cry uncle.

"So, Bree, what'd you do in school today?" Sloane angled her shoulder against the passenger seat to get a good view of Bree in the back, but her body faced him full-on. Okay, he was an adult. He could focus on the conversation. And he could absolutely forget that Sloane was wearing the sheerest pale pink bra he'd ever seen underneath that black sweater. He knew, because he'd taken it off of her just after lunch.

She shifted her weight next to him, and it was all Gavin could do to suppress a groan at the petal-colored strap peeking out from beneath her V-neck in the world's prettiest taunt.

Bree leaned forward from the backseat, mercifully snagging his attention as she answered. "We're getting ready to dissect frogs next week in biology, which is totally wrong, not to mention gross. Caitlin and Sadie and I were thinking of boycotting."

"Boycotting, huh? Well, that's one way to make your voices heard, I suppose." The inflection in Sloane's voice told him she'd chosen her words with care, and it piqued the hell out of his curiosity. Still, no way was he going to let Bree stir up trouble in biology.

He frowned, but held on to his protest for a minute despite the urge to flat-out tell her she had to participate. "Would that save the life of your amphibian subject?"

Bree's sigh was a gusty, drawn-out number. "No. They're already dead when they ship them to the school. We asked Mr. Morrison all about it. He said they're . . . what's the word for killing them nicely?"

"Euthanized?" Sloane supplied, and Gavin caught Bree's nod in the rearview mirror.

"Yeah. Euthanized with a chemical that makes them basically fall asleep first. He promised they really don't feel anything, and that even with a computer program, we wouldn't learn the same stuff as doing the real dissection."

Sloane tipped her head, her dark, silky hair tumbling within his reach. Christ, what was *wrong* with him?

"Hmm. Guess it wouldn't be entirely bad to take it as a learning experience then," she said.

"Doing animal dissections is where veterinarians start out," Gavin added. It might have been ages ago, but he firmly remembered an eight-year-old Bree claiming her life's goal was to care for animals. By the time he moved to San Francisco, he'd had nearly every show on Animal

Planet down cold just from watching with her during his precious few off-hours.

Bree paused. "I guess you're right. And it's okay anyway. Lucas Ford said he'd be my lab partner, and he promised to do the actual dissecting if I'd write up the lab. That way I don't have to butcher poor Kermit but I'll still get credit for participating."

"That was awfully nice." Relief flooded Gavin, and he was grateful that he didn't have to directly intervene to save Bree's science grade. The emotion was short-lived, however, when he caught the distinctive change in her sigh.

"Yeah. Lucas is pretty nice."

Oh, *hell* no. Gavin didn't care if she failed science ten times in a row. No way was this Lucas kid getting within a twelve-foot radius of his sister.

His knuckles went white over the steering wheel. "On second thought, maybe—"

"Oooh, look! The perfect parking spot," Sloane interjected, flinging her arm toward the passenger side window and effectively bringing his train of thought to a screeching halt. He maneuvered the Audi between a sleek, red sports car and a minivan, realizing only after the fact that the lot was littered with empty spaces. He opened his mouth to revisit the argument in his head with fresh vigor, but Bree was already happily chatting with Sloane about some TV show they'd watched together the other night, and his window of opportunity had clearly passed. It might be just as well, though. If Bree was only willing to give this Lucas kid two seconds worth of airtime, he probably wasn't worth having an argument and wrecking their afternoon.

"Okay. What do you two want to shop for first?" Gavin asked, sliding out of the car.

"Shoes," Sloane said, with a look that suggested this was the only possible answer to the question.

"A new cell phone," Bree added excitedly, and he nearly pitched to a stop on the pavement.

"You have a cell phone so you can reach me if there's an emergency," he reminded her. "And it works perfectly fine."

Their feet kept time on the black pavement in the parking lot, and Bree jumped over a crack between two spaces. "My cell phone is a total dinosaur. It doesn't even get e-mail."

"Neither do you, really. Except from the people you could call on the phone."

But she set her face with a pleading expression, and damn, it took a potshot right at his ribs. "But if I had my own iPhone, then I wouldn't have to borrow Sloane's."

He swung a look of surprise at Sloane. "You let her have your iPhone?"

She went wide-eyed as they all hopped the curb and headed toward the brightly lit mall entrance. "Well, Sadie and Caitlin got iPhones for their birthday last week, and we were just testing out FaceTime. You know, the person-to-person chat thing? I'm sorry. I didn't think you'd have a problem with it, but I shouldn't have assumed."

Gavin shrugged. "There are worse things than video chatting with friends," he said, holding the glass-paned door open to usher them both into the mall. "Plus, I trust you to make those kinds of judgment calls, anyway. I just don't want Bree killing your battery or monopolizing your phone."

Sloane's pace slowed for a second, and as she scrambled to make up the few strides she'd lost, Bree intervened.

"I didn't monopolize. I borrowed," she said, and Sloane nodded in agreement.

"It was fine, really." She lifted an eyebrow in Bree's direction and bumped Bree's hip with a gentle nudge.

"You're just lucky I have a high tolerance for extended discussions about who got kicked off *Survivor,* kid."

"Whatever." But Bree bumped her back with a laugh of her own, and the familiar ease lit something uncontrollably happy in Gavin's chest. By the time they got a third of the way through the aisles in the Target next to the mall, their effortless banter had turned his mood damn near unbreakable.

Sloane got a wicked glint in her eye as they rounded a huge display of sunglasses, and she snapped a pair of purple aviator shades from the wall. "A girl can never have too many pairs of sunglasses," she crooned, popping them over her face and fluffing her hair in the display mirror.

Gavin laughed. "Those are totally ridiculous." And yet she still managed to look irresistible in them.

"Not as ridiculous as these," Bree chimed in, grabbing a pair of lime green Wayfarers.

"Between the two of you, I think the sun would be tempted to cry rather than shine." And yet his laughter kept welling up with no end in sight.

Sloane took a step back, propping the purple glasses on her forehead in order to scan the rest of the display. "Okay. Let's find a pair for you, then."

His amusement veered toward nervousness, but he had a funny feeling Sloane could smell fear like most people could smell cookies in the oven, so he made an effort to keep his expression neutral. "No thanks. I'm all set."

"Oh, come on! You have to play, too." Bree wasted less than five seconds before gleefully pointing out some of the ugliest sunglasses on the planet to Sloane, and shit, how was he going to get out of this now?

He took a quick survey of the neighboring aisles, noting with chagrin that they were dotted with shoppers all well within sight of them. "Really. Those look so much better on you guys. I'll just let you have all the glory."

"Nice try, you old smoothie." Sloane plucked a pair of huge shades from the rack that looked like they should come with an optional disco ball, and Gavin took a step backward.

"No way. Not a chance those are going on my face." He gestured to the plastic monstrosity in her hand.

Velvety laughter spilled from her lips. "Relax. These are for me. These"—she paused, reaching around Bree's shoulder to slip a pair of strangely normal-looking men's sunglasses from the backlit display—"are for you."

"Oh, you let him off easy," Bree complained with a giggle, but Sloane just smiled and swapped her purple glasses for the bug-eyed disco pair.

"What do you say, boss? Do you want to give these a shot?" She held out the pair she'd chosen for him, and even in those completely ludicrous sunglasses she'd pulled from the display, she looked so sweetly endearing, so completely *Sloane,* that he took the purple aviators from her other hand without a second thought.

"Nope. If I'm going to look ridiculous, I might as well go all in." He shoved the frames over his nose in one smooth gesture, savoring the shock on both of the faces in front of him as he turned to the rack of hats and scarves behind them.

"As a matter of fact, while we're at it, why don't we try this?" He skimmed the shelves of hats, his violet-tinted gaze snagging on the perfect example of turnabout being fair play. He placed a floppy, daisy-studded rain hat on Bree's head, eliciting a fresh round of giggles from her.

"Pick one for Sloane," she chanted, her girlish face lit up sweetly despite the garish hat-and-glasses combination she wore.

Gavin tapped a finger to his chin, feigning deep thought.

"One for Sloane. Hmmm." He picked up a dramatic bright red fedora and twirled it menacingly in his hand.

"Hey, don't forget I was nice to you. You're the one who stole my aviators," Sloane reminded him with a laugh.

"So I am." He returned the fedora to the shelf, even though he had a sneaking suspicion it would've looked more attractive than comical on her. Finally, out of the corner of his eye, a snippet of color caught his attention. Oh, yeah. Freaking perfect.

He picked up the delicately crocheted sky blue beret, and the soft cotton threads felt just right in his hands as he lifted it to Sloane's head. "But I think this ought to do it. How about you?"

Gavin slipped the stupid purple glasses off his face at the same time Sloane removed her own sunglasses, both of them staring into the mirror nestled between the shelves. The beret framed her face with just enough color to make her eyes shine, and she blinked first at her own reflection, then at his.

"Wow," she murmured, and when she leaned against him, his arm went around her as if it couldn't possibly belong anywhere else. "Thank you."

"Well, I know you're a bit partial to the hat you already have, but . . ."

Her eyes glittered, never wavering from his in the mirror. "It's perfect. I love it."

"Oh, that looks really pretty, Sloane. You should totally get it." Bree looked at her, suddenly reverent, and she slipped the daisy hat from the crown of her honey-colored waves. The sensation of tight, incredible breathlessness he'd felt before in the living room invaded Gavin's senses once again, only this time he didn't fight it.

After all, if he was going to be in love with her, he might as well go all in there, too.

* * *

Sloane padded down the hallway, her bare feet shushing over the cottage floorboards like a secret as she headed toward Bree's room. She knew that Bree was fine, of course—the kid was made of tougher stuff than most of the adults Sloane had met—but occasionally Bree fell asleep with her lights on or her radio going. It wouldn't really hurt to double-check, just in case. Plus, she could use a break from the relentlessly blank pages of legal paper spread across the breakfast bar, just waiting for a Greece book outline to fill them up.

Fat chance of that happening. God, her writer's block on that book could give Stonehenge a run for its money right about now.

"Bree? You awake?" Sloane tapped lightly on the glossy white frame outlining Bree's door, tipping her ear toward the cracked-open panel for a response. The hushed tones of a local radio show were the sole reply, and Sloane broke into a knowing smile as she poked her head into the room with caution.

Sure enough, Bree was sprawled, out cold, over her twin bed. Her quilt covered more of the floor than her body, and Sloane bent to lift the patchwork edge from the cherrywood boards. Bree's face was soft with the telltale mark of deep sleep, and the pink flannel pajamas that Gavin had bought her on their shopping excursion a few days ago threatened to swallow her whole. Sloane's smile made itself comfortable on her lips as she drew the quilt over Bree's slumbering frame. Considering how fast pre-teen girls grew, she'd be shocked if the pajamas made it to the end of the year without becoming high-waters.

She froze in place, mid-tuck. Since when did she have a clue what the growth curve of a thirteen-year-old looked like? Four weeks' worth of not endangering one kid didn't exactly earn her the Caregiver of the Year award. She might do just fine helping out with essay questions and rides to the library or the movies, but that was a far cry from actually thinking she was any good at this.

Judging by the two missed calls from her mother that she had accidentally-on-purpose not yet returned this week, Sloane still wasn't much of a candidate for good daughterhood, despite Gavin's arguments to the contrary.

And yet, something about the way he continually trusted her with Bree's well-being kept rising up in her mind, daring her in quiet moments like this one to believe that she might be good enough anyway.

"You're losing it," she muttered and silenced the radio with a flick of her wrist. After clicking off the light, she retraced her footsteps down the hall. Her stomach took a swan dive at the sight of the blank pages gracing the granite countertop, ones with headings that read *Hero's Internal Conflict* and *Setting: Research and Description.*

She picked up the latter with a frown. Not since she'd started writing had she had a book fight her so hard on its way out. Short of being smack in the middle of Athens, Sloane had done everything she could think of to bring the beautiful Greek city to the forefront of her imagination. But the harder she tried, the more difficult it became, to the point that she was starting to feel like one of those salmon that fought tooth and nail just to get inches up-stream.

Her only hope was to fight the good fight, the only way she knew how. Either that, or she was going to be eaten by a bear.

Sloane caught sight of her propped-open laptop on the kitchen table, and it stirred equal parts frustration and longing in the space beneath her rib cage. If the Greece book counted as a dry spell, then the unnamed project spilling out of her was a total deluge. Even now, the ideas called to her, begging to be splashed over the screen. As much as she'd thought she could get one book out of the way to pave the path for the other, she was starting to think that maybe there was more to it than that. She was beginning to believe the book that was taking shape in front of her was good enough to pitch despite the fact that it was the complete opposite of what her editor had asked for.

On pure impulse, Sloane's fingers found her laptop keyboard, and she tapped the screen to life with a quick keystroke. If she could compose a smart enough proposal and put some extra polish on that first chapter, Belinda would have no choice but to see how good this project was. Okay, so it wasn't Sloane's usual fare, and yes, they'd have to work out a new spin on the marketing, but in the end, it would be worth it. Something about this book just sang, and while her others had certainly been strong, this one just felt *right*.

As if the ideas coming from within her really were good enough.

She angled the cursor over the icon for her e-mail, gaining momentum as she clicked. God, she couldn't wait to tell Gavin about this. Of course, she'd probably have to endure some good-natured ribbing over not believing in herself in the first place, but that was fine. The look on his face when she told him she'd really pitched the book would be worth it.

Sloane's computer dinged with an unread e-mail message, and she nearly laughed out loud when she clicked on her inbox and saw Belinda's name flashing in bold, blue letters.

"Must be kismet," she told the screen, clicking on the message with happy abandon. But what she found made her mouth go dry before she got past the second sentence.

Dear Sloane,

*I hope this finds you well and hard at work. I
need a copy of your Greece proposal ASAP—
marketing is dying to get their hands on it. Also,
our sales rep hinted to one of our biggest accounts
that you had your nose to the grindstone on
another Europe book, and they've expressed
interest in some major placement within their
stores, as well as hosting a series of high-profile
signings. You are a fan favorite! Not that I'm
surprised, of course. But I'd like to get moving on
your contract, so the sooner I get that proposal,
the sooner we can dive right in.*

*   Best,*
*   Belinda*

*P.S. Just between you and me, I told Martin you'd
decided to head to Greece to write another book
for us, and he's thrilled.*

She lifted her hands to her mouth, trying to swallow
the bitter combination of unease and dread starting to
form within her. Martin Abernathy, whom Sloane had
met exactly once in her tenure with Morton House Publishers, was thrilled about her Greece book? According to
his reputation, the serious-as-a-heart-attack editor in chief
didn't even crack a polite smile at the biggest of sales, and
yet he was *thrilled* over the prospect of her project? And
she'd barely been a blip on the big chains' radar when her
first book had been released. Now they wanted her for
book signings in big cities?

All for a novel she hadn't written a single word of, despite putting almost a month's worth of effort into trying.
Oh, God, there was no way Sloane could sell Belinda on

the idea of this other story now, no matter how seamlessly it was falling out of her brain and onto the screen.

It made no difference how much she wanted to stay in Pine Mountain, to sit right here in the cottage with Gavin and Bree where she felt so completely at home for the first time in . . . well, ever, and write this book of her heart. All the pure, uncut happiness she felt when she talked about it with Gavin—hell, when she was just near Gavin— didn't matter when held up against the fact that she was going to be jobless and homeless and maybe jobless again in a couple of weeks if she didn't get her act together.

She needed the Greece book, and she needed it *now*.

Sloane pinched the bridge of her nose between her thumb and forefinger, using her free hand to close the e-mail from Belinda. She slid her mouse across the screen, and it only took a handful of clicks to pull up her favorite travel planning Web site. Locating a one-way flight to Athens proved all too easy, although her usual giddy anticipation at planning a trip was conspicuously absent, replaced instead by the dread bottoming out in her gut.

Her hand shook over the mouse, causing the tiny white arrow to waver over the *Confirm Flight Now* button. But all the self-belief in the universe wasn't going to get her out of this, and to be honest, Gavin really had given her too much credit. She just wasn't cut out for sticking around, not even when sticking around felt good, right down to her pedicure. It was time to face what she'd known was coming all along. Her time in Pine Mountain was drawing to a bittersweet close.

Sloane had no sooner clicked the button to print her confirmation and flight itinerary when Bree's blood-curdling scream ripped through the cottage.

Chapter Twenty-Four

Acting on nothing but sheer instinct and undiluted adrenaline, Sloane bolted through the kitchen at a dead run. Her bare feet slapped against the floor hard enough to send a jolt up the length of her spine, yet she didn't break stride on her direct path to Bree's room. She vaguely noticed that the front door was still bolted shut, just as it had been all night, and that nothing in the cottage seemed even a hair out of place.

Bree screamed again, an unholy sound that sent Sloane's blood vibrating in her veins, and she ran even faster.

"Bree!" Sloane kicked through the entryway, far past the pleasantries of knocking. The door clattered against the adjacent wall in noisy protest, but Sloane barely heard the racket. She zeroed in on Bree's bed, where she could just make out her shaking outline from the scant light filtering in from the hallway.

"Bree, what's the matter? What is it?" Oh, God. She'd been sleeping like the dead only half an hour ago when Sloane had come in to turn off the light. What the hell could've happened this fast? She yanked back the quilt, determined to figure it out, but her movements skidded to a stop as soon as the image in front of her registered.

Bree was curled around her pillow, with her back to Sloane and her hands jammed over her ears, seeming to be caught in the limbo of dream-level sleep. She thrashed over the sheets, her damp hair sticking to her forehead as she jerked into full view, and it occurred to Sloane all at once that Bree wasn't sick or hurt. Not in the traditional sense, anyway.

She was having the mother of all nightmares.

"Bree," Sloane tried tentatively, afraid to scare her awake and do more damage. "Bree, can you hear me? It's Sloane."

Bree's only response was to follow her writhing with a low whimper, and Sloane's heart threatened to shatter.

"Don't . . . don't go . . ." Bree mumbled into her pillow, eyes squeezed shut as she grasped at the fabric around her. It was impossible to tell if she was waking up or still stuck in dream mode, and Sloane stood, mired to her spot with ice-cold fear. Clearly, Bree was so far in the throes of sleep that she thought her dream was real, but would waking her with a start knock her out of the nightmare, or make things even worse?

Bree twisted the edge of her pillowcase in a tight fist, her whimper growing louder, and Sloane moved on gut-driven impulse to make it stop. She rounded the far side of the bed to sit on the twin mattress right next to Bree's curled-up form. A fresh round of cries began welling up from Bree's chest, but this time Sloane was prepared. Bree might not be able to take on this nightmare, but Sloane sure as hell could.

No way was Bree going to be frightened like that. Not on her watch.

"Shhh. It's okay, Bree. You're having a bad dream. I'm right here." Sloane reached down to smooth the wild threads of Bree's hair back from her temples, repeating the same words over and over again. "Shhh, I'm right here."

Bree's sleep-furrowed brow softened for a breath before her eyes flew open with a gasp that sounded as if she'd surfaced from the bottom of the ocean.

"Don't go!" Bree flailed for a moment, certainly stuck between sleep and waking, and she grabbed for Sloane with what had to be all her might. Sloane's breath left her on a sharp exhale, but she refused to be toppled as Bree launched herself forward, hanging on for dear life.

"Hey, hey, it's okay. I'm right here. It was just a nightmare." Sloane pulled away to cradle Bree's face between her palms in an effort to soothe her back to consciousness. It took every ounce of strength for Sloane to keep her hands from visibly shaking, but she dug deep. If she wasn't steady, Bree might get even more frightened, and that just couldn't happen.

"Sloane?" The thick veil of confusion began to lift from Bree's features, and she blinked through the soft shadows as if trying to gain her bearings.

"Hi, sweetheart." Sloane tried on a crooked smile, praying it would hold. "You okay?"

Bree exhaled and dropped her chin to the notch of her rumpled pajama top, realization trickling over her face. "I have nightmares sometimes." Her body tensed as she let go of Sloane and curled back up against the mattress, and in that moment, Sloane caught a firm snapshot of the little girl she'd once been.

"I see that. It's kind of scary, huh?" She reached around and placed a hand on Bree's back, rubbing a gentle circle between her shoulder blades just like her own mother used to do when Sloane was a kid.

"I guess," Bree said, in a clear bid to try to appear tough. She hugged her knees to her chest, capturing the pillow in the unyielding knot of her arms. "Sorry if I made a lot of noise."

Tears pricked Sloane's eyes. "It's all right. You filled my excitement quota for the night."

She felt the razor-wire tension start to slip from Bree's shoulders, one tiny degree at a time. Hushed quiet folded around them, punctuated only by the whisper of Sloane's hand on the flannel as she continued her soft, steadfast circles. Finally, just when she thought maybe Bree had dropped back off to sleep, the girl's barely there voice broke the silence.

"Am I ever going to stop missing my mom?"

Sloane halted, but didn't remove her hand from Bree's back. "I still miss my dad sometimes," she admitted on a quivery breath. "And it's okay to miss her. You don't have to pretend that you don't."

Bree nodded into her pillow. "So what do you do? When you miss your dad?"

"I write to him," she confessed, surprised at how easily the admission flowed out of her.

"But he can't get the letters," Bree said, her confusion plain even in the dim light from the hallway.

"I know. But the letters aren't for him, really." Sloane turned the idea over in her mind with a wistful smile. She'd never told anyone about the letters she wrote to her *papa*, not even her mother or sisters. Somehow, it had never occurred to her that anyone would really get the importance of it—until now.

Bree peered up at Sloane, her brows knit together. "I don't understand. You write the letters to your dad, right?"

"Well, the letters are *to* him, but they're more for me. To help me feel close to him still. Like I'm filling him in on my life. I know he can't answer, but it makes me feel that he's heard me anyway. And then I miss him a little less."

Bree hesitated before eking out a small nod. "Do you think that would help me? If I wrote to my mom, I mean?"

"That's really a question only you can answer. But I don't think it would hurt to try," Sloane said, pulling the quilt around Bree's shoulders.

She burrowed down into the covers, the traces of brutal sadness disappearing from her face. "Sometimes I . . . think about talking to her. You know, when no one else is around."

"It's the same idea. And a good one."

"You don't think I'm crazy? For wanting to talk to my mom when she's not here?"

Sloane shook her head, meeting Bree's eyes even though she had tears in her own. "Not at all."

"Oh. Well, maybe I could give it a try, then." Bree's eyelids drooped, but she fluttered them open in a battle against her exhaustion and emotions.

"You should get some sleep." Sloane fought the urge to give an ironic laugh. Never in a million years had she thought such motherly advice would come out of her mouth. Kind of funny how much sense it made, though. The poor kid looked weary to the point of being wrecked.

"I know," Bree said, yet still, she struggled to keep her eyes open, darting her gaze around the darkened room as if she was trying to keep her eyes busy.

Not one for pretenses anyway, Sloane threw them to the back of her mind, simply asking, "Are you afraid to go back to sleep?"

"No. Not really. It's just that normally when I have a really bad dream, Gavin, um . . . stays with me for a while."

Her heart smacked against her ribs. "He does?"

Bree nodded, her hair whispering against the bedsheets. "I don't think he knows I know. But he stands in the doorway and waits for me to go back to sleep."

Realization hit Sloane with the full force of the implication, but she didn't even hesitate. Right now, in this moment, Bree needed to be taken care of. Not by grabbing a ride to the mall, and not by getting help with an essay, but by having someone she trusted protect her heart.

And she wanted Sloane to do it.

"Don't worry, sweetie. I'll be right here for as long as it takes."

Sloane fought the urge to drift into twilight sleep, even though Bree had conked out about four seconds after Sloane settled into the overstuffed chair by her bed. The sound of Bree's slow, rhythmic breathing was the calm on the surface of Sloane's churning mind, like a summer breeze over deceptive undertow.

The idea of leaving now made Sloane's heart ache, but she'd be a fool not to face facts. Yes, she'd been able to wing her way through comforting Bree, but in two weeks, Gavin's regular babysitter would be back in the picture. It would probably be a matter of days before Bree readjusted to the older, more experienced woman again. And no matter how purely good being with both Bree and Gavin felt, she still needed a job. She hadn't worked endlessly to carve out a successful career only to toss it aside at a little writer's block that could be easily fixed on location.

Even though she was needed in the here and now, Sloane knew better than anyone that the here and now couldn't last forever.

The sound of movement at the front door pulled her from her gloom, and the familiar cadence of Gavin's footfalls through the cottage told her that he was home. Sloane's heart kicked in her chest. Even though she wanted to do its bidding and wrap herself up in Gavin's safe, experienced arms, she also realized that doing so would only prolong the inevitable. They might not have any commitment to each other beyond the next two weeks, but she owed him the truth. Telling him about Greece was long overdue, and she had no choice but to go.

"Is everything okay?"

Even though she'd heard him enter the cottage, Gavin's troubled whisper still startled her. He stood in the doorframe, his pale blue dress shirt not showing nearly as many creases as his worried brow.

"Oh." Sloane snapped upright in the chair, nodding a quick reassurance. She whispered back, "Yeah. She had a nightmare." She gestured to Bree and unfolded herself from the cream-colored cushions of the chair, pausing to tuck the quilt a little tighter over the girl's shoulder before moving toward the door.

But Gavin stood there, stock-still. "She hadn't had one in a while, so I thought maybe she was past them. But I should've told you, just in case. Was it bad?"

His sculpted jaw ticked with worry, and Sloane slipped an arm around him for comfort before it struck her that she shouldn't. But God, he felt so warm and undeniably good pressed up against her, each of them giving the other the perfect amount of support, and she simply couldn't let go.

"She's okay now. I just figured I'd stay with her until she fell back to sleep."

"Thank you." He guided her into the hallway, reaching back to close Bree's door with a hushed *snick*.

"Just doing my job," she said, but he stopped her short in the shadowy entrance to the foyer.

"You're doing a lot more than your job, Sloane. Bree trusts you. She needs you."

Gavin's words brought her feet to a clumsy halt. She blinked in the ambient light. "It was just a little comforting. That's all. Anyone would've done it."

He pinned her with a dark gaze that arrowed right to her very center. "But she wouldn't have *let* just anyone do it. It's not about having whoever's available sit by her bedside when she has a bad dream. It's about you. She wants *you*."

Something Sloane couldn't name rushed through her, but she couldn't look away, not even when Gavin stepped so close she could feel the intensity of the heat coming off of him.

"And *I* want you. I want you to stay, here with us. Just like this." He stroked her face, skating his fingers down the line of her neck to rest right over her heart. "Please. Say you'll stay."

Sloane's time-tested defenses formed the word *run* in the back of her mind, but she knew all at once she wouldn't honor them. Not this time. Despite the near-impossible odds stacked against her, she had to find a way to stay in Pine Mountain, to soothe Bree's nightmares and spend her nights in Gavin's arms. There had to be some way to make it work.

Because she'd finally found where she belonged, and in this place, despite it all, she was good enough.

"Yes." She wrapped her arms around him, diving in headfirst even though she couldn't see the bottom.

"I'll stay."

Sloane reached up in one fluid surge, fitting herself against him with gorgeous precision that could only belong to their bodies, and she slanted her lips over his in just a hint of a kiss. Breath left her body on a sigh, twining around his softly until he couldn't tell where she ended and he began, and he realized in a rush that it didn't matter.

Sloane, with her go-where-the-wind-takes-me lifestyle, wanted to stay, to hold on to something right here with him and Bree.

And despite his fear of screwing things up with his emotions, Gavin didn't want to ever let her go.

He cupped her face between his palms, capturing her lips more fully. Each stroke of his tongue against hers, every taste of her exquisitely plump bottom lip held gently between his teeth, all of it made him want her with raw intensity he couldn't explain. And the more he had, the more he wanted, until he was certain that the only way he'd slake his need for her was to just have her indefinitely.

Starting right now.

Gavin guided Sloane wordlessly to his room, pausing only long enough to shut and lock the door before turning his attention back to her. He could just make out the lean silhouette of her body in the scant glow of moonlight spilling in from the windows, but his mind's eye filled in the blanks with luscious detail. The golden, graceful column of her neck, the tight curve of cinnamon-sweet skin where her shoulder eased into her collarbone, the waterfall of delicate bones in her spine—each lay unfurled in front of him like a feast. And knowing it was all right there, covered in nothing more than shadows, made him desperate to start tasting, layer by flawless layer.

"Come here." There was no hiding the gravel in his voice as he met her halfway despite his words. They moved, fusing their pent-up need together in one single, white-hot point. Sloane's lips parted easily, granting him permission to take her mouth with deep, unyielding strokes, and he wasn't about to deny her. He cupped the back of her neck with a hot palm, knotting his fingers through the tumble of her hair as he kissed her, exploring the sweet nuances of her mouth. Christ, he could do this a million times and still find himself blown away with want at her hot little whimpers and the drawn-out exhalation of her sighs.

Sloane's nimble fingers worked first at the knot of his

tie, then his shirt buttons before she gripped his shoulders over the thin cotton of his T-shirt with tight fists. A low sound worked the back of his throat, somewhere between a moan and a growl, and she met it with a laugh that sounded like liquid sin.

"Guess that answers the question of whether or not you like that." She stood on her toes, lifting off his T-shirt and pressing her breasts to his chest to produce the most infuriatingly sexy friction he'd ever felt. He reached down to grab the hem of her sweater, and with a swift yank, he was one glorious step closer to being inside her.

"I like this even better."

Testing the weight of her breasts with his palms, he caressed her with firm intention, skimming his thumbs over the barely there cups of her bra. It didn't take much encouraging to free her nipples from their lacy haven, and he stroked her until she arced against him with a groan.

"Gavin, please," Sloane whispered, and anything else she was going to say got lost on the tide of her sigh. He eased her toward the bed, lowering her to the soft down comforter while settling at the cradle of her hips, but she surprised him by placing both hands on his shoulders and giving a sharp push. Before he could even put his stunned thoughts into action, Sloane had looped a leg over his hip and turned him squarely to his back.

"You know what I think?" she asked, and her voice was such a sensual purr that he could barely keep himself from pushing back to regain his original position.

He groaned, all pleasure. "What?"

Sloane seated herself right in the heat of his lap, and he was certain he'd lose his mind. Christ, he wasn't going to make it like this.

"I think it's about time someone turned the tables on you." She slid the seam of her jeans up the length of his aching cock, and his gruff laugh popped out without warning.

"We're not going to be here long if you do that again." But Gavin gripped her hips, guiding her roughly over him again anyway because she felt *that* fucking good, even through their clothes.

Bracketing his shoulders with her palms, Sloane leaned seductively over his chest, brushing his skin with just the sheer suggestion of lace and hard nipples. "I don't care. For once, I want to see *you* get a little reckless."

Between the slow, hard thrust of her hips and the silky, sweet brush of her breasts on his chest, Gavin's resolve disappeared as if it had never existed. He answered every thrust in turn, pushing against her with dwindling control. When she dipped a hand between them to release the button on his pants, he reached out to return the favor, only to be denied.

"Uh-uh." Sloane shifted to her knees beside him, removing his pants with one economical tug but leaving her own in place. She ran her hands down his midsection, curling them around the waistband of his boxers with obvious intent. "Not this time."

"Sloane." He propped himself on his forearms, tracing his eyes over her in the gauzy moonlight just in time to watch as she freed him from his last remaining article of clothing. Nestling on her side right by his hips, she wrapped her fingers around his erection, and he released a tight exhale. "You're a little overdressed, don't you think?"

But her grin became wicked, just a flash of white teeth. A look of sexy longing took over her features, enhanced by the velvety shadows of the room. She peered up between her lashes, meeting his eyes for the briefest of seconds before treating him to an erotic pump of her fist.

"Not for what I have in mind."

And then her mouth was on him, and he couldn't think, let alone speak to reply.

Sloane swept her tongue down his length in one un- remitting line, and it was all Gavin had not to cant his hips off the bed at the white-hot sensation ripping through him. She stroked him again, first with her tongue, then with her hand, letting one follow the other until they blended together to become a blur of total intensity.

Sloane alternated the most feather-soft kisses with harder, unyielding friction from deft fingers, and when she took him deeply into the heat of her mouth, a hoarse groan broke free from the darkest part of his chest. Unre- pentant need rose from low in his belly, but he buckled down over it even though it took willpower he questioned, absolutely determined not to climax until she did.

"Sloane." He ground out her name, but even then it came out like a prayer. "Ah, *God,* you have to stop."

Her movements stilled, and the reprieve from her heated ministrations allowed him just a few seconds of clear thought.

She looked up at him, her expression laced with sexy abandon. "Go ahead," she murmured, her grin both wicked and sweet. "Lose control."

The irony of it hit him full-on, and he sat up, pulling her close until their eyes were mere inches apart.

"I haven't had any control since the minute I walked through the door tonight, Sloane. I want you. I want to make love to *you* and only you. That's what will make me completely lose my mind." He kissed his way from her jaw to her neck, finding that honey-sweet spot below the shell of her ear that made her moan softly when he tasted it.

All the sexy acrobatics in the world couldn't shred Gavin's composure like the sounds this woman made under his hands, his mouth, his lovemaking. There was only one thing he wanted, pure and simple.

"Just you."

With a few well-placed maneuvers, the rest of Sloane's clothes joined his in the dark shadows of the room. He quickly grabbed a condom from his bedside table and settled back on the bed beside her, but she repeated her earlier move by pushing him flat on his back. Parting her thighs, she rested her core over the lower threshold of his belly, just out of reach of his rock-hard erection.

Sloane glided over the crest of his hips with friction so utterly hot, he nearly saw stars from how badly he wanted to bury himself inside of her, and she leaned in close to whisper in his ear.

"If having me is what's going to send you over the edge," she said, her breath as ragged as his felt, "then I want you to watch every second of it."

She seated herself in his lap in one smooth stroke, and Gavin nearly lost it right there at how her words coupled with the movement. Her body, so tight yet pliant and wanting, surrounded him in a flawless give and take as she lifted herself over him only to lower back down until they were completely joined. He grasped her hips, but immediately wanted more. Encouraging her forward with the bend of his knees, he slid his hands to her backside until she filled his palms, guiding her to a rhythm that had both of them panting.

He stilled beneath Sloane's exquisite movement, watching her wanton expression break open further with each thrust. He took in the modest curve of her breasts, the dip of her belly, the velvety curls between her legs, branding it all on his memory just as she'd told him to. This time, when the urge rushed up from within him, he didn't hold back. With one last push upward, he razored into an orgasm so hard, it blurred the line between pleasure and pain.

Sloane's heady gasp and the quickening of her body

around him heightened the raw intensity, and Gavin held her tightly as she tumbled apart. Her gasp became a pleasured sigh, which then became his name, repeated over and again in the same honest, dulcet tones of the laugh he loved so much. After a moment of stillness, she unwound her body from his. But rather than moving away or turning to get dressed, she simply settled against him, matching his slowing, awe-filled breaths with her own.

And as he held her and listened to the rise and fall of her body lulling her to sleep, Gavin knew he could just as soon live without her as he could move the moon.

Chapter Twenty-Five

Sloane tugged at the gaping waistband of the plaid pajama pants she'd borrowed from Gavin, retying the drawstring below her belly button in an effort to keep them settled over her hips. She knotted her legs beneath her as she readjusted her position at the kitchen table for conservatively the sixtieth time in ten minutes. Her stare was certainly as blank as the screen in front of her, and she didn't even try to stop the sigh in her chest from rolling past her lips.

Of all the things she'd even written, this e-mail to Belinda was proving by far the most difficult. She'd rather take on ten Greece books than pen the missive that might well tank her hard-earned career. Oh, God, how had she not thought of this last night when she'd recklessly said she'd stay?

The answer was easy enough. She might've said it recklessly, but she meant it right down to her marrow. Sloane had said she wouldn't leave Pine Mountain, and it was because she was head over heels insane for Gavin Carmichael.

That falling unexpectedly in love would end up being the one thing that kept her from writing a romance novel was so ironic, she had no choice but to laugh, even though the sound emerged as flat as an old party balloon. It wasn't the decision to stay that was difficult—on the contrary, *that* had felt as right and natural as taking a deep breath upon waking to a new day.

It was the fallout that threatened to swallow her whole.

Eyeing the hallway down which Bree still lay blissfully asleep, Sloane scooped her cell phone into her hand and tiptoed onto the porch.

"Hey, it's me," she whispered after dialing, wishing in hindsight she'd grabbed a sweatshirt to brace herself against the Saturday-morning cold. She paced over the sun-bleached slate of the porch floor. "Do you have a minute?"

Carly's laugh held all the warmth Sloane's had lacked only a few minutes ago. "I have exactly ten, and then I have to leave for the restaurant. What's up?"

Sloane closed her eyes, and her words barged out without apology or grace. "I'm in love with Gavin."

Silence buzzed softly over the line for a second, then two before Carly replied, "Well. I've got to give you credit, *cucciola*. When you go swimming, you sure as hell jump in with both feet. Does he know?"

"You mean have I said it?"

"Yeah."

Sloane hesitated. "He asked me to stay here with him and Bree, and I said yes."

"You told him about Greece?" Surprise colored Carly's words, but whether it was at the notion of Sloane telling him about her intended trip or the fact that she wasn't taking it, Sloane couldn't be sure.

"No, but it doesn't matter. I'm not going. I don't want to go," she corrected, and God, her thoughts couldn't get any more muddled if she paid them outright to confuse her.

"Those are two different things," Carly offered gently, and Sloane pinched the bridge of her nose hard enough to feel the bite of her fingernails there.

"I know." She stopped pacing and flicked a glance at the front door. It was closed snug in the frame, but Sloane dropped her voice to a whisper anyway. "I just never expected any of this. I want to stay so much, but what if I screw things up? Then what?"

But Carly didn't even pause. "Gavin trusts you, Sloane. Maybe it's about time you started returning the favor."

Sloane could count on exactly two fingers the number of times she'd been shocked speechless in her entire life, and this moment made the list. "What?"

"Look, I know that sticking around scares the hell out of you, and I also know you have your reasons for that. But when you weed away all the doubt and what-ifs, it's still totally clear that Gavin trusts you with the most important thing in his life. All I'm saying is that it might not be a bad idea to believe—*really* believe—that he trusts you for good reasons."

"You mean that I'm good at taking care of Bree," Sloane said, the combination of mutinously bright sunlight and rising emotion making her eyes water.

"For one thing, yes. But he doesn't just want you to stick around to take care of his sister, does he?"

Carly's words hit a bull's-eye and broke open in Sloane's chest. "No," she whispered.

"Okay, then. How about maybe you trust that, too?" Carly whispered back.

The flash of emotion she'd felt when she'd promised to stay last night returned, surging over her in full force.

"Oh my God, you're right," Sloane blurted. "How did I not see this before?"

All at once, her emotions fell into place with such startling accuracy, she couldn't believe they'd eluded her in the first place. After all, it had been Gavin's faith in her that had kicked her desire into motion in the first place. How could she not trust it now, when she needed it the most?

Carly's slight chuckle returned Sloane's attention to the here-and-now. "Because you're human, and falling in love makes even the best of people prone to total lunacy."

Sloane barked out a snap of laughter. "Um, thank you, I think."

"My pleasure. You forget, it wasn't that long ago that I was the Queen Mother of raving lunatics when it came to being in love. But Jackson and I worked things out, and you and Gavin will too."

Sloane stuttered to a stop at the corner of the porch, bracing her hand on the weather-beaten white railing. "Do you really think so?"

"I really do," Carly confirmed.

For the first time, Sloane allowed herself a glimmer of hope. "Thanks." Her impulses booted up, heading directly for *right now* mode, and she bit her lip before continuing. "Hey, I don't mean to pull an emotional drive-by on you, but I should probably go get this Greece thing settled."

"Any idea how you're going to spin that?" Carly asked gently.

Sloane squared her shoulders with absolute surety. "Not a one. But I'll work at it until I figure it out. You're right. It's time I started trusting myself. And the people who care about me."

"Hey. What were you doing out on the porch?"

The sound of Bree's sleep-laden voice scared Sloane clean out of her skin, and she swung around so fast that she caught her elbow on the doorjamb with a merciless bang.

"Ow! Mother—" She clamped down on her tongue with all her might so as to not finish her sentence, even though the pain shooting up her arm begged for expression.

"Are you okay?" Bree asked, genuine concern washing over her sleepy face.

"Who, me? Sure." Sloane made a sour face and flexed her elbow a few times, grateful that the throbbing joint cooperated. For the most part, anyway. She looked at Bree, her grimace easing up considerably at the sight of her well-rested face. "You look like you slept pretty well, huh?"

If Bree had fallen prey to another nightmare after Sloane left her room last night, it had been the silent variety. Sloane had insisted Gavin leave his bedroom door cracked open before they fell asleep though, just in case.

Bree nodded, gesturing to Sloane's borrowed sleepwear. "You stayed."

"Oh." Sloane glanced down at the pajamas. It was painfully obvious from the baggy fit and masculine plaid that they were Gavin's, but she didn't bat an eye. "Yeah. I was worried about you, and then your brother, ah, asked me to stay. So I did."

While the conversation had a dangerous amount of awkward potential, being straight with Bree just made sense. After all, Gavin wasn't the only person Sloane was staying here for, and dancing around the situation didn't seem fair. Bree deserved to know the truth.

Sloane wanted to be part of their lives, plain and simple.

"Cool." A smile twitched at the corners of Bree's mouth, making a liar out of her indifferent shrug. "So do you want breakfast? I don't know how to make doughnuts like Gavin, but I could make bacon and eggs or something." Her eyes lit up with a tawny flicker. "I could even teach you how to make it if you want."

Sloane thought of her laptop sitting on the kitchen table, and she hesitated. She didn't want to wait another minute to write that e-mail now that she'd decided to take the plunge, but it wasn't something she could just rattle off and send. "Well, breakfast sounds great, but . . ."

Bree's expression faltered. "It's okay if you don't want to. I just thought the cooking part might be kind of fun. Sometimes we do it, you know. As a family."

The true implication of what Bree wanted knocked into Sloane with all the force of a palpable shove. How could she not have remembered how much the idea of making doughnuts with Bree had meant to Gavin? Or how reverently he'd left her that omelet the first time she'd stayed over, wrapped up nice and neat in the fridge?

For Gavin, food was an expression of caring, and whether or not he realized it, he'd passed it on to Bree.

"In that case, you're on. But I'm telling you now, the best thing I know how to make is reservations."

Sloane frowned at the sheer volume of food items and kitchen-type gadgets covering the butcher block island. Simplicity, it seemed, was not the theme of the day.

"Are you sure we need all this? It's just bacon and eggs." She picked up a stainless steel whisk, surprised at its lightness in her hand despite the heavy-looking handle.

Bree shot a grin over her shoulder from her station in front of the fridge. "This is nothing. You should see Gavin make his home fries casserole."

Sloane's stomach spoke up with a growl. "That sounds good."

"It is. But you don't want to be on cleanup duty afterward. It takes forever to wash all the stuff he uses." She joined Sloane at the butcher block, plopping a half-gallon of milk on the careworn surface. "Okay. So the first thing you do is get the egg mixture ready."

"That doesn't sound so bad." Sloane popped the top of the Styrofoam carton and passed an egg to Bree. She cracked it easily against the butcher block and emptied the contents into the bowl one-handed.

"Now you try."

Okay, this was going to be a piece of cake. Sloane took an egg between her fingers and mimicked Bree's movements. Right up until the egg exploded all over the countertop.

"Shit," Sloane muttered, her head springing up at the sound of Bree's giggle. "I mean, uh, darn." She looked down at the mess and winced.

"It's okay." Bree laughed. "We can just clean it up." She passed over the paper towels, and Sloane wondered if Bree had them so handy out of luck or because she'd suspected they'd need them.

Sloane wiped the mess from the counter to the trash can. "So I take it there's a trick to that."

Bree nodded, and showed her. "You learn it by feel. And by crushing a bunch of eggs in practice."

By the time they got to the sixth egg, Sloane got the hang of it. "You're pretty good at this, you know." She watched Bree add some milk and start whisking.

"We used to cook a lot, even when I was little."

Sloane clamped down on her ironic chuckle, not wanting to discourage Bree from talking. "Ah. Well, no wonder you're so good then." She paused, letting the metal on metal rhythm of the whisk against the bowl thread between them. A thought that had taken root as Sloane sat curled in the chair by Bree's bedside worked back through her brain, and she gave it voice.

"I've been thinking about something you said last night. I'd like to talk to you about it a little, if that's okay."

Bree's hand stilled over the bowl. "About my nightmare, you mean?"

"Yes." Sloane took the bowl from Bree's hands, her own attempts at whisking horribly clumsy in comparison. "Have you ever talked to Gavin about it? Like right afterward, when it's scariest?"

"No." Bree's forehead creased with lines way too worried for her thirteen-year-old face.

Sloane gentled her voice until it was one notch above a whisper. "Can I ask why not?"

"Because," Bree said, but then jerked to a halt. "Just because."

"He would understand, Bree. And he really wants to help you." Despite her efforts to stay calm, tears pricked Sloane's eyes, threatening to spill. Bree looked up at her, and the girl's stony façade crumbled.

"I know, but he's sad too. And it's not . . . fair. He quit his job to take me, and he works a lot so we can have the stuff we need. I used to hate him for that, before, because I felt like he left me and my mom behind. But now I don't want to tell him because I know he misses her, too. And he's already sad about giving up his life."

For a second, Sloane was so stunned, she couldn't breathe. "Oh, Bree. Don't you see? Honey, you *are* his life." She moved to take the bowl from Bree's shaking hands and set it on the counter. "Yes, he loves his career, but he loves you so much more. And even though he misses your mom, he wants to help you when you do, too. If you two talk about it, it might make it easier on both of you."

"I never thought about it like that," Bree whispered, tears streaking her delicately freckled cheeks. "I mean, he said I could talk to him if I felt like it. But I didn't think maybe *he'd* want to."

Sloane's words spilled right from her very center. "I wouldn't say it if it wasn't the truth. You can still talk to your mom or write her letters when you're feeling sad, but don't shut Gavin out. He needs you, too."

Bree wiped her face with the back of one hand. "Thanks. For understanding, and . . . well, everything."

"Anytime." Sloane reached out to capture the tears on Bree's other cheek with her thumb, surprised at how natural the comforting movement felt. She folded her into a quick embrace, which Bree readily returned. "I've got your back, kid."

"Promise?"

Sloane pulled back, but only so she could look Bree right in the eye. "I promise."

"Okay." Bree nodded.

Sloane broke into a slow smile, one that migrated all the way down to her heart and filled her completely. "Now what do you say we get back to it? These eggs aren't going to smash themselves."

They spent the rest of the morning and early afternoon puttering around the cottage, painting their toenails outrageous colors, and watching various shows on TV. When Bree settled in to start on her weekend homework, Sloane took advantage of the break and finally powered up her laptop.

Dear Belinda,

   I got your message, and I'm glad everyone's so enthusiastic about my writing. I'd like to talk to you about the direction of the project, but I think it would be best if we discussed it by phone. Can you call me at your earliest convenience? I'll have a proposal for you ASAP.

                              Thanks,
                              Sloane

Hitting *send* was shockingly easier than she'd expected, and relief filled Sloane's chest as she stared at the flashing message telling her it had been delivered. The book she'd tried so hard to fight was fresh and dynamic, and it was time to put her faith in it.

It was time to put her faith in herself.

Her fingers flew over the keyboard, forming the proposal she'd promised Belinda with ease. She described the story with rich details and poignant touches, losing herself in every layer until it burst with emotion, both in her mind and on the page. For the first time ever, what was around her didn't matter nearly as much as what was inside of her, and as she laid the story out like a tapestry, Sloane believed in it.

The sound of a voice being cleared snagged her from her thoughts, and although Sloane had been certain she'd only been on the couch for a few minutes, she was startled to see that the graying shadows of evening had been replaced by nightfall.

"Oh, jeez! I didn't realize it was so late." She blinked up at Bree, her eyes slowly adjusting from the glare of the computer screen to the soft lamplight of the cottage. "How did your homework go?"

"Fine." Bree shrugged, shifting her weight on the floorboards, and a pang of remorse worked through Sloane's belly.

"Sorry I didn't check on you sooner. I guess this book thing kind of got away from me. But I can read that *Macbeth* assignment over if you want." Damn it, she should've kept a better eye on the time. Bree had been struggling a little with the latest round of essays, and her bone-deep desire for independence could make asking for help a little dicey, even on their good days. "Here, I'll just take a quick look."

"No! I don't need any help. I just wanted to tell you I'm going to my room. You don't need to check on me."

Whoa. Speaking of preteen pride. Sloane tucked her surprise into a bittersweet smile. She might be an old geezer as far as Bree was concerned, but it hadn't been *that* long since Sloane's teen years. And if anyone understood the need for independence, it was certainly her. Still, the guilt kicking up in her chest refused to back all the way down.

"Tell you what," she said, sliding her laptop to the coffee table. "My *Macbeth* is pretty rusty. Maybe if you let me read it, I'll learn something new. Then when we're done, we can see what looks good in the Netflix queue. What do you say?"

For a second, Bree went wide-eyed and completely still. But then she threaded her arms into a tight knot over the chest of her thermal pajama top, and Sloane knew she'd lost this round of homework wars squarely to Team Hormones.

"I already printed the essay, so no big deal. I'm going to go work on the final write-up for my biology lab."

Sloane laughed in a last-ditch effort to smooth over Bree's crabby mood. "On a Saturday night?"

Bree responded with a blush and scowl combo that was probably visible from the moon before giving an exasperated sigh. "It's due on Tuesday. Plus, I'm supposed to call Lucas so I can get the rest of his notes and stuff for the PowerPoint slides."

Ahhh. Well at least her mood made sense now. And so did her bid for privacy. Sloane bit her lip and tried to decide how to proceed. Gavin would probably have a kitten at the whole boys-on-the-phone thing, but really, Bree seemed edgy enough about it without Sloane giving her a hard time.

Still, something about the hard flash in Bree's eyes made Sloane pause. "Hey, are you sure you're okay?"

"Fine," Bree said, with enough frost to make it sound like the other f-word. "Can I go now? Please?"

Even though Sloane's radar was on full alert, she knew that pushing Bree was only going to get her pushed back. "Sure," she said slowly. "We can do the Shakespeare thing tomorrow. Just let me know if you need anything."

"Yeah. Whatever."

The shock of Bree's words knocked Sloane for a loop, and by the time the retort registered, Bree had beat a hasty retreat to her room.

She popped up from the couch with every intention of calling Bree back to take her to task, but the spurt of irritation flickered hard in her chest, and she froze to the floorboards. They'd spent an awful lot of time together over the last couple of days, and Bree's adolescent emotions had more hairpin turns than the freaking Grand Prix. While Sloane wasn't nuts about the eye-rolling attitude, it *was* pretty common fare for the broody moody set. Bree probably just needed a break to hang out with someone else. The last thing she wanted to do was breathe down the kid's neck. Hell, even the most even-keeled thirteen-year-old would get testy at that.

And anyway, it would probably be long forgotten by morning.

Chapter Twenty-Six

Gavin shook the late-February chill from his coat as he slipped his key in the lock and crossed the threshold into the warmth of the cottage. The sight of Sloane, curled up in a blanket by the fireplace with her fingers going a mile a minute on her laptop, sent a shot of heat through him that had nothing to do with escaping the elements. Man, she was sweet to come home to.

He wanted to come home to her every night, exactly like this, just so they could fall asleep together and wake up to do it all over again.

For the rest of their lives.

"Oh, hey. You're home early." A grin broke over Sloane's face as she unfolded into a stretch against the couch cushions, and no way was he passing up that hot glimpse of skin peeking out from the hem of her shirt.

"I'm home early," he agreed, but his mouth was already on her, testing the column of her neck as he pulled her close. Christ, nothing had ever tasted so pure and right and downright good as this woman.

She let out a melted-butter laugh and wrapped her arms around his shoulders, her body fitting against his in a way that had them halfway to the bedroom in his brain.

"That's not like you, Mr. Responsibility. Are you sure the restaurant didn't burn down or something?"

He slid his tongue over the delicate vein in her neck, just to feel her pulse jump. "No."

"Mmm. And Carly didn't fire you?" Her teasing lost its edge as he worked his way to the curve of her ear, the bold push of satisfaction and want combining low in his belly as she ended her question on a sigh.

"No." Gavin lifted his head, placing his mouth just inches from hers. "I just left early."

"That's awfully impulsive for someone so serious," Sloane said, making it sound every inch a compliment.

He kissed her with just enough pressure to make it a promise of things to come. "What can I say? I learned from the best."

"Are you trying to woo me with flattery?" Leave it to Sloane to make a decent vocabulary sound sexy as hell. He unwound an arm from her waist and pulled back to pin her with a serious stare.

"Absolutely. Is it working?"

She arched a brow, but her smile gave her away. "Absolutely. Too bad for you, I can't stay."

"You can't?" Gavin froze. Maybe he shouldn't have come on so strong right out of the gate like that, especially after how intense things had been last night. Then again, this was a woman who wanted to go to the South Pacific sans apparel, for God's sake. As much as she liked her independence, it wasn't like a little reckless emotion should really scare her.

Which was good, considering he was pretty much overflowing with it.

Sloane shook her head, dark hair tumbling as she took a step back toward the couch. "Despite how much I want to stick around and let you flatter me 'til the sun comes up,

I think I might've worn out my welcome with your sister. It might be best if I leave you guys alone for a night."

"Wait, you mean with Bree? Are you serious?" No way could he have heard her right. Bree was nuts about Sloane, right down to her crazy purple boots.

But Sloane's expression was strangely devoid of her trademark laughter as she closed her laptop and slipped it into her bag. "'Fraid so. She was in a hell of a mood before she went to bed. I went to check on her a little while ago, but her door was locked and her light was out." She paused, her blue eyes flicking over him carefully before adding, "She might just need someone to talk to. After all, she's had kind of an emotional weekend with that nightmare and everything."

Gavin's memory stuttered back a few hours, snagging hard. "She texted me earlier."

"She did?" Sloane's lips parted in surprise. Clearly, it was news to her.

"Yeah, but . . ." He unearthed his phone from his back pocket, tapping the touch screen to life to pull up the message. "It was really vague, see? To be honest, I didn't think anything of it. I mean, I knew if she really needed anything, she'd ask you."

Sloane leaned in, reading the message over his shoulder while he reread the scant line of text from the screen.

Something 2 ask u about. Maybe 2nite at home?
Don't need 2 call, no big.

"Did you talk to her after this?" Sloane asked, her pretty face shadowed in thought.

"No. We were slammed, and by the time I got it, I was already halfway out the door. Plus, she said it wasn't a big deal. She didn't say anything about this to you?" Concern filtered into out-and-out worry, percolating like day-old diner coffee in his gut.

"No, but . . ." Sloane broke off with a blink. "I did tell her this morning that she could talk to you no matter what, even if it was about the hard stuff like missing your mom. Maybe she's ready to open up and just doesn't know how to say it."

Gavin's worry became something else entirely, and his breath left him in a rush of surprise. "She talked to you about our mom?"

"A little, but I think she's still got a lot inside of her." She brushed her fingers over his forearm, and the gentle squeeze was all he needed to let loose the emotions crowding his brain.

"I'm scared to push her. God, she seems so fragile sometimes, and all I want to do is keep her safe." The words stuck in his throat like sand on wet skin, but he'd shoved them down long enough. And baring them to Sloane just felt right.

"There's nothing wrong with that," she said. "She's been through a lot."

Gavin let out a shaky breath. "I know. Sometimes talking to her feels like navigating a minefield. If I leave it alone, there's always the potential for danger later, but if I bug her, she might blow up in my face. I can't win."

"Maybe you should just ask her about it. She can't really blow up at you for being concerned about her."

He coughed out a humorless laugh. "This is Bree we're talking about here. I love her, but she's not exactly a paragon of logical thinking, especially when it comes to anything emotional. I have no idea how to get her to open up without pissing her off, or worse, having her shut me out. Sometimes I wonder how the hell my mother thought I'd be any good at this," he admitted. "Every time I think

I've made progress with Bree, something pops up to show me I'm completely full of shit."

"You're not full of shit just because you want to protect her, Gavin." Sloane's eyes sparked with dark blue conviction, fierce in the low light from the fireplace. "And you're allowed to grieve, too. It's okay for her to see that."

"What if it makes her worse? The nightmares are already pretty horrific. You saw for yourself." No matter what, he couldn't put Bree through more of that. No way.

Sloane stepped in, her gaze unrelenting on his. "And what if it gives her permission to start letting it go?"

For a split second, Gavin couldn't breathe. Oh, hell. *Hell*.

It made all the sense in the world. He'd tried to protect Bree for all the right reasons, but really, what she needed was to know how he felt, to see that he grieved and felt sad sometimes, and know that finding moments of new happiness didn't mean trading in the old ones.

And he needed to show her that. Starting with his own feelings.

"I don't know what to say to her," he finally managed, but Sloane just shook her head.

"You don't have to know what to say. Just tell her how you feel. The rest will come." She leaned in to place a kiss on his lips, soft and quick.

Gavin cupped her cheeks, returning the kiss just as sweetly before taking a step back. "How do you always know what to do?"

Her smile threaded through every last part of him as she said, "Just doing my job, boss. Now go talk to that kid. I'll see you in the morning."

Gavin stood on the threshold of Bree's door with one hand on the cool wood panel and his heart in his throat. It was now or never, and really, all the preparation in the world wouldn't make a damned bit of difference. She'd reached out to him the only way she knew how, and it was up to him to catch her.

"Bree?" He knocked softly and scraped in a deep breath. "You awake?"

A muffled thump sounded off on the other side of the door, and he heard the metallic click of the lock being released. She swung the door open just a crack, barely enough to send a wary peek out into the hallway. "Is Sloane still here?"

"No, she decided to go back to her place tonight." Damn it, maybe he should've asked her to stay, just in case it made Bree feel more comfortable. "She, ah, said you seemed a little upset about something, though. You want to talk about it?"

Bree's eyes widened, and Gavin realized with a pang that she'd been crying. "She said that?"

Man, he didn't want to put her on the spot, but they weren't going to get very far by skirting the subject. "Yeah. She thought you might be feeling a little out of sorts, and was worried about you."

But then her mouth snapped into a scowl, and she said with a shrug, "Whatever."

Something strange tickled at the back of Gavin's mind, but he pushed it aside. He couldn't shy away from this conversation now. Not when Bree needed him.

"So, can I come in?" He softened his voice a notch and just told the truth. "Because I'm worried about you, too."

Bree dropped her chin into her thermal pajama top, but thankfully, she didn't rebuff him. "Okay." She sat down on her rumpled bed and hugged her flannel-clad legs to her chest, silently staring at her toes.

Right. Clearly Sloane had underestimated the awkward factor of this whole thing when she'd assured him he'd know what to say. He sat on the edge of the bed and opened his mouth before he lost his nerve. "Listen, I know that sometimes—"

"Are you in love with Sloane?"

The question startled him into complete freeze. "What?"

"I don't mean to be nosy. I just . . . I need to know." Bree's voice wavered, and the emotion infusing her words did nothing to help him focus.

"I don't understand. Is this what you wanted to talk to me about?" Gavin's brain scrambled to play catch-up, but it was completely useless. If anything, he'd thought Bree would be thrilled about the idea of him and Sloane getting serious. So why was she looking at him with so much trepidation?

"Yeah. I need to know if you want her to stay. Like forever."

He paused. No, it wasn't what he'd been expecting, but he still owed it to Bree to be honest. After all, having Sloane around for the long haul would affect Bree's life, too. He pulled in a breath and looked her right in the eye.

"To answer your question, yes, I'm in love with Sloane. And yes, even though I think it's something we should talk about together, I want her to stay. Forever."

"But she won't," Bree whispered, and finally, Gavin got it.

"Bree, you don't have to be afraid that anything will happen to Sloane." He picked up her hand and gave it a tight squeeze. "It's perfectly understandable that you'd be worried after how suddenly Mom got sick. But I promise, Sloane's not going anywhere."

She let go of his hand to take a sheet of paper from her nightstand, pressing her eyes shut as she held it out with shaking fingers.

"Tell that to her. She's leaving for Greece next week."

Chapter Twenty-Seven

A bolt of unadulterated shock straightened Gavin's spine, and he barked out a completely involuntary laugh at Bree's words.

"That's ridiculous. Why on earth would you think she was going to Greece?"

"Because she booked a one-way ticket. It says so right here. She's leaving next Friday, and she's not coming back." Bree held the paper out, eyes brimming with tears. "She was never going to stay. See for yourself."

A deep-seated voice at the back of his mind screamed at Gavin not to take the paper from Bree's trembling fingers. Sloane wouldn't leave. Sure, she'd traveled the world on a whim in the past, but things were different now. She knew how much Bree needed her, how much he needed her. She wouldn't do that to him.

She wouldn't do that to *them*.

He took the paper from her shaking hands, but didn't look at it. "Bree, I think this is a misunderstanding. Where did you even get this?" The single piece of paper felt like a ten-ton weight between his suddenly unsteady fingers.

"I found it on the printer when I went to get my English

homework. And it's not a misunderstanding. Have you looked at Sloane's Web site?"

His confusion deepened, shifting and kicking like a live entity. "What does her Web site have to do with any of this?"

Tears spilled over Bree's cheeks, her mouth an angry line. "All her books are set in foreign places. And her biography page says she's been to all of them, you know, for research and stuff. That part of what inspires her is being in all these countries and experiencing them firsthand. And *that's* how she writes a book."

Gavin's mind took a hard tumble back to the morning when Sloane had run her fingers so reverently over the picture frames in the living room, telling him she'd walked the Via Francigena in Tuscany. France . . . Spain . . . Italy . . . she went wherever the wind carried her, whenever she felt like going. And she wrote a book, fueling her livelihood every time she went.

Oh, I spent time in Venice and Milan, too. But the whole point of the trip was to find inspiration . . .

Oh, God. Sloane had specifically mentioned the six-week time frame when he'd asked her to take care of Bree. And at the time, he'd assumed she'd say no because she had a book to write.

But a lifetime of things had happened since then. Bree had opened up to her, *trusted* her. And he had trusted her with the most important thing—the only thing—in his life.

Not to mention his heart.

In that moment, as Gavin finally dropped his eyes and saw Sloane's betrayal right there in black and white, his gut seized with realization. He'd made a huge error in his assumption.

He'd never thought she would agree to stay, but then leave him and Bree anyway.

* * *

Sloane made a mad dash for Gavin's porch, doing her best to dodge the steadily falling raindrops. She was cutting it a little close on the time for Gavin's Sunday morning shift, but in all likelihood, if he and Bree had spent some time talking last night, then Bree would probably sleep late this morning anyway. God, she really hoped he'd been able to coax something out of Bree to ease her mind. The poor kid was probably aching for someone to talk to, and even though Sloane was more than happy to let Bree bend her ear for the girl stuff, at some point, she and Gavin were going to have to connect, especially about their mom. Sloane shook the cold rain from her blue beret, running her fingers over the soft threads with a smile as she closed her hand around the doorknob to let herself into the cottage.

The door was locked.

"What the heck?" Sloane tried the knob again, but before she could follow the failed attempt with a knock, it twisted in her palm, slipping from her grasp with a firm pull.

"Oh! Jeez, you startled me." She laughed, but the sound met a quick end in her throat when she walked into the foyer and saw the serious look etched on Gavin's face. "How did it go with Bree last night? Did you guys get a chance to talk?"

"Yes." His expression betrayed nothing, as impeccably pressed as his pale blue dress shirt, but she froze midstep on the dark wood of the floorboards.

His expression might not let anything show, but his voice was a dead giveaway that something was horribly wrong.

Sloane's heart fumbled against her ribs. "Oh, God,

Gavin. Is she okay? I mean, I know she's not *okay* okay, but—"

"No, she's not." A muscle ticked in his angular jaw, and her worry snowballed into fear.

"What's going on? Where is she?"

"Jeannie picked her up about ten minutes ago. She was nice enough to help me out until Mrs. Teasdale comes back next week." Gavin's voice was utterly detached, as if he were reading a produce order over the phone.

Sloane pulled back, trying to make sense of what he was saying. Finally, she was forced to admit defeat. "I'm sorry, I don't understand."

"It's simple, really. Bree is staying with Jeannie this week while I'm at work. We just thought you might need the extra week to close up the bungalow and pack all of your things. Since you're headed to Greece, and everything."

His words slammed into her with tangible force, knocking her breath loose on a gasp. "What?"

He eyed her with steely disdain as he produced a piece of paper from his back pocket, unfolding it from its precise creases. "You should probably be more careful about where you leave your flight confirmation. After all, you're going to need it when you skip town next Friday."

Sloane's mind dipped and spun, screeching to a halt with realization that turned her blood to ice water. "I left it on the printer," she blurted, remembering too late how she'd clicked the icon to print the flight itinerary the night Bree had woken from her nightmare.

Oh, God. He thought she was leaving. Which meant he thought . . .

"Gavin, I can explain." Sloane took a wobbly step toward him, but he cut her off with a tight wave of his hand.

"I don't want you to." The words arrowed into her, burrowing deep in her bones and stealing her voice as he continued. "You don't owe me any explanations. In fact, you don't owe me anything. We had a short-term business agreement. What you do now that it's over is none of my concern."

"That's what you think we had? A business agreement?" Sloane forced herself to breathe, even though both her lungs and her throat had their own agenda. No, she and Gavin had never actually discussed what was going on between them, but it sure as hell hadn't been just business.

It hadn't been *just* anything.

"You're the one who made it clear from the beginning that sticking around wasn't your thing, Sloane," Gavin said, folding his arms into an impenetrable knot over his chest. "And Mrs. Teasdale will be back next week, so you're off the hook. Feel free to go." He aimed a pointed, icy gaze at the door, and the move kick-started her mouth into motion.

"I wasn't *going* to go. I mean, originally, I was, but—"

"The flight was booked three days ago." A hint of something dark and thoroughly angry flashed over Gavin's face as he lifted the paper. "So forgive me if I have trouble believing you."

She squeezed her eyes shut, partly to escape from his expression and partly so she could think. Pure survival instinct swirled at the back of her mind, whispering that she should run, but she quashed it.

She could fix this. She had to fix it.

"I know how this looks, but you have to believe me. I wasn't going to leave. I'm sorry that you and Bree found out like this, but I didn't think—"

Gavin stiffened at the sound of Bree's name, cutting her off completely. "That's the trouble, isn't it? You don't think. You live your life from one impulsive decision to the next, just stirring up trouble and never thinking about the consequences. Well, I hate to break it to you, but that's not how the real world works. Not that you'd know, because you're too busy racking up frequent flyer mileage to sit still long enough to get it."

Sloane winced. Just because she'd earned his anger didn't mean it stung any less upon impact. "I know I hurt you, and I'm sorry."

"You think this is about me?" Gavin's frosty stare became downright glacial. "I don't give a shit if you want to hurt me, Sloane. But if you think I'm going to sit around and listen to anything you have to say after you just destroyed my sister's trust, you're out of your mind. That kid cared about you, but you're too stuck in your own selfish world to see it."

Sloane's eyes filled with tears, and they breached her lids to track down both cheeks as she said the only thing she could think of to make it right.

"I'm so sorry, Gavin. I never meant to hurt either of you."

For just a breath, time melted into slow motion, a flicker of emotion making the tiniest dent in Gavin's expression, and her chest surged with possibility and hope.

But then it disappeared, his words ripping at her as the banked emotion in his eyes turned to solid ice and he said, "Your apology isn't good enough."

He walked to the front door without pause and held it open, and Sloane had no choice but to walk through it and leave her heart behind.

Sloane's suitcase had seen better days, but that had never stopped her from shoving all her worldly possessions into it. Granted, she usually had an idea of where she was headed when she zipped it up, but having a destination didn't seem nearly as important right now as getting away from Pine Mountain. Once she was on the road, she'd be able to think, to lift the boulder-sized block of sadness off her chest and at least breathe.

Oh, God, she had to get *out* of here.

Windshield wipers flashed across the rain-slicked glass, the rhythmic *thump-THUMP* keeping time in Sloane's head like a bad-weather metronome. She reached forward to turn the knob to the next setting, her breath leaking out of her in a slow sigh when she realized it wasn't the rain blurring her vision, but a fresh round of tears spilling involuntarily from beneath her eyelids.

She guided the Fiat carefully down Rural Route Four. While her deeply ingrained survival instinct hollered at her to get out of Dodge as fast as possible, she wasn't stupid enough to go speeding down the mountain like her hair was on fire. Those guardrails were high and tight for a reason, and it wasn't to block the gorgeous views.

And besides, the slower you go, the longer you have to change your mind.

Sloane stuffed down the thought about two seconds after it surfaced. Her impulsive ways had gotten her into enough trouble, thank you very much. Recklessly turning around and begging Gavin and Bree for another chance blew right past the border of pointlessness, landing directly in the lap of total frickin' insanity. He'd made it crystal-goblet clear that he wasn't interested in anything she had to say, and in hindsight, Sloane couldn't blame him.

After all, she'd proved the whole *not good enough* thing in spades.

As she turned off the gravel mountain road and her tires found the smooth ribbon of highway beneath them, Sloane began to cry in earnest.

* * *

Gavin sat at La Dolce Vita's polished mahogany bar, wishing the stack of inventory sheets in front of him was a double shot of Grey Goose over ice. He'd had enough emotion in the past twenty-four hours to last him a lifetime. Considering where it had gotten him, he'd give his right arm to forget the pleasantries of his palate and go right for numb.

"Hey." Adrian's gruff voice yanked Gavin out of his wishful thinking, and his head snapped up in surprise. "You've got a visitor."

Gavin's pulse clattered through his veins. "We're not open for dinner shift for another hour and a half."

One corner of Adrian's mouth kicked up into a half smile. "Yeah, I figured you'd make an exception for this one." He took a step back, ushering Bree into the bar area from the dining room, with Jeannie right behind her.

"Is everything okay?" Gavin asked, concern flooding through him, but Bree was quick to head it off.

"I'm not hurt or anything. I just . . ." She turned and looked at Jeannie, who put a comforting arm around Bree's shoulders. "We were all skiing, but the trails are really crummy from the rain, so we came inside and Mrs. Carter said maybe we could catch you in between lunch and dinner. You know, to just say hi."

"Oh. Sure." Gavin's brows slid together, his worry deepening as he caught Jeannie's troubled expression. "Are you sure everything is okay?"

Bree nodded, but Jeannie shook her head. "Bree seemed a little down, so I thought maybe coming over for a minute would cheer her up." She gave Bree's shoulder a squeeze before letting her go. "I'll give you two a minute. Just come find me when you're ready to head back to the lodge."

Gavin's heart took a nosedive toward his shoes as he watched Jeannie slip through the entrance to the dining room. If he was begging to be numb, it made sense that Bree would be feeling the same way. He looked at her red-rimmed eyes and sullen face, and his words came tumbling out without a second thought.

"Tell you what. Why don't you stick around here tonight? Dinner rush is earlier on Sundays, and I can probably sneak out as soon as it starts to slow down. Plus, I bet if you play your cards right with Bellamy, she'll let you taste some of the dessert specials for tonight. Someone in the lunch crowd actually threatened to lick her plate clean after eating a slice of her mocha cheesecake. So what do you say?"

Okay, so it was a pretty transparent attempt to comfort her, which he knew from experience would probably make her feel like a baby, but he was grasping at straws. Keeping her close and feeding her were the only two ways he really knew how to make her feel better, and selfishly, he knew it would make him feel better to have her close by. Gavin steeled himself for her response, fully expecting her to push him away.

But she shocked the hell out of him by giving a tiny nod. "Yeah. I'd really like that." His surprise threatened to overwhelm him completely when she took a few steps forward and wrapped her arms around him, tucking her head into his shoulder.

There had been a time, God, barely months ago, when putting his emotions on display like this would've made him shrink back and hide. But if anything, Gavin knew now more than ever that if he wanted to be a good parent, he had to take a risk every now and then.

So he said, "Okay, sweetheart. I've got you. You stay right here with me, for as long as you want."

And he held her, just like that while she cried.

Chapter Twenty-Eight

Sloane got exactly twelve miles down the highway before her cell phone rang, simultaneously scaring the shit out of her and sending her hope through the roof of the Fiat. Both emotions twisted together into a tight pretzel of dread as the caller ID popped up on the hands-free touch screen in front of her.

Jacobs, Belinda, Morton House Publishers

In the flurry of wild emotions that had encompassed her morning, Sloane had completely blanked on the e-mail she'd sent Belinda about her book. Oh, God, her *book*. The one that had flowed right out of her, despite where she was. The one that was the exact opposite of what Belinda had asked for, and could ruin her future at Morton House in a single pitch.

The one she didn't have to write, because there was nothing keeping her from getting on that plane and writing the Greece book, just like she'd said she would.

Her career was on the line, and it was the only thing she had left.

Just as Sloane was about to open her mouth to tell

Belinda to forget the e-mail, her vision caught on the Fiat's passenger seat. Brightly colored Post-it notes covered the outline she'd hastily shoved in her bag, but the purple square in the center of the page froze the breath to her lungs.

Heroine risks all for love.

Oh, God. Her career *wasn't* the only thing she had left. Sloane had her heart, and even if it was broken, it was past time to start trusting that heart to be good enough. Even if it meant risking everything.

"Hi, Belinda," Sloane finally said as she guided the Fiat toward the nearest U-turn. "I'm so glad you called. I've got a lot to tell you."

Gavin made his way back to the pass in La Dolce Vita's kitchen, narrowly dodging a harried-looking server with a full tray on her shoulder.

"Please tell me that's table seven," he said, hoping like hell to get an affirmative. Although they were keeping a smooth schedule, the dining room was absolutely packed for a Sunday, and the good timing they were currently enjoying could turn on a dime without warning. The server hollered a *table seven, out* over her free shoulder, slipping confidently through the swinging doors toward the dining room. Gavin grabbed a pair of plates from the expanse of stainless steel counter in front of him, taking the briefest of seconds to admire the pan-seared sea scallops and sunflower-yellow polenta in his hands.

"Table thirteen, scallops and polenta out the door," he clipped, raising his voice over the din of metallic cacophony from the pots and pans being maneuvered through the kitchen.

"Wait!" Carly's shrill command stopped him in his tracks, and he swung toward her, brows upturned.

"Mushroom sauce on the scallops," she said, and they both frowned at his miss.

"Fuck. Sorry, chef." He slid the dish back up to the pass so she could finish plating it. This special had been on the tasting menu barely three hours ago, and Carly always went out of her way to make sure the staff knew what everything was supposed to look like when it went out the door. How had he missed something so obvious?

Kind of easy when all you can think about is what you're not going home to.

"Is Bree doing okay in the break room?" Carly worked her magic with efficient hands, finishing the scallops with just a few simple touches.

"She's actually in the dining room with Jeannie and the twins. They came by for dessert. Said Bellamy's chocolate torte was incredible." Actually, Jeannie had said it, and the twins had agreed. Bree just pushed hers around on her plate.

"Are you going to tell me what's going on here, or am I going to have to pry?" Carly held out the finished plate of sea scallops, but didn't let go when Gavin reached for it.

"Nothing's going on." He might be coming to terms in the emotions-sharing department with Bree, but letting loose with his boss while his dinner service crashed down around him was not on his to-do list.

Plus, all the talking in the world wouldn't change the fact that Sloane was gone, and he should've known better than to think she'd stay.

One of Carly's shadowy brows winged skyward. "Nothing," she repeated, looking as doubtful as she sounded as she let go of the plate.

But Gavin didn't budge. "No. Table thirteen, out the door."

The next few hours passed in a mercifully mind-numbing

blur, and he went through the motions with fast feet and a heart full of broken glass. In time, he knew he'd get used to Sloane not being around—in truth, she'd spent less than two months with them, so it shouldn't be such a daunting task. Eventually, he'd be able to walk past the guest bedroom without thinking of that first night they'd made love, urgent and beautiful against luxurious bedsheets. He'd be able to look at the fireplace and not remember how the soft light reflected in her eyes to make them sparkle when she typed furiously on her laptop. And he'd be able to look at Bree and not see the bottomless sadness on her face as she looked around the cottage and saw Sloane in every corner, too.

Christ, it had to get better than this, because it sure as hell couldn't get worse.

"Hey, chef. We're starting to wind down in the dining room. If it's okay with you, I'm going to leave some of the paperwork for the morning and head home with Bree." While Gavin was less than thrilled at the prospect of crossing the threshold to his empty cottage with his head full of memories, it was time to start facing the facts.

Sloane was gone, and she wasn't coming back. No matter how in love with her he was.

Carly wiped her hands on her apron and fastened him with a glance. "Sure." Her gaze shifted over his shoulder, eyes going momentarily wide before she blanked her expression again, and he turned in confusion.

"Oh, hey, Stephanie." Gavin looked at the bartender with a tired smile. "I'm heading out for the night, so just update your tallies before you leave. I'll grab them in the morning."

The bartender split a look between Carly and Gavin before holding up a bar slip between her first two fingers. "You're not out the door yet. Someone ordered a bottle of red that's gonna cost big bucks. Inventory says we have one in the wine cellar, so here you go."

It was standard operating procedure any time an order came in for a bottle of wine costing over a hundred dollars for the manager to handle the service from cellar to glass. Given his penchant for finer vintages, this was never a rule Gavin balked at; on the contrary, it always gave him a bit of a thrill to have his hands on a bottle of something that could be so well appreciated.

For the first time ever, he couldn't care less.

"Okay. What am I getting?"

Stephanie's eyes darted to the pass, where Carly and Adrian were suddenly busy with a round of last-minute dishes heading out the door. "Um, looks like a really pricey Bordeaux. Glad you're opening it. Personally, those expensive bottles give me the shakes. Enjoy."

A really pricey Bordeaux. Wait a second . . . there were only a couple really high-end reds on their wine list. He turned the bar slip Stephanie had put in his hand. No way it could be—

1999 Château Bellevue Mondotte.

It was the same bottle of wine he and Sloane had impulsively enjoyed on the night of Carly's wedding. The same bottle of wine that, given the chance, he would pick above all others.

For a second, Gavin's world tilted on an angle he had no hope of reconciling. Then his head snapped up to meet Carly's clear-as-a-bell gaze.

"Someone order a doozy?" she asked, but he clamped down on the feeling surging in his chest.

"Just a nice bottle of red. I'll grab it from the wine cellar. See you tomorrow."

Gavin made his way to the back of the kitchen, taking the steps to the wine cellar with his mind spinning. They hadn't sold a bottle of Bellevue Mondotte in almost a year, and he'd even wondered if it made sense to replace the one he had bought that night. Except as the chief consultant for wine orders, he'd known that they should have one on-hand. It was one of the best Bordeaux in that price range. No better experience for your money.

And apparently he wasn't the only one who thought so.

Gavin stopped at the dimly lit section where they housed the reds and inhaled the dry, crisp scent of wood and cork. His fingers found the grooved space where the bottle reclined, delicately notched in the resting place where he'd put it upon delivery, and he slid it from the shelf. He stuffed back the memory of the last time he'd been down here to take a bottle from this spot, and the delicious possibility he'd felt upon doing something so capricious.

Hell of a lot of irony in how right something could feel, only to leave you picking up the pieces once it shattered in your hands.

"Enough," he told himself, closing his fingers over the neck of the bottle and covering the space back up to La Dolce Vita in even strides. He placed the bottle on the bar while he grabbed a wine key and two glasses, running his eyes over the crystal with quick care to make sure it was ready to go.

"Hey. Is that a good one?" Bree asked, coming up across from him to prop her elbows on the polished mahogany bar.

Gavin laughed, even though there was little humor in it. "You could say that. You want to watch me open it? It's not every day you see the cork come out of a two-hundred-fifty-dollar bottle of red."

"Holy moly," Bree gasped, eyeing him as if he were nuts. "Why do grown-ups do such crazy stuff?"

Now his laugh was genuine, albeit soft. "Good question. I'm headed to the dining room with this, but after I'm done, we can go home if you want."

"Okay. Can I really watch you open it?"

Gavin did a mental tally of open tables. "Sure. Table fourteen should be close enough, and it's empty. You know the one by the fireplace in front?"

Bree nodded. "Yeah. Just let me get my backpack from the office."

"Go up to the pass and ask Carly to get you through the kitchen. It's slow enough back there now that she can help you. I'll go talk up this customer." He jerked his head toward the dining room. "See you in a minute."

With a slow exhale, Gavin looped his fingers around the delicate stems of the wineglasses and put them on a clean bar tray. The bottle was smooth and comforting in his hand as he headed through the glowing half light of La Dolce Vita's dining room, taking in the handful of still-occupied tables and quietly chatting diners. Table sixteen was a cozy little two-top, close to the front entrance. Probably a couple celebrating a birthday or anniversary, he thought as he gave the bottle a glance.

Maybe he'd get a little impulsive and take Bree somewhere really nice for her birthday next month, even round up the twins and take them all into Philly for the weekend. A grin poked at the edges of his mouth despite his weary mood. He could just hear the delighted preteen squeals that would accompany that suggestion, followed by a deep, velvety belly laugh that he'd come up with such a good idea on his own . . .

Gavin's thoughts crashed to a halt, his grip tightening over the bottle in his hand. Damn it, he needed to figure out a better way to purge Sloane from his memory, otherwise he was never going to get over this. She'd made her decision, made it weeks ago and stuck to it despite everything between them. No matter how much he hated it, he needed to get rid of everything Sloane-related in his brain, once and for all.

Starting right now.

* * *

Sloane's cell phone buzzed softly, but the vibration in her palm was nothing compared to the jackhammer of her pulse as she read the incoming text message.

> All set. 2 mins, tops. Hope u know what u r doing.
> Good luck, C.

She released a shaky breath. She had no *idea* what she was doing, but it didn't matter.

She was tired of running away when things got tough. It was time to run back and trust that what she had to say was good enough.

As soon as she saw Gavin, with his crisp suit and serious-as-a-tax-audit face, her heart launched against her ribs, but she sat firmly in her seat. She might not know what she was doing, but she sure as hell knew what she wanted, and it was high time she made a decision she could stand by without changing her mind.

He looked up as he approached the table that Carly had carefully selected, stopping short a few feet away.

"You ordered this?"

Sloane nodded, eternally grateful she was sitting down. "I owe you a bottle. Since we never finished the first one."

Gavin's eyes flashed, dark and unreadable. "You don't owe me anything."

"Oh, yes, I do. But the wine isn't the half of it."

Now or never, now or never, now or . . .

"For starters, I owe you an apology. I kept things from you, and although at the time I thought I had good reasons for it, there's no excuse for what I did. I know that it hurt you and Bree, and I'm sorry."

"You're sorry," he repeated, and *God,* his expression was a wall of stone.

But Sloane continued, not allowing it to throw her. "The next thing I owe you is that bottle of wine. I didn't realize it at the time, but you taught me a really valuable lesson about slowing down. So I wanted to let you know how grateful I am by repaying the bottle you didn't get to finish."

"You don't owe me anything," he said again, and everything around her fluttered as she stood.

"You're wrong, Gavin. I owe you everything." Tears filled her eyes, but she didn't fight them as they slipped silently down her face. "You trusted me, with Bree, with your feelings, with all of it, and you believed in me when I didn't even believe in myself. I should've trusted you back, but I was scared, and by the time I wasn't scared, it was too late. But late is better than never, and I couldn't let another minute go by without telling you that I'm in love with you. I don't want to be anywhere other than with you and Bree. I don't want to live my life jumping from one place to the next. I want you. All I want is . . . you."

Sloane's throat closed around the last word, refusing to allow anything else past her lips, which was probably just as well. She ran a hand over her face, realizing that everyone within earshot was unabashedly staring at her. She forced herself to unfold her spine and lift her head.

Her days of running from the tough stuff were over.

"Anyway. I just wanted to say that." She lowered her eyes, which only sent more tears down her face and more stares in her direction, but she was so far past caring. It was time to stick around and be accountable for her feelings rather than take off at the first sign of trouble or unease.

Even if it broke her heart in the process.

"You just ran up one hell of a bar tab."

Gavin's words washed over her slowly, and she blinked in confusion. "I'm sorry?"

He held up the bottle in his hand, but didn't take his eyes off her as he said, "This is a really expensive bottle of wine. I'm just wondering if you can afford it, since last I heard, you were unemployed."

Sloane's brows slid together. "Oh. Well, actually—"

But Gavin took a step toward her, then two, and her words faded away.

"I might be able to solve your problem. See, I'm looking for a babysitter." He sent a pointed glance over his shoulder, and holy crap, Bree was sitting right there at the table behind him, her brown eyes wide and tearstained.

"As long as that's okay with you," Gavin said to Bree, and she looked at Sloane and nodded.

"Yeah. That's okay with me."

Sloane blinked, her lips parting in shock. "You want me back?"

Gavin was beside her in an instant. "I believe you, Sloane, and I love you, too. I want to come home to you every night, and wake up next to you every morning. I don't just want you back. I want you forever. What do you say?"

"Yes. God, yes!"

His arms felt perfect as they slid around her, and perfect got even better as Bree's arms folded over them both. They stood there in the middle of the restaurant, tangled together and laughing like gleeful idiots until finally, Gavin pulled back with a mischievous grin.

"Okay, big spender. Let's open this bottle up and celebrate your homecoming, shall we?"

Sloane's laughter bubbled out of her, all the way from her toes. "We can celebrate more than that."

"We can?" Bree asked. "Like what?"

"Let's just say my latest proposal went over incredibly well with Belinda. She gave me the green light to write the book I've been working on. So it looks like I'm gainfully employed twice."

"I don't think I can compete with a major publishing house," Gavin said with a shake of his head.

But Sloane just threw her head back and laughed. "They can't hold a candle to you, boss. Now open up that bottle, would you? I'm ready to stir up a little trouble, one sip at a time."

Gavin's Swiss Omelet Recipe

Breakfast is a big-time meal in our house, and we often have it for dinner as well as in the morning. It's one of those meals where even the youngest chefs in the house can take part in preparations. So when I was searching for something that Gavin, the hero in book three of the Pine Mountain series, could make with his thirteen-year-old half sister Bree, my brain immediately went the breakfast route. Gavin may not always have the right words as he raises his sister, especially as Bree goes from pigtails to puberty, but they share a bond through food, and this omelet makes several appearances in *Stirring Up Trouble*. Of course, they share it—and all the emotion that goes with their family—with unlikely "antinanny" Sloane Russo, too.

Ingredients:
    2 large eggs
    2 Tablespoons milk (whole preferred)
    1 Tablespoon butter
    ¼ cup diced onion
    ⅓ cup cooked ham, cubed or sliced into ribbons
    ¼ cup shredded Swiss cheese
    1 teaspoon each freshly chopped tarragon and thyme
    Extra Swiss and sprigs of thyme for garnish

Gently whisk eggs and milk in a small bowl; set aside. In an omelet pan over medium heat, melt butter and cook onion until soft and translucent, about 5 minutes (stir often). Add ham, then cover with egg mixture. With the heat between medium and medium-high, swirl the egg mixture evenly through the pan with other ingredients distributed throughout. Use a fork to stir the mixture carefully as it cooks (eggs will begin to set up and mixture will thicken). When the mixture has set up but is still wet, add cheese and herbs. Using a spatula or your mad omelet flipping skills, flip the omelet to form a half-moon shape. Cook for another minute, then slide to a plate, garnish, and share with someone you love!

Bree's Best Doughnut Holes Recipe

In *Stirring Up Trouble*, Gavin and his half-sister Bree talk
about making doughnuts. Doing this from scratch takes a
lot of time and even more patience, but doughnut holes
are a fantastic shortcut to a tasty treat. The only equip-
ment you'll need is a food-safe thermometer and heavy-
bottomed stock pot, plus a wire-mesh scoop or slotted
spoon for frying.

<u>Ingredients:</u>
   1¼ cups all-purpose flour
   ½ cup sugar
   2 teaspoons baking powder
   ½ teaspoon ground cinnamon
   ½ teaspoon kosher salt
   1 egg
   ½ cup milk
   2 Tablespoons butter, room temperature at least
   Enough canola oil to measure 3 inches deep in your
      pot / fry vessel

*Combine dry ingredients, through salt, in a large bowl
(preferably with a stand mixer). Add egg, milk and
butter until all ingredients are well combined but not
over-mixed (think doughnuts . . . not doorstops!). Heat
oil in stock pot over medium heat until a food-safe
thermometer registers 375. This is tricky—you may need*

to adjust as you go, but that is okay. Carefully drop rounded teaspoonfuls of dough into the oil (only 6 at a time maximum to avoid crowding). Cook one minute, then flip with a slotted spoon or wire-mesh scoop. Cook one additional minute, then remove the dough from the oil. Place cooked doughnut holes on a paper towel to remove excess oil.

Toppings for these can vary. Gavin and Bree do glazed, which is easy to make with milk and powdered sugar. Start with a cup of powdered sugar, and add just enough milk until you reach your desired consistency. Adding sprinkles to these is fun for the younger set too. But I am a sucker for cinnamon and sugar topping, which can be made by combining ½ cup sugar with 1 teaspoon cinnamon (double as necessary) and stirring well. Place in a shallow bowl, and roll just-cooled doughnut holes in the mixture. There won't be leftovers. Promise!

Don't miss Kimberly Kincaid's next
Pine Mountain novel,

Fire Me Up,

coming next February.

"Sorry to interrupt, gentlemen, but I heard this was where the party is." Without a second thought, Teagan slipped into the hairsbreadth of space between the cop and her irritated patient, assessing the latter with a critical eye. Her subconscious gave up a whisper of recognition as she looked at his ruggedly stubbled face, but the tickle of familiarity took a backseat to the visual assessment she needed to do in order to gauge his injuries.

The guy had nearly a foot on her, which was pretty freaking impressive considering she clocked in at five-foot-seven. The physique that went with his height left impressive in the dust, though, especially since his chest was as thick as a double-wide trailer and every ounce of it looked to be muscle.

Make that leather-clad muscle, which had probably saved his ass, quite literally. As best she could tell, thanks to his now-banged-up jacket, the guy's road rash appeared shockingly minimal, although she'd have to get the garment off to be sure.

Too bad the rest of his injuries didn't look to match, namely that arm he was cradling like a helpless newborn.

She didn't even want to get started on the laundry list of other injuries that could be lurking beneath the dirt-streaked denim and leather.

She passed the first-in bag to Jeff, who caught it without looking while the police officer stepped to the background to give them a wide berth.

"My name is Teagan O'Malley, and I'm a paramedic with Pine Mountain Fire and Rescue," she said, her hands a flurry of movement as she geared up to do a rapid trauma assessment. "Can you tell me your name?"

The guy lifted a pierced eyebrow toward his spiky platinum hairline and speared her with a stare caught somewhere between hazel and cold gray. God, how did she *know* him?

"I'm fine," he ground out, his voice pure gravel and aggravation. "Which I already told that fucking jarhead, but he wouldn't let me leave."

Yeah. It was going to take a little more than a bad attitude and some uncut testosterone to get her to back down. "That fucking jarhead, as you so eloquently put it, might've saved your life by keeping you here until you can be medically cleared. While I doubt there's a gift registry for that kind of thing, a simple thank-you might be nice. Just to be on the safe side."

Her would-be patient took a step back, his stare going from cutting to calculating in the span of a breath. "I don't need to be medically cleared," he said, although it didn't escape her notice that he caught the cop's attention to toss him a deferent nod.

Teagan bit back the temptation to point out that, from the looks of things, he was a walking, talking version of the board game Operation with that arm bent up like it was. "Okay. Why don't you let me give you a quick once-over to be sure?"

"No." The word fell between them without subtlety,

and she drew back with a frown. The tough-guy routine was cute, really, but nobody was indestructible.

"Look, I know this isn't fun, but it's necessary, so—"

"If you think I'm getting in that ambulance, then you don't know shit."

Jeff locked eyes on her in a nonverbal translation of *say the word,* but Teagan gave a tight, singular shake of her head. She'd handled enough tough guys to fill a stadium, and this one was no different.

She craned her neck and stepped close enough to see the numerous abrasions peppered in with the guy's dark stubble, meeting his stare head-on even though it sent an involuntary shiver down the plumb line of her spine.

"Let me tell you what I *do* know." She dropped her voice to just a notch above a whisper and threw on a smile as thick and sweet as store-bought frosting. "I know your arm is broken, and I think you know it, too. I know you don't want me to look at it even though it hurts like a bitch. And I also know that's not an option, because it's possible that broken arm is the least of your worries. So here it is. You can either cooperate with me and we'll do this the easy way, or I can sedate you and work you over so thoroughly, I'll be on a first-name basis with every last part of you. Are we clear?"

A muscle tightened in the hard line of his jaw, drawing out the silence for a beat, then two before he turned toward her ever so slightly, as if waiting for her to get on with it.

Good enough, she thought as she lifted her hands to start checking him out.

But before Teagan could even start on his pulse, the guy's free hand had turned to form an ironclad circle around her wrist.